THE MISSING SPOKE

David Geiger

First Edition May 14th, 2011

ISBN: 978-09836522-0-5

This is a fictional account of a very real and dangerous time.
Contact : http://themissingspoke.blogspot.com

Front cover and back cover design by R. Gargallo

Maresa Publishing

This book is dedicated to two people: my mother Rose
and my beloved, Raquel.
Mom, you taught me courage and perseverance,
and Raquel, you taught me love.

INTRODUCTION

It was something for which I had been waiting a very long time. I had been a teacher at a small alternative school for the past eight years. During that time, I had taught middle school students and the daily strain of the job had been wearing on me. In my first few years of teaching, I was energetic and creative, but after that it had been a real struggle; I was burnt out. I applied for and was given a sabbatical to travel for a year.

I had planned to travel around the world. First, I was going to visit an old girlfriend in Hong Kong. Then I'd fly to Bombay, India, to try and become a Bollywood film star named hanumanji. I had been to India the previous summer and I thought I'd go back there with the intent of making some cheesy movies and having my fifteen minutes of fame.

After Bombay, I'd fly to Egypt and visit the pyramids. I had recently taught my students about ancient Egypt and I was anxious to see the sites in person. Then I'd fly to Greece and explore Europe by land, flying out of London and heading home to San Francisco after nine months of travel.

But the events of September 11th, 2001, changed all of those plans. Bombay now seemed much too close to Afghanistan and I was afraid that the tension between India and Pakistan might escalate into something worse. Egypt did not seem like a good idea either. I was afraid that we were headed for a third world war.

I needed to travel, though. It was in my agreement. I loved traveling. It was one of the reasons that I had become a teacher. I decided to spend my entire nine months in Europe. I would fly into Spain and stay near the Mediterranean Sea during the winter months, head north in the spring and fly out of Amsterdam to head back to San Francisco.

I was traveling alone again. That is how I said that I preferred to travel. That way I didn't have to make any compromises and I was free to do what I wanted, when I wanted. It had been good traveling that way for many years, but the loneliness was beginning to wear on me. Somehow I had aged from twenty three to forty three years old in what seemed like a very short time. I now desired more companionship.

I shaved off my long beard and began to grow back the hair on my head that I had been shaving. In India last summer, many people had approached me and inquired whether I was a Muslim. In Europe, I didn't want people to be suspicious of me and fearful to rent me a room. So I took the look of Everyman with short hair and a neatly trimmed goatee.

The inspiration for this story began with one word and I'm not sure whether or not I heard it correctly, but the word was spoken and it inspired me in the strange way that I became. And so now, if you choose, you will listen to my fantasy and the music that was sung to me and you will do with it whatever you wish.

Part I: Island

I walked into an old bookshop in ol' Palma on the island of Mallorca looking for a copy of James Michener's, 'Iberia'. Four Spaniards, three men and a woman, were seated in a circle in the center of the shop having a discussion. I said, "Bon dia," and headed to the back of the shop. They nodded to me and continued their discussion, none of which I could understand.

All of the books in the shop were very old and there was one small section of books in English, but no 'Iberia'. I turned to leave and as I was exiting, I softly said, "Adios" and the woman smiled and replied, "Hago." I looked confused and she said in English, "It's short for hasta luego, see you later."

"Oh yes, of course," I said. I thought that I remembered hearing that somewhere before. She asked me if I was English and I replied that I was American.

The big man with dark wild hair and dark wild eyes stood up and exclaimed, "American, come sit down and join us," as he added another chair to the circle. I sat down between him and a thin, very serious man with eyes that always pierced through me even though his face was never directed toward me. The other man had a dark, bushy mustache and even darker, bushier eyebrows.

I nervously asked, "Como se llama?" and the two hairy men and the girl laughed and the big guy replied, "No, no names and we will speak in English, like Americans," and the three laughed again.

The girl said, "I'll start, why are you here..."

"I was looking for a book called..."

"No, why are you here in Palma?"

"I am on a break from my work."

Bushy Eyebrows- "In what city do you live?"

"San Francisco."

They all looked at each other very mysteriously and silently with slight smiles on their faces.

Big Guy - "What do you do?"

"I do many things, but my job for the last eight years has been as a teacher."

I then began to ask my question because I assumed that this was the way that this discussion group worked; going clockwise with one question at a time. But they waved me off and the big guy said that I could ask one question, but it would be after they had finished all of their questions.

Bushy Eyebrows added, "This is an inquisition," and they all laughed again except for the thin one, who questioned me next.

"What is it you teach?"

"I teach history."

Girl- "What do you know about history?"

"I know very little, but I am trying to learn more."

Bushy Eyebrows- "What is it that you fear most?"

Long pause, then I replied, "I fear nothing." More laughter from the three and even a slight smile from the thin one.

Big Guy-"Why is it that you sweat?"

"I sweat because I am hot."

Thin One—"Would you like a drink of my tea?"

"No, thank you. I have my own water." I nervously got out my water bottle and had a drink while all of their eyes were fixed upon me. Water dripped out of my mouth and onto my pants, but there was no reaction from them.

Girl-"How do you like to live?"

"I like to live with the joyfulness of simple things."

Bushy Eyebrows—"What is simple for you?"

"A walk in the park, the warmth of the sun on my face."

Big Guy—"How would you like to die?"

"I would like to die slowly, so that I can fight 'til my last breath."

Thin One-"When would you like to die?"

"When it is my time."

The big guy then clapped his big hands together and proclaimed, "Inquisition over. Now it is time for your one question."

I decided to ask the same question that I was going to ask from the very start.

"For what purpose do the four of you meet?"

They all looked at each other and then the three gestured for the thin one to answer. He turned his face toward me for the first time and replied, "We meet to discuss the obliteration of all capitalist pigs of the world." He then laughed hysterically, exposing his yellow, crooked teeth while the other three sat silently and still, without expression. The big guy told me that it was time for me to go and he took my chair from the circle. As I exited, I said goodbye and they responded, "Hago."

I went back to my room at the Hostel Ritzi and decided to try to take a nap because I felt exhausted; I had gotten very little sleep since my arrival at the island. I lay in bed but had a hard time falling asleep because I kept thinking about the scary encounter that I just had. Was my life in danger?

I dreamed that I was sitting in a room with a bunch of terrorists. They were venting their anger at the evil American empire and kept asking me where I was from, but I kept replying, "No se'."

A holograph of some spiritual leader appeared on the wall and one after one, the terrorists would climb upon a stool placed in front of the holograph and raise themselves until their heads entered into the fractured glass ceiling, and then they would disappear. One of the terrorists pushed me toward the stool and forced me to stand upon it.

He said, "Now raise yourself."

I replied, "I don't want to. I will damage my head."

He answered, "If you are a true believer, you will feel no pain."

"But I can't," I protested.

"But you must," he demanded, "or you will die."

I raised myself and the sharp glass pierced into my head and blood poured out over my face.

That night I decided to go to a chamber music recital at Sa Nostra, the Palma cultural center. I took a seat in the center of the small balcony. The first part of the program, music by Janacek and Mozart, was very slow and I found my eyelids getting very heavy. By the time the orchestra was into Mozart's # 12 in K Major, I was constantly nodding off with my chin dropping down to my chest and then back up again in rhythm to the music.

I awoke when the audience applauded and the houselights came on for intermission. I decided to walk around outside and I found the courtyard in the back, where the other audience members stood smoking cigarettes and drinking wine. I bought a wine and gazed at the crescent moon which glowed in the evening sky. The audience started moving back into the concert hall, so I followed.

Back in my seat now, the orchestra returned with woodwinds being added to the strings and a woman in a shawl sat down and began the narration to DeFalla's "El Amor Brujo" (The Bewitching Love). She narrated and sang with great intensity and the strings and woodwinds backed her with passionate fervor. When they got to the fourth movement, Danza Ritual del Fuego (Ritual Dance of the Fire), the bows of the stringed instruments appeared to be leaving the stage and crashing into the ceiling, while the woman's face changed colors. From the ninth movement, El Terror (The Terror) to the eleventh movement, Alucinaciones (Hallucinations), all the faces in the orchestra changed colors and the woman was no longer in human form but was some strange primeval beast. The bows were now just flashes of fire and the woodwinds serpentined toward me with seething satanicism. I think I let out a scream, but after it happened nobody in the audience seemed to have noticed.

They were all sitting upright watching the performance as if it was just another night of sophisticated chamber music. Everybody. Everybody that is except for the four people who were a few rows behind me and to the left: the Girl, the Big Guy, Bushy Eyebrows, and the Thin One. They were all looking at me with big smiles and waving.

The rest, I don't remember. I woke up to the finale, Las Campanas del Amanecer (the Bells of Dawn) and everything seemed to be normal again. The four came over to me with great friendliness. The girl said that I looked a bit ill and suggested that the four of them accompany me. As we were walking down the Passeig del Born, they apologized for their behavior at the bookstore and said that they were just having a little fun.

Frederico (the Big Guy), who wanted me to call him Freddy, was the owner of the bookshop. Jorge, "but call me George" (Bushy Eyebrows) was a construction worker, Constanza (the Girl) was a painter, and Izmael (the Thin One) was a former farmer but was currently unemployed. They told me that they met each Thursday afternoon to discuss literature and have a few laughs. "Yesterday's laughs," I told them, "were at my expense."

They told me about a bar that they said I would love and talked me into going there with them. Suddenly, we turned into a maze of alleys, left, then right, then left again, many times over until we got to the Escape, a bar much like my neighborhood bar in San Francisco with friendly people, a pool table, pretty girls, and two couches facing each other, where we placed ourselves.

Constanza sat next to me on one couch, while the other three faced us. Freddy brought two pitchers of wine mixed with coke and when I offered to pay, he replied, "I don't want your money." The drink, which seemed repugnant to me at first, was actually quite tasty.

We talked about simple things. George asked me, "What's the business about baseball? Why do people get so excited about it?"

"It moves so slow," Izmael added, "Now futbol, there's a game; constant movement."

Freddy scoffed at that, "They run around and kick the ball for eternity and bounce it off their little heads and get their little yellow cards. Rugby's the game. American football is good, but in rugby the players hit just as hard and they don't need no stinkin' helmets."

I agreed with Freddy. Rugby was becoming more and more interesting to me each time that I watched it and American football was very hard to see here in Spain. Constanza hardly talked at all; she filled our glasses from the pitchers and held my arm.

After a few too many pitchers more, we five left the bar. I held Constanza with my arm around her shoulder and her hand went around my waist. We turned right outside of the bar and walked down an alley. The three amigos clowned around ahead of Constanza and me. Izmael jumped upon a thrown out washing machine and rode it like a horse proclaiming that he was Don Quijote, while George became Sancho, and Freddy was Dulcinea.

We, five musketeers, danced along the alley some ten meters more, when suddenly I noticed that we were beside the Bar Dia Tapas bar, which was just a minute up the alley from my hostel, the Ritzi. I proclaimed, "There's my hostel, right there." We got to the gate and the three amigos became even more clownish. Blowing kisses to Constanza and me and wishing us lovebirds well, they continued leap-frogging each other until they were out of sight.

I asked Constanza if she'd like to come and see my room. She replied, "What is there to see?" I told her that I had music and other things. She said, "I like music," and so we went upstairs.

The next morning I woke up to find that Constanza was no longer there. Was it only a dream? My head was throbbing with pain. I turned to the nightstand and there was a note from her. It read, "David, please meet me at the Escape bar at 9 pm." I lay on my back for a while and then fell asleep.

I had a dream in which I think I was John Lindh Walker, whom I had recently read about in the newspaper. He was a young American who had converted to Islam in 1997 and regularly attended a mosque in San Francisco. He traveled to Yemen in 1998 and 2000 and then joined the Taliban in Afghanistan in May of 2001. He was recently captured by Afghan Northern Alliance forces who were working with the USA. In my dream the CIA was interviewing me and seemed to know that I was an American. They kept offering for me to call my family back home, but I continually refused as I spoke in Arabic and kept repeating that my name was Abd-al-Hamid.

I awoke to a vacuum cleaner outside of my door and looked at my watch which read 8:42 pm. I had just enough time for a quick shower before meeting Constanza. I rushed up Apuntadores to the Escape.

The bar was empty except for the bartender and Constanza and the other three who were seated in the back on the couches. Izmael was sitting next to Freddy and George was next to Constanza. I kind of expected George to move over to the other couch, so that we could sit as the previous night, but he didn't budge, so I squeezed in at the end of the couch next to Constanza. She poured me a wine and coke and the five of us sat there rather glum.

Finally, Freddy said, "Let's blow this joint," and we did.

We walked along the Passeig del Maritim, where cars sped by along the waterfront. Weaving right we walked up a hill and walked over a bridge before entering the beautiful Plaza La Feixina, with its water fountains of constantly changing colors. We crossed Argentina Street and walked along Carrer de Sant Magi. I asked where we were going and Freddy pointed ahead and said, "There." Up ahead I saw a glowing crescent moon. As we got closer, I saw that this moon was made from broken mirrors and was the sign for the cocktail lounge, Crescent Moon.

Inside the Crescent Moon, things were very festive with balloons and crepe paper everywhere. The jukebox played Cuban music and the young revelers shook their booties and kissed passionately. We went to the back room where there was another bar, and the young people who were sitting there stood up, and we took their seats. Hermina, the bartendress, was very attractive with long black hair and glitter on her face. She served us drinks of many colors in tall glasses and we had the first of many. There was something very strange about this place. Mirrors were everywhere in many different shapes and sizes and everyone seemed to be conversing with the person's reflection in the mirror rather than looking directly at the person.

The six of us left the bar and walked up Sant Magi. I was arm in arm with both of the girls and the men followed. The girls turned me to the left and said, "We are home."

Home was a very old, dark building with iron terraces and iron spears throughout its front. The borders of the windows were decorated with what looked like giant wings of bats. The street level of the building was a hardware store, but it was unlike any hardware store that I had ever seen before. Displayed in the windows were regular hardware items such as electrical plugs and hooks to hang keys, but there were also muzzles and whips and blades of various shapes and sizes.

The six of us walked up a spiral staircase made of iron. Hermina led the way and held my hand, while I held Constanza's. The three men exited onto the second floor, but the girls and I continued up to the third. Hermina opened the door to the third floor and turned on the light. Paintings were everywhere with dark, grotesque figures and iron sculptures of spears and fire. I remember going to a large bed with red satin sheets and watching the girls undress themselves and me, but that's all I can remember.

The next morning I awoke to bright sunshine in my face and another massive headache. The girls were gone, but Izmael was sitting in a wicker chair facing me. He said that Constanza had business and suggested that since it was Sunday, we should go to the Cathedral of Palma for the 10:30 mass, and so we did.

We entered the Cathedral, which was filled to capacity, and sat near the back. I noticed a rodent-like old man with dark sunglasses and a suit with a wool sweater buttoned up to his neck, standing by a pillar. He appeared to have nodded to Izmael and Izmael appeared to have nodded back to him.

The ceremony began with the priests entering amid smoky incense. During his sermon the priest talked about el reino (the kingdom) and sumision (submission), which he emphasized with great emotion. A woman about fifteen meters to my left began to cough and then the man sitting about ten rows ahead of me coughed as well. Soon it was dueling coughers. The woman, "Cough, cough," the man, "Cough, cough." This continued for a minute or more and then more coughers were added to this coucoughony. By the time the sermon had ended, the cathedral was reverberating with coughers of sopranos and altos and tenors and bass.

I looked at the frail Jesus Christ dying on the cross for our sins and I noticed the green and yellow rays of light shooting out from the stained glass toward the ceiling of the altar and I shuddered, recalling how the bows of the strings had done the same thing two nights earlier. Was it only two nights? It seemed like an eternity. Then the altar boys brought out the chalices filled with wine and hosts, which was followed by more smoky incense. Men in red and white robes came around collecting money from the congregation and I noticed that the man, in whose basket I dropped my coin, was the 'rodent' now dressed in red and white. The priest changed the bread and wine into the body and blood of Christ amid more smoky incense. We shook hands with our neighbors for peace and Izmael grabbed my hand with both of his and said, "Eternal bliss, my comrade."

I stood up to go and receive communion, but Izmael grabbed my arm and gestured for me to sit back down. I looked at him with confusion. Was it because I was a foreigner? No, other foreigners were receiving communion. I had not been a practicing Catholic for many years, but I thought it would be nice to receive the body and blood of Christ. Well, no matter, I watched the others come back to their seats after having received the red wine and white host. The ceremony ended with the pipe organ playing a terrifying song of long, distorted tones.

I walked around the stations of the cross and was standing in front of the one where Christ was tied to a log, when a small door opened from this station and out stepped the 'rodent', now wearing his suit and buttoned-up sweater and dark sunglasses.

Izmael and I stepped outside and walked along the Palau del Almudaina, which was next to the Cathedral. "The palace," Izmael told me, "was Islamic. On the land where the Cathedral is now, there once stood a mosque. This whole island, this whole Spain, this whole everything was Islamic."

We walked past the entrance to the palace; two cannons were there pointing at the Cathedral. We walked down to Ses Voltes, an outdoor auditorium, where a young brass band played the American classic that Sinatra had made famous, 'New York, New York'.

We sat down for the rest of the brass concert and during Pastor's 'El Arte de Cuchares', Izmael received a call on his cell phone. He talked loudly into it, oblivious to the stares of disdain being directed his way from the other audience members. He put the phone in his jacket and said, "We must depart."

We walked up a steep flight of old stone steps and passed through tunnels until we came to Los Bany Arabes (the Arab Baths) where tourists stood in line awaiting admittance. Izmael and I slipped through a small green door and walked through dark passages 'til we came to a dimly-lit cave dwelling where a small man with a freshly-shaven head sat. Izmael introduced him as Edmundo, but Edmundo said, "You can call me Eddie," and he shook my hand with great vigor.

We sat on some rocks and Izmael and Eddie got into a conversation (in Spanish I think). The sounds from their mouths were shooting out muy rapido and sometimes the conversation seemed to get very heated with increased volume and large gestures. Some type of negotiation seemed to be taking place. Finally, it ended and both were happy and shook hands.

Eddie invited me to join him on a drive to the other side of the island. He was so exuberant that I could not refuse. As we drove past numerous fallen trees and collapsed rural shacks, I told him about my arrival onto Mallorca on the day after the huge hurricane. I told him, "I find the island to be magical of both black and white. It is most dense with coincidence."

He said, "I have been nowhere, but sometime soon I will take a boat to anywhere." He did not like living on Mallorca because he said that most of the people on the island- the Germans, the English, and the Spanish- lived in bubbles; money bubbles and beauty bubbles and fame bubbles and no one could enter their bubbles because otherwise they would burst and there would be no more bubbles. "They bounce off of their bubbles and allow no one to enter," he said.

He talked about a former girlfriend of his from a poor family in England who had become a Christian. "Once I was driving her in a jeep through some mountains, when a man came out with a large gun and demanded that we get off of his land. I got all shook up and accidentally drove the jeep into another man's car. The damage was minimal and I gave the man enough money to cover the expenses and everything was fine, except the girl then created a bubble. She thought that I had made an irreparable mistake and she no longer wanted to be with me. She's still in Mallorca and is very rich living in her money bubble. Sometimes we pass along the street, but we don't talk. Our bubbles bounce off of each other. I don't like Christians because those who think that they are the truest Christians are the least truthful. The earth is Truth. It is where we come from and to where we will return."

The conversation changed to September 11th and the war in Afghanistan, which he did not like. "I'm not a nationalist," he said. "It makes no sense for some people to be rich while other people are very poor. The war in Afghanistan is without sense."

I told him that I usually considered myself to be a pacifist, but the reality of the situation was that we had to fight or the evil would become worse. I compared the Taliban rule of Afghanistan to Europe in the 1930's and 40's. I said, "I feel that if America had gotten involved in the fight against Hitler and the other Fascists earlier, not so many innocent people would have perished. We learned from that war and we learned a valuable lesson from the Vietnam War. Although I feel that we should never have gotten involved in Vietnam, we did, but we went about it all wrong. We kept gradually bringing in more troops and the war lasted forever and we never won it. Later in the 90's when George Sr. was president, we acted swiftly and carried a big stick against Iraq. George Sr. never finished the job by capturing Sadaam Hussein, but I feel that Junior is going to finish his dad's job after the bloody mess in Afghanistan is resolved."

I explained that my philosophy came from my interest in Hinduism and in particular the holy tale, the Mahabharata. In the famous chapter of this tale, the Bhagavad-Gita, Krishna, the Enlightened One, says to the noble warrior, Arjuna, as he drives their chariot into battle, "To a warrior, there is nothing nobler than a righteous war because it opens a door to Heaven."

I said, "I hope that our cause is righteous. Unfortunately, I believe that there are no enlightened leaders in the world today. My candidate for U.S. president, Bill Bradley, lost because he spoke the truth, and the American people were not interested in hearing the truth."

Eddie said, "September 11th did not surprise me at all. America, a nation that began by pillaging and raping their native people, cannot expect to continue its peaceful existence without painful retaliation. It's Karma: What goes around, comes around."

We turned on the radio and listened to Leonard Cohen's, 'The Land of Plenty'.

We drove into Pollensa and I slipped into a nearby bar to take the edge off, while Eddie rested in the car. I was drinking a glass of vino rosado when a South African man, whose name was Brun, sat down next to me and asked, "What has four legs in the morning, two at midday, and three in the evening?"

I thought about it but could not come up with an answer. He then took out a coin and requested that I bet my soul on the outcome if he flipped it. I said that I was not a betting man and if I were, I would not make any bet when it meant that I might lose my soul. He said, "You bet heads," and flipped the coin and it came up tails. He said, "It's a good thing that you did not bet."

I replied, "That's why I don't bet."

He said, "You bet heads."

I replied, "I don't bet anything." He flipped the coin and it came up tails again. He said that I lost the bet, but I said that I did not make any bet. He grabbed for his beer but spilled it all over the bar and onto my pants."

He said, "Let's make a bet for a beer," and I reiterated that I did not bet. He said, "Well, buy me a beer anyway."

I said, "I will buy you a beer, if you tell me the answer to the 4,2,3 legs riddle." He said that he would tell me the answer after I bought him the beer. I said that I would buy him the beer after he told me the answer. The woman behind him, a friend of his I assume, gestured to me not to buy him a beer and pointed to her head signifying that he was not well in the head. He told me that a baby has four legs in the morning, then walks with two at midday, and needs a walking stick in the evening. I bought him his beer.

He asked me if I understood the answer. I replied that I thought I did, "A baby crawls with four legs, and as it gets older, it uses two legs to walk, and when it becomes old, it needs a third leg or a walking stick."

He replied, "You don't understand."

"I don't?"

"No, you don't."

"What don't I understand?"

"You don't understand the answer."

"I don't?"

"No, you don't."

"Well then, explain it to me."

"I cannot."

"Why not?"

"Because you don't understand"

"I'm not sure if I want to understand."

"Oh yes, you do."

"No, I don't think I do." There was a long pause as he drank from his beer and grabbed my cigarettes and took three.

He said, "I was born."

"You were born?"

"No, I WAS born."

"You were born."

"NO, I WAS born."

"You were born." We repeated the same exchange for about five minutes and the woman behind us and the bartender shook their heads and prayed that we would stop. He told me that I reminded him of someone. I replied that I hoped that it was someone that he felt well about and he replied that no, it was not. He said that he was no danger to me and that he was not a violent man. I told him that I was very happy to hear that. He told me that he was born in Born.

"You were born in Born?"

"Yes, I was born in Born. Do you know where Born is?"

"No, I don't know where Born is. Where is it?"

"Born is in bloody England. Do you know where it is?"

"I guess from what you say that it is in England."

"YES, it's in BLOODY England ...... There's more than one Born"

"There is?"

"Yes, there's East Born and then there's West Born."

"But no North and South Born?"

"YES, there's North Born...and South Born. . .and East Born...and West Born." He asked me what Born I was born. I replied that I was not born in Born. He insisted that I was born in Born and inquired, "Which Born were you born?"

I answered that I was born in the Midwest."

"So," he said, "You were born in West Born."

"If you say so."

He brought out his coin again and told me to bet my soul on its outcome. I said that I would not.

He said, "Where's my hat?" and looked around his barstool on the floor.

I said, "Is it on your head?" and he checked his head, but it was not there.

He saw my hat on my head and asked, "Is that my hat?"

"No, it's my hat. Is your hat black as well?"

He looked confused and replied, "I have special powers. I know things that you do not know."

"And perhaps," I replied, "I know things that you do not know."

"I have SPECIAL powers. I know things that you cannot know."

"Do I want to know these things?"

"Oh, yes, you do."

"No, I don't think that I do."

He took out his grey hat from his coat pocket and put it on his head and told me to tell him about myself, where I was from. I replied that I was born in Wisconsin and moved to California.

"NO, talk to me."

"I am talking to you."

"NO, talk to me. You're NOT talking to me."

"I am an island."

"NO, I am an island. If you were an island, I would blow you out of the bloody water."

"But, you're not a violent person."

"No, I'm not."

"Am I a violent person?"

"No, you're not a violent person."

"I'm not?"

"No, you're not."

I grabbed my cigarettes and went back to the car, where Eddie was sleeping in the back seat. I drove back to Palma and then walked to the Ritzi, where I slept.

I dreamt that I was a defendant on trial. I sat alone at the table for the defense and my hands were behind me and handcuffed to the chair. The judge, Constanza, sat at a very tall desk and said, "Mr. Geiger, where is your attorney?"

I answered, "Nobody will represent me."

"I can't blame them," she replied. "Let's proceed. Mr. Geiger, you are on trial for being an adventurer."

"Not just an adventurer, Your Honor," Brun, the prosecutor interrupted, "but an adventurer in the third degree, a sole adventurer." The audience in the courtroom gasped. Brun continued, "Mr. Geiger not only goes on adventures, but he does it alone."

The audience became very loud and outraged and Judge Constanza banged on her gigantic gavel and said, "Order in the court, order in the court. Mr. Geiger, no man is an island. You are guilty of adventure in the third degree. Your sentence is..." and I woke up.

I lay awake for the rest of the night and thought about the dream. I had been an adventurer for as long as I could remember. What was the crime in that? I thought about the time when I was three years old and the neighbor girls, Marla and Amy Smolinsky, and I each had a penny. We remembered that there was a bubble gum machine outside of the Red Owl grocery store on Highway 47 about a half a mile away, so I suggested that we trade in our change for some chewable delight.

We walked down London Street and turned right on Ninth Street when a man, who was mowing his lawn, asked us where we were going. We each held up our shiny pennies and told him about the bubblegum machine and continued our journey despite his protestations. We turned left on Highway 47 and marched alongside the busy road, until the bubblegum machine was within sight. I urged the girls to pick up the pace and soon enough the bubblegum balls were so close that we could almost taste them.

Suddenly, a police car pulled up alongside us and the officer ordered us to get into the back of the car. The girls complied, but I argued and wanted to get my gum first. He picked me up and threw me into the backseat with the girls, where I continued to scream and shake the cage that stood between the front and back seat.

The police car slowly passed by our house as my mother was shaking out a rug. She recognized my white head and screamed for the officer to stop. The officer said to my mom, "What have you told your son about the police? Doesn't he know that the police are here to help him? He acted as though I were the enemy. I thought I might have to put handcuffs on him."

I thought of my other misadventures as a child. The time that I went to my first movie with my brother and sister, and I watched the cartoons preceding the movie and thought that the show was over. So, I exited the theatre by myself and walked across town to my grandma's house. And my first day in first grade when I walked home at lunchtime because I thought that school was over. After all, kindergarten was only a half day. And the time that my family visited the Chicago Museum of Science and History; I drifted away from them and after a long frantic search, I was found sitting happily inside a German U-boat.

Throughout my life I had been wandering around on my own. I started to think about what the cop had said to my mom about putting handcuffs on me. In the past few years, I began having obsessive thoughts about being handcuffed. It wasn't the kinky kind of Sadomasochistic obsession, but something that seemed inevitable and preordained. I envisioned officers forcibly pulling my arms behind my back and slapping on the cuffs.

Why was I obsessing about this? Obviously I felt guilty about something. Growing up as a Catholic, I recognized that guilt was a way of life.

I felt guilty that I had spilled water on the floor when I was three, and my mother slipped on it and separated her shoulder and had a nervous breakdown shortly afterwards. Sure, my dad had recently died and that probably caused the breakdown, but I always felt the guilt because of the water that I had failed to wipe up.

The next day, I ran into Constanza and we decided to go to the symphony together, the two of us; not George, not Freddy, not Izmael, only Constanza and I walking together arm in arm on air. We sat in a private box and held hands as the program began. The first part was called Canco De Amor i De Guerra (Song of Love and of War). The operetta featured a soprano, a tenor, and a baritone backed by a large chorus. The voices lamented of their painful existence in the highlands but proclaimed their devotion to their cause for a dignified life. They sang of battles and victories, the immaculate emblem of their eternal existence.

The second part of the program was a comedy about a thin man, who was constantly swinging from place to place, from Mallorca to Barcelona to America and back again. I thought, as I held Constanza's hand, 'How happy I am now that I don't need to be hopping around from place to place, a solitary traveler. I have found my place in the sun.'

After the show, we walked back to Constanza's place and I noticed that there were far fewer paintings and sculptures than the time that I had been there before. Constanza said that she had a very enthusiastic British buyer, who had purchased nearly everything. I commented that the paints that she used were unlike any I had ever seen before. I asked how she did it, but she smiled and said, "It's my secret recipe," and refused to tell me anything else.

The next morning, I awoke to find Constanza packing a bag. She said that she needed to leave for a couple of days on business. I told her that I would accompany her, but she said that I could not. We walked down the stairs to the door and onto the street where George was sitting in an old pickup truck with the engine running. Constanza said, "Don't worry, I'll be back soon," and kissed me and rode off in George's truck.

Four days had passed and still there was no sign of Constanza. I hung out at cafes and bars in her neighborhood, but it was to no avail. So, I spent the week drinking and smoking way too much. The next Sunday afternoon, I went to the symphony again only this time alone again, naturally.

The first part of the program was four interludes from Benjamin Britten's English opera, Peter Grimes. The first interlude, Dawn, began very peacefully with violins and flutes, but I started to sweat and struggle with my breathing. During the second interlude, Sunday Morning, I felt numbness in my left arm. In the third interlude, Moonlight, all of my clothing were drenched in sweat and my entire body seemed paralyzed. In the fourth interlude, Storm, the orchestra played with presto con fuoco, and each time that the marimba player struck the keys, a sharp pain pierced into my heart. The ceiling above turned into dark storm clouds and the audience applauded, but I could not move.

The second part of the program was Joaquin Rodrigo's "Fantasia para un Gentilhombre" which premiered in 1958, the year of my birth. The ceiling above the orchestra became the face of a very angry God. God seemed to be telling me that the time had come for me to die. There was applause and the audience walked out for intermission, but I could not move. I sat there, in my pool of sweat, looking at the face of God.

After intermission, the audience returned for Antonin Dvorak's 8th symphony which the program said, he had composed in 1889 in his Bohemian country home amid a flow of inspiration so swift that his pen could barely keep pace with it. I didn't remember any of it. I awoke and the auditorium was empty and the face of God was now benevolent and behind the stage, the scrim was lit like a beautiful blue sky with white billowy clouds and a bright orange and yellow sun.

My heart was now beating at a normal rate and my breathing was without effort. I stood up and walked out of the auditorium, throwing my newly purchased pack of cigarettes into the garbage bin.

The sun had set and the church bells from up the street at Sant Magi started to ring. I decided to follow the bells and ask for God's forgiveness of my sins. I tried to enter the church from the front entrance, but a vicious black dog stood at the gate and howled wildly and arched its back and revealed its frothing mouth and sharp teeth. I walked around the Placa de la Verge del Miracle and entered the church from the rear.

I was now wearing my six-pointed Star of David outside of my shirt rather than on the inside like I had usually worn it. I'm not Jewish, but my name is David and it was given to me by a trusted Jewish friend as good luck before my journey into India last year. As I sat down in the pew, I discovered that my copy of the Bhagavad-Gita was in my back pants pocket. I removed it and placed it on the pew face down.

The altar at Sant Magi was magnificent. At the bottom was the sacred arc surrounded by haloed old and young holding double-barred crucifixes and keys, while Christ above ascended to the golden crown on which a real live black bird stood.

I noticed a man, who looked like the 'rodent' from the cathedral, slip behind a door into the sacristy. He had the same face and dark sunglasses as the rodent, but now was wearing a young man's black and gold athletic jacket with a golden eagle on its back.

The ceremony began and a very humble priest led us through the service. Although it was in Spanish, I found myself remembering the responses in English and making signs of the cross across my forehead, mouth, and heart very naturally.

When the priest delivered his sermon, he stared directly into my eyes without once looking away. I understood exactly what he was saying to me, although many of the words, I could not comprehend. He talked to me about alegria y alegria falsa (happiness and false happiness). He contrasted between the fiesta, which is temporary, and eternal bliss. Paraiso (Paradise) can be yours, but you must do penitencia (penance) for your sins. The gates to Heaven will open for you, but you must first get the llave (key).

The priest began to change the bread and the wine into the body and blood of Christ, as the assistants collected donations from the congregation. I dropped a 500 peseta coin into the basket held by the 'rodent' now dressed in a red and white robe.

I walked in the line for Holy Communion and said, "Amen" to the priest who placed the powdery white host into my mouth. The ceremony ended, but I decided to kneel down on the wooden plank and repent for my sins. Two snobby women in full length mink coats looked at me as they passed as if I were repugnant. They were the "True Christians".

I asked God's forgiveness for all of my past sins and told him that I would be good from this moment forward. I prayed while thinking about my Wheel of Life that I had created while hiking alone through the Himalayan Mountains in Nepal last summer. The Wheel had eight spokes. The first spoke of Truth, to be honest in words, action and thought; the second spoke of Honor, to live with dignity; the third spoke of Justice, to be fair in all dealings; the fourth spoke of Duty, to fulfill responsibilities; the fifth spoke of Service, to help others; the sixth spoke of Courage, to not fear adversity; the seventh spoke of Humility, to be humble, and the eighth spoke of Joy, to rejoice in all these things.

I thought about the undignified way that I had been behaving, and the insolent brashness and flaunting of my supposed superiority. I asked God to please forgive me.

The black bird, which had been perched upon the golden crown, began to fly furiously around the alcove above the altar. The walls of the alcove were sculptured into eight gigantic keys. An old woman opened the side door, which led to Plaza de la Verge del Miracle, and the bird flew out.

I walked around the interior of the church while an invisible woman's voice led the old women in prayer. Familiar words such as San Francisco and California were spoken by the invisible voice and each statement was followed by "el senor es contigo", which I believe means "and the Lord is with you."

I looked at an old painting of Sant Magi. He was a peaceful-looking man with a long beard wearing a long brown robe. The painting showed smaller men doing acts of violence, such as beheading others, while other men kneeled and prayed. Below the painting was an eight-pointed star with a fossil in the shape of Spain with the words of Sant Magi inscribed and a small Sant Magi statue standing on top.

At another side altar stood a small white marble statue of the Virgin Mary and the Christ child. Two cherubs held a small round mirror which was angled, so that it reflected my image amid the tiny white flowers. I lit a candle and prayed for the health of my mother.

On the back wall of the church was a painting with men floundering in the flames of Hades. They were each wearing necklaces of black and white. Below the painting was a small confessional, where the priest sat waiting for me. I tried to speak in Spanish to him, but he said, "Speak to me in English, which is the language that you speak."

"Bless me, Father, for I have sinned. My last confession was many years ago, when I was a small child." I told him about the lying and the stealing and the debauchery that has plagued me throughout most of my life. I talked about my enormous ego and my selfish behavior toward others. I talked about my drug and alcohol abuse and my fear of dying."

He said, "My son, your sins will be forgiven, but first, you must pay a penance."

I replied, "I understand. I will do anything."

He said, "You must provide service to the young. Some are without homes, without families, without food, without souls. You must provide these things for these young people and your sins will be forgiven."

I thought silently, 'Didn't penance used to be ten Our Fathers and ten Hail Marys?'

The priest said, "Ten Our Fathers and ten Hail Marys will not suffice. You must provide service with humility for the young who are in need, and then you will discover that eighth spoke on your wheel."

I got startled by his knowledge of my Wheel, but then composed myself and replied, "I understand, Father. Thank you."

"Go in peace, my son," he said as he made the sign of the cross on my forehead, mouth and heart with holy water. I exited as the door slammed thunderously behind me.

Beside the church in Placa de la Verge del Miracle, a very thin woman, dressed in black feathers and darting eyes, played guitar and sang the Beatles' song, Blackbird. The vicious, black dog, that I had encountered earlier in the evening, now lay serenely at her feet wagging its tail and smiling at me.

I walked back to the Escape, but Constanza was not there, so I decided to walk to Sa Posada to see a musical duo that was advertised in the daily. As I walked, I thought about all that had happened in the church, and what my penance was that the priest had given me, and how I could fulfill it. I must have walked at least thirty minutes even though Sa Posada was only ten minutes away.

I took out my map and opened it to try to figure out where I was, when a strong gust of wind blew my map through the iron gate that stood in front of an old, deserted two story building with a small roofed terrace above part of the second level. I reached for the map but could not get it because the gate was chained. Two dog-like gargoyles sat above the gate, protecting the building from intruders. Beneath the leaves of a palm tree, I noticed that there was a small for sale sign with a phone number. I thought, 'This will be the place where I will provide service for the young that are in need. This will be the place that I will serve my penance.'

But the sinfulness continued. One night I was moping around in my room and listening to Bob Dylan's 'Devil Shuffle', when I noticed that there was a Devil Festival going on that night. I put on my red T-shirt that had Buddha on the front with bloodshot eyes. The eyes had gotten that way because I had once washed the shirt in hot water and the red mixed into the whites of his eyes. His eyes now matched mine.

I put on my black coat and tied my scarf into a large, black bowtie. My black stocking cap looked different on my head as if it was covering two small horns. My eyebrows seemed bushier and more arched and my goatee was now very pointed and very silver. Walking to the Devil Festival, I felt very powerful and dangerous.

Inside, Sala Sonotone was one very large room of red and black with mirrors and mirror balls everywhere. The large mirrors on the wall hung in front of dark, cave-like circles. Flame-like lightbulbs hung from the ceiling as well as empty bird cages, coiled, snake-like springs, and rectangles blowing silver horns. The rectangles had faces of young people with missing eyes, ears, noses, and mouths.

The crowd was very young and they wore greased, spikey hair or stocking caps with words like Sepultura, Kreator, Diablo, Nirvana, and Kamakaze emblazoned across the front. They were all dancing near the stage while the lights flashed and the punk bands screamed, "War, War, War, Fire, Fire, Fire!" The place was scorching hot like an inferno, but I continued to wear my black jacket, black bowtie scarf, and black horny hat. I stood alone at the bar in the back and ordered tequila after tequila. And then I blacked out.

Sunday came again and found me entering a small house near the Ritzi where readings from the muse, Sofia, were advertised. She lit a white candle that was in the shape of a female torso and we sat on cushions beside a small octagonal wooden table.

She asked me, "How do you feel about death?"

I replied, "I do not fear it because I feel that I have lived a good life, so I will be rewarded rather than condemned." I told her how I had hiked through the Himalayan Mountains alone against the advice of others, because if bandits were to confront me, I would say, "I know that you are thieves, but are you murderers as well? Because in order to take even one Nepali rupee from me, you will have to kill me and live with that sin in your next life."

She said, "You say that you do not fear death, but you are obsessed with the thought of it. All your life, since your father's young death when you were only three years old, you have feared that you have a weak heart as well."

I thought, 'How does she know about my father's heart attack? I did not tell her this.'

"Your heart is weak, Beloved One," said she, "but you can make it strong."

"How?"

"I cannot tell you. You must listen to your heart." I looked befuddled. "Let us talk about something that you feel very strongly, Perennial Philosophy," said she.

"Perennial Philosophy? I know nothing about it"

"You know much about it; you just don't realize that it has a name. In your travels, you have discovered the commonalities among all of the religions and cultures; Hindu, Muslim, Buddhist, Christian, Jew. You have recognized their true common spirit in their pure state without government or business."

"Yes, that is true."

"Universal Truth flows from one single divine source. This single source is interpreted in many different ways through not only inference, but direct intuition as well. The true purpose of all humans is to discover our eternal selves which is what and who we truly are."

"Yes, I understand."

"In Hinduism, the Eternal Truth is Brahman, which is manifested by the Holy Trinity; Brahma -the creator, Vishnu -the preserver, and Shiva -the destroyer. Christians have their Holy Trinity as well; the Father, Son and Holy Ghost. In Christianity, God has purified human spirit through an act of grace. In Buddhism, the focus is on the spiritual quest for Nirvana. In the Islamic philosophy, the Eternal Truth is called al hagg — the Unity of Allah."

"I need to write this down" "

"No, there's no need for that. You already have the words and have underlined and starred the most important parts."

"Where?"

"In the book in your black bag."

"What book? I have many books in the bag."

"The book that is falling apart because you keep putting it in your back pocket and then you sit down on it. The book that you have barely opened."

"The Bhagavad-Gita?"

She nodded silently. I took out the book and, sure enough, the parts that I found interesting were already underlined and the most important parts had beside them in pen a six pointed star, the Star of David. She told me to close the book, and I did.

She said, "You must learn to write with your right hand."

"I can't. My right hand is useless. I will only be able to scribble incomprehensibly."

"No, you must do it," and she placed a small silver ring upon my right pinkie. "This ring has a six-pointed star like the medal that you wear around your neck. When you have learned how to write with your right hand, two more points will appear on the star like your wheel of life which has eight points..."

"My Wheel of Life? How do you know about my Wheel of Life?"

"It is written all over your face."

"You are strong in six of your spokes but in two you are very weak."

"Which two?"

"You know which two, numbers five and seven."

"Service and humility?"

"Yes, service and humility. You will acquire these spokes when you begin to help others, those who are in need of your service, the young who are without a home and a soul. You must provide these things for these needy or you will perish in darkness."

"How should I do this?"

"I cannot tell you how, but don't worry. You will not find the way; the way will find you. Now we begin with something very simple. With your right hand, you will underline and star the parts in the Gita that you find to be of most interest to you."

"But it's already been done," I said as I reopened the book, but the markings had disappeared.

"Read slowly the book with care and place your markings. You stay here and I will sit in the far corner. Begin now."

The vein on the inside of my right elbow began to pulsate very strongly as I underlined and starred with my right hand. I silently read the first chapter entitled, 'The Sorrow of Arjuna' and became confused when Arjuna was described as the conqueror of sloth. Without asking her, Sofia answered my question, "Arjuna lived without sleep. He overcame his need for sleep or rest."

Outside a church bell rang eight times. She said, "You must go now and follow the bells and attend the service of your family's religion. There, you will discover knowledge in your heart that no book can ever teach you."

I walked to where I thought that I had heard the bells, but the doors to the small church were locked. When I pushed on the door, another bell sounded, so I continued my search. The bell seemed to have rung from my left, so I kept looking in that direction. I walked over the same street blocks over and over again, but there was no sign of a church; only restaurants, bars, and shops. I glanced to my right and there was the church, the enormous Cathedral of Palma. A large crowd of lemmings were standing in a stagnant line waiting to enter the Cathedral through one door, but I remembered from my earlier visit with Izmael that there was another door ten feet away. I followed three school girls in long plaid skirts and entered from the other door.

I sat down in a pew with a black man and woman and noticed that nearly all of the congregation were Anglos. This seemed unusual to me because when I had visited the Cathedral the previous time, the congregation appeared to be Spanish in the majority.

My pew filled up with a German man and his young daughter sitting to my right and two upper-class English women sat between me and the black people.

I discovered that this was not a church service but an ecumenical gathering to celebrate Christmas in song and word. The celebration began with the congregation singing 'Once in Royal David's City'. I turned my program over to see the lyrics, but I discovered that they were missing from my page. Everybody else in the area had lyrics except for me and an elderly French woman who sat in front of me. The woman looked with confusion at the paper as did I, and the woman next to her gave the old woman her program. I was hoping that the couples next to me would offer me one of their programs as well, but they did not, so I leaned forward and sang the words from the old woman's paper, "...with the poor and mean and lowly, lived on earth our Savior holy..."

The first reading was from the third verse of Genesis in which the serpent tricked Eve into eating God's forbidden fruit. God then proclaimed that humans would from then on toil in their labor amid thorns and thistles and then die, proclaiming, "Dust you are and to dust you will return."

The pipe organ then reverberated throughout the Cathedral as a young boy wearing a long purple turban and carrying a long sword sang about the wizard from the Old Testament, Sybilla. The content of the music was about the Day of Judgment in which mountains would collapse, and rivers would flood, and terrible creatures would appear.

I turned to the side and watched a grey haired man in his fifties, wearing a blue trenchcoat, pacing back and forth and obsessively doing the sign of the cross and then prostrating himself. The man's feet kept shifting and he constantly turned his head from side to side; his eyes revealing a paranoiac terror. This was in sharp contrast to the baby that sat in its carriage beside its family. The baby sat calmly with a smiling open mouth and his eyes were bright and enthusiastic, as Sybilla sang that men shall be distinguished as good or bad due to their service to God.

The celebration ended with the congregation singing the first verse of Silent Night in English, followed by Catalan, German, French, then Castilian. I no longer needed to peek over the shoulder of the woman in front of me. The words magically materialized from my mouth, as the rays of colored light from the stained glass window shone down upon the people.

Since the Ecumenical Celebration wasn't really a church service, I decided to walk to Sant Magi Church for Mass. Before the service began, I knelt on a wooden plank and prayed for my family. I thought about how I had prayed with such remorse during my first visit to this church. Now I felt much more at peace with myself.

I wanted to see if the priest would again direct his sermon to me, so I sat along the side rather than directly in front of him. He turned to his right and again glued his eyes onto mine. He talked about redencion (Redemption) and said that my corazon esta debil (Heart is weak) and I needed to make my heart fuerte (Strong), by being a mensajero de la palabra (Messenger of the word) y del mundo (and of the world).

I thought that I was sitting in front of a poor-looking black man, but when I turned around to offer him my greeting of peace there stood a fresh-faced young Spanish boy. Just before the service ended, however, a black man sat in front of me, and we lowered our heads in submission to the Lord. After the service, we simultaneously put coins into the candle holder to light a candle, but there was only one available candle, so we lit it simultaneously and knelt down on each side of the candle and prayed with our heads bowed. The cracks of the floor below me revealed faces of suffering men and sympathetic gods of all denominations.

I see faces in just about anything that I look at. I remember in high school the teacher gave each of us a paper with a drawing on it, and he asked us what we saw. Immediately, students raised their hands and answered that they saw a woman.

"What type of woman?"

"Young," said one.

"Old", said another.

"Beautiful," said she,

"Ugly," said he.

Young and old, beautiful and ugly; they were all there in that famous picture of perception, but I didn't know what they were talking about. I was looking at the white border around the picture and saw many faces. Funny, sad, happy, mad, skinny and fat, a dog and a cat. If I stare at a wall, my eyes unfocus and the faces appear. When I close my eyes, still more faces sparkle in the darkness like stars in the night.

I picked up a newspaper and some flowers and went back to the Escape hoping to find Constanza, but she was not there. I really missed her and I wanted to ask her out again. I sat out on the terrace and read the news while watching the street for any sign of her or any of her friends.

The newspaper that day was giving me a not too subtle message about remembering to serve my penance. It started with my horoscope, which read, "Parents or people who work with children are nudged by today's new moon to think of better ways of teaching. Shaping young minds is an important responsibility."

Nearly every article was about young people dealing with difficult circumstances. "In the United States, two Vermont teenagers were charged with stabbing to death a 63 year old man and his 55 year old wife. They were stabbed multiple times in the face, neck and chest, and found lying in pools of blood. In Britain, the 42 year old alleged killer of 8 year old Sarah Payne said that he had the inside of his van pressure cleaned the day after Sarah was snatched, but he had nothing to hide. Also in the U.K., a 46 year old man denied murdering 17 year old dance student, Heather Tell. He says that he spent two days sleeping on a towpath near his home drinking only canal water. In Lima, Peru, 13 year old Diego wakes up early to go to the dump to collect recyclables."

I had a relatively sleepless night back at the Ritzi. I thought about the way that my days and nights were spent. I had scheduled to have a tattoo that would be on my left arm and depict the face of a red-nosed sad clown with a bloody heart. I reflected that having a sad clown tattoo was not such a good idea. A large red pimple had appeared at the tip of my nose, and I began to look more and more like the sad clown. I worried that if my nose now resembled the clown, perhaps my heart would bleed as well, like the clown's.

Finally, I fell asleep and awoke to the alarm clock at 11:30 and set off for the Tainted Soul Tattoo Parlor for my 12 noon appointment. As I walked there, I was still undecided whether or not I would have the tattoo applied. I looked up an adjoining street and saw a sign entitled True Love. I thought, 'Is it true love that I have for Constanza or is it only an illusion?'

I walked further past an antique jewelry shop and then an unusual flower shop and saw along the next adjoining street another sign that advertised True Love from another shop. Again, I stopped and thought about the reality or illusion of our relationship and I determined that it was only an illusion and not permanent. Most things in life were only temporary, except tattoos; they stayed with you forever. Did I really want this tragic clown to be with me forever. No, I determined; I did not. I went to the parlor and canceled my appointment. And I felt lonely again.

The next day, I attended a school concert at the San Francesc Church in old Palma, where the voices were a bit off key, but it was very enjoyable watching the teachers guide their students through the rather complicated songs. The concert ended with a Hallelujah medley, in which the kids did some unusual sound effects with some very some unusual and never in-rhythm dance movements. It was very good.

Then, I rushed over to the Sa Nostra Cultural Center to catch another free concert. This evening's performance was by a quartet of two violins, a viola, and a cellist from Prague. I entered the building just before the concert was to begin. Two very loud Italians were shouting at each other in what looked like a normal conversation for them. I passed the noise pollution and walked up the stairs to get to my usual spot up in the balcony, but the door was locked. I started to run back down the stairs to go to the main level, but an usher came with a key and unlocked the door, and I entered followed by the two obnoxious men. The men stormed ahead of me and sat in the back row, and I went to the first row across the aisle and down from them.

Just after the lights went down, a very pretty young woman in a long dark blue coat sat in the front row seat right across the aisle from me. I thought it was a bit unusual because the balcony was almost empty and, usually, women seemed to try to avoid me for reasons that I don't understand. She looked to be Eastern European to me and I hypothesized that she was probably from Prague, a friend of the musicians.

The two noisy Italians talked very loudly as the musicians were tuning their instruments. When the music began, they shut up for a while. During the second song composed by Vranicky, the jerks started talking loudly again, and I looked back at them and gave them an evil stare, and they closed their mouths. I glanced at the pretty woman, and she was still sitting serenely with her eyes closed, listening to the music.

I felt a very strong attraction toward her, and I remembered my horoscope for that day (the 14th of December, my lucky number, because of my boyhood baseball hero, Mr. Sunshine, Mr. Cub, number 14 on your program, Ernie Banks!). The horoscope said something about me being highly attracted to someone that day, but that I needed to display courage and aim very carefully at my target.

The music was hypnotic and induced me to sleep, but just before I would doze off, the high bee buzzing sounds of the violins would wake me up. I continually glanced over at the woman, and she continued to sit serenely with eyes closed.

I knew that my horoscope was about her, and I tried to think of a way that I could begin a conversation with her without scaring her away. The musicians played Smetana's, "From My Life", while I thought about all the loser feeble openers, I had attempted with women in the past.

Intermission came, and I waited to see if the woman was going to walk outside. She stayed in her seat and brought out a book from her bag and began to read. I looked at her, and she looked at me, and I became scared and looked away. 'Where are your balls, Geigerman?' I thought. I picked up my bag and went to the men's room. Returning to my seat, I brought out some breath mints and made it obvious so that, hopefully, she would look over and I could offer her one, but she continued reading.

In the second part of the program, the musicians performed Ravel's Quartet number 1 by finger plucking their instruments, and the broken springs boooiiingged in my head of opening line ideas. About 10 seconds before the final number ended in a very quiet moment of heavy concentration by the musicians, the two brainless morons stood up and exited, slamming the door behind them.

The musicians looked up to the balcony and then finished to huge applause and took two curtain calls as the audience shouted for more. The quartet came back to do an encore which was not listed in the program. The woman cellist spoke, "We will now perform blank, blank, blank in 7 major by blank, blank.

I loved the encore, not so much because the music was magnificent, but because it had given me an opening line, "Who was the composer of the encore?"

The musicians left the stage to great applause, and I saw that the woman was slowly repacking her bag, so I did the same. When she stood up, I did as well, and asked while trying not to look scary, "Senorita, hablas ingles?"

She answered, "Yes, a little."

"Do you know the composer's name of the encore piece?"

"Encore?" she asked confused.

"The finido, the end, se llama de composer" I said very nervously.

"Oh, the finale,...I think...Mozart. I'm not sure," she said calmly.

"Ah, Mozart," I said too excitedly.

She began to walk away, and I said, "Are you French?"

"French, no,"

"Ah, ah, ah, de donde esta usted?"

"Barcelona, pero ahora Palma. Y tu?"

"Si, mi tambien, pero primero vivo en San Francisco."

"Oh, an American," she replied smiling. We walked down the stairs together, but some people separated us at the bottom. I caught up to her as she was looking at some pamphlets, and I did the same. She exited, and I followed alongside her.

I said, "The music was wonderful, wasn't it? I liked the finger-plucking in the third part."

She replied, "I liked best the first part." which was the music where I kept falling asleep.

The woman, whose name was Ana, continued to walk along the street, as I tried to muster up the courage to ask her out for a drink. She asked what I did. I said, "I'm a teacher on a one year sabbatical, paid vacation."

"I know what a sabbatical is," she said with confidence.

I continued, "I am a writer creating a story."

"What kind of story?"

"It's fiction with a lot of reality."

"Oh really, I want to hear about it. Shall we go somewhere and have a beer?"

"Yes, that would be very nice," I replied with relief.

She suggested McDougall's, but I envisioned a bunch of drunken, obnoxious white guys screaming at the soccer game on television while I tried to have a meaningful conversation. "Or we can go somewhere else," she said.

"Yes, I know some good places where we can talk," I answered and thought, 'It's like she is reading my mind.'

We walked up Apuntadores past the Ritzi, and I said, "Here's where I live."

"Oh, the Ritzi," she said, "We are very close to one another." We headed toward the Escape, but I was afraid that maybe Constanza or her friends would show up there, so I suggested that we go to the Corner Bar, which I had just recently discovered. It was noisy in there, but we found a relatively quiet spot at the bar in the back room. We ordered two pints of beer, and I paid for them, but Ana wanted to buy her own, so she set her coins on the bar.

"Now," she said, "tell me about your book."

"It's not a book yet," I said, knocking on the wooden bottom of the bar, "and I can't tell you much detail of the story until it is finished because I am very superstitious."

"Oh, yes, I understand. Tell me what you want to tell me."

"I started it about three weeks ago when I first came to Palma. I became inspired by one word. I think it's a slang word that was spoken to me, and after that my imagination and strange coincidences took over."

"What was the word, and who spoke it?"

"It was spoken by a woman, I saw at a bookshop."

She smiled mischievously and said, "And the word?"

"I think it was 'hago' which is slang."

"I don't know this word."

"I think it's short for hasta luego, see you later, so it means something like 'later'."

"I never heard such a word."

"I think I saw it used in a book once, but I don't know where."

"What is your story about?"

"All I can say is, it's about the struggle between good and evil."

"Oh, okay," she said, "I like that idea. Do you have a name for the book?"

"I have a tentative title and subtitle, but it's very boring and no one seems to like it but me."

"Tell it to me."

I wrote 'The Book Club' on a pad, while explaining it. "The title has three words but two of the words have multiple meanings. Book has many meanings because there are many types of books; good, bad, fiction, reality, religion, propaganda, and on and on. It's also a verb which means to charge a person with a crime. Hawaii 5-O. 'Book him, Danno'. Club means an organization, so 'Book Club' is a place where people get together and talk about books. But another meaning of club is as a weapon, to hit someone and hurt him."

"I don't understand."

"Big stick, bam, bam, bam," I spoke and gestured.

"Oh, yes, I like the title," Ana said with great brightness of being.

"The subtitle is longer but in short letters, 'the words with music of an american in europe'. The words are my own, but some of the ideas I get from newspapers about world and local affairs. 'With music' is important, because I don't think that any of the music is my own, but it influences what I write, and what my character does, both good and evil. It is my character's and my muse; our inspiration."

Ana smiled and said, "I like your title very much. Tell me about you and your family."

"Well, I come from a middle-class family in Wisconsin. We are certainly not rich, and we are certainly not poor. We are right in the middle. My father died, when I was three years old of a heart attack at the age of thirty. My mother loved him very much, and she was very young, only 25, I think, with four young children and a dead husband."

"Tell me the names of your family and write them down please."

I wrote as I spoke, "I have one brother and two sisters. It goes boy, girl, boy, girl. My brother, Jeff, is eldest, then my sister, Sandy, then me, David, then Lisa, my sister, who was just a baby when my father died. Our last name is Geiger, which means Violin in German. My first name in Hebrew means Beloved."

"So your name is Beloved Violinist. Do you play the violin?"

"No, just a little guitar. My mother's name is Lily"

"Tell me about her," she said.

"My mother is very strong and very funny. She's gotten older now, but she is still very lively. She is in a singing group that goes to old folks' homes and entertains the residents. She has married three times. My father, Bill Geiger, that I told you about, I only have one memory of him."

"Tell me."

"We were in the living room, and I was riding on his shoulders, and he was acting like a horse, and my brother, Jeff, and sister, Sandy, were begging for him to give them a ride."

"That's a very nice memory."

"Six years later, when I was nine, my mother married a man named Jed Modine, who was the father I remembered most. He lived as a bachelor most of his life and was very set in his ways. We had many conflicts but many things in common, as well. He loved horses, golf, football, Hershey chocolate kisses and his lazy boy chair, where he always reclined. He died of a heart attack just before he was to retire, which was very tragic, because in retirement he would have been very happy with golf every day."

"That is very sad."

"My mother's third husband, Bill Burbank, was a very strong man, but now he is very ill."

"You have experienced many difficult things."

"I think about death often. I guess I'm obsessed with it. I never thought I would live to see thirty years, and when I did, my friends in San Francisco had a very nice surprise party for me."

"Do you still fear death?"

I then talked about my discovery of courage, while hiking through the mountains of Nepal, and drew my Wheel of Life, and explained each of the eight spokes. When I came to the final spoke, Joy, I had difficulty explaining it, and Ana said, "I think your wheel is missing something."

"What's that?"

"Love," she said, "You have no love."

"But there's love in service and joy."

"Yes, but love is very important. Perhaps, you don't want it."

"I want it, but I have accepted living without it."

"Yes, we do that."

She pointed out the six-pointed star that I wore around my neck and my finger and asked me whether I was Jewish. I said, "I don't think so. I wear them because they are the Star of David, and that is my name."

"I love the Jewish people."

"But a French girl, that I lived with in San Francisco, was convinced that I had Jewish blood because of the way I looked, and she thought that Geiger was a common German Jewish name."

"I think you do," she said. "I have a very close Jewish friend, who lives in Berkeley."

She mentioned to me a Jewish Chanukah celebration that was taking place on Sunday. I grabbed my post-it notes, and I showed her that on the second page I had written down the details of the event, and that I had already planned to go. "I am going too. Will I you see there?" I asked.

"Yes," she answered. "I am very interested in Jewish people. They have struggled very much, yet they are very successful."

We finished our drinks and I walked her home. I couldn't help feeling jealous of this young Jewish man in Berkeley because I thought that they were probably lovers, but I didn't ask about it because I didn't want to appear possessive.

She invited me up to her apartment, which she shared with a friendly gay Spaniard, named Andreu. She showed me her paintings of people from South Africa, each of which were based upon a different chakra; the part of our body that gives us energy.

She asked, "Do you like real or not real?"

I didn't know if she was talking about art or life or love, and I responded, "What do you mean?"

She said, "I make these paintings from photographs that I have taken in South Africa, but I don't like them. They are only copies of photographs."

"I think they are very good. Why do you paint from photographs?"

"Because I am afraid to do otherwise."

"Why are you afraid?"

"I don't know...I don't know what will happen to me. It frightens me."

"You need to discover courage and abandon your fears."

"I know but it is very difficult."

"Yes, I know."

She showed me the painting, she was currently working on, showing a black woman. "It is not finished. I don't like it. The eyes are not right."

"I like it very much. It is my favorite. I like the eyes, especially. They are very mysterious."

"You like?"

"Very much."

Ana made café con leche for us, and we sat down at a small round table in her living room. "Where do you paint?" I asked.

"I like to paint on the terrace or here in this room and play music to inspire me. I open the doors to the terrace and sit at this table and drink coffee and read and write. It is very good to be here. The landlord lives next door, and she is a very kind and wise grandmother. She is my mentor."

"Yes, it is very nice here."

She brought out a book and explained to me the chakras. She said that she was a solitary person like me, but that she was happy.

She asked me about my opinion of the war in Afghanistan. I said, "I don't think that I want to talk about it because when I do, people get angry at me."

"I won't get angry, tell me."

I explained that I thought that America had a just cause and explained my belief in Hinduism and my philosophy of perennialism. I continued, "I think that the most important part is not the fighting in Afghanistan, but what will happen in the world after the war. We need to create a balance in this world. There is too much inequality which creates hatred. But our leaders are not enlightened. They don't see the cause of the problem."

"I agree with you," Ana said. Then she said that she was very tired and that she needed to work in the morning so we stood up to leave. At the doorway, I noticed that her table had many small golden stones and I asked about them.

"Here, this is for you. It will give you good luck," she said, while giving me one. "They are from my flower shop." We kissed each other softly on the cheeks, and I left.

I went back to my room, and I lay on my bed and thought about the magical night. I placed the small golden stone that she had given me and felt its energy being transferred into my heart. My mind and heart were racing, and thoughts kept jumping in and out of my head, but they kept coming back to one idea, which was Ana's, about my Wheel of Life not having a place for love.

I had tried to have love in my past relationships with women, but it was never realized. I had been hurt, and I had hurt others, and I had resigned myself some five years ago that my life would have to continue without it. I would find joy in other things; helping others, expanding my creativity, and exploring my spirituality.

But tonight, those things were no longer sufficient. I wanted love, and I wanted my love to be with Ana. She was so bright (intelligent and illuminating), and funny in her talk, expressions, and movements, and she displayed a wisdom much beyond her 28 years, and her beauty, oh her beauty.

I stayed up most of the night and early morning, day-dreaming about my future with Ana. She would travel with me across Europe and live with me in San Francisco or Europe, or wherever we chose. We would have beautiful children with blue eyes like ours. The first will be a boy and the second, a girl. One would have blonde hair like me and the other brown hair like Ana. We would spend some holidays with her family in Barcelona, and other holidays with my family in Wisconsin. We would grow old together, and our features would become more and more similar to each other, and strangers would think we were brother and sister. We would die together and then return to earth in mortal form as even more beautiful, enlightened beings. We would be soul-mates for eternity.

Finally, I fell asleep around half past ten in the morning and awoke suddenly at 12 noon. I stared at my brown pants, hanging from the foot of my bed. With the light coming in through the window and the way the pants were wrinkled, they looked like the face of some wise, bearded dog god. The Brown Pants God stared at me, wearing a grave expression on his face. He said, "Your thoughts are too high, they're in the air. This is not love, you're feeling; it's only infatuation. You are only dreaming in the ideal. You must get real and come down to earth. You are an old man and she is a young woman. Stop dreaming. Get real."

I thought that the Brown Pants God was probably giving me some good advice because I knew that since I had only known Ana for one night, my feelings could be only infatuation and not true love. But, I also suspected that perhaps this god, that had appeared to me in the form of my brown pants, may have actually been the devil in disguise, trying to squash my dreams. I decided to restrain myself from expressing the emotions that I felt through voice and decided instead to write Ana a simple rhyme, that I hoped would let her know my feelings about her without scaring her away. I needed to aim carefully with Cupid as my guide.

I looked at the photograph that I had taken of myself a couple of weeks earlier in front of an artistic sculpture in Palma. It was a large concrete wheel, but one eighth of it was empty, and this part I thought to be the love that was missing from my Wheel of Life. In the corner of the photo, I was hiding behind another small structure, and I looked very serious and mysterious in a black hat, coat, pants, shoes and dark sunglasses.

I wrote my Rhyme for Love and attached it to the photo. The rhyme went like this:

I placed the magic stone close to my heart

and thought about a fresh new start.

The stone is golden and purple too,

with mountains and trees in morning dew.

It's round like my wheel, yet needs no spokes;

it reflects my desires, it shows no hoax.

It's love my wheel is missing,

your lips that I'm not kissing.

I hope that this rhyme brings you no fear,

I'm harmless and patient for you, my dear.

I then lay back down and fell asleep throughout the day and night until I awoke on Sunday morning. I went outside, but had to return to my room, to get what I call my blue Krishna poncho because it was raining with great intensity. I walked to one of the few stores, that was open on this Sunday, and bought a newspaper, put it underneath my poncho, and walked briskly back to my hostel. On the other side of Borne, walking in the opposite direction very quickly, I thought that I saw Ana with her long dark blue coat and funny black hat, but I wasn't sure if it was her because of the distance and the rain. I thought about calling her name, but decided against that because I was in my pajamas and was unshaven with bloodshot eyes. Perhaps I would frighten her, if she saw me. 'One must aim carefully,' I thought and walked back to my room.

I listened to the tranquil music of the Santo Domingo monks for a couple of hours to relieve my restlessness, then showered, shaved, applied eye drops to my bloodshot eyes and dressed in blue. I still had about 40 minutes before the celebration was to begin, so I decided to walk to Sant Miquel's Church to pray and see where Ana had told me that she sang in the church choir.

The doors to the church were locked, so I sat on a bench praying for help in winning Ana's heart. While I prayed, a squatter who looked like Kris

Kringle sat at the church's door and read a Bible with his lips moving for each word that he silently read. I watched him for a while and thought, 'He is not uneducated because his lips move as he reads. The words on the page are not just words on a page. There's a spirit behind those words that come alive from his shriveled, bloody lips.' I walked over to him and dropped some coins into his filthy hands. He thanked me and told me that his name was Nick.

"Mucho gusto, Nick," I said, "muchas gracias."

He replied, "De nada," and I departed to the Chanukah celebration.

I arrived at the Arca for the Chanukah celebration, but there was no sign of Ana. I thought that perhaps she had decided not to attend because perhaps she had seen me in the rain and became frightened. I smoked a cigarette to relax myself and rested against a cold wall.

Suddenly, Ana appeared with her roommate, Andreu. She looked tired and sad and did not kiss me on the cheeks, as I had expected. I asked, "Como estas?"

And she replied, "Oh, not too well." She didn't appear to be happy to be with me like I thought she was two nights ago. I thought that the Brown Pants God had spoken the truth, and we would be 'just friends', those words that every relatively nice guy like me detests hearing from a woman in whom he is interested.

We unsteadily walked upstairs and sat on the rear wooden bench, while Andreu sat on a metal chair a row in front of us. Ana asked him to sit with us, but he declined, saying, "I want to be near the heater." It was very cold in the auditorium, but I suspected that this was a good sign; he wanted to let us sit alone. Perhaps, I thought, I have a chance with her.

Suddenly, a well-dressed and manicured Spanish (perhaps Jewish) man named Pere sat down next to Ana and began to converse with her and looked longingly into her eyes with passionate lust. I didn't understand anything that they said, but Ana responded to his remarks with sweet laughter and I became very jealous, although I tried not to show it. How I wished now that Andreu had chosen to sit next to us rather than the heater. I felt like I was being ignored by Ana, although she did speak to me briefly and translated to me what I hoped was their true conversation. I suspected that they had arranged a rendezvous, and she was keeping this information from me, but I tried to appear friendly and unconcerned.

The program began with a middle-aged Jewish man, with a long black beard, speaking in a high-pitched tone about the reason for this celebration. While he spoke, his dark penetrating eyes seemed to never leave mine. I didn't understand a thing that he said, although his constant gestures toward the Menorah gave me the impression that he was talking about the miracle of the eternal light.

The second man that spoke was much easier to understand because he spoke more slowly, his voice was of a lower tone, and his eyes did not mesmerize me. He talked about the battle that the Israelites had fought against the much more powerful Greeks. The Jews had very little oil for their lamps, but the lamps remained lit, hence the miracle. He talked about Truth and Justice being the fundamental beliefs of all Jewish people.

The man with the penetrating eyes then spoke again. He recruited children to light the candles of the menorah. Skullcaps were placed upon the boys' heads. One father placed his decorated skullcap on his son's head and then brought out a black handkerchief for the top of his own head. The children lit the candles in order from left to right. One impatient girl tried to light a candle before it was her turn, and the other children became testy, but the bearded man calmly explained to the girl, that it was not yet her turn, and that she needed to follow the tradition. The bearded man announced that they would now prepare the food downstairs, while the children would play with their traditional wooden toys. Pere and Andreu stood up and asked Ana and me if we wanted to go to a bar for a drink. I replied, "No, I'd rather stay up here for a while and watch the children play." Ana agreed with me and Pere and Andreu walked downstairs.

The children started pounding their wooden hammers against the wooden blocks, as Ana and I talked over the cacophony. I took out my photo album that I had brought from the States, and asked Ana if she'd like to look at it. We looked at the photos of my family, friends, adventures, and the different phases of my life. She was very curious and asked me many questions and judged the people in the photos, based upon their facial expressions.

Then we went downstairs to taste the traditional Jewish food. We stood with Pere and Andreu, and I could sense that there was a competition between Pere and myself. He criticized all American movies and politicians. I could not disagree with him although my opinion was much less extreme. Ana mentioned that she very much liked the movie, 'American Beauty' and Andreu and I agreed, which shut Pere up for a while.

We walked back upstairs for traditional Jewish music played by a violinist and a guitarist in a funny black hat. As they sang, a face in the blue curtain behind them appeared to me. The blue curtain god smiled at me tenderly and gave me reassurance that all would be well.

Above the stage, stood a placard with an angel holding a piece of land in one hand and a sword in the other. Around the placard on the plastered wall, faces of Jewish spirits wailed at me of their struggle with everlasting persecution and despair. I, with the rest of the audience, wailed the cathartic refrain with the musicians, "Ay, Ay, Ay, Ay."

Then, the tablets of the Ten Commandments appeared on the wall, and I tried to recall what they were, but I could only remember two: Thou shall not kill, and thou shall not covet thy neighbor's wife.

Afterwards, we went to The Escape, so that I could watch my NFL San Francisco 49ers play on television. Pere said that when he was younger, he dreamed of studying three things, Architecture, Astronomy and Archeology.

"And what did you choose?" Ana asked.

"Architecture," answered Pere.

"You chose the most practical profession," Ana replied. I felt relieved because I knew that practicality did not impress her.

Ana asked us what animals we thought that we would be in our next lives. She thought that I would be a dog in my next life, but I replied, "I believe that I was a dog in my past life before becoming me, but I hope that in the next life I will be a more enlightened human."

"No," she said, "my question is what animal."

"But human beings are animals," I countered.

"They are?" she asked, "But no, say another animal."

"Well then," I answered, "I wish to be a dove, a symbol of peace. And you Ana?"

"I will be a cat," she answered as she purred at me. "And you, Andreu, what animal will you be?"

"I will be an elephant," he answered proudly.

"In India," I said, "the elephant is a very sacred and well-loved creature."

"And you, Pere," Ana asked, "What animal will you be?"

We waited for a long time as Pere sat with a blank stare.

"I will be a dog," Pere proudly proclaimed.

"Why?" I asked.

"Because I want to chase after the cat," he answered while smiling at Ana.

Ana talked about her boss at the flower shop, whom she described as being rigid and unfriendly. "I am the only woman at the flower shop and the men all express themselves very seriously and close their lives off from one another," she said, "but I try to bring a little light and warmth into the shop."

I related to her the idea about people living in bubbles and added, "Bubbles are translucent and your light can enter through them," and she smiled warmly at me.

We walked back to Ana's home and at the entrance I gave her an envelope with my Rhyme for Love enclosed.

I said, "Look at it later, goodnight," and we kissed on the cheeks as Pere stood wide-eyed like a big fish ready to swallow a small one. Then we went our separate ways.

The next day, I went to Bar Bosch to have coffee and read the newspaper. Bin Laden was still not captured by the American troops. The paper said that it was believed that he was now hiding in Pakistan. Andreu, Ana's roommate, walked by and gave me a very friendly "Hola," which encouraged me to think that the Rhyme for Love went over well with Ana. About 30 minutes later, a smiling Ana appeared and sat at the table with me. I asked her whether she liked the rhyme and she smiled more and said, "Very much."

We talked more about the chakras, which are the elements that she was using for the foundation of her South African paintings. She said that chakras were a confluence of waves of energy and compared them to streets in the city. "People show the opposite of what their chakra is," she explained, "but they are capable of changing their energy waves through the body, mind, and spirit."

We agreed to meet again at the Corner Bar at 8 pm. I went back to my room at the Ritzi and took a nap. I awoke at 7:45 and rushed into the shower because I looked very tired and greasy. It was important to me not to be late for my 8 o'clock appointment because I considered this to be our first real date and I didn't know how she would react with my tardiness. I left the hostel at 8 pm and ran to the bar and arrived at 8:02, but she was not there. I hoped that she had not yet arrived. She didn't seem like the type that would be insulted by only two minutes of tardiness. 'No, she did not yet arrive. Everybody in Spain is always late for everything,' I thought.

I ordered a red wine and sat on a couch in the lounge trying to look nonchalant while smoking a cigarette. At 8:20 Ana arrived with Andreu and sat down on the chair beside me.

She said, "Andreu made me late. He always moves so slowly."

I replied, "His chakras must be moving very fast."

Andreu asked me to tell him about Hinduism. I said, "It has numerous gods and Hindus tend to have their own personal gods. For example, my personal Hindu god is Hanuman, the monkey god."

"And me?" asked Andreu.

"Yours would be Ganesha, the elephant god, the remover of obstacles."

"And what would mine be?" inquired Ana.

"Yours would be Lakshmi, the goddess of beauty."

A Chinese woman entered the bar selling roses and I decided that I wanted to buy one for Ana since I considered this our first date. I knew that she would say "no" because she worked in a flower shop and could get roses whenever she wanted them, but I wanted to get her one anyway.

To lessen her objection, I decided that when the Chinese woman came to us, I would buy Andreu one as well, but before the woman got to us, Andreu stood up and wished us good night.

The Chinese woman approached us and I said, "I want to buy a rose tonight. Which one would you like?"

Ana said, "I don't want any."

I said, "Please let me buy you one. I need to practice at giving and you need to practice at receiving." Ana raised her eyebrows and I said, "I'll pick one out for you and one for me, okay?"

"Vale," she replied.

"What?"

"Vale, it means okay," she answered. I picked out a small pink one for her and a red one for myself.

I invited Ana up to my room to listen to some music. She sat on my bed and looked very pretty in a tight red V-neck sweater with a white blouse underneath. As Van Morrison sang, 'Caravan', I sat on the bed beside her.

She said, "I liked your rhyme very much, but some parts I found confusing. For example, what is this magic stone that you write about?"

I brought out the small Buddhist pouch from underneath my shirt and showed her the golden stone that she had given me on the night that we had met.

"And what is ho-ax?" she asked.

"It's pronounced hoax," I answered, "It means that my intentions for you are honest and pure."

"The line that I liked the best is 'It's love my wheel is missing, your lips that I'm not kissing.' "

"May I kiss your lips now?" I asked.

"Yes," she replied and we kissed tenderly.

The next morning I walked up Borne to the newsstand to get a daily and noticed a small smiling ceramic angel lying on her back with her legs spread out in a window at a gift shop and decided to buy it for Ana. At the newsstand, I purchased the daily and turned to our horoscopes. Ana's read, "An unexpected gift will come your way." Once again the daily horoscope spoke the truth. This island was so incredibly magical.

I went back to my room to make a card to accompany the angel. I cut out a small blue heart and wrote on it, "Ana, you are an angel sent down from Heaven to rescue my tortured heart and show me love. I adore your funny ways, your serious thoughts, and your very pretty face. Con amor, David."

We planned to meet at her place at 8:10 pm and go out for dinner, which we did in the company of Andreu and Pere. After some time we escaped to my hostel, and I brought out the daily and read Ana's horoscope aloud. "Did you receive a gift today?" I asked.

"No, I guess that horoscope did not come true," she answered.

"Wait, it says that it could benefit through your partner. I received a Christmas gift from my family today,"

"Was it unexpected?" she asked.

"No," I frowned, "my brother e-mailed me yesterday and told me to expect it. Oh, well." I put the newspaper back into my bag and said, "Oh, what's this?"

"What's what?" she asked.

"I don't know. I found it mysteriously in my bag. It has your name on it, so it must be for you." She unwrapped the angel and read the poem, and we lay down and kissed some more.

Ana's roommate, Andreu, flew to Germany for the holidays to visit his boyfriend, Klaus, a flight attendant. He was very enthusiastic about seeing Klaus again and was trying to learn some English since Klaus spoke no Spanish. Andreu also bought lots of new clothing, which he had purchased from a women's clothing store, which was where he liked to shop. Ana was relieved that he had found someone because she said he had gotten very dependent upon her as he had been with his past female friends.

I moved into Ana's apartment while Andreu was away, and in our love nest Ana painted as I wrote and the music played. Ana said that she wished that it could always be like this. I agreed. We had dinner on the terrace and Ana said, "When you leave Palma, we will need to talk on the telephone each day."

"No," I replied, "I don't want to talk with you on the phone."

"But we must. How else can our relationship grow?"

"I don't want to talk with you on the phone. I want you to travel across Europe and return to San Francisco with me."

"But I have my job."

"There are other jobs, and you always speak of travel and adventure being more important than work. I think that this is a great opportunity for the both of us. Do you agree?"

"I don't disagree, but this is a major step and I must think about it. I have very little money."

"I have enough money for the both of us."

"No, I want to pay my share."

"I can lend it to you then. I really want you to be with me as I see Europe for the first time."

"Maybe I could get jobs in Italy and Greece. I must pay my own way."

We discussed the places that we would want to visit and I said, "Take your time and think it over. I do not expect an immediate answer."

"I will think about it. It may be possible, but I need to think."

I walked her to the flower shop which stood right between the two True Love signs, and we kissed goodbye. Then I stood in front of one the True Love signs and prayed. I walked past the flower shop to pray to the second True Love sign and on my way I noticed in the window of an antique store next to the flower shop, an interesting and beautiful blue-beaded bracelet. I went inside and asked the Jewish proprietress if it was made from gems and silver. She replied, "No, it is made of glass beads and non-allergic metal. It is expensive because of the craftsmanship put into it. It was made in Israel." Immediately my eyes lit up; I knew that this would be the perfect Christmas gift for Ana; it was made of simple materials, it was blue like her eyes, and it was Jewish.

I asked to sit down so that I could count the beads. "You want to do what?" inquired Madge Dawson, the proprietress.

"I wish to count the number of beads in each arrangement. Numbers are very significant to me and my beloved."

"Do as you wish," she replied and looked at her assistant with raised eyebrows.

The numbers were good. Some of the arrangements had 14 and 8 beads, which are good numbers for me and some of the arrangements had 9 and 22 beads, which are good for Ana. The shop was closing for siesta, and I didn't have the necessary cash with me, so I told them that I would be back with the money after siesta.

As I was walking to Ana's place to meet her for lunch, I composed the poem that would accompany the bracelet. It went like this:

I looked for a sign

And found two.

I looked for True Love

And found you.

Blue is the sky,

Blue is the sea,

I'll never be blue

If you are with me.

We had lunch on the terrace again and painted and wrote. I told Ana that I needed to go outside alone and that I would return within 14 minutes.

"Where are you going?" she asked.

"It's a secret." I answered and gave her a short kiss.

The antique shop had just opened as I got there. Madge looked surprised when I said, "I'll buy the blue bracelet." She put it in a small suede pouch and I headed back to my hostel to hide it in my room.

When I came back to Ana's place, we started preparing dinner and after eating, we did more paintings and writing. Ana was becoming frustrated with her paintings so I surprised her with a new canvas and said, "With this canvas, you will use no photo. Paint it from your imagination and your heart." She painted in an unrestrained style her image of our twin children inside her body that we named Josiah and Jedeidah. The music embraced us as we did our art and it filled us with romantic love. By the next morning we had promised faithfulness to each other and gave our marriage vows under a canopy made out of white gauze from Ana's bed. It was the 22nd of December, just one day over a week since our first meeting.

That evening I met Ana outside of Saint Miguel's church after the choir practice. We walked to the Cellar to have some soup since it was a cold night. Ana sang her songs in Catalan as we walked, while I threw in the English versions of the songs that I could recognize.

At the Cellar, Ana showed me the lyrics to a song that she had copied down from a CD and asked me if I knew the song. I recognized it immediately since it was one of my favorites from the '70s and I sang it to her. It was Elton John's love ballad, 'Your Song'.

After we finished eating, Ana asked me again to tell her about my family. As I talked, Ana turned over the paper placemat and wrote out my family tree. She put symbols next to some of the names. For example, she put a crucifix if they were deceased or teardrops if they had a tragic life. Then we did the same thing with her family and noticed similarities and differences between our families. We each had two boys and two girls in our immediate families. We each had stepfathers and mothers with strong personalities. She still had three surviving grandparents, while mine had died when I was very young. She folded the placemat and we headed back to our love nest.

On Christmas Eve day, I surprised her at lunchtime with the table already set with pate', cheese, and crackers and a large bowl of fruit salad that I had put together. She was very surprised when she saw it and was happy with the cuisine since we had decided that we would try to eat healthier food.

"I have some news that I do not think you will like," she said as she served up the salad. She looked very nervous and I was afraid that she was going to break up with me because she had found another lover or had grown tired of me. "Pere came to the flower shop today…" she said.

'Oh, not Pere. You're not going to dump me for Pere, the bore,' I thought.

"He wants to go to St. Miguel tonight to hear my choir sing. Afterwards, I told him that he could join us for a drink."

Greatly relieved at the insignificance of the news, I said, "Sure, that's fine, but I have a feeling that we'll both be very tired tonight and will have the energy for only one drink."

"Claro," Ana replied with a smile.

In the evening we walked to St. Miguel and had a cigarette before entering. At the top of the entrance was St. Miguel standing on top of a fearless serpent and below that stood the Virgin Mary holding the Christ child surrounded by angels. At the bottom of the entrance sat Squatter Nick, once again begging for coins. He smiled at us as I handed him some money and thanked him again.

Ana introduced me to a man whom she described as her favorite priest and then went up to the choir loft. I sat near the back of the church so that lonely Pere could join me when he came. The mass began with a Catalan version of 'O Come All Ye Faithful' and I sang along with the choir and congregation using the lyrics that were written on my program. A woman stood at the pulpit and sang off-beat into the microphone, which made it difficult for me and I suppose everyone else to sing with the joy in which it was intended.

In the middle of a very dramatic rendition of Sybilla by a dark, statuesque woman, a small boy wearing a Santa Claus hat and bright yellow gloves noisily ran down the aisle and stopped at my pew and waved and yelled for his parents to hurry up and join him. The boy sat next to me and kicked the back of the seat in front of him and kept looking at me, but I sat calmly looking forward and following the proceedings.

I thought that his parents might remove his hat since it is inappropriate for males to hear headwear in church, but they did nothing. I began to stare at the paper snowflakes that spun counter-clockwise as the choir sang and thought how beautiful it was, but that it would be more beautiful if they spun clockwise like the prayer wheels and monks around the stupas in Nepal. Instantly, the snowflakes changed direction and now spun clockwise, and the boy removed his hat.

We then stood up and sang, 'Cant de Gloria'. I noticed that the boy was looking around because he had no program and I held mine so that he could read the words as well. With gusto I sang the refrain, 'Gloria in Excelsis Deo' as the boy looked up at me and we smiled.

Ana's favorite priest stood at the pulpit and spoke about the need for justice for everyone. He talked about the events of September 11th in New York and then quoted from the Bible, "The meek shall inherit the earth."

Beside him stood a man in a long blue trench coat and dark sunglasses who continually swung the smoky incense out to the congregation.

When it was time to offer peace to those around us, the boy turned away from me, so I tapped him on the shoulder and said, " Paz a tu y Feliz Navidad." He gave me a confused look and moved to the other side of his father.

During Holy Communion, I received the powdery host from Ana's favorite priest and expected him to say the Catalan equivalent to The Body of Christ, but he said nothing. I watched the people who followed me in the communion line and the priest continued to hand out the powdery host in complete silence. Then he placed the extra hosts back into the tabernacle, and the boy started to clown around again by standing on the pew and violently kicking the back of the seat, as the congregation sang, 'Silent Night'.

Outside of church, Pere was standing with Ana and Ana's friend and choir mate, Lucia, as well as Lucia's boyfriend, Marcos, who looked very ill at ease. Ana later told me that Marcos had recently had a falling out with religion and was very uncomfortable being near churches.

Ana asked Lucia and Marcos if they'd like to join the three of us for a drink and Lucia replied, "No, we need to go home. Marcos is very sick and needs to rest."

Pere, Ana, and I went to Bar Latitude 59 and as Ana went to the restrooms, Pere turned to me and said, "So, when is it that you leave Mallorca?"

"I plan to leave on January 10th."

"Ah, the 10th!" Pere said with excitement and added, "You will love Europe very much. The women are very beautiful in the north."

"I am not going there to meet women. I already have one that I love very much."

"Who?"

"Ana, the woman in the restroom."

"We shall see," said Pere. "All things change."

Ana returned to our table and asked, "What were you talking about?"

I replied, "Pere was wishing me a happy trip."

"We say to David, 'So long'," Pere said and laughed uproariously at his supposed joke.

I asked Pere about his beliefs in a god and he replied, "God is the bag of seeds, and he mixes the seeds together and then throws them to the earth to see how they will grow." Both Ana and I were impressed with his unique answer.

I asked him if he was a Christian, and he replied, "Of course not, religions were created to promote fear. Are you a Christian?"

I replied, "Yes, I consider myself a Christian as well as a Jew, a Muslim, a Hindu, and a Buddhist."

"You can't be a Christian," Ana protested, "because you don't go to church regularly."

I countered, "Since I've arrived into Spain, I've gone to church at least once a week. But that it is not what is important. That is only dogma and ritual. I believe that you are a Christian or whatever if your belief comes from the heart."

"For me, church serves as a reminder, a union," said Ana, "but God really does not exist except within ourselves."

"I agree that God exists within all of us," I replied, "but I also think that He or She or It or the Common Ground or whatever name you give, also exists outside of us."

Pere and Ana both looked disapprovingly at me and I suggested that we have another drink at Bluesville. Ana raised her eyebrows at me and shifted her eyes toward Pere but agreed to my suggestion. "It'll only be a quick drink, Ana, because I am very tired and you look very tired as well."

"Yes," she replied, "I am very tired," and gave out a yawn.

At Bluesville, we talked about God and religion some more. I said, "I think that human life is God's favorite game or pastime. And He gives us happiness, anger, sadness, and tragedy to see how we will react. If we react to these things well with humility and acceptance, we will get rewarded in our next life."

Pere remarked, "In my next life, I speak very good English," and we laughed.

Ana excused herself again to go to the restroom and Pere turned to me and asked," How old are you?"

"I am 43 years young," I replied. "How young are you?"

"I am only 37. I am much younger than you, like Ana," and his chest inflated.

After we left and arrived at Ana's building, I shook Pere's hand and said that I enjoyed our talk and Ana kissed him on both cheeks as Pere smiled at me and strutted away. Inside Ana's apartment, I told Ana that I was sure that Pere was after her and told her about the talks Pere and I had while she went to the restrooms. She agreed with me saying that when he had been visiting the flower shop, the phone rang and he said, "Who can that be, perhaps another suitor?"

We lay back in bed and on the next day, a beautiful Christmas morning, I told Ana that I didn't want to share the pillow with her like before. I grabbed the pillow and pulled it away from her as she looked at me with fear. Suddenly she noticed that her head was resting on a small package and I said, "Merry Christmas, my love." Her terrified face turned to jubilation as she opened up the package and pressed the Jewish bracelet against her heart and read the blue poem.

I told her that it was handmade from Israel and she proclaimed, "This is the best Christmas gift that I have ever received." We cuddled and watched the blue glass beads sparkle off the rays of the sun.

We decided that we would go for a walk and analyze sculptures on this day. On the Passeig del Born, stood a large iron structure that I did not like. "What do you see?" Ana asked.

"I see a stack of metal that impedes foot traffic," I replied.

"Say something positive about it" she demanded.

"I see a place to set down my camera on the structure," and I took a time-released photo of ourselves. "What do you see, Ana?"

"I see a beautiful house in the mountains with flowing rivers," she answered.

"Oh, yes, I see that too," I replied, "but now I see something else."

"What?"

"I see Heaven and Hell and here in between is Purgatory. And if people in Purgatory do not seek redemption for their sins, they slide down into Hell and spend their eternity in damnation."

"Must you always be so dark?"

"No, not always, but sometimes. I feel that the darkness suits me."

We decided to walk up to 86 Joan Miro because Ana wanted to check out my dream house/youth center. We imagined ourselves renovating the old abandoned house and giving direction to young people who had lost their way. Ana could help the kids express themselves through art, and I could teach them about the commonalities in all the world's philosophies. We envisioned closing off that part of Joan Miro to street traffic and making it into a pedestrian passage. This small section of Joan Miro, amid the strip clubs and casinos and discotheques, would be a sanctuary for goodness. We would try to bring a little light to all of the darkness.

We walked back to our love nest holding hands and read our horoscopes for that day. Ana's read, "You can derive great benefits from a trip to a destination that you have never been before," and Ana stated, "It's true. Our trip to Joan Miro was very special for me. This has been our best day yet."

My horoscope read, "Your most intimate relationships take on a more affectionate and tender quality now. You know that what was merely physical can become a vehicle for transformation and inner change."

"My horoscope came true as well," I proclaimed, "I feel much less darkness."

For dinner we went to the Cellar again for some soup. I talked about my hometown, Menasha, Wisconsin, as being a good place to have a marriage ceremony in the States. Ana turned over the paper placemat and drew the design for the dress that she would make for our celebration of love. It would be medium-length and cream-colored and subtly decorated with flowers. I would wear cream-colored pants and a blue shirt with my Star of David and red Hindu beads hanging across the front. Both of us would grow our hair long.

We both already felt like we were married, as we had promised our vows under God, but we wanted to celebrate our love with our families in a simple way, without gifts or stuffiness. We agreed that it was important to be legally married before our first child was born.

The next day my horoscope read, "Buy appropriate clothes so that you feel confident in yourself and the image you project to others." I already felt confident in myself and I really didn't want to buy any more clothing because my backpack was already too heavy, but Ana and I agreed that if I bought anything, a new hat would be nice. I admired the funny black hat that she wore the first night that I had met her and I wanted to find something similar to that. I thought of pictures of John and Yoko wearing the same black caps and compared them to us. She was an artist, like Ana, and I was, well I was not John Lennon, but I liked to write, and make funny jokes, and think about religion.

I found a black Jewish cap like Barbara Streisand had worn in the movie, Yentl, when she disguised herself as a boy. I also bought a long, blue wool coat, which was similar to Ana's. I thought that it might seem strange wearing such similar clothing as Ana because I always thought that it was comical when I saw older couples wearing the same clothing, but it didn't matter to me. In fact, I liked it.

I passed a music shop and saw a small guitar hanging in the window and decided to buy that as well. I missed not having my guitar with me and thought that it would be nice not to just listen to other's people's music, but also to create my own.

It was almost time for Ana to get out of work for her siesta break, so I sat down next to the monument in Plaza Wyler by the flower shop and began to play my new guitar while singing ' Poems, Prayers, and Promises' by John Denver. There were very few people in the area but within a moment, a sweet little Spanish boy with thick eyeglasses walked out of his way and dropped thirty pesetas upon the top of my guitar case. We smiled and nodded at each other and he walked away. During the next minute a bearded German man about 50 and his Spanish wife about 35 stood and listened to me sing as we smiled at each other. We wished each other a Happy New Year and they dropped 100 pesetas on my guitar case and walked away holding hands.

Ana came out of the flower shop and we discussed that we'd like to sing in the parks and streets as we traveled across Europe. We would wear our black Jewish caps and long, blue coats and become known as 'The Gypsy Angels'. We went to a music shop and I bought a violin for Ana. She now became like my name, my Beloved Violinist.

The violin, like anything for Ana, was a test of her patience. She was so brilliant and quick of thought that she always expected things to be achieved within a small matter of time. The violin, Ana found, would take a great amount of time and practice before she was able to produce the sounds that she wished to make. We would practice and play our music in the parks of Palma where very few people would pass. We never expected people to give us money. All we wished for was a smile in return.

A couple of nights later, we went to see the Edward's Burns' movie, 'The Sidewalks of New York'. The movie was described on the billboards as a romantic comedy, but I found it to be very sad. It depicted the temporary state of most relationships and the lack of communication between couples. We talked about the movie afterwards at a pizza joint and tried to devise a strategy so that our own relationship would not become temporary like the characters in the movie.

Ana, a former chemistry and psychology student, was very methodical and analytical in charting out the different levels of love, beginning with the physical, then the emotional, then the spiritual, then the selfless love. We hoped that our love of only 14 days, which seemed to each of us like 14 years would progress to this final stage slowly but at a very quick pace.

On New Year' Eve Day, Palma celebrated the Christian conquest over the Muslim Empire. It began in the Cathedral with children hopping and spinning down the aisle while playing flutes. They were followed by men riding phony ponies while swinging whips with bells attached to the end of them. Drums and more flutes followed along with a man playing a bagpipe. In the front of the Cathedral, the men on the phony ponies circled a woman riding a white 'horse' and did an elaborate dance.

The mass followed with the bishop of the region conducting the ceremony amid much smoky incense that floated in the air and engulfed the congregation that was filled to capacity. The pipe organ played a very loud atonal requiem and as I was looking at it, I noticed Izmael slipping out of the side door. It had been a long time since I had seen my old friend. He looked very mysterious and terrifying like he did when I had first met him in the bookshop six weeks earlier.

After the mass the phony ponies paraded throughout the streets of Palma, but they were joined by real black horses with conquistadores riding upon them and men dressed as monks and women and children in traditional peasant dresses. The parade ended at Plaza Cort where a woman told the story of the Conquest as the children sat around her on the ground.

A band then played traditional Catalan music as the crowd became circles and danced with castanets clicking the rhythm of the music, as the dignitaries stood on the balcony looking very important and unmoved. They were served drinks and aperitifs by the waiters dressed in black and white. I noticed that two of the waiters were Izmael and Eddie.

Izmael looked very out of place and uncomfortable in his role as a waiter. His eyes were very shifty and diabolical as he moved from one dignitary to another with his platter of aperitifs. I could not have imagined that Izmael would ever take a job where he would have to serve others, but perhaps he was desperate for money.

Ana and I had decided that we wanted to spend a quiet night alone for New Year's Eve so we had a simple candle-lit dinner. But ten minutes before midnight, we decided to go and see the New Year's festivities and set off for the main celebration at Plaza Cort.

We arrived just before midnight and swallowed a grape for each of the twelve times that the bell rang. Rock music followed with a Mallorcan band singing the song, 'Love Me Do' as Ana danced with me and we kissed. It felt so good to have someone to kiss at New Year's Eve; it had been so many years since I had last done that. I couldn't recall when was the last time and with whom. The fairy tale continued.

It was time to start our journey. We embarked on the large Transmediterranean boat and lay alongside the swimming pool on the top floor and basked in the sun which shone down upon us through the transparent roof. Ana and I held hands while we rested our eyes and we awoke just in time to watch another beautiful sunset before arriving at the harbor in Barcelona.

We needed to carry Ana's paintings as well as our other heavy luggage but with a strap that I constructed, it was not so great a problem. The previous day Ana and I had taken the paintings to the post office to be shipped, but they were oversize. Ana became upset and said, "Let's just throw them in the garbage!"

I tried to calm her by saying, "I think that it's better that we carry them. There will be less of a chance of them getting damaged or arriving late. I'll make a strap so that we can easily carry them."

"You don't understand. It's impossible," she argued.

"No, it's not impossible," I countered, "It will take only a bit of ingenuity, faith and patience. You'll see." And I was right. The paintings and the luggage were very heavy and cumbersome but we decided to walk from the port to Ana's family home rather than hail a taxi. Ana proudly carried her paintings up Las Ramblas and through the Barri Gotic.

We stood outside the family's wine shop, Vinoteca, which was below the family home and Ana said, "Wait, I want to pause here for a moment before entering. I need to gather my strength because I become very weak and not like myself when I am with my family." I took the moment to collect my strength as well since meeting with a girlfriend's family was a very unusual occurrence for me and I did not know how they would behave toward me. I thought that they might be suspicious of me because of my being an American and 15 years older than Ana.

We entered the wine shop and Ana's mother, Carme and stepfather, Antoni, greeted us. They seemed to be relieved when I took off my hat and they saw that I still had hair on my head. We removed our coats and my blue shirt was drenched with sweat, which caused me some embarrassment. We were led to the second level where Antoni's father Gerard, and Ana's sister Sara lived. Gerard, was a kind, little man with sparkling blue eyes, who greeted us warmly.

I went to my bedroom across from Ana's and undressed for a shower. Ana came in and said, "Gerard says that we should make ourselves at home and act as we normally would." She then looked down at my bare feet and gave a disapproving look.

The next morning, Ana had a private breakfast with her mother at Café de la Opera. Ana told her about our plans to marry in Wisconsin and her mother said that she'd try to change the family's holiday plans, so that they could attend. She also asked if she could participate in some way. Ana agreed that Carme could make her wedding dress as long as she did it according to Ana's design. Carme was very pleased to be participating and said, "I will make it exactly as you want it."

Meanwhile I walked over to Las Ramblas and bought a newspaper and sat on a bench reading it, while the characters and tourists of Barcelona passed by. The cover story in the paper told about the United States frustration in their failure to capture bin Laden. Grumbled a U.S. intelligence official, "One hour we're told he's in Afghanistan, another hour he's in Pakistan, Yemen, or even Paris."

Ana felt that a heavy load had been lifted from her shoulders after talking with her mother and we walked to the Parc de la Ciutadella to play guitar and violin and bask in the sun. Ana did not like that there were so many people in the park, so she refused to play the violin, and we lay alongside a tree to nap.

Some teenagers sat near us and had a picnic while we rested with our belongings between us. I heard the sound of Velcro, such as I have on my black bag, and looked around. My bag was now on the other side of Ana. I saw no one else around and I thought that Ana must have moved the bag for some reason but thought nothing of it and lay back down. I heard the teenagers talking more seriously and looked up again and they indicated that someone had taken my black bag with my camera, video camera, books, and two months of writing. I asked, "Quien?" They pointed to a guy with a horizontally-striped shirt exiting the park about 100 meters away. I put on my untied shoes, told Ana to stay with our other things and began to run after him. He didn't notice at first that I was after him so I gained some ground. He looked back and saw me rushing toward him about 40 meters back and started to run away. Even though my shoes were untied, I was still wearing my heavy wool coat, and he was younger and thinner than me, I kept up with him because my adrenaline was very high.

We ran through many deserted blocks and whenever I saw another person, I would yell, "Policia!" But they would do nothing and looked as if they were enjoying another one of Barcelona's most common sporting events, Moroccan Thief Running from Tourist Victim. He kept turning around corners and each time that I turned onto a new block, I would see his black and white striped shirt disappear around another corner.

On one deserted street he looked back at me with surprise that I was still behind him. I yelled to him with Shakesperian ferocity, "You better keep running you motherf*!ker, because if I don't get my bag back with all my things, I'm going to catch up with you and beat the motherf*!king shit out of you!" He looked back at me, his face filled with terror, and he threw the bag down and continued running.

I got the bag and saw that everything was still there except my camera so I ran in his direction for another two blocks, but he had disappeared. I looked around and had no idea where I was and began to walk in the direction that I thought Ana would be. Several Moroccan street toughs walked by me and looked at my bag, and I gave them a menacing look and they walked away.

It had been at least thirty minutes since I had last seen Ana and I imagined she was worried about me. I pictured her as thinking that I was lying in a street somewhere in a pool of blood. Finally I saw a sign directing me to the Cathedral, so I followed it and oriented myself back to the park and Ana.

She stood waiting at the spot where I had left her and was very relieved to see me in good health. "I was so worried about you," she said. "I imagined that you were dead somewhere. I thought about how I was just talking with my mother about our marriage and suddenly over a stupid bag, you would be gone."

"I was not going to put myself in a dangerous position. If the thief had brought out a knife, I would have said, 'Okay, it's yours, keep my stuff. I have a beautiful woman who loves me. I don't need those things. Have a wonderful afterlife in hell, you stinking thief.' But I felt that if I could safely get them back, then it was my duty to do so."

We walked back to Ana's family home, and she said, "I have now seen a whole new side to you. You will protect me and keep me safe. I love you."

"I love you too, babe," I replied. "Now, roll me a cigarette."

The next morning Ana's parents invited us to have breakfast with them. Ana warned me that they might ask us to change our wedding date so that it would not conflict with their holiday plans. She asked me not to be rigid with the date and be willing to compromise with them. I told her that it would be no problem for me and we could move the wedding to a week later if that was what her parents desired.

We sat at the breakfast table and they offered wine for us to drink. It was an early hour in the morning and I declined although I did not know if it was Spanish custom to have wine with breakfast. I think that they were testing me to see if I would like alcohol in the morning. They suspected that I had Russian ancestry due to my Lenin-like appearance and they thought that Russians like to imbibe a lot.

After breakfast, Ana and her mother went to another room as Antoni and I remained. He asked me about our plans together and I described to him our itinerary for traveling across Europe, and returning to San Francisco, and then getting married in Wisconsin. I asked him about their holiday plans to give him an opening to request a change in the marriage date, but he told me that they had decided to visit the States rather than Brazil as originally planned. The date seemed good for Antoni because he preferred to make the holiday shorter than usual as he often became bored with traveling for long periods of time.

Throughout our conversation, Antoni kept repeating that he had been married three times and I replied, "That's nice." Finally I figured out why he was telling me this information and I replied, "I have never been married before. A couple of times I came close but it did not feel right in the heart for me, so I called it off. With Ana I feel a deep love and it feels very right for me in my heart. I want to be a good husband for her and hopefully raise a family with her." Immediately he called for the women and announced that they were going to be in Wisconsin on August 11th. Apparently I had passed the test.

Ana had warned me earlier that Antoni might take me into his study surrounded by animal heads and skins and guns and knives to try to frighten me. I had expected that and I had expected a more rigorous interrogation but was relieved that the pre-marital discussion between the men had been in such a relaxed atmosphere.

In the afternoon, we met for a formal family luncheon and Ana and I were served fish with bones while the rest of the family ate another type of fish without bones. I thought that this was another test to see whether I had acceptable table manners. In the past, I would use my right hand to help me gather the food onto the fork of my left hand, but I used Ana as a guide and used a knife or bread rather than my bare hand. I also followed how Gerard, the grandfather, ate since he was the oldest and probably followed the customary etiquette. I watched which forks and spoons that Gerard used with each entrée and tried not to lean into the food but let it come to me, although I found this very difficult to do.

After dinner, the men drank strong liquor, although I declined because I was feeling rather tipsy from the very good wine that I had already drunk. The family seemed slightly offended that I had declined and Ana explained later to me that it probably would have been more polite to accept a little bit so that I would be on the same level with the others and would be able to speak more openly.

The next afternoon we walked with Gerard around the old Jewish quarter and he showed us where the synagogue originally stood before King Ferdinand expelled the Jews from Spain. Ana placed her hand on the wall of the old synagogue which was now a hostel, and felt energy from the past. Gerard explained that under Muslim rule, the Muslims, Jews, and Christians had lived peacefully together, but after the Christian conquest, Jews and Muslims were driven out of the area and their temples were destroyed and replaced with Christian churches.

In the evening, Antoni and Carme invited Ana and me to the Gran Teatre de Liceu to see what is considered the first opera, 'L'Orfeo' by Monteverdi. The opera is based upon the myth of Orpheus, a poet and musician, who charmed wild animals and nature with his singing, and descended into the underworld to rescue his wife, Eurydice, who had died from snakebite.

Ana and I sat in the front row of the family's box with Carme's best friend, Monica, as Antoni, Carme, and Aunt Angela sat behind us. I could feel their eyes watching me to see how an uncultured American would react to the sophistication of European opera. At intermission Monica and Ana expressed that they thought that the opera was boring and although I heartily agreed with them, I chose to use the euphemistic terms, soothing and tranquil.

Antoni gave us a tour of the studies and art galleries for select members and their guests and I was given a tie to wear before entering. Without difficulty, I swung the tie around my neck and made a perfect knot and hopefully impressed Antoni that I had been taught something in my uncultured country. The room that Ana and I liked best was called the Aquarium, where men would sit in a study next to a one-way mirror which looked out onto Las Ramblas. I joked that the Chief of Police should sit there so that he could observe the daily crime and the inattentiveness of his officers, but Antoni was not amused.

Monica needed to leave the opera early due to another appointment and became very emotional and teary-eyed when she talked about our wedding plans. Ana said to me privately that she wished that her mother could display less self-control like Monica.

In the final act of the opera, Orfeo asks Apollo to return Eurydice to him, but Apollo reminds him that earthly joys are fleeting and only immortality can bring enduring happiness. He invites Orfeo to ascend with him to the heavens where he can contemplate the celestial image of Eurydice forever amid the sun and stars. As I watched them ascend to the heavens, I thought about the prospect of my immortal love with Ana and was elated that the opera was over because my neck and buttocks had become very sore from sitting with such rigid sophistication.

We had dinner afterwards in the opera house's private restaurant and I slowly ate and tried to follow the proper etiquette by not using my fingers. Ana brought up the subject of all of the paperwork that was required for her to become my wife in America and her family discoursed in Catalan and then suggested that we should change our marriage plans and marry in Spain instead. I explained that this option would also be difficult since I did not have my original birth certificate and was shocked that plans seemed to be changing so rapidly without my awareness. Antoni began to criticize the American government and talk about politics, and I replied, "I like the philosophy of your father, Gerard, that dinner conversations should be about simple matters such as the weather so that we can concentrate on the taste of the food." He gave me an icy stare.

We walked back to the family home as Ana and I walked together in silence while Antoni and Carme conversed with each other. Ana asked, "Do you have something to say to me?"

I replied, "No, do you have something to say to me?" I wondered whether I had forgotten to say something important because she seemed to be upset with me. In the past we had said that we liked walking together in silence because we were comfortable with one another, but now Ana seemed to be forcing me to talk.

"If you want me to talk to you, ask me a question and I will reply because now I can't think of anything to say."

She coldly replied, "No, it is not my position to begin."

We walked further in silence and I could see that Ana's strong character had become weakened by the presence of her family. I said, "I prefer classical music because it is the universal language. There are no problems with understanding the words because there are no words. The music speaks to your heart and it either moves you or it doesn't."

Ana replied, "In opera it is not necessary to know the language. Lucia's boyfriend, Marcos, loves opera although he doesn't understand Italian."

"I wish that in the opera we saw, there would have been more movement and expression. The characters tend to just stand and sing and I find that not very exciting," I said as I could feel Antoni tuning in on us. I continued, "I would have liked to have seen Orfeo taming the wild animals with his song. Instead, all we saw were little fairies prancing around."

"You want wild animals on stage?" asked Ana.

"No," I answered, "I would have liked to have seen the actors portraying wild animals and I would have liked to have seen the transformation from ferociousness to serenity. It all seemed too tranquil to me. And the expressions of the characters' faces never seemed to change. I was trained in the theatre and that's probably why I prefer it over opera."

"You just don't understand opera," Ana replied, "because you are uncultured."

I saw that Antoni and Carme were now walking separately, so I decided to catch up with him so Ana could talk with her mother. I accelerated and Ana complained, "Don't leave me. I have high heels. Walk with me." I slowed down but did not walk next to her. I had heard enough about my lack of culture.

Back in the apartment that we shared with Gerard and Sara, Ana asked me for a cigarette and then walked to the sitting room, expecting me to follow her. Instead I walked down the hall in the opposite direction and sat on the toilet. I thought about how tired I had become with dinner conversations criticizing my country. And I was disturbed that an important conversation about changing the date and place of the wedding had taken place in a language that I could not understand. When people converse in a foreign language for a long time, I become hypnotized by it and suddenly when I'm asked a question in English, I find it very difficult to reply because I have no idea what was said before me.

I opened the door to the sitting room and saw Ana smoking a cigarette and I said, "We need to talk," as I shut the door behind me.

Ana asked, "Are you angry with me?"

And I replied, "Yes, I think that I am. Perhaps you don't want to come to America with me if you find it so offensive."

"No, I want to go there."

"I found your behavior very unusual tonight. You're forcing me to talk and saying how great opera is, when yesterday you said that you didn't like it. You were not yourself tonight. You were very weak and demanding. I know that this is not aiming carefully, but I feel that I must ask you this. Are you happy with me or do I make you sad?"

She paused for a moment and appeared to be shocked, then took out a pen and drew a small circle on a napkin, saying, "This small circle was me before I met you." Then she drew an asymmetrical shape with many bumps and valleys, saying, "This is me now. I'm growing in parts, but I'm out of balance. Over time I hope to become this," and she drew a large perfect circle. We kissed and went to our separate rooms.

The next day we went to various offices of bureaucracy to deal with the paperwork required for our impending marriage. We visited the high-security U.S. Consulate office and received the fiancé visa application. Although the paperwork was immense, we thought that it was manageable and decided that our plan for marriage in Wisconsin was the best option. Although Ana would need to go to Madrid sometime in the coming months for an interview, we figured that it would be best to apply for a fiancé visa now. Otherwise, we would not be allowed to visit each other's countries until six months had elapsed, and we could not bear to be apart from each other for that long of a time.

I was shocked to find out that visa requirements for me had changed with the recent start of the European Union. I did not get a visa when I was in San Francisco because I was told there that I could spend up to three months in any European country without needing one. "I thought that I could spend 3 months in Spain, then 3 months in Italy, then…"

"You are wrong," said the woman behind the glass shield, "you must leave Europe after 3 months without a visa. The European Union has what is called the Schengen Agreement whereby the countries of the E.U. are like the States. You must leave Europe by February 2, 2002."

"Can I get a visa now?"

She smiled and pointed to the document that stated, "You MUST obtain a visa from the Spanish Embassy or Consulate in the U.S. BEFORE coming to Spain."

"But the office in San Francisco told me…"

"I don't care what they told you. There are no exceptions to this rule."

Ana and I left the office and decided that I would need to travel across Europe illegally.

Ana picked up her birth certificate at the civil office and then we went to the Office of Penal and Justice Tribunals to get a document verifying that she did not have a criminal record. Ana gave her passport to a small, nervous, balding man with thick eyeglasses, whose head was always darting from side to side with paranoiac suspicion. He looked at the passport from behind the thin glass shield and then told us to sit down and wait.

Ana became visibly nervous as we waited for over two hours. Different men and women would peer at us from the door of the inner office and Ana's legs began to tremble. I asked Ana, "Did you murder someone or do you have a dark secret that you have not yet told me?"

"No!" She replied much too loudly. "I have a clean record. I have not hidden anything."

The man with the thick eyeglasses returned to the window and indicated for Ana to come to the inner office and for me to stay in the lobby. They closed the door behind her but I could hear much argument taking place between Ana and the others, although I could not understand anything that they said.

Ana burst out of the room, teary-eyed and walked past me and across the heavily-trafficked street, as I ran in front of automobiles to catch up with her. "What's the problem, Ana?" I asked, "Please explain to me and we'll come up with a solution."

"I don't want to talk now," she answered, "I want to think alone. Please leave me alone." She sped up and left me in her dust. I walked back to the family home and found no Ana, so I began to roll cigarettes in the sitting room and smoke them.

Six cigarettes later, Ana returned and sat down beside me and explained her situation. "When I was at the university, I became involved with a man who was an anarchist. I followed him in his activities and did some bad things because I thought that I loved him. I was never charged with anything, but the authorities have a file on me and are very suspicious."

"What kind of bad things did you do?" I asked.

"I would go into government buildings and flirt with the security guards to distract them, while my lover and his friends sabotaged the building," she explained.

"But they have no evidence of any wrong-doing on your part?"

"No, none, but they are very suspicious."

"Well, if they have no evidence and you have no criminal record, they can do nothing. The bureaucratic paperwork may take a bit longer because of this, but it'll turn out alright in the end."

The next day we had another luncheon with Ana's family. At dessert, Ana formally announced our wedding plans to the entire family. We then drank champagne to celebrate the occasion and I was again offered liquor to drink with the other men and I replied, "Porque no, why not?"

The family responded with laughter echoing me, "Porque no, why not?"

Ana's mother, Carme, said that she was going to wear a flamboyant wide-brimmed hat to the wedding because "Por que no, no one will know me." Antoni brought out a panama hat that he planned to wear to the wedding and asked me to try it on. He said, "You should wear a hat like this, you look much younger with this hat than your other one." I thought about the disapproving look that he had given me when I wore my Jewish hat to the opera.

He said, "Last night we went to the theatre but it was very bad; too much movement. In opera, the performers stand still and it is much better."

Carme turned to me and said, "Opera es muy bonita."

"Sí," I replied with a smile, "muy bonita."

Carme walked with us to the train station and she urged Ana that if we had children, Ana should teach them to speak Catalan. Ana promised her that she would and we got on the train to Girona and sighed with relief that our visit with the family was over and our journey would now begin.

At one of the stops, I noticed a very nervous looking Middle Eastern man looking into the cars on the train. He wore what looked like a satchel strapped around his shoulders. I could not see what the bulky thing was that was in front of his chest because it was concealed with a piece of red material. He jumped into our car just before it departed and tore off the red material, which revealed an accordion, which he played rather badly and loudly as he stomped his feet not in rhythm to the music. He then went throughout the car asking for donations and exited sheepishly at the next stop.

We carried our bags up the steep stairs to the fourth floor of Pensión Viladomat in the old part of Girona and then walked a few blocks to the old Jewish Quarter. We visited the Centre Bonastruc Ca Porta, which was named after the thirteenth century Cabbalist philosopher and mystic. The museum told the story of Jewish life in Girona before their expulsion from Spain in 1492.

We used our intuition as we walked through the narrow medieval streets searching for a bowl of soup. Two barking German shepherd dogs denied our entrance through a tunnel. Ana began to sing the song, 'All You Need is Love' and the dogs lay down passively and wagged their tails as we passed. We came upon an odd little restaurant that had the limited menu written on bar disks and ordered the best fish soup since my travels had begun.

We walked back to the hotel and went to bed. Ana slept and I thought about how my life had changed because of the September 11th tragedy. Before that date my plan was to first stop into Hong Kong to visit my old girlfriend, Kooki, and personally break up with her so that she could get on with her life. Perhaps, because of my loneliness, I would have given in and decided to continue my relationship with her, although I knew that my heart wasn't in it.

Now I was lying in bed with the woman that I knew I loved. I had not planned to visit Spain, much less Mallorca, before the terrorist attack in New

York. So in a very small, very personal way, some good had come from the tragedy. I had found my true love at last.

The next day we stopped off at an Internet center to check our emails and Kooki had written to me saying that she was very hurt by my letter to her about my impending marriage to Ana. She gave me a phone number and said that I must call her immediately because it was "a matter of life or death." I felt badly that she was hurt even though I had written and told her many times before that she should not depend on me and that she should find another lover.

Ana warned me, "She is trying to make you into the victim by making you feel guilty. She is like a vampire who wants to suck the life out of you."

"Do you feel that I should not call her?" I asked.

"Would it bother you greatly if I said that you shouldn't call her?"

"No, it wouldn't bother me. I agree with you that she's been acting like a vampire with me."

"Then you can call her. I just don't want you to become the victim."

In the afternoon we set off for the village of Llagostera to have lunch with Ana's maternal grandparents, Tomasa and Pep. We walked along the beautiful country roads as I followed Ana who seemed not entirely certain if we were walking in the right direction. I had noticed from previous occasions that Ana seemed to lack in the navigational skills but I thought, "What the heck, if we're walking the wrong way, we can always call her grandparents on the telephone and have them pick us up."

We found a shaded, secluded area along the way and sat down to play guitar and violin. It had been a couple of weeks since Ana last played the violin, so I took a more aggressive approach in getting her to practice. I told her that from now on she must play or practice the violin for at least 22 (her favorite number) minutes each day. She submissively agreed to my order by saying with a bit of playfulness, "Yes, I will do that, oh wise and noble teacher." The spot that we picked to play was perfect because there were no other people around, so Ana did not become self-conscious.

We arrived for the three o'clock luncheon on time and Ana's aunt, Elisabet, joined us to have some wine and engage in the discussion. She seemed to always be at odds with the opinion of her mother. The dinner discussion was like I had imagined would only take place in a Luis Bunuél film, but never in reality. They talked in Catalan of philosophies, Carl Jung's 'The Collective Unconscious,' education, spirits, and herbal remedies. Whenever Tomasa began to talk about herbal remedies, Pep would raise his eyebrows at me as if he had heard this discussion a thousand times before.

Tomasa had very wise, green eyes that matched her sweater and a calm manner that included me in the discussions. Although they did not speak English and I did not speak Catalan, I felt that I got the basic gist of the discussion. Ana seemed much more relaxed with her grandmother than she had been with her family in Barcelona. Although the luncheon was very traditional with various spoons and forks, Tomasa urged me to use my hands if I desired, but I did not.

After champagne and coffee, Pep drove us back to Girona. We settled into bed and sighed with relief that now, for sure, the family visits would be over until the week of our wedding. We talked of growing old together and fell asleep in each other's arms.

Part II   Honeymoon

We left Girona the next morning and stopped into Figueres to visit the Dali museum before heading into France, destination Nimes. The museum was very unusual like the artist, although, I was not as moved by it as I had been during my early years of experimenting with drugs. Much of the artwork featured paintings of Dali's wife, Gala. Their marriage must have been very unusual, Ana and I hypothesized, much like ours.

On the train to Nimes, a lazy looking man that I thought looked French was reclining in the seats that were reserved for Ana and me. He didn't want to move and requested that Ana and I sit opposite from him. Although I wasn't very happy with the idea because I wanted to keep my eyes on our bags, we complied and sat down.

Ana asked if he was German since he was reading a German translation of Noah Chomsky's 'Economy and Violence.' He replied that he was Swiss and his name was Mats. He immediately recognized my American accent and asked, "Don't you feel in danger traveling in Europe as an American?"

I replied with a question, "Should I be?" and he gave me a very sly smile. He seemed to be very interested in me and I became suspicious of the ulterior motive behind his numerous questions.

He requested that I read the Chomsky book, saying, "This book is about the killing machine, the U.S. government and how it has profited from each of the wars. You must read it and learn the motives behind your country's actions." I started to ignore him and began to focus on a North African man who was standing by our bags. He seemed to be making eye signals with someone behind us, but I could not tell who it was. It turned out that it was a dark-haired, young woman that he was apparently trying to pick up. She joined him and they appeared to be engaging in a flirtatious encounter. They kept looking back at us and I suspected that the flirtatious encounter was only a ruse for them to steal our bags, so I kept my eyes focused on their hands.

The train stopped into the Nimes station and the pair departed without our luggage but an old black man with a white walking stick, who was apparently blind, stood up from the front row by our luggage. The old man moved very slowly and caused a log jam of people who were trying to depart. A short, greasy-haired North African grabbed Mats' luggage and took off running. I told Mats what had happened and he lay back down in our seats and said, "Screw it, I don't care. Everything I need is right here," as he pointed to his head and slyly smiled.

Ana and I found Nimes to be a very unusual city. There were many restaurants that were open, but none of them seemed to be serving food. We searched the city during lunchtime and dinnertime but were unsuccessful in finding a place that would feed us. We looked for markets to purchase food to eat in our hotel room, but did not find a single one. There were hair salons and sexy underwear shops everywhere but no places to get food.

Finally, on our second day in Nimes, after visiting the Jardins de la Fontaine, we found a café that was willing to provide us with salads. The food was delicious but Ana and I became constipated. I hypothesized that I now understood the reason why the French appear so snobby and higher than thou and why French restaurants do not seem to serve food. "They're all constipated."

We arrived into Nice on Friday and were surprised to find that Carnaval was being celebrated there during the weekend. We were excited that there were some interesting events planned for the weekend but had a difficult time finding a room, since most of the hotels were already fully booked. Finally, we found a satisfactory room in Hotel D'Orsay and relaxed.

Both Ana and I were feeling very weak and had the same sharp pains along the sides of our heads. We noticed that a very unusual growth was festering below my lower lip. We thought that perhaps it was a cold sore due to lack of sufficient water and an inadequate diet, but it did not look like any cold sores that I had before. Besides the usual colors of irritated red skin with white pus, there also appeared to be a very strange greenish hue.

We went out for dinner at Restaurant LeToscan since we were not satisfied with our experiences with French cuisine and were looking forward to going to Italy. As I was eating my ravioli, Ana complained, "You always eat with your mouth open."

I became annoyed and said, "I do not always eat with my mouth open, sometimes I know that I do, but sometimes I know that I do not. When people use absolutes such as 'always' and 'never', usually conflict results. When you say things such as 'you're always sleeping' or 'you're never working', I become insulted because I know that what is spoken is untrue and it seems more like nagging than constructive criticism."

"I'm sorry," she replied, "it's a problem that we have with our different languages." We ate the rest of the meal in silence with closed mouths. It appeared that the honeymoon was over. Ana was becoming more annoyed by my table manners and I was becoming more annoyed by her nagging.

The next day we walked to the Russian Orthodox Cathedral of Saint Nicholas and arrived just as a service was about to begin. The priest chanted melodically out of view from the congregation, as the choir responded. Suddenly the doors to the altar opened and out stepped the priest with Rasputin-like hair, beard, and eyes holding the chalice. I noticed that he had a growth below his lip like mine. He drank from the chalice and then the congregation lined up before him to receive a small portion of wine from a long silver spoon that he held. They then went to a small table and helped themselves with bread and water.

A strange looking, little man with beady eyes brought a large golden bowl onto the altar. The priest started to wash himself from the bowl and then began to cough uncontrollably. He turned to the congregation, looked up at the choir, then turned to the large painting of Jesus above the altar, and fell on his back and was dead.

Everyone was shocked. The women and children wailed while the men looked suspiciously around the cathedral and especially at Ana and me, the only outsiders. The police and ambulance came and it was determined that he had died from a heart attack, so we were free to leave. As we were walking, we passed a hospital and I decided that I wanted a doctor to look at the growth below my lip. We waited for over two hours until I met with a doctor. He dismissed my growth as a common cold sore and when I questioned him about the strange green color, he said, "It's nothing. Go to the pharmacy and get some Activir crème," and left.

I wanted to get a second opinion, but Ana said, "Don't be ridiculous, you're over-reacting like you always do. You are not only depressive, you're paranoid."

We walked to the Marc Chagall Museum to look at his paintings from 1954-67, which depicted events from the first two books of the Old Testament; Genesis and Exodus. Among Chagall's paintings were 'The Creation of Man,' 'Noah's Ark,' 'The Sacrifice of Isaac,' 'Paradise,' and 'Adam and Eve's Expulsion from Paradise.'

A group of orthodox Jewish people were looking at the paintings at the same time as us. The men wore long black coats and wide-brimmed black hats and long black beards from which their paises dangled. They left the museum right before us and we decided to follow them because we were curious to see where they would go next. With our dark hats and coats, we had the appearance of being Jewish as well and people who crossed our path looked at both the Jews and us with curiosity.

We kept a safe distance behind them to avoid suspicion although Ana kept saying, "You must walk faster. You always walk so slow." After following them for quite a while, one of the Jewish men looked back at us

73

with suspicion and said something to his mates and they accelerated their pace. We continued to follow them because as Ana said, "There is no law against walking down a public street."

The Jews turned off of Rue Guglia and entered the Jardin Alsace Lorraine as we followed. In the park, I saw a statue that interested me and held onto Ana so that she would not walk ahead of me. She complained, "We're going to lose them; you and your stupid statues." She pulled on my arm and we walked briskly to catch up with them.

The Jews exited the park and turned up Avenue des Fleurs. Suddenly a large black car with tinted windows crept up beside them and two men with black skin masks shot down the three Jewish men and two small boys with automatic rifles. One of them yelled, "Vive Hezbollah," and the car sped away. The women knelt down beside their dead husbands and cried while the little girl stood solemnly beside her dead brothers lying in a bed of red flowers.

Ana and I stood there in shock like the little girl, as we heard the sounds of the French sirens approaching. The same police that questioned us at the Russian Cathedral arrived on the scene and were astonished to see us again. They checked our passports and questioned us about our travel plans and talked to various French witnesses while pointing at us. The witnesses shook their heads and shrugged their shoulders and then the officers approached us again. One of them said, "You say that tomorrow night you will be leaving for Italy? To what city are you going?"

"Florence," Ana and I replied in unison.

The officer looked us over and said, "I hope that death does not follow you in your travels. You are free to go. I hope that we do not see you again. Enjoy your final night in Nice, but be careful where you go. These are dangerous times, especially for Americans."

He said the last statement with a strange smile which made me feel very uncomfortable. I mentioned it to Ana and she replied, "There you go again with your paranoia. You always think that someone is plotting against you."

"No, not always, sometimes I feel that there may be more than meets the eyes. The French cop probably just hates Americans like I hate the French. But his eyes were very strange and my intuition tells me that something unusual is happening. I don't know what it is, but I feel a real sense of danger."

We walked back to our room and I refused to leave it until our train was scheduled to depart. Ana spent the night with me but was very agitated. I offered her money so she could have some dinner, but she refused. I took a sleeping pill and immediately fell asleep.

I dreamt that there was a black shadow always in pursuit of me. I'd run through dark alleys, hop onto trains, and climb mountains but he was always there lurking in the shadows. At one point, he grabbed my shoulder and turned me around and was ready to expose his face when I suddenly awoke.

Ana was standing beside me with her ear plugs attached and a scornful scowl on her face. "You took your sleeping pills again. Every time that you get paranoid, you go right to the drugs to sleep and escape reality. You snore so loud when you take the drugs. Roll over and turn away from me now. I can't stand that noise."

I rolled over and fell back asleep. The next morning, I woke up and saw that I was alone. Ana had left me a note which said, "I went for a walk around the city and then I'm going to watch the Carnaval parade. I'm sure that you're too paranoid to leave the room, so I'll meet you at the train station at 6pm. I still love you and want to be with you, but you are beginning to drive me crazy."

I stayed in the room throughout most of the day wondering whether the gun shots had been intended for me and obsessively looking into the mirror at my festering growth. "This is not an ordinary cold sore," I said aloud, "Something very strange is happening and I don't like it."

I read an article in the newspaper about an American journalist named Dan Pearl, who was kidnapped and beheaded by Al-Qaeda. He was in Mumbai (Bombay), India, investigating the alleged links between Richard Reid (the shoe bomber) and Al-Qaeda. I thought about my original plan to fly to Bombay to become a Bollywood film star. If 911 had not happened, I would have been in the same place as Pearl. I wouldn't have been there investigating terrorism, though. I would have been displaying my talents as a triple threat in acting, singing, and dancing. Who knows? After seeing me do that, somebody might have wanted to kill me, too.

I mustered up some courage and decided to check out the Carnaval parade because I was driving myself nuts in that tiny, dismal room. I wore my black stocking cap below my ears and put on my sunglasses for the first time since I had been going out with Ana. In San Francisco, I wore sunglasses frequently, even at night, but Ana told me that she liked to look at my pretty eyes, so I packed them away. Now, though, I felt that they had become necessary again because I needed to live incognito.

I walked along the parade's route, Avenue Jean Médecin, and weaved through the crowd of people until I found an inconspicuous spot along the Basilique Notre Dame. The floats passed by and I stood unimpressed. I had expected beautiful dancers and live, spirited music like the Carnavals in Brazil and San Francisco, but here in Nice each parade entrant focused on the subject of Euros. There were walking Euro coins and bills, huge Euro floats, and my favorite, a man eating Euros and simultaneously pooping them into a toilet. The French had something to learn about the concept of Carnaval, I thought.

The biggest joy that both the adults and children got from the event was spraying aerosol string into people's faces. One French ass shot some straight into my eyes from six inches away when I saw Ana talking with someone. From the back it looked as if it could have been Mats, the curious Swiss guy from the train, but I wasn't sure.

As I approached them, Ana noticed me and said something to the guy and he took off. When I got to her, I asked, "Who were you talking to?"

She answered, "Just some obnoxious French guy that was trying to seduce me. I told him to piss off."

"It looked like that Swiss guy from the train, Mats. It wasn't him, was it?"

"Don't be ridiculous!" she screamed, "He didn't look anything like him. You need to get help from a psychiatrist. You're very sick."

She turned to leave, but I grabbed her violently on her arm and pulled her face in front of mine and said, "I am not sick. I see deception in your eyes. There is something that you are keeping from me." She refused to talk to me as we walked to the train station and boarded the train for Florence.

We found ourselves a private cabin and lay down on our separate seats and fell asleep. When the train stopped at the border town, Menton, two Italian police officers burst into our cabin and looked at us as if they had made a discovery and asked us from what countries we were. "I'm from Spain and he's from the USA," Ana replied.

"America," I added as we started to bring out our passports, but the officers had already left.

"Did you notice the way the officers looked at us when they entered?" I asked Ana.

"I didn't notice anything," she replied.

"They looked as if they had been looking for us," I said. "The French police probably told them to keep an eye on us."

"Can you just once react without paranoia?" Ana argued, "Border patrols are very common even with the European Union."

"I just think that it was strange that they didn't even look at our passports. They seemed as if they already knew us."

"Shut up and go to sleep," Ana said with a look of disgust and rolled away.

At the next train stop, a strange-looking man with a long black coat and black fedora hat paced along the platform looking into the windows of the train. He had a thick, silver mustache and dark-tinted glasses and I imagined that he was Mats in disguise, but I kept it to myself because I knew that Ana would only protest against my paranoia.

The man entered our car and glanced into our cabin as he passed, then he took the cabin next to ours and lowered the blinds so that there was only a slight opening. Why is Mats (if that's his real name) following us? Are he and Ana in cahoots with each other? Is my life in danger? These thoughts ran endlessly in my brain as I thought about bringing out my knife and sneaking into the next cabin and slashing Mats' throat. "No, don't be crazy. You're not a killer. You don't even know if that man is following you. You are paranoid. Ana's right. You need help," I said to myself as I noticed that my clothes were drenched in sweat.

I changed my clothes and noticed that Ana was sleeping deeply and I got the idea to move all of our luggage to the exit and then grab Ana at the last minute and get off at the next station to lose the spy. When the train stopped, I quickly threw down the luggage to the platform, then returned to the cabin and placed my hand over Ana's mouth as I pulled her to the exit. She fought with me and tried to make noise, but I was able to restrain her and we exited the train without the spy noticing that we had left.

Once the train was gone, Ana screamed at me, "You're crazy!"

"If you don't want to travel with me anymore," I replied, "that's fine. I'll buy you a ticket to wherever you want to go."

"No," she answered. "I want to stay with you. I love you." Something in her eyes made me suspect that her feelings were not real and that she only wished to travel with me for another reason, but what?

We were now in Empoli and we decided to catch another train to Siena in Tuscany but had to wait for three hours. A little Italian man holding Jehovah Witness's pamphlets told us about a bakery that was open down the street. Ana's face brightened with thoughts of croissants and hot coffee. The croissants came straight out of the oven and melted in our mouths as we each had three. Some very elaborately uniformed Italian motorcycle cops entered the bakery and although I acted paranoiacally, Ana didn't get bothered because she was in the ecstatic splendor of croissant heaven.

All of the guidebooks described Siena as one of the most beautiful towns in all of Italy and it was very interesting with its many gothic buildings in various shades of burnt sienna and its main square, the shell-shaped Piazza del Campo, and the imposing black and white striped Dubino Cathedral. But something was very peculiar about this town. Everyone in it appeared to be very ill. Their skin was very pale, their eyes were bloodshot, they were constantly coughing, and many of them had sores below their lips like I did. The guidebook told me that Siena went through a great plague in the Middle Ages and it appeared to me that history was repeating itself.

I stayed in my hotel room most of the time because I was feeling ill, but whenever I went out, I was shocked at the masks of death that the people wore. Ana urged me to go out for pizza and pasta, but I could barely keep my food down whenever I looked around at anyone.

Ana told me that she had found a good library to do some research on the Kabbalah, so she left me in the hotel room each day and spent hours away from me. I had no desire to go outside since I was feeling very weak and the weather was mostly rainy and miserable.

One day, however, the sun peaked out and so I decided to go for a walk and try to find the bottinis that I had read about in the guidebooks. Bottinis were underground aqueducts that were constructed in medieval times because of the lack of rivers in the Tuscany area. An entire subterranean culture was said to have existed with underground tunnels much like the Christian catacombs.

I found an entrance near the Basilica di Sant Francesco and used a small flashlight to make my way through the dark, twisting tunnels that branched off into numerous directions. Along the walls there appeared to be names of people etched in the stone. It was obviously not graffiti but appeared to be an underground cemetery. I became spooked by the eerie atmosphere and turned around to depart, when suddenly I heard the hushed voices of men and a woman.

The woman's voice sounded very similar to Ana's although the language was neither Catalan, Castilian, English, nor French; the languages that Ana told me that she spoke. I turned my flashlight off so that they would not detect me and slowly inched closer to them.

It was very dark, but I could make out the outlines of their bodies. There appeared to be three men and a woman and the woman's profile resembled Ana's with her Streisand-like nose and large hips. One man was rotund like Freddie, the other was small and thin like Izmael, and the third appeared to have the same muscular physique as George.

The language sounded Arabic or Moroccan or some type of Islamic language, although I could not be sure since I am so inept at foreign languages. The woman appeared to be arguing with the men who appeared to be trying to convince her to do something. She stood firmly with her hand on her hips and her chin raised and shook her head just like Ana when she took on the persona of the know-it-all little girl from the Harry Potter movie.

It was very damp in the tunnel and I began to feel as if I was going to sneeze, so I slowly crept back and eventually found my way out of the bottini. Thoughts were running through my head of some devious plot that

Ana and the others were planning for me to be a part of, but I could not figure out what it was. Perhaps my imagination had gotten the better of me and I had only imagined resemblances of the four people below. I stood beside the wall of the Basilica and waited for the four to exit from the underground, but night fell and it began to rain again and no one appeared, so I went back to the hotel.

Immediately I dropped upon the bed and fell asleep. I dreamt that I was lying on a slab of stone and walls of sienna bricks were being built around me. At each wall, the bricklayer was a different person: Ana, Freddie, Izmael, and George. Izmael said, "Are you sure that he's dead?"

George answered, "Yes, my knife went right into his heart and blood gushed out from his aorta."

Ana argued, "He's not dead, I know it. He's only pretending to sleep like he always does. I can smell his endorphins; I can sense his fear." She then began to howl like a wild wolf.

I awoke and Ana was sitting at the table beside me smoking a cigarette and writing. I asked her, "What are you doing?"

And she answered, "Nothing, just doing research on the Kabbalah, but the information I found today was no good." She crumpled up the paper and threw it into the wastebasket.

She cuddled up next to me and asked, "What were you dreaming? It sounded very scary. I thought that perhaps I should wake you."

"I don't remember," I answered, "Did I say anything?"

"No, you were just breathing very heavily and your feet were moving as if you were running away from something."

"I don't remember anything. I don't feel well. I'm going to sleep some more." I rolled away and pretended to fall asleep.

Ana got up and grabbed her toiletries and headed to the bathroom. Within a moment, I arose from the bed and looked at the crumpled paper in the wastebasket. The writing was of another language that I did not recognize; Arabic, perhaps. The only non-Arabic writing seemed to be some type of chemical formula, which was $Fe^2 (HCN)^- K+ H+Cl^- \rightarrow HCN^- \uparrow$. "What does this formula have to do with the Kabbalah?" I asked myself. Ana was always sketching diagrams and trying to figure out complex problems. Perhaps she was trying to figure out some connection between physical properties and spiritual growth. Perhaps not. I took the paper and placed it inside my backpack and lay back on the bed.

Ana returned and she suggested that we go to Rome the next day. "Don't you like it here?" I asked.

"No, I'm bored. I want to see Rome," she answered like a spoiled child.

"Okay, honey. We'll go to Rome tomorrow if that's what you want. Whatever my baby wants, my baby gets." She smiled and kissed me and I began to feel better.

We found a room near the main train station in Rome and then went out for pizza. A pizzeria offered what we thought were slices of pizza for one Euro each, but when the bill came we discovered that the price was actually one Euro per gram, which made our dinner quite a bit more expensive than we had expected. Que sera, sera.

The next morning I told Ana that I wanted to visit the Vatican, but she replied, "I don't want to see all of the monuments in gold that were created from people's fears. I want to visit the library and do more research on the Kabbalah."

So I went alone. I walked across a bridge over the Tevere River and suddenly the heavy traffic congestion of Rome was replaced with the hordes of tourists snapping pictures and asking in obnoxious American accents, "Where's the Sistine Chapel? I want to see the Sistine Chapel." I entered St. Peter's Cathedral and looked at the many painted domes showing recreations of religious events. The cathedral was quite spectacular with gold shining everywhere, even from the pews.

I saw that a religious service was taking place at the main chapel so I sat down in a pew behind three nuns. The priest, a small, old, gray-haired man, spoke in Italian as the congregation responded and I sat silently. Suddenly the three nuns stood up and walked by me and I was shocked to see that one of the nuns looked exactly like Hermina, the bartendress from the Crescent Moon Bar in Palma.

The service continued and I became mesmerized by the background of the altar. It showed a red glowing sun with a dove in the center that was surrounded by statues of angels. All of a sudden, the sun exploded, the dove disintegrated, and the beheaded angels with broken wings flew toward the congregation and crashed upon them. The entire cathedral was in chaos as people rushed over each other and pushed to get to the outside. I sat both in shock and fascination at the event until an angel's head crashed down between my legs. Immediately, I stood and made for the exit.

As I stood in the mass of terrified tourists at the exit, another explosion occurred; this time from the direction of the Sistine Chapel. Once outside, most of the tourists made a mass exodus from Vatican City, but I stood in the center of the square alongside the obelisk. Two panic-stricken Canadians collapsed beside me and reported that an explosion in the Sistine Chapel had obliterated Michelangelo's Last Judgment. They kept repeating, "The Horror, eh, the horror, eh."

I suspected that Hermina the bartendress had something to do with the explosion, but I decided to tell no one because 1. I had no proof, 2. I was in Europe illegally, and 3. Trouble seemed to be following me wherever I went, and I would become a suspect for these crimes. So I went back to the hotel and waited for Ana to return.

She returned after darkness had set and I told her about the tragedy at the Vatican. She stood dispassionately smoking a cigarette and said, "It doesn't surprise me at all. The Vatican is corrupt and the Cathedral should be demolished."

I said, "I almost got hit between my legs by a marble angel head."

"But you didn't," she replied, "so stop whining. I'm hungry. Let's get something to eat." I was shocked by her reply, but her suggestion seemed reasonable since I had not eaten the entire day.

We went to a cheap Chinese restaurant where everything on the menu appeared to be four Euros or less. Since it was Friday, we decided to order fish, which was very delicious, but when the bill came, again we were surprised to discover that in very small print on the menu, the fish were priced per gram. Again we paid much more than we had expected, and decided that from now on, we would look more carefully at each menu before ordering. Otherwise, we would be broke and stuck up crap creek without a paddle.

After dinner, we went to see the movie, 'The Believer.' The main character was a Jewish boy, who had become a skinhead and had great hatred for the Jews. When other skinheads questioned him why he knew so much about Jewish tradition, he replied, "One needs to know the enemy."

After the movie, Ana and I meandered back to our hotel and I asked, "Ana, why is it that you are so interested in Jewish things?"

She replied, "I find it interesting that they have been able to overcome so much adversity and have made such great accomplishments."

"So it's not like the character in the movie?" I questioned. "You are not doing it to know the enemy."

"The enemy?" she replied. "They're not my enemy. I think that perhaps I am Jewish."

"He was a Jew, too." I added.

"What?" Ana asked.

"Nothing," I replied and we walked in silence.

The next morning we visited the Roman Coliseum and Forum and were looking for an internet café to check out whether my friend in

Wisconsin had information about a polka band for our wedding, when Ana spotted a Hard Rock Café on Via Veneto and insisted that we have lunch there. "Okay, sweetheart," I replied, "but let's be sure to look carefully at the menus this time."

We each had a burger and fries with no surprises when the bill came and had an after-dinner smoke. Ana noticed an American flag flying from the building across the street and said, "That must be the American Embassy. Let's go there and see if they can help us with our paperwork for our marriage."

"Ana," I replied, "this is Italy. They can't do anything for us that we haven't already done in Spain. We'll just have to be patient and wait for the reply from Madrid." Ana started to pout like a little girl and I said, "Okay, honey bunny, we'll go to the Embassy and see if they can help us. Don't cry, baby, we'll go right now." Ana's pout immediately turned into a broad smile, and she gave me a big kiss.

When we got through security at the Embassy and were headed for the appropriate office, Ana suddenly said, "I have to use the ladies' room. I'm having my period. I saw a restroom back that way. You go ahead and I'll meet you in the office."

"I can wait outside the restroom until you're ready."

"No, you go ahead," she answered, "sometimes this woman business gets messy and takes a while. You go to the office and I'll be right there when I finish." She gave me a big kiss and I continued onto the office.

When I got there, I took my time stepping up to the counter because I knew that they really couldn't help me and that it was all a waste of time. I only agreed to go there to pacify Ana. I told the woman our situation and she replied, "What do you expect from me? You'll need to wait for the reply from Madrid. Case closed." She turned from me and I said, "Is it okay if I wait here for my fiancé to join me? She needed to use the bathroom. It's that time of the month. You understand."

She scowled at me and replied sourly, "I suppose," and went back to her desk.

Forty minutes passed and still Ana had not shown up. The woman kept looking at me and I sheepishly pointed down to my groin area and gestured like my hands were in a sticky mess and the woman sighed, shook her head and went back to her work. Ana finally arrived and I told her that they couldn't help us and she replied, "Okay, let's go," and rushed me to the exit. Once outside, Ana said that she needed to do more research at the library, so she kissed me goodbye and departed.

I went back to our room for a siesta. I dreamt that I was Remus, and George was Romulus, and Ana was the she-wolf that raised us. The she-wolf's howling seemed to be directing Romulus to do his villainous deed. I awoke drenched in sweat and saw that the night had fallen and Ana was lying beside me snoring loudly. I put in my earplugs and fell back asleep.

The next morning we were sitting at an outdoor café outside of the Parthenon drinking café lattes for four Euros each, when I grabbed an international newspaper and read to Ana the top headline, "U.S. Embassy in Rome a Target of Terrorist Plot." Her face turned white as snow and she grabbed the paper from me as I read the article from over her shoulder. It stated that three Tunisian nationals with nearly nine pounds of a cyanide compound and a map indicating the location of water pipes that leads to the U.S. Embassy were arrested for having more than 100 fake residence permits. Officials reported that the men had enough potassium ferro cyanide to have caused dozens of deaths and that a possible bio-terror attack had been averted with their arrest.

"I can't believe it," I stated. "We were just at the Embassy yesterday..."

Ana interrupted, "I hate Italy; four Euros for one cup of coffee. Let's leave for Greece today. We can take the train to Brindisi and then the night ferry to Greece. Please." She gave me her big puppy dog blue eyes and put her hands close to me and I acquiesced. Within two hours we were on the train to Brindisi, and when night fell again we were in our cabin on the ferry to Greece.

That night I dreamt about our wedding in Wisconsin. All of Ana's family and friends as well as my own were gathered on the little island in Jefferson Park as Ana and I exchanged our vows. Then George, the justice of peace, said, "Do you, David, take Ana to be your wife?" I replied, "I do with all of my heart." George continued, "Do you, Ana, take David to be your husband?" "I do until the end of time," she replied. George then said, "I now pronounce you husband and wife. You may kiss." And we kissed passionately but as we did so, I opened my eyes and saw that it was not Ana that I was kissing, but Constanza. I awoke and Ana was sleeping beside me with a devilish grin.

Just what did I know about her anyway? I met her family and they seemed like respectable people. She seemed so angelic when I had first met her, but she was becoming more and more a bitch as I got to know her. Was that really her in the bottini or had my imagination and paranoia gotten the best of me? Just who was this woman that I had fallen in love with? I needed to find out.

From the port in Pabras, we took a train to Corinth and then a bus to the beautiful town, Napflio, along the Argolic Bay. We decided to try to find an apartment where we could veg out and relax for maybe a month because we were both tired of continually packing and unpacking. We found a domatia from a Greek at the tourist office and decided to pay on a weekly basis. The place had a big kitchen that we would need to share with the other renters from the other two rooms, and there was a nice back porch.

The next morning Ana and I walked to a café for some coffee. The café offered a choice of either Greek coffee or Nescafe, so we decided to try the Greek blend. The waiter brought our coffees, which tasted as if they had been filtered through my dirty socks, along with two tall glasses of water. Ana told me that the water in Greece was very good as I took a large swig. After I finished my glass, I noticed that she hadn't touched hers and I inquired about that, but she replied, "I'm not thirsty, here, have mine." I looked at her eyes as she offered me her glass and again I became suspicious of her and declined. She seemed to be too eager for me to drink the water. What was she trying to do to me?

She said, "I want to go to the library and see if I can find any information about the Kabbalah."

I replied, "You go alone. I'll get a newspaper and go to the back porch to read it." We walked to the newsstand together, kissed goodbye, and I bought my newspaper and then watched her walk in the direction of the public library. But instead of going to the back porch, I decided to sit in the park for a while and then sneak into the library to see if she was really doing what she had said.

I looked at the top headline in the newspaper and read that more than 500 people had been killed in the past few days in the Indian state of Gujarat in riots between the Hindus and the Muslims. The riots had begun when some Hindu activists began to taunt Muslims on a train called the Sabarmati Express. The activists pulled the head scarves off of Muslim women, shouted slogans such as, "Wipe out every Muslim," and refused to pay for the tea and snacks that they consumed at the train stops, where the vendors were young Muslim men.

The train was traveling from Ajodhya, where the activists had been rallying in support of building a temple for the Hindu god, Rama. At this site in 1992, a mosque had been demolished by Hindus, and fighting broke out and 3000 people were killed.

The Muslim vendors refused to be victimized by the Hindu activists. They jumped onto the train and started a fire on one of the cars. 58 people, most of them women and children, died from that incident. Then the Hindus retaliated and set fire to a block of Muslim homes, killing at least 38 people. Since then, more rioting broke out and the state government issued shoot-on-sight orders to the police against rioters.

This article stunned me because I had been in Ahmadabad, the town where most of the rioting had occurred, just a year ago. I went there to visit Mohandas Gandhi's Sabarmati Ashram and became very touched by the peaceful atmosphere of the place. Birds sang, beautiful butterflies flew from one colorful flower to another, and school children planted trees.

The ashram was now a museum dedicated to Gandhi and it showed his historical struggle in trying to get the Indian people to live with honor and tolerance. I thought of the school girls with the red ribbons in their hair and thought about all of the innocent blood that had been shed because the people had ignored or forgotten Gandhi's message of peace. What a tragedy, what a mess, was the world coming apart at its seams? All throughout the world, rioting and senseless killing were taking place, and most of it seemed to be caused by religious differences. But it was not the pure essence of the religions that caused the violence. The religions were polluted with business and politics and greed.

Each day the newspaper would basically say the same thing: Palestinian kills Jews, Jews retaliate and kill Palestinians, Palestinians retaliate and kill Jews, and on and on in this vicious cycle of hate. Why could these people not recognize that they each prayed to the same God and that their religions had many similarities? Why did they not respond to the messages of love and respect in all of their holy books? As Rodney King, the black who was beaten up by the Los Angeles cops said, "Can't we just get along?" Apparently not.

I folded up the newspaper and quietly snuck into the library and saw Ana sitting alone at a table and studying a book. She sat with perfect posture and her concentration was undoubtedly very deep, so I decided to not disturb her and sneaked back out. How could I have suspected that my sweet angel, Ana, could have any devious intent? What a paranoid, delusional person I had become. For the first time in my life, I had discovered True Love and now I was trying to destroy it with my misconceived fantasies. I walked back to the apartment and continued to read the newspaper on the back porch.

There was an article in the newspaper about the growing number of Islamic schools in the United States. In the past, most Islamic students would attend public schools but due to taunting from other students, these private schools were created to provide a safer haven for the young Muslims. The Muslim educators compared it to the same thing that Catholics, Jews, and Mormons experienced in the past two hundred years.

All of the schools said that they taught history and good values and what it takes to be a good Muslim and emphasized the practice of tolerance. But when looking at some of the textbooks, religious tolerance advocates found passages that promoted hatred of non-Muslims. For example, an eleventh grade textbook said that on the Day of Judgment, Muslims will kill Jews, who will hide behind trees that say, "O' Muslim, O' servant of God, here is a Jew hiding behind me. Come here and kill me."

Suddenly, Ana's hands touched me on my shoulders from behind and I jumped up from my chair. I thought that she was going to try and strangle me, but I could tell from her sweet, angelic eyes that there was no evil intent. She sat on my lap as I told her about the news. She replied with a question, "Why do people have the need for religion?"

I answered, "I think that they have fears and that they want to feel protected by some greater force and then want to be directed toward having good, moral values, so that they will be rewarded in their afterlife."

"So they want to be rewarded," she replied. "What if there is no God, no afterlife? All of their efforts toward leading a righteous life will then have been all in vain."

"Not necessarily," I countered, "I believe that there is an energy force that we all are a part of, and if we disseminate negative energy, karma will come and haunt us for our misdeeds. I believe in reincarnation and my goal is to perform good deeds in this short span of time that I have been given, so that I may evolve into a higher being in my next life."

"But what if there is no next life?" she asked. "Your good deeds will have been a waste of time. You could have spent your time cheating and killing others, but because of your fears and your expectation of a gift from God or your energy force or whatever you want to call it, you will have wasted your time with morals."

"I don't think that it's a waste of time to try to treat people with respect," I countered. "We, as humans, cannot conceive of God's purpose for us but if we have faith, we can believe that the Ten Commandments were handed down from God to Moses and we can choose to follow this directive."

"But I have no faith," she answered back. "I see nothing beyond this life and when I think about it, it makes me very sad. I don't feel that I need religion because all that it does is play upon people's guilt and fears. I don't know what I need."

"All yah need is love, baby," I replied, and we went to bed.

The next day Ana and I hiked up to the imposing Palamidi fortress and discussed its interesting history. I said between breaths, "Palamidis was the son of Nafplios, who was the son of the Greek god of the sea, Poseidon.

The fortress was built to defend against first the Byzantines, then the Venetians, then the Franks, then the Turkish Ottoman Empire…"

"Which controlled it for many years," Ana finished my sentence.

"Then a secret society was formed that educated young Greeks with strategies to overcome the Ottomans."

"This secret society," Ana stopped and asked, "did it succeed?"

"Yes, the Turks surrendered. But then ten years after that, the governor was assassinated in the church of Saint Spyridon and anarchy broke out. European powers declared that Otto of Bavaria would become king and the capital was moved from Nafplio to Athens."

After reaching the top, we hiked back down to our apartment with a bag of groceries to prepare lunch. However, we saw that the kitchen was vacated by a young, dark-haired woman, who had rented the bedroom across from us and was now preparing her own lunch. She said that her name was Pastora and that she was from Madrid and instantly she and Ana began to speak in Castilian very rapidly. I had no idea what they were saying although they seemed to like each other very much and acted as if they were old friends. I excused myself to go to the bedroom and took a siesta.

I dreamt that I was standing on top of a large ship that was sailing to Israel over a tumultuous sea and below a dark-clouded sky. The dark clouds turned into large menacing birds that appeared to be dropping their feces upon my ship. But when the droppings landed upon the deck, they exploded and created huge orifices from which water gushed out at me. I recognized the large bird in the front to be Yassar Arafat, the Palestinian leader, and the two birds that were following him appeared to be Ana and Pastora. I screamed at them, "You can drop all the shit you want upon me, but I will not sink. I am invincible!" I looked forward at the sea ahead of me and saw another large bird flying directly at me. It appeared to be on a suicide mission. I stood frozen, unable to move or speak as the bird with the white turban and dark beard and unmistakable bin Laden eyes made its descent upon me.

I awoke and Ana was sitting beside me in the bed and she said, "Honey, Pastora is going to the island named Crete and it sounds wonderful. I'm bored here. There's nothing to do. Rethymno, where Pastora is going, has a university, so I can study at the library there. The library here is terrible. Can we go to Rethymno, honey, please honey, please?"

"Yeah, baby, sure baby, whatever my baby wants, baby, sure baby, yeah."

Pastora left the next morning to go to Athens to catch the evening ferry to Rethymno and Ana begged me for us to join her, but I insisted that I wanted to visit the ancient theatre in Epidaurus before leaving the island. Ana pouted like a little girl and said, "I don't want to see no stupid old theatre. I want to go to Crete."

I replied, "We'll go to Crete, little baby. Tomorrow night we'll set sail, but today we're going to Epidaurus."

"We're not going anywhere," she argued. "You can go if you want, but I'm going to stay here and pack for Crete. I don't want to see no stupid, old theatre."

"Okay, baby, I'll go alone," I said and that's what I did.

I arrived in Epidaurus after a 40 minute bus ride and walked through the wooded area to the theatre. I felt very depressed that Ana had chosen not to join me. My heart felt as if it had been torn out from me and my eyes were watering as I stood on the stage and looked about at the groups of Greek and Asian tourists that sat as my audience, and I recited a speech from Shakespeare's 'Richard II'. I said, "Play I in one person, many people and none contented. Sometimes am I king, then treasons make me wish myself a beggar, and so I am. Then crushing penury persuades me I was better when a king, then I am kinged again. And by and by think that I am unkinged by Bolingbroke and straight am nothing. But whate'er I be, nor I, nor any man that but man is, with nothing shall be pleased 'til he be eased with being nothing."

I looked up at the audience who were all focused upon me and thought about continuing the speech but instead turned away and walked dejectedly back to the bus stop. In the backseat of the bus I sat alone and depressed as it entered Napflio and passed the café where Ana and I had our first Greek coffee and water. My depression turned into shocking suspicion as I saw Ana conversing with the waiter who had served us. She handed him an envelope. Just what the hell was going on?

I ran back to the apartment and saw that Ana had not yet packed. I started to go through her things and searched for evidence that could answer my question. I found one small piece of paper that seemed to have writing in some type of Arabic language, so I crammed it into the hidden pocket of my coat as I heard the door open and saw Ana enter. She seemed startled by my appearance and said, "Hi, honey, you're back so soon. I thought that you'd be gone all day."

"And I thought that you'd be all packed and ready to go," I replied.

"Oh, I got bored and went for a walk," she answered.

"Anything interesting on your walk?" I asked. "You talk with anyone?"

"No, no one," she answered. "There's nobody here and nothing to do. I'm so bored, but I'm happy that you're back." She lay down on the bed and I joined her as day became night and what was wrong became right.

The next morning, we entered Athens via bus and stored our luggage at the bus terminal and then hastily toured through the garbage strewn streets (due to a garbage workers' strike) and checked out the Acropolis and neighboring Plaka neighborhood. By mid-afternoon we were on the ferry and inside our cabin for our boat ride to Crete. We were both very tired, so after showering we lay down to sleep in our bunk beds with Ana on top.

In my dream, our wedding was on the ship and I was teaching Ana how to dance to the polka music. We danced and laughed with joy as the musicians played and jugs of wine were passed throughout the crowd. I grabbed Ana's hand and led her to the bow of the ship. I said like Leonardo DiCaprio from the Titanic movie, "I will teach you how to fly. Step up on the railing and you will experience something unbelievable."

"I'm scared," Ana said with child-like fear.

"There is nothing to be afraid of," I assured her, "I will be right behind you to protect you." And we stood up on the railing and spread our arms like they did in the movie, and suddenly Ana flew up into the air and laughed as I plunged below into the dark, cold, endless sea.

The ship docked at the Port of Rethymnon in the early morning and Ana and I walked through the old part of town until we found a café that was open near the Rimondi Fountain and sat down at an outdoor table and consumed coffee, ham and cheese toasted sandwiches, and of course, water. I noticed that since our arrival into Greece, anything that we ordered would always be accompanied with a tall glass of tap water on the side. The Greeks seemed very proud of their water. When I would buy tobacco at the kiosk, I half expected to be given a glass of water to go with my Drum.

Before we had finished our breakfast, Pastora appeared from around the corner and joined us. She and Ana spoke to each other very animatedly in Castilian, I assumed. Pastora then turned to me and said in English, "I need to go to the University now, but I will see you soon. I'm so excited that you have chosen to come here." She then embraced me and kissed me on the cheek and briskly marched up Abratzoylou Street.

I remarked to Ana, "What a coincidence it is that we arrive here in the early morning, and the streets are deserted, and we should come across the one person in this entire town that we know."

"It's not so unusual," Ana answered with her cigarette hanging from her mouth. "After all, this is a small town. Honey, you look so comfortable sitting here with your coffee. I'll walk around and see if I can find a place for us to stay."

"I don't know if that's such a good idea, sweetie. Your sense of direction leaves a bit to be desired. I'm afraid you might get lost. Perhaps I should go."

"No," she answered vehemently, "I'll go. You stay and relax, honey."

Her manner turned very sweet as she kissed me and sped up Abratzoglou. I stood up and cautioned her, "Be careful. Don't get lost," and looked up the street, but she was gone.

I sat back down at the table and nursed my coffee while I read an article from yesterday's newspaper that reported that U.S. Naval warships and aircraft were trying to locate the three crew members from a U.S. Navy SH – 60B Seahawk helicopter that had plunged into the Mediterranean Sea. The helicopter, which specialized in anti-submarine warfare, had been on a routine maintenance flight when it mysteriously crashed near Peloponnese.

This was the second 'accident' involving U.S. Naval aircraft in the Greek waters in less than a month, the newspaper reported. Two weeks earlier an F-14 Tomcat fighter jet crashed into the Mediterranean Sea fifty miles south of Crete after taking off from the flight deck of the aircraft carrier, USS John F. Kennedy. The jet was on a routine training exercise and the carrier had just left the U.S. Naval base at Souda Bay to participate in Operation Enduring Freedom in Afghanistan. The pilot of the Tomcat jet was killed upon impact, while his co-pilot managed to eject safely.

"This is very strange," I thought aloud, "Two 'accidents' in two weeks. I think not. Something's rotten here and it's not just this acerbic coffee."

"What are you saying, honey?" Ana asked from behind me.

"Nothing, sweetie," I answered as I put the newspaper back into my bag. "I'm just marveling at the tasty nectar that the Greek coffee god, Vomitrius, has bestowed upon us."

She gave me a look indicating incomprehension and then changed the subject. "I have wonderful news, honey. I found for us a really nice studio along the waterfront where we can stay for a month. It has a terrace overlooking the sea, and a kitchen, and a television, and a big romantic bed. You'll love it."

"A television you say," I replied. "That's great, but it sounds like something that will be very expensive."

"No, honey," Ana answered, "it's only 293 Euros for a whole month. That's less than 10 Euros a day. Did I do good, honey?"

"You did great, baby," I answered and gave her a big bear hug. "When can we move in?"

"Right now," she replied. "The real estate agent is waiting for us in his car just up the street. He's going to drive us there now."

"Let's go then," I said as I grabbed my bags and left my cup of coffee which stared back at me like a jilted bride that had been left at the altar because of her foul stench.

The real estate agent, who introduced himself as Ambrose, had dark, slicked-back hair, and eyebrows that joined above his hawk-like nose. He showed us the studio in an apartment complex that looked as if it was closed down until the high season. I offered to pay for the month in advance, but he said, "Don't pay me. Spend a night or two here and if you feel comfortable, the owner will come in a few days to collect the money. Whatever you do, do not give the money to the cleaning lady." He gave us the key and left without even requesting that we show him any form of identification.

The place was great. We sat on the small couch in front of the T.V. which reported on CNN the latest number of casualties in the Middle East. We then retired to the bed and I think I fell asleep. Suddenly I heard a key in the door and Ambrose and an unidentified man that I thought to be the owner entered our room and grabbed Ana and carried her away. I lay paralyzed, unable to move as the door slammed behind them. My brother, Jeff, appeared in the bed next to me and I twisted his arm and screamed, "Where have they taken her?"

Suddenly, Ana and I were down at the beach across from our studio. I was sitting in the shaded area underneath the pedestrian walkway while Ana lay on her back basking in the sun. I looked up from my book and noticed that a grey-haired man with steely blue eyes and sun-baked skin in a grey turtleneck sweater was slowly approaching in the direction of Ana. I gave the man a cold stare to indicate to him to leave my girl alone, when all of a sudden a strong gust of wind blew sand into my eyes. When I cleared the sand away, I saw the man in grey running away from the perfectly still body of Ana. I ran to her and saw blood gushing out from a slit in her heart. The blood was the only thing that moved as Ana lay perfectly still without life. I screamed to the man in grey who gradually disappeared from my sight, "Why? Why?" and awoke to find Ana lying inanimately alongside me in bed.

I shook her violently and she awoke and screamed, "What are you doing?"

"I thought that you were dead," I answered. "I think that I had a very bad dream."

"Tell me about it," she requested.

"I can't remember it," I lied to her. "It just happened, but I can't remember anything." I lay back down and tried to figure out who that grey-haired murderer was from my dream whose face appeared to be so familiar to me. I knew that I had seen that face before, but where? Who was that blue-eyed devil?

The next morning Ana and I took a bus to the university a few kilometers west of the town. We went into the library and Ana located some philosophy books in the reference section and then sat down at a table. I said, "I'm going to roam around the shelves for a while and see what I can find," and left her.

The library had a good supply of non-fiction books, mainly in Greek and English. I looked down from the second level and noticed that Ana had moved over to a computer. 'She's probably trying to locate books on the Kabbalah,' I thought and then continued to amble. At one time I turned a corner and almost ran into a young student with a long, dark beard and no mustache. I said in a friendly Wisconsin-accented manner, "Sorry, Excuse me." He looked up at me and then squinted his eyes at the Star of David medallion that hung around my neck and scowled. As I quickly descended the stairs to the lower level, I thought, 'I really need to learn to speak another language or at least speak in a European accent. I don't think that many of the Greeks have a very friendly attitude towards Americans.'

On the lowest level of the library, I located a Jewish section of books and wrote down the call numbers for Ana. The opposite side of those shelves, befittingly held books about Islamic history and I wondered whether the books ever fought with each other over the limited amount of shelf space.

I went back up to the first level and saw that Ana was back in her seat and that Pastora had joined her at the table. They were engaged in another animated discussion and I felt like a third wheel, so I said, "Sweetie, I'm going back to the studio. Do you want to come along with me or do you want to stay here?"

"No, honey, you go alone. I want to stay here and do some more research," she said with a smile.

I went to the locker to get my bag, noticed that Ana's bag was in the same locker, and realized that she would need the key, so I returned to the table but found that it was vacant. I looked throughout the library but could not find Ana or Pastora.

Ana returned to the studio a couple of hours after me and I asked, "So how was your day at the library? Anything exciting happen? How's Pastora?"

"Just another day of research. The Kabbalah is so complicated. I don't know if I'll ever begin to understand it," she replied. "I need to take a bath. Then we go out for dinner for our three month anniversary, right, honey?"

"That's right, baby," I answered, "You've had a hard day. You take a nice long bath and then we'll celebrate in style."

After Ana finished bathing, we went to a nice Italian restaurant along the waterfront for a romantic candlelit dinner. The waiter first brought us wine and salad, and Ana's face radiated in the soft candle light as the sea surged behind her. I noticed that she hadn't touched her lasagna and she began looking out the window with a sad, faraway look in her eyes. "What's the matter, honey?" I asked. "The lasagna's very good. You'll like it."

"I can't eat now," she said with a very sad face.

"What's wrong, baby?"

Her eyes stared into mine as she took a long pause and asked me whether I ever had any close gay friends. I told her about an actor friend of mine from San Francisco who came out of the closet a few years after I had met him. I then talked at length about a show that Calvin and I produced and acted in together.

The production was Georg Büchner's 'Woyzeck' and when I described the part where I, as the doctor, used Woyzeck (Calvin) as a guinea pig for my experiments by allowing him to eat only peas, her eyes became big with excitement. I explained to her that as a result of his limited diet, Woyzeck began to hallucinate and become crazy. I told her that in reality there was discovered to be found in peas some kind of chemical reaction that produced psychosis, and her sadness turned to glee as she polished off the lasagna. I could not give her any more details about the scientific cause of such a reaction from peas, but she said that she had some friends who worked in a lab that could provide her with some answers.

She changed the subject and said, "I really love you. I became sad earlier because I know that I've become obsessed with having children and I don't think that it's healthy and I want to stop having this obsession. What can I do?"

My mind flashed to a hadith (Islamic edict) that I had read earlier in the day at the library. It said, "Copulate and procreate for I shall gain glory from your numbers at the Day of Judgment."

I answered, "Perhaps meditation would help."

"Will you help me learn how to meditate?" she asked.

"Sure, baby," I answered, "Breathe in, breathe out, take in everything, and retain nothing."

"What?" she asked.

"Look at the sea," I answered, "it's so soothing to watch and listen to the surf constantly washing upon the shore. It moves in rhythm to our breathing and we find it relaxing. But the sea is also a deadly, frigid, swirling mass of chaos at the same time. Accept both and you accept the reality of the sea. Accept that you have a need for children and accept the struggle involved in getting them, and I don't think that you will be so bothered about it."

"You talk shit," she replied, "but I really love you. And you?"

"Me too, baby," I answered, "I love me, too."

The next morning Ana left for the university library and I told her that I was going to stay all day at the studio, although I had no intention of doing so. I stayed for an hour after she had left and then caught the bus to the university with the hope of seeing what she and Pastora were doing. When I got there, I saw Ana sitting alone at a table studying a book on the Kabbalah. I came from behind her and put my hand on her shoulders. She said, "What took you so long?" and turned around as her face turned to shock when she saw that it was me.

"Expecting someone else?" I asked.

"No, of course not," she tried to compose herself. "I knew that you'd show up. I was missing you and I knew that magically you'd appear."

"But you looked shocked when you saw me."

"It's just...it's just," she stammered, "I was just wondering where you were now and suddenly you appeared. I'm so happy to see you."

I sat down for a while and then decided to stroll around the library in the hope that Pastora would appear. I went to the newspaper section and was surprised when I saw in the local entertainment section that a production of Woyzeck was being performed the next evening at a local theatre. 'How odd,' I thought, 'that one day after talking about Woyzeck with Ana, a production of such an obscure play should be performed here in Crete. What a coincidence!'

I returned to Ana's table to tell her the news and saw Pastora was talking with her. I slowly moved to the table in hope of catching their conversation, but they spotted me. I said, "Hi, Pastora. It's great to see you again. You really should come to our studio sometime for dinner."

"Sure, sometime," she said. "I have to go to class now. I'll see you," and she left.

The following night Ana and I went to see Woyzeck at the small Minotaur Theatre. The production was in Greek but was very easy for me to follow since I was so familiar with it. The play began with Woyzeck shaving the Captain as the Captain warned, "The world is a dangerous place, Woyzeck, a dangerous place." The production was very similar to ours in San Francisco, but I became astounded in the scene with Woyzeck and the Doctor when I noticed that the Doctor had an uncanny resemblance to Calvin (Woyzeck in our production) and Woyzeck looked eerily like me although his hair was much thicker and grey.

My astonishment turned to horror in the scene where Woyzeck stabs Maria to death because of her affair with the Drum Major. The terrible dream that I had a couple of nights before came back to me and I recognized who the grey-haired murderer on the beach was. It was me.

Afterwards, Ana and I went to a nearby bar and we discussed the play although I did not reveal to her the horror that I felt. She stated, "Woyzeck had no right to kill Maria. He was not giving her pleasure, so she had a right to go somewhere else for it."

All I could respond to that was, "It was not Maria's adultery that caused the murder. It was the peas, the peas."

"The peas," a familiar voice echoed behind me, "the peas," and then laughter ensued. The laughter came from the three men sitting at the table behind us; the actors who portrayed Woyzeck, the Doctor, and the Drum Major. They invited us to join them and shared with us their bottle of ouzo, a very strong, aniseed-flavored spirit. They were very impressed when I related my experience with 'Woyzeck' because they too had produced the play themselves. Emanuil (Woyzeck) sat next to Ana and became involved in a discussion of the Kabbalah, which he said he was also researching. I didn't like the way his eyes stared into Ana's as he talked and especially did not like the way hers stared back at him.

Aleksandhros (the Doctor) said, "Come with us. We are going to Otekes."

"Otekes?" I asked. "Where's that?"

"Otekes is a smoking den," the good doctor explained, "You must join us. It will be like nothing that you have ever experienced before."

Ana, who by now was very drunk from the ouzo, said, "Come on, honey. Let's do it. It'll be fun," and so I complied.

The smoking den was just a few doors down from the bar and before we entered, I warned Ana, "There are very severe penalties for drug use in Greece."

Emanuil protested while grabbing Ana by the arm, "Don't be such a wet blanket, David."

Ana echoed, "Don't be such a wet blanket, David," and entered the den as I followed.

The smoking den was very dark with only candles and flashing lighters providing illumination. The air was thick with the fragrance of ganja as dark, scary-looking guys sat on cushions around the short, circular tables inhaling and exhaling the pungent smoke.

We sat down at a table and Konstandinos (the Drum Major) brought out a large switchblade to cut hashish and then stuck its blade into the top of the table next to the hookah. He requested that I give my opinion about the war in Afghanistan. I originally declined to comment upon it but after much baiting, I gave in and said, "I do not believe in the killing of innocent people, but I believe that the American forces are justified in their military involvement."

Konstandinos and Aleksandhros asked me to explain my reasoning and I began when Ana stood up with Emanuil and said, "Emanuil's going to show me a painting about the Kabbalah in the next room. I'll be right back."

"I'll join you, baby," I replied, but the combination of the ouzo and the protestations from Konstandinos and Aleksandhros kept me on my cushion. I explained, "Wealth is distributed unevenly throughout the world and the impoverished have a right to rebel, but killing thousands of innocent people is not the right means to that end."

"Sachlamare, rubbish," Aleksandhros protested, "Apokliete, no way!"

Konstandinos added, "Equality and the truth must be realized through any means necessary." His eyes pierced into mine and for the first time I realized that he too resembled someone familiar. His eyes glowed with the same demonical essence as those of George.

I stood up, grabbed the switchblade, and said, "Where's Ana?" and started to search through the adjoining rooms. Every time I opened a curtain, dangerous-looking fiends would stare back at me and scare me away.

I stood behind a final curtain and heard Ana say, "Ochi," the Greek word meaning 'no'. She followed with "Mi mangiziz aliti! (Don't touch me bastard!)" and I swung the curtain open to see Emanuil forcing himself upon her. Konstandinos came from behind and snatched the switchblade from me so I grabbed a hookah and hit Emanuil over his head and he collapsed. I grabbed Ana and yelled at Emanuil, "Ande Ghamisu!" (Go screw yourself!) and kicked him squarely in the balls, and then added, "If you can, malaka (wanker)." As we exited the den, I turned back to Aleksandhros and Konstandinos and screamed, "Kaneta lathos, kanete sachlamare! (You're wrong, you're garbage!)" and slammed the door behind us.

The next day Rethymno celebrated Carnaval with a huge parade that went down Koundouriotou, the main street of the city. Young people dressed as ancient Greeks, hairy pigs, and bug-eyed calamari drank from bottles of whiskey, wine, and ouzo as they danced and stumbled past us. Ana and I sat on a ledge alongside the street wearing our George Jr and Sr masks that we had recently purchased at one of the many small shops that displayed mainly Osama bin Laden masks in their windows. One menacing, tank-like float with the words, 'I anisotita epikinhonos' (dangerous inequality) passed by us with three costumed figures standing on top of the tank. I recognized immediately underneath the beards and turbans of Arafat, bin Laden, and the eye-patched Mullah Omar were the faces of Aleksandhros, Konstandinos, and Emanuil. They pointed their guns at us as they passed and we reciprocated with the middle finger salute.

The following day was Clean Monday, which marked the beginning of Lent in Greece. I stayed at the studio and asked Ana to pick up a newspaper for me while she went on her daily ritual, a walk along the coast. However, she returned empty-handed and explained that because of the holiday, there weren't any papers printed. I turned on the television to watch CNN, but the television did not appear to be working. I surmised that because of the beginning of Lent, all media had taken a break in observance to the holiday.

Later in the day, I went for a walk by myself and asked at the newsstand for my paper, but the man said that they were already sold out. I stopped at a café for a beer and noticed a copy of an English newspaper at the vacant table next to me and grabbed it. I was surprised to see that the date on it was that day. Why had Ana lied to me about the newspaper? Why were all the newspapers sold out at the newsstand? Why was there no television news? What was Ana trying to keep from me?

I searched through the newspaper until I thought that I had found my answer. An article stated that the U.S. government was warning its citizens that were living abroad that they were being endangered by a greater risk of terrorist acts. One paragraph that particularly got my attention stated that some terrorists would feign love with American citizens in order to enter the country, which had become much more difficult since September 11th, and then commit their terrorist acts. Is this what Ana was plotting all along? Was our meeting on December 14th by chance and good fortune or had it all been arranged by a terrorist network? I needed to find answers, but I didn't know where or how to find them. I remembered the small piece of paper that I had stolen from Ana's bag in Napflio and thought that perhaps that would be a start. I planned to go to the university library the next day to try to decipher the message using an English-Arabic dictionary but was unable to go because Ana pouted like a child and demanded that we take an excursion to the southern part of the island at Ayía Galíni. The message would have to wait and perhaps Ayía Galíni might give me some answers. Why was it so important for her to go there on that day? Perhaps I'd find out.

We got into town and I was expecting a relaxing day at the beach but Ana led me through an excruciating hike along and through a river, up hills and down valleys until we reached the highest point in the vicinity. Ana kept asking me for the time as we hiked and sped up each time after I answered. She appeared to be on a deadline and seemed to know exactly where her destination was; but why?

As we were sitting on top of a hill at 3:30 pm two American fighter jets flew by in the distance and suddenly exploded in the sky. Ana turned to me and asked again, "What time is it?"

"Its 3:33," I answered in shock. "We have to go," she informed me and set back down the hill as I stumbled behind her. Was this coincidence or had Ana been sent here on surveillance? Tomorrow, perhaps, the scrap of paper would give me some clues.

The next morning I set off for the university library alone because Ana complained that she was not feeling well and wanted to stay in bed for the day and rest. I asked her if she'd like for me to stay and care for her, but she insisted that I leave. Immediately after leaving the studio, I heard the sound of a television coming from what appeared to be our room. Was the television working again because we had passed Clean Monday or did Ana rig it so that I could not watch it that day? No matter, I had bigger fish to fry, with trying to decipher the note in my hidden pocket. In the back of my mind and in my heart, I hoped that it would amount to nothing, and that Ana and I stood on firm ground without any terrorist intrigue or deception. But coincidence after coincidence seemed to be adding up to suggest otherwise. Who was it that said, 'There is no coincidence'? We all determine our own fate. What was mine?

I picked up a newspaper on my way to the library. It reported that the two jets, that we saw explode, were F-14 Tomcats like the one that crashed into the sea a few weeks before. A military spokesman said, "This was no accident. Four human lives were brutally murdered through an act of sabotage by unknown killers. They are unknown now, but not for long. They will be caught and prosecuted." Was Ana a part of this terrorist act? Should I report to the authorities what I saw? No, I needed to wait and gather evidence before I accused the love of my life for murder. I needed hard evidence not just circumstantial coincidence.

I went to the Islamic section of the library and located an English-Arabic dictionary and found a secluded area to begin my work. The first part of the message appeared to be numbers ח٩٣ and I deciphered it as best as I could and came up with 1 19 3. Immediately I thought that these numbers meant yesterday's date, March 19, 2001. Wait, it's 2002, not 2001. What does the 1 mean? I looked more closely at the note and saw that perhaps the two ones belonged together rather than with the nine. 11 9 3. 11-9, September 11th and the 3, the three planes that crashed on that tragic day. Was my sweet, angel-eyed Ana involved with that massacre? How could she be? My imagination was getting the better of me. I needed to decipher further to get stronger evidence before I could call my bride-to-be a part of such a monumental mass murder.

Suddenly, Pastora appeared at my table with a bright smile on her face that contrasted with her dark, sensuous eyes and jet-black hair that flowed down her bare back. She touched my shoulder and asked, "How are you, David?"

I said, "Fine. How are you, Pastora?"

"I'm good, David. I was thinking about your dinner invitation and thought that maybe tonight might be a good time for me to come over."

"Tonight, yes, tonight at 8 is perfect! I'll tell Ana. We'll, I mean, she'll be so happy. Me too. Well, I'm happy now. We'll have fish and vegetables and some dessert. I'll get something sweet with crème and cherries. You like crème, you like cherries, don't you?"

"Oh, David," she remarked, "You're so funny. I'll like whatever you give me."

She then kissed me on the cheeks and said, "I have a class now. "I'll see you tonight," and left. I sat down and tried to get back back to work. But I couldn't continue to decipher the message. It had mysteriously disappeared.

Pastora arrived at our studio at 8 sharp as I began to prepare the fish and vegetables. I poured some white wine for her and Ana, put on an Alanis Morrisette CD and then began to cook the dinner. Ana and Pastora sat on the loveseat conversing and I came back to pour them more wine but noticed that they hadn't touched their first glasses. I said, "This wine is really good. You really should try it. Do you like the music? It's Alanis Morrisette. What do you think?"

Ana answered, "I think that your fish are burning, that is what I think."

I ran back to the stove and lowered the heat and turned the fish over as Ana and Pastora began to watch CNN on the television. The reporter talked about the exploding American jets, but I didn't hear much because of the sizzling of the fish and the girls' Castilian conversation.

Dinner was served and the three of us sat on the loveseat and watched a rerun of 'Ally McBeal.' Pastora stood up and said, "I have to go. I have a test tomorrow. Dinner was great, David. Thanks a lot."

"But we haven't had dessert yet. I have cake with cherries and crème."

"Sorry, I've got to go," she said as she kissed me and Ana on our cheeks and left.

The next morning, Ana said, "I am sure that I am now pregnant. I can feel our baby inside of me." She seemed to be convinced that we had conceived our child on the night of our three month anniversary of being together.

I would kiss her and the baby at the end of each night. When I served dessert, I would cut out one piece for myself and two for Ana and the baby. I was convinced that I would become a father in December and I felt very proud and happy about the prospect.

One night I lay awake in bed thinking about the names for our children. Josiah seemed perfect; he had been a great Jewish king, and two of our grandfathers were named Joseph. For our daughter's name, I began to feel apprehensive about our choice, Jedeidah. I could picture Jedeidah's classmates making fun of her by saying JedeiDuh, indicating that she was stupid. When Ana awoke, I expressed my thoughts to her and she suggested that we change it to Jediah, which pleased me. It sounded prettier than Jedeidah and was easier to pronounce and most importantly, it did not give other children the opportunity to be unkind. "Children can be so cruel toward one another. We, as parents, must not make it easy for our children to become victims of other's brutality," I told Ana.

The next day we went to an internet café and the screen came on with an ad that asked whether we'd like to sign up for a program that kept a calendar of the baby's development during pregnancy. We immediately signed up for this program and Ana typed in the date that we thought the baby had been conceived. The program told us that we could now take a pregnancy test, so we looked for a pharmacy but found none that were open. So we walked back to our studio.

Ana decided not to smoke cigarettes or drink wine anymore so as not to hinder the baby's development. She was glowing with beauty and was convinced that our child would be a boy because "Expectant mothers that show beauty have sons, while those that do not look so well have daughters."

She requested that I kiss the baby goodnight and I hesitated before doing so and then said, "Honey, I'm a bit worried. You're feeling so high right now because you think that you're pregnant. I'm afraid that if you find out that you're not pregnant, you're going to become very depressed. Let's try to keep things on an even keel until we know for sure."

She reacted very emotionally and said, "You think that I need a test to tell me that I'm pregnant? I know my body and I know what my body is telling me."

I answered, "Yeah, you're right honey. The signs are indicating that you're pregnant, but let's not get too excited until we're sure."

She sat up and went to the table and said, "Well, if I'm not pregnant, I'll have a cigarette then," and rolled one and smoked it. I tried to make her feel better by reassuring her that her instincts and feelings were probably right, but she continued to smoke and said, "I don't want to talk about it anymore," so I went to the bed and tried to fall asleep. That night we slept separately for the first time in a long while. Ana took her pillow and slept on the couch.

The next morning Ana asked me to express my feelings. I said, "Having a baby seems like such a top priority now even though we've known each other for only 3 ½ months. I'm afraid that if you're not able to have a child with me, you'll leave me and find another who can get the job done."

She kissed me and assured me that she would never leave me, saying, "God has provided us with a great gift, the gift of love. I will never leave you. We are forever bonded together."

We walked to the pharmacy and purchased a pregnancy test. I nervously sat outside the bathroom while Ana administered the test. She came out of the bathroom and shook her head no. She smiled at me although the look of disappointment was apparent in her eyes.

We discussed that now was probably not the best time to become pregnant anyway. We still had over three months to travel through Europe and did not have access to a doctor that could monitor our baby's development. Also, the paperwork for our marriage was still up in the air. There was the possibility that it would take longer than we had anticipated and we would be forced to live separately from each other for a while. That would be hellish for us both.

We decided that we would hold off on trying to have a baby until we were officially married. Things with us, such as marriage, citizenship, a house, were already moving very rapidly without adding a baby into the equation. We just needed to be patient. When the time was right, hopefully we would be blessed.

Ana rolled a cigarette and noticed that there was only one paper. Although I was desiring a cigarette as well, I said, "You have it. I think that you desire it more than me."

She replied, "We'll share it," which we did. After smoking, Ana lay across my lap and reflected, "I think that we just shared our strongest act of love yet. I know that it's only a stupid cigarette but we both desired it, yet acted unselfishly. I love you, David,"

"I love you, Ana."

In the evening we went to see an American movie called 'Serendipity' in which a couple meets in Manhattan and are attracted toward one another. The woman decides that they need to test fate by going on separate elevators and if they both press the same floor button, fate will have told them that they should be together. They get into their separate elevators and they both press the 23rd floor but the man's elevator gets loaded with many other people and he gets delayed. The woman waits on the 23rd floor for the man to arrive but sadly gives up hope and leaves just before the man arrives. Three years pass and they don't see each other again. They become engaged with others but cannot help but think about each other. Before their weddings, they each make one last, desperate attempt to find one another and at the movie's end, they happily reunite.

Throughout the movie I kept thinking about the night that Ana and I had met. I felt so grateful that she didn't play those fate games with me like the characters in the movie. I felt very strongly that it was fate that brought us together and I knew that if we hadn't talked that first night at the Czech quartet recital, we would have met two nights later at the Chanukah celebration, but what if? What if one of us felt ill that night and we never saw each other again? If I was in Greece right now without Ana as I had planned to be, I would be bored out of my mind. Being alone no longer suited me. Something inside of me would feel empty and my purpose in life would be cloudy. Sure, I might have found another, but I was convinced that I would be like the characters in the movie wondering, "What if?"

On the way back to the studio, we passed a machine that was called The Mouth of Truth. It looked kind of like that Coney Island machine from the Tom Hanks' movie, 'Big'. We each placed our hands inside the mouth and then received a computer print-out that analyzed each of us. Amazingly, both of our print-outs were exactly the same. Some of the things that the Mouth of Truth said about us were that we keep making mistakes that could jeopardize our future and that we seem almost incapable of achieving tranquility.

Ana and I designed our wedding invitations. We photocopied the painting of Josiah and Jediah and wrote above it, passages from the Sohar book of the Kabbalah and the Ecclesiastes. It read, "Each soul and spirit, prior to its entering into this world, consists of a male and female united into one being. When it descends on this earth, the two parts separate and animate two different bodies. At the time of marriage, the Holy One, blessed be He, who knows all souls and spirits, unites them again as they were before, and they again constitute one body and one soul, forming as it were the right and left of one individual; Therefore there is nothing new under the sun."

I was convinced that I had found my soul-mate and that it was Ana. She said the same about me. We were very lucky, we thought.

This morning's newspaper reported that two suspects were being held for the sabotage of the F-14 Tomcats that Ana and I saw explode in the sky a week ago. Very little detail about the suspects was given; only that they were male and female Crete University students who were studying abroad. Immediately I thought of Pastora. Then the face of the unfriendly bearded man that I ran into at the library also appeared in my mind. The article stated that the two were on an academic field trip when they disappeared from their group. Pastora had told me that she was studying in Rethymno to become an English teacher, but it didn't make much sense. Her ability in English appeared to me to be less than adequate.

I suggested to Ana that we visit the university library. For the first time since we had arrived into Rethymno, she did not seem eager to go there, but she grudgingly came along. Ana's face had turned white when I showed her the newspaper article and her tenseness was apparent during our entire bus ride to the university. She said that her nervousness was caused by an insufficient amount of sleep.

She awoke from a dream at 1:30 am and was unable to fall back asleep. "In my dream," she said, "an old classmate of mine named Sylvia and I shared an apartment. We each had our own bedrooms and mine was larger than hers but her room had cupboards while mine did not. I became jealous of her and suggested that I move the cupboards from the kitchen to my room, but she did not like that idea. She suggested that I wait to see the landlord and talk about the problem with him, but he never came. It was a silly dream, but for some reason it disturbed me and I couldn't fall back asleep."

"What are the cupboards?" I asked.

She sat silently for a moment and then said, "I don't know. What are they?"

"Your friend Sylvia, is she married? Does she have any children?"

"I would imagine so," she answered. "She was always very successful. But what are the cupboards? Oh, you think that the cupboards are babies and I'm jealous of her because she has babies, but I do not. That's what you think, don't you?"

"What do you think?"

"I think that maybe you're right. I still want children," and she began to cry like a small child.

"Patience, baby," I replied while hugging her, "We must have patience."

While Ana sat at a table reading about the Kabbalah, I wandered around the library looking for Pastora or the bearded man but did not see either of them. I tried looking for her name in the computer, but I only knew her first name and was not able to get anywhere with my search. I thought about going to the administration building and asking about her, but if she was the terrorist I was afraid that red flags would fly up and I would be escorted away by the police as another suspect, so I didn't go there. Somehow I needed to get the information from Ana.

I sat back down at her table and leafed through one of her books while trying to think of a subtle way to get this information, but came up with nothing. I pointed at a long-haired girl standing by the bookshelves and said, "There's Pastora!"

Ana's head shot up and looked at the girl. The expression on her face changed immediately from astonishment to disappointment and agitation. She said, "That girl looks nothing like Pastora. Are you crazy?"

"Oh, I thought that it was her," I replied, "but you're right. Pastora is taller. Have you seen her here today?"

"No," Ana scowled back at me.

"That's strange," I remarked. "We usually see her here at this time. I wonder where she is."

"I don't know," Ana scowled back at me again, "Please stop disturbing me. I'm trying to read."

"Do you know Pastora's last name?" I asked. "We should invite her for dinner again."

"I think that she went back to Spain for the Easter holidays."

"But Easter in Greece isn't until the first week of May."

"But in Spain, it is not," Ana seethed. "Now stop bothering me."

"I only think that it's strange that she should travel here and then go back to Spain after three weeks for a brief holiday."

"It's not strange at all," Ana fumed at me. "Easter is a very important holiday for Christians."

"Why's that?" I asked with child-like ignorance.

"Because that's the damn day that Jesus Christ supposedly rose from the dead. Now shut the hell up!" she answered me with raging eyes and clenched teeth.

"Okay, I'm sorry. It only seemed strange. No matter. I'll be quiet now...really." I continued to leaf through the Kabbalah book while I watched Ana from the corner of my eye as she pretended to read, but I could tell that her mind was a million miles away from the printed page.

The next few days, Ana remained secluded in our studio. The only time that she left was when she went to the nearby supermarket to get some groceries and some red hair dye. Her new image changed as dramatically as her new hair color. She wore her hair up for the first time since I had known her and also she began to dress in dark suits rather than the bright and flowery outfits that she had previously worn.

Each morning when I would come back to the studio with the newspaper, she would grab it from me and anxiously look through the pages. I would ask, "What are you looking for, honey?"

She would always answer, "Nothing, I'm just so bored."

"Let's go for a walk then," I would suggest.

"No!" she would shout, "I don't want to go outside."

This was very unusual because previously Ana loved being out in the sun and frolicking around the town. It was obvious to me that she had gone into hiding.

One day Ana suggested that we leave Rethymno and move to Anóyin, a small village that sits beneath the Psilorítis Mountain Range. We were getting near the end of our month stay in Rethymno and I was getting the itch to travel again, so I agreed with her idea. We thought that we would stay for a few days there and then take a bus to Iráklion, Crete's largest city and fly from there to Budapest.

We found a nice room in the upper village overlooking the lower village and the mountains and then went out for dinner at the only restaurant that appeared to be open. The menu was very limited so we each ordered portions of lamb and a Greek salad that we shared. The loudspeakers hanging from the steeple of the Adios Ioánnis Church blared out the service across the entire village as we ate and I drank a beer.

Ana started to complain about me being a loser and said that she worried how our children would turn out with me as their father. I shrugged off her comments without getting annoyed because I knew that they were without foundation. I had cleaned up my act. I was no longer abusing drugs and boozing it up like I had done in the past. I was devoted to her and to our family if we should ever have one.

Ana finished her dinner early and then stared coldly at me as I ate. In a snobbish tone she said, "Perhaps the reason why you always eat with your mouth open is that you can't breathe through your nose."

I was in no mood to have a conversation like this. I was irritable because I was on my third day of trying not to smoke cigarettes, I was tired from the long bus ride, and I was disappointed with the lamb that consisted mainly of bone and fat. I put my money on the table and said, "I'm done. I'm going," and started to walk away.

Ana yelled, "You can't leave me like this."

And I replied, "I can do anything that I want to do and so can you," and I walked away.

I had expected her to follow me to have another one of our 'discussions' but when I turned around, she was nowhere in sight. I hiked uphill to our room but she wasn't there, so I perched myself at the top of the hill and looked over the entire village as the loudspeaker from the church continued to resound. The village seemed empty except for three men wearing the traditional saríki black headdresses and vraka trousers tucked into their high black boots.

In the distance I saw a solitary figure walking along the road heading out of town. It could have been Ana, but it was impossible to tell because of the distance. An old truck pulled up alongside the walking person, who got into the truck, which then winded around a curve and out of my sight.

That could not have been Ana, I thought, she would never have gotten into a stranger's truck. But perhaps it wasn't a stranger. Perhaps she had arranged to meet this fellow terrorist here and she started the argument with me on purpose, so that she would have a chance to be away from me. She knew that complaining about me eating with an open mouth would push my buttons and I would become irritated. She disappeared so quickly from the restaurant. It was as if she was on a timetable and late for an appointment.

I walked around the village and then returned to the room and sat alone on the dark terrace overlooking the sleepy village. At 10:32 pm, Ana opened the door and apologized for making me angry and said that she had been in the church crying and then after the service she had tried walking back to the hotel but got lost.

"Where did you go?" I asked.

"I turned the wrong way and headed out of town."

"Did any cars or trucks stop as you were walking?"

"No," she answered, "I was all alone. I became frightened and saw the lights of the village and turned around."

She hugged and kissed me and said, "This place scares me. Can we please go to Irákilo tomorrow?"

I was surprised because earlier I had gotten the impression that she wanted to stay here for a few days and do some hiking, but I only answered, "Sure, baby, we'll leave tomorrow."

In Irakilo we went to a travel agent to check about flights to Budapest but Ana was looking at a ferry schedule and saw that there was a boat going to Israel. "Please, honey, can we go to Israel, please?" she pleaded.

But I would have none of that. I said, "There is no way in hell that I am going to Israel now. Don't you read the newspapers, Ana? Innocent people are getting blown to pieces there each day. That's about the last place that I want to go."

"But I want to go on a boat again. On airplanes, we don't get our own cabin. I want our own cabin," she pouted like a small child.

"Okay, okay, we'll take a boat, but where?"

"There's a boat tonight for Thessaloniki," she suggested, "From there we can take a bus into Bulgaria."

"Bulgaria?" I asked, "Why do you want to go to Bulgaria?"

"I don't know," she answered, "There are gypsies there. I want to see the gypsies sing and dance. Can we go there, please?"

"Okay, baby, Bulgaria it will be," I said and she gave me a big kiss, as I thought, 'Was it Bulgaria that she had intended to go all along? Did she only bring up Israel to make Bulgaria seem more attractive to me? All that she needed to do was kiss me and I was like putty ready to be molded. Oh, hell, enjoy it while you can. Go with the flow.'

We found a hotel in Thessaloniki and then went out for dinner. On the way back to the hotel we bought a gift for the both of us, Angel Cards. We would each ask a question and then randomly pick one card from each of the two decks. The card from the first deck would reassure us and give us advice and the card from the second deck would give us a certain power or tell us how we needed to act.

Ana asked the angels whether we would have a baby. The first card answered that "changes are coming," while the second said that one needed to "act with patience and consistency."

Ana frowned and said, "Everyone's always telling me that I need to be patient; first with the painting, now with having a baby."

"Having a baby is a very special event and anything that special takes a great amount of effort and perseverance."

"I know but I wanted a better answer."

"I think that the angels answered very wisely. Rome was not built in a day."

"What?"

"Building the great Roman Empire took great effort and many years. It did not just magically appear. Great art takes many hours of reflection and hard work. Anything good is worth waiting for."

"I know but I want to be pregnant now!"

My question for the angels was, "Will Ana's and my love last throughout our lifetimes?" The first card answered that I needed to trust the angel and the second card told me to act with freedom and detachment.

I thought that this second card forebode a very bleak future for us, but Ana saw it in a different light. She explained, "You must keep your independence because I love that quality in you. And we must not become too dependent upon each other, otherwise we will lose our wholeness."

Ana said that I had of late been slacking off with my writing, so she suggested, "You should go for a walk and find a nice bar where you can do your writing like you used to. I miss you doing that." So I left her at the hotel.

I found a strange, little subterranean bar that still had all of its Christmas decorations up. Behind the bar was a very grumpy-looking woman. I noticed a sign that said, 'Happy Hour, 2 for 1 all drinks.' The clientele consisted of a wide assortment of young and old, Greek and foreign, but all inebriated.

The grumpy bartender grunted, "What yah want?"

I said, "Is it Happy Hour?"

"Yeah," she frowned.

"Well, let's get happy then. I'll take some red wine."

I took my glasses of wine and sat down at a table and began to write as the people at the bar turned in their seats and watched me. Midway through my second paragraph, a very sad-looking woman named Akeldama came to my table and asked me to tell her what my story was about. I gave the standard response, "Fiction with a lot of reality about the struggle between good and evil."

"Yes," said Akeldama, "life must have both good and evil, otherwise there is an imbalance."

"I agree."

"You know what that medal means that you wear around your neck?" she asked about the crucifix with the rounded top.

"Yes, I believe that it is a symbol for many things. For the Christians, it is a crucifix, but also I think, a key to the gates of paradise."

"Yes, that's correct," said Akeldama, "but it is much more."

"A man told me," I continued, "that it is a symbol of fertility: the round part at the top being the woman's vagina and the shaft is the man's penis."

"Yes, but there is more."

"Tell me."

"It is Egyptian. The top represents Upper Egypt and the bottom represents Lower Egypt."

"Of course," I replied, "I had taught that to my middle school students, but I had forgotten all about it. The pharaoh's crown was decorated with that symbol."

"Yes," she replied, "upper and lower, everything needs its opposite. Otherwise there is no balance and it cannot exist; it will die."

I asked about the four necklaces that she wore: three of cats and the fourth, a small silver harp. "I wear the cats," she replied, "because I have many cats whom I love and love me."

"Also," I added, "the cat was considered a sacred god in Egypt."

"Oh yes," she agreed with a smile of momentary serenity.

"And the harp?" I asked, "Are you a musician?"

"Oh no, I was a dancer of ballet." Her eyes reflected her past beauty. "My life has been very bad. When I was younger, it was very good, but now it is very bad. It has some balance, but there is too much bad."

"Yes, I can see that, but perhaps it will become good again."

"No, it is too late for that. Perhaps in my next life, I will see good again."

"I will pray for you."

"It will do no good. There is no god and religions are useless."

"I don't agree. I believe that there is a God and that God exists in many forms."

"No, there is no god. All that exists is you and your energy."

"I don't believe that God exists like some books show him as an old man with a long beard. I agree with you that an energy or common ground or God exists within us, but I think that He/She/It exists without us as well."

"No, there is no god. There is only you alone."

"I think that God is benevolent but God sometimes appears in an evil form because God is constantly testing us in God's game that we call life."

"Yes but no, good cannot exist without evil."

"And evil cannot exist without good."

"Yes, but there is no god, no devil, there is only you. I leave you to write now but I want to talk with you again. I have no one to talk to. No one understands me."

"Yes, we will talk again. I enjoyed our talk."

She went back to her seat at the bar and I began to write again. I wrote for maybe two seconds when a young woman with long blonde hair, who was dancing wildly by herself, sat down beside me as I continued to write. She said rather loudly, "People do not come to bars to write. People come to bars to meet other people and drink so that they will forget."

I replied, "I think that I am a person and I have met some people here already, but now I am here to write," and I continued writing.

"But you have not met me and I have my story to tell you," she persisted. I finished writing my sentence and closed my notebook and grabbed my post-it notes.

"What is it that you wish to tell me?" I asked.

"Oh, I don't know. I'm very drunk."

"Why is it that you are very drunk?" I calmly asked.

"Oh, you're going to get American on me," she screeched. "I hate it when they do that."

"I don't understand what you mean by 'getting American'. What does it mean?"

"You Americans think that you know everything, but you know nothing."

"All Americans know nothing?"

"There you go again, getting American on me. I hate that."

"I'm sorry," I replied, "and I'll try not to do whatever it is that I'm doing. Now I think that I will write some more."

"No!" she screamed, "You must listen to me talk."

"I must not do anything. I'll decide what I want to do because I have a free will."

"Stop getting American on me!" she screamed, "I hate that."

"I'm sorry. Please say what you want to say to me, but I ask that you be brief because I really want to finish this chapter.

"I'll talk as long as I want," she loudly retaliated.

"And I'll listen for as long as I want," I calmly counter-attacked.

"There you go again," she said.

"What do you want to say?" I asked. A blank look came over her face as we sat in silence. "Perhaps I'll start. Tell me about yourself."

"I'll talk about my job," she said with excitement.

"Vale," I answered.

"What?" she asked.

"Vale, it means okay in Spanish."

"I don't care about that. Talk English, you're not Spanish."

"And what is my language?"

"English, you stupid fool. You speak only English."

"I speak some Spanish. I speak it very poorly but I am trying to get better and practice makes perfect. I love to learn at least the greetings in foreign tongue of the countries that I am visiting."

"That's stupid!"

"Why?"

"There you go again!" she screamed then she said with a very pleasant smile, "I have lived in Japan."

"Oh really, why did you decide to live in Japan?"

"I went there to study the Japanese language."

"That's exciting, so you speak Japanese?"

"No, you stupid fool, I don't speak Japanese. I'm not Japanese."

"What is your name and from what country are you?"

"I'm Tarah and I'm a Kiwi," she answered proudly, "but you don't know what that is."

"I think I do. You're from New Zealand. My best friend is from there as well."

"We're talking about me, not him, so shut the hell up," she answered in a way that I thought was other than polite.

I stated, "I think I will continue with my chapter now. It was interesting for me to chat with you, but now I want to write."

"I'm not going anywhere."

"That's fine, but now I write."

I started to write a word when she grabbed my pen to keep me from writing any further and said, "I want to talk about...(blank stare) my job. Yes, I'll tell you about my job." She smiled with pride.

"Okay," I remarked, "you tell me about your job, and I'll appear to be listening. But first you must release my pen because I'll perhaps want to take notes of what you say."

"Okay," she replied happily, "I'll tell you about...(another blank stare)...what am I talking about?"

"Your job which you enjoy so much."

"Yes, my job," she said and her face went blank again.

"What is your duty?" I asked.

She replied, "I work on a German diving boat, but the equipment has never been used."

"Why is that?"

"What?"

"Why is it that the equipment has never been used?"

"Because," she loudly answered, "nobody knows what the hell they're doing."

"What is your duty on this boat? Are you the skipper?"

"Don't be stupid. I'm not the skipper; I'm a deckhand, a stewardess."

"Oh, and what is the duty of the deckhand/stewardess?"

"I fold towels, but the German bitch always says that I do it wrong and she shows me how to do it and it's just like I've already done it."

"How is it that the German bitch wishes you to fold the towels?"

She then explained the highly-complicated technique while holding an invisible towel, "You first fold it in half and then you fold it in half again. No wait, you fold it in half, then you fold it three times."

"Into thirds?"

"Yes...no...maybe...I don't know. I need a towel to show you," she answered with maybe more than a slight hint of confusion.

I held up a post-it note and said, "Let's pretend that this paper is the towel. Is the towel square like this paper?"

She thought for a while with her well-oiled mind and then said, "No, you stupid idiot, it's a rectangle. Towels are rectangles, not squares. Haven't you been anywhere?"

"I guess not," I replied and continued, "Your towels are rectangles, so I'll tear off this left third, and now this paper has become your rectangular towel."

"It's too small," she protested.

"Yes, it is a small towel, but it is for a small diver," I answered. "Now please fold the small towel for me the way in which the German bitch wants it to be done."

She folded the small towel in half three times, then screamed, "That's not right!" Then she folded it in half two times and then folded it into thirds. "Shit, that's not right either."

"Perhaps," said I, "you should ask the German bitch to explain it to you very slowly tomorrow."

"Slowly," she said as if enlightened of a great truth.

"Yes, slowly," I said, "and if you get confused, ask the bitch to show you again until you are no longer confused. Now Tarah, I have a question for you. Why did you choose to wear a small stone on the right side of your nose?"

"Oh this? This is my rebellion stone," she answered.

"So, you are a rebel."

"I don't know what I am."

"I'm also curious about the design on your shirt."

"What design?" she asked while surveying her shirt.

"The one on the front of your shirt below your neck," I answered as I pointed at the large circle with a small circle in the center, which was surrounded on four sides by smaller circles, which were partnered with curved lines. "Why do you wear this symbol on your shirt?"

"It has no symbolic meaning for me. I wear it because it is trendy."

"Oh, you are a trendy person as well?"

"What?"

"You are a rebel because you wear the stone in your nose and you are a trendy person because you wear the trendy shirt."

"No, I'm not either. I'm just Tarah, that's who I am."

A young man in an obvious state of inebriation weaved toward our table and rested his elbows on my writing pad. "This is my boyfriend, Mike. He's an Aussie," Tarah informed me.

"Pleased to meet you, Mike. I'm David," said I. Mike looked at me with disdain, then appeared as if he was going to vomit all over me and my writing. Then he weaved back to the bar.

"Well, it was a pleasure talking with you, Tarah, but now I'd like to continue writing. So, you may leave me now and be with your beloved," I said.

"My What?"

"Your beloved, your loved one, your boyfriend." She still looked confused. "Mike, the man that you just introduced me to."

"Oh Mike," something within her finally connected, "he's my boyfriend."

"Yes, you make a very lovely couple. Now please join him, so that I can continue to write."

"I'm not going anywhere. I'm going to stay here and bother you, so that you can't write."

"Tarah," I said very calmly, "Piss off."

"What?"

"Piss off."

She stood up and went to the bar and told everybody what I had said and they all laughed except for Mike, who scowled at me.

I continued to write for a short time when Akeldama stood at my table again and said, "We need to go to the Untruth to get to the Truth. The Truth is like a spiral; it's constantly moving. Religion does not get to the Truth; it's dogmatic, it's used to satisfy the mortal world. The Bible is only a fairy tale."

"Do you believe that Christ lived?" I asked.

"I believe that there may have been a good man named Jesus," she answered, "but he was not Christ; he was no god, he was only a symbol. The word Christ means light or understanding."

"I understand," I replied.

"I must go now," she said, "but we must talk again. I can't talk about these things to anyone else."

"I have met many people while I've been traveling that like to talk philosophy," I said.

"I have met no one," she said and left.

Mike, the drunken Aussie, collapsed at my table again and pressed his booze-scented body against mine. I asked him if we had a problem. He answered that there was no problem, but that now he wanted to tell me his story. I brought out my post-it notes and asked, "What is it that you wish to tell me?" He then grabbed my notebook and tried to destroy it, but I took it from his hands. I said, "I think you've said enough," and grabbed my things and sat at the bar and continued to write.

A few minutes later, Mike approached me again with a bottle of red wine. He asked me if I wanted some. I told him that my glass was still three quarters full. He grabbed my glass and gulped it down and then walked away with his bottle, falling over the decorated Christmas tree that crashed to the ground. He bellowed, "I have the most important thing to say!"

The bus left the next morning at 7:30 and we arrived at the Bulgarian border at around 10:30. But there was a long delay at the border. All of the passengers on the bus had gotten back their passports except for Ana and me. I suspected that it was because of my illegally extended stay in the European Union, but it turned out that I wasn't the problem.

The border agents thought that Ana's passport looked suspicious and kept putting it through an X-ray machine to see if the original photo had been replaced. She was told to show another photo ID and she provided her Spanish driver's license, but that was insufficient for the agents because the photo was only stapled on a piece of paper. It wasn't like my California driver's license, which had a holograph and was very difficult to forge. Finally, after two hours of looking through manuals, and putting the passports in and out of the X-ray machine, and looking at us suspiciously without hardly any interrogation, the agents let us pass the border.

Back on the bus, I asked Ana, "What's wrong with your passport?"

"Nothing's wrong with it," she snapped. "It's an old passport and it's a little bit worn at the edges. They thought that the photo had been replaced."

"Yeah," I replied, "it is pretty beat up. You probably should get a new one."

"I know," she snapped again, "I didn't have time."

The bus dropped us off at Blagoevgrad, which was the closest bus stop to the Sila Monastery where we were headed. Ana had suggested that we stay at the monastery for a few days to rejuvenate our spirits, since we were both feeling a bit burnt out. In Blagoevgrad, we didn't know where to go. The city did not look anything like the images of opulent buildings and the American University that we saw on the internet the previous night. Instead, it looked like a slum area with publicly-funded highrises with broken windows and tattered laundry hanging in the dusty air.

A little, old lady with kindly eyes started to talk to us in Bulgarian and pointed her cane in the direction further up the street. I thought that perhaps she was just a busybody who was going to lead us astray, but Ana stood and paid careful attention to her. The lady started to walk in that direction and urged us with her cane to hurry up and follow her. She led us straight to the bus that was just ready to depart for the monastery.

I got on the bus first and paid for our tickets and then looked back at Ana and thought that I saw the old lady slip a piece of paper into Ana's hand. But when we got to our seats, I asked Ana about it and she denied that she had received anything from the lady. She said, "We only shook hands. You probably saw the old lady's white, wrinkly hands because there was nothing more."

We arrived at the Sila Monastery, which is situated 149 kilometers south of Sofia. The monastery, a gigantic four-level structure with numerous arches and balconies, was founded by a colony of hermits and then during the Turkish rule from the 15th to 19th centuries, it served as a refuge to help keep alive the Bulgarian culture.

Ana was able to have a room for herself since she was the only woman staying at the monastery, but I was told that I would need to share a room with one of the monks. I entered my room and saw my new roommate, Brother Todor, sitting on a chair in the back of the darkened room. Brother Todor had long black hair and beard and hypnotic eyes that stared at me and caused me to jump back with off-guarded fear. With his right hand, he silently indicated which was to be my bed and I clumsily dropped my guitar and small backpack on it, which caused him to grimace. Again with his right hand, he indicated my closet space which stood in the back of the room beside my bed. I tried to carefully place my things there by hanging my shirts and pants on the hangers and hooks that were provided and stuffing my underwear and socks on the shelves.

From Brother Todor's expressions, it was obvious that I was not doing it correctly. He stood up and opened the door to his closet and I saw his clothing very neatly arranged in perfect symmetry. The gowns flowed down from the hangers, the two hats sat on the top shelf and below that, the undergarments were folded with a meticulousness that I had not witnessed in the finest of any laundry establishments. He looked at me with pride and I tried to show him that I was impressed by nodding my head and saying, "Nice, very nice, muy perfecto."

He abruptly closed the closet door and sat back down in his chair. I sat down on my bed and he grimaced again, so I moved to the wooden chair that stood beside his. We both sat there silently in our chairs for about ten minutes. I was hoping to get a feeling of peace come over me but all that I felt was an ever-increasing tension. I stood up and said, "I'm going to go for a walk," and indicated a walking motion with my fingers. He sat without expression as I exited and closed the door behind me.

I saw Ana sitting in the courtyard and rushed down to her. She appeared to be meditating, but I interrupted her anyway and said, "Ana, can we go for a walk?" She grimaced but agreed to join me. We walked through the small village of restaurants and souvenir shops that stood behind the monastery as I told her about my meeting with Brother Todor. I said, "I don't want to stay here long. This Brother Todor really gives me the creeps. I have a really bad feeling about him."

Ana answered, "I think that you need to show more patience. Perhaps you will learn something very important from him. It sounded to me like a very spiritual encounter that you had with him, but you were not yet ready for it."

"There was nothing spiritual about it. He's a control freak and that I do not need."

"Perhaps that is exactly what you need; more discipline. Perhaps Brother Todor will help you find it."

"I don't know," I replied. "The dude really gives me the creeps."

We walked back into the monastery and were met by another monk, Brother Ivan, who was about forty years old with rather short brown hair and beard and a sharp hawk-like nose. He said, "Please forgive me, but it is now dinnertime and you should come to the dining room."

We followed Brother Ivan into the cavernous dining room which was lined with large wooden tables and numerous chairs. However, only one other person besides the three of us was there, Brother Petár. Brother Petár was an albino with long white flowing hair and beard, ashen skin, and pink eyes. The way that the hair flowed over his head and with his closely set eyes and long, flat nose, he looked like an albino lion king.

He greeted us very warmly and invited us to sit down beside him. I looked around at all of the empty chairs and asked, "Where are all of the others?"

Brother Petár replied, "Brother Todor is fixing the meal."

"There are no others here?"

"No, it is very quiet here now," Brother Petár answered.

"But there are so many rooms…"

I began to ask why I needed to share one with Brother Todor, but Brother Ivan interrupted me and said, "Please forgive my interruption, but Brother Todor is now approaching with our meal and we must be silent."

Brother Todor walked across the large room carrying a wooden tray, which held five bowls, five cups, five spoons, and five pieces of bread. He perfectly placed each of the articles in front of each of us as we sat in perfect stillness and silence. He sat down and Ana and I watched as the three monks closed their eyes and prayed in silence. At exactly the same moment, they opened their eyes and we began to eat.

In the bowl was the least tasty lentil soup that I had ever had. The lentils appeared to have been boiled in water, nothing more. No spices, not even salt. When we had all finished with our soup, bread, and water, Brother Ivan said, "Please forgive me, Brother David and Sister Ana, but it is now our duty to clean the kitchen and dining room."

Brother Petár went with Ana to the kitchen to do the dishes as Brother Ivan and I washed the tables and swept the floor of the dining room. I noticed that no dirt or dust was collected from my broom and said, "Is this really necessary, Brother Ivan? This room is perfectly clean. There is no dust."

"Please forgive me, Brother David," replied Brother Ivan, "but it is our duty to wash and sweep the dining room and so we must," and we continued to sweep over the entire floor. We then carried our empty dustpans to the wastebasket and poured out the nothingness that we had collected.

I asked Brother Ivan about Brother Todor and he replied, "Brother Todor is a great holy man and a great teacher. He is perfection personified. He has no vices, no weaknesses. He is pure."

"Don't you find his rigidness and perfection a bit scary?" I asked.

Brother Ivan replied, "Please forgive me, Brother David, but I think that perhaps you find Brother Todor scary because he makes you see the weakness in yourself." I could not think of a response, so I remained silent. I went to the kitchen to see Ana but it was empty, so I made my way back to my room with great trepidation.

I entered the room with my pocket flashlight turned on, so that I could be quiet and not disturb Brother Todor. He seemed to be sleeping in his bed, so I crept to my closet to get my pajamas. When I opened the closet, I was astonished to see that my clothes were now hung and folded in perfect symmetry; obviously the work of Brother Todor. I carefully removed my clothing and silently laid them on the chair so that I would not awaken Brother Todor and slipped on my pajamas and went down into my hard bed which made springy sounds whenever I moved. I lay still and noticed a strong scent, which smelled like brandy. I lay on my back trying not to make a sound. The room was silent. I heard no breathing coming from Brother Todor. I sensed that he was awake and listening for any sound that I would make. Each time that the bed springs sounded, I could imagine Brother Todor's expression of disapproval. Some two hours later, I fell asleep.

I dreamed that Ana and the three brothers were sitting at a table in the dining room although now it looked more like a medieval beer hall. Brother Todor kept pouring shots of brandy into the four glasses. The four of them would raise their glasses into the air and say, "Nazdrave!" and then they would spill the brandy across the floor. I would come rushing out of the kitchen wearing an apron and carrying a broom and dustpan. Every time that

I had collected all of the brandy, it would suddenly disappear and more brandy would splash across the floor. This sequence would continue over and over again and Ana and the three monks would laugh louder and louder as they would watch me scramble across the floor to collect every drop of brandy.

I awoke and saw Brother Todor standing over my bed. For the first time, he spoke to me. He said, in a harsh tone, "This is totally unacceptable. You come into the room late at night and awaken me with your noisy, irreverent behavior. You place your clothing on the chair. Do you know the purpose of a closet? Of course you don't. A closet is for storing clothing. Yet you place your clothing on the chair. You really are an ignorant fool, aren't you?"

"But I…" I tried to explain that I placed my clothes on the chair so that I would not awaken him, but Brother Todor would not let me continue.

"Your behavior is totally unacceptable. Perhaps in time, you will learn the just way," he said and then walked out of the room without closing the door.

I lay back down in bed and tried to figure out how I had gotten myself in such a ridiculous situation. I felt as if I was a little kid again and I was being chastised for having a messy room. I didn't need this crap. I'm a grown man. I decided I was going to get the hell out of there that day.

I put on my clothes and walked out to the terrace that faced the central courtyard. There I saw Ana and Brother Petár filling plastic water bottles from the well. They were working very efficiently with Ana holding the bottle until it was filled and Brother Petár capping it and placing it in a crate.

I walked down the stairs and joined them and asked, "What are you doing?"

Ana answered, "Brother Petár has been bottling the mountain water that flows down here to the monastery. He's been selling it to help support the monastery. It's been very successful."

"Well, that's wonderful," I answered and tried to grab an empty bottle from the crate, but Brother Petár gave me a full, capped bottle and said, "Here, have one of these with my compliments." The bottle showed a rendering of the monastery with the mountains in the background and words in English that said, 'Sila Monastery Mountain Spring Water – God's Gift to Man.'

"Why are the words in English?" I asked.

"Our water is very popular in London," Brother Petár replied. "It's considered a delicacy among the elite. I have put my love into each bottle that I have produced and God has rewarded me by having this product be in great demand. Thus, I can, as you Americans say, charge an arm and a leg for each bottle." He then let out an unusually high-pitched laugh and put his hand on my shoulder and said, "Now, if you'll excuse me. I need to get back to work. I have a huge shipment that needs to be sent out today."

"May I help?" I asked.

"No," he replied, "Only two bottlers are needed here and Sister Ana and I are working very well together. Brother Ivan is in the infirmary attending to the sick. I'm sure that you would be of great assistance to him there." I thought about asking Ana to walk with me for a talk about leaving, but I could see that she was enjoying herself too much, so I decided to save that for later.

I walked to the infirmary expecting to see a room full of Bulgarian peasants and their children, but instead I saw a large group of rich-looking tourists. "Brother Petár said that perhaps you could use my assistance, Brother Ivan."

"Yes, yes, of course, thank you, Brother David," said Brother Ivan with a wide smile, "With your assistance, we will be done in no time." I held a vial for Brother Ivan as he injected each of the tourists with a syringe and said a short prayer.

After we had finished and were cleaning up, I asked, "Where did these patients come from and why?"

He answered, "Mostly they come from Sofia although sometimes I get busloads from other parts of Europe. They come here to rid themselves of various illnesses. I'm happy to say that I have had great success with the results."

"What do you give them that their own doctors don't?"

"My remedy has not yet been approved, but I administer it anyway because I can't stand to see the people suffering. But actually, I feel that the prayer that accompanies each injection is the missing ingredient that they can't get from any of their doctors."

"What is the prayer?"

"I'm sorry, Brother David, but that I cannot tell you."

"Brother Ivan, I'm having great difficulties in sharing a room with Brother Todor. He is such a perfectionist and makes me very nervous. Do you think that I may have a room for myself?"

"I'm sorry, Brother David, but it is the policy here that visitors room with one of the monks."

"Can I room with you then, Brother Ivan?"

"No, that's impossible. It has already been decided."

"By whom?"

He didn't answer me but only looked towards the heavens with a serene smile. He then said, "We must forgive Brother Todor for his harshness. He suffers greatly and sometimes we need to suffer for it. Be patient and show mercy and everything will turn out well."

I walked out to the courtyard and saw Ana standing outside of the church studying the frescoes. "Hey, Ana, what are you doing?"

She answered, "I think that I have solved one of my important questions about the Kabbalah. Remember when I told you about the faces of the ox, lion, man, and eagle? What do you see above?"

I looked up and in each corner of this section of the ceiling, I saw a man writing accompanied by one of the four creatures. "Yes, I see them," I answered.

"The writer in all four pictures is the same man, but he has aged. When he is young, he is with the ox, then the lion, then the man, then the eagle, which is the highest level in the development of wisdom. That is what the book meant at the library. I did not understand it, but now this fresco explains it for me. I'm so happy. I love it here, don't you?"

"Actually, Ana, I was hoping that we could leave. Brother Todor is a real pain. I really need to leave here before I lose it and kill him."

"Please, honey," she pleaded, "Let's stay here just a couple of days more. Then we can leave for Transylvania. I'm learning so much here and I so enjoy working with Brother Petár. He's such a sweet soul."

"Alright, sweetie," I relented, "I suppose I can stick it out for two more days, but after that we're out of here."

We walked around the church some more and stopped in front of a fresco that showed three long-haired bearded men. "These men are Abraham, Isaac, and Jacob," Ana pointed out. "Each of them is an archetype for a Sephiroth in the Kabbalah. Abraham is the archetype for mercy, Isaac is justice, and Jacob is love."

"Now, how do you think that the animals from the other painting would match with these three men?" I asked.

"Well, I would say that justice seems to be a very human concept so I would match the man with Isaac," she answered. "Mercy seems to be a higher, more sophisticated concept, so I'd put that with the eagle. The eagle flies from above and does not distinguish between colors, whereas the man does. That leaves the lion for love which is Jacob. I think that probably these three men are at too high a level of be associated with the ox. The lion has a strong family network which is based on love."

"And Jacob wrestled like a lion with the angel before his name was changed to Israel," I added.

"Yeah, I suppose," Ana said although I felt that she was not so impressed with my observation.

"You know, these three archetypes seem to match up pretty well with the three monks here," I observed again.

"Explain," Ana stated in her direct way.

"Well, first of all Brother Petár looks like a lion and he seems to put so much love into anything he does like the bottling of the water. Ivan is, of course, mercy. He's always saying 'please forgive me' and 'we must forgive him' and he looks like an eagle. Todor is justice. Everything must be done the correct way, which for him is his way."

"Please forgive the interruption," said Brother Ivan, "but it is now time to eat."

We followed him to the dining room and once again went through the ritual of silence as Brother Todor placed before us the blandest bread that I have ever tasted. Afterwards, while Brother Ivan and I were sweeping up the air, I said, "Brother Ivan, who was it that determined it would be our duty to clean the dining room after each meal?" He only smiled at me. "It was Brother Todor, wasn't it?" I continued, "You know, Brother Todor is so obsessed with cleanliness that I think he would be of better use doing the cleaning. His talent certainly is not in cooking. The food is totally tasteless."

"Forgive me, Brother David," Brother Ivan replied, "but I think that your anger is making you say things that are intended to be cruel. The food is simple, yes, that is how things should be in a monastery, but it is not tasteless. Perhaps you should look further into yourself to see what is the cause for your anger."

I walked through the mountains until it got dark and returned to my room and fell asleep with an empty stomach. That night I remember having three different dreams, which seemed to have been influenced by the conversation that Ana and I had outside the church earlier in the day.

In the first dream Ivan was Abraham and he was sacrificing Isaac (Petár) to God, but an angel appeared and told him that he had proved his loyalty to God and that he should sacrifice a ram in place of Isaac.

In the second dream Petár was Isaac again only this time he was very old and on his death bed. His son, Jacob, who was Todor, approached the bed disguised as his older brother, Esau. He wore animal fur over his arms and hands to make Isaac think that he was giving his blessing to the eldest son as he had intended.

In the third dream Petár was Isaac again, but this time as a young man. He was standing beside a well and waiting for his servant to come with his bride-to-be, Rebekah. In the dream I was the servant riding a camel toward the well and on the camel beside me was Ana as Isaac's future bride, Rebekah. Suddenly, the dream turned into a negative image and Petar's white hair and skin turned dark. He no longer looked like a benevolent, albino monk but looked like a monster version of America's Most Wanted, Osama bin Laden.

I awoke screaming but found that it was now morning and I was alone in the room. I lay in bed and thought about the three dreams. Ivan was Abraham like I had told Ana the previous day but in the dreams, Todor's and Petar's roles were reversed. Todor was Jacob and Petár was Isaac in all three of the dreams. Did that mean that Todor actually signified Love and Petár signified Justice? What were my dreams trying to tell me? Was the negative image of Petár turning into a monstrous bin Laden warning me that he was not actually the saintly figure that he seemed to be?

I walked out onto the terrace and saw Petár and Ana at the well filling and capping their bottles. They looked so happy as they were doing their work. They looked too happy. What evil intent lied beneath their smiles? What mysterious killing agent was capped into each of those bottles of water that were being sent to the elite of London?

I had evidence in the bottle that Petár had given me the previous day. I only needed to keep it and have it analyzed at a lab to prove that my suspicions were justified. But it would be a while before I could get to a lab, so I would have to wait. Meanwhile, I wanted to get the hell out of here. Petár seemed like a really good man, but my dream was telling me otherwise. Todor seemed like an ass and probably was. Ivan was the only one that remained consistent with my initial observations. He seemed merciful and appeared to have good intentions. But what was really in the syringes that he applied to all of those people? Were any of these three monks to be trusted? Was Ana in cahoots with them? Was she to be trusted?

The next bus leaving from the monastery would be early the next morning. I was going to be on that bus whether Ana joined me or not. I walked to the well and told Ana that I was leaving the next morning. She and Petár looked at each other and she tried to convince me to stay for one more day, but I refused to give in. I said, "I'm taking the morning bus at 6 tomorrow. You can either be with me or you can stay here. It's your choice. I'm going into the mountains now. I'll see you later," and I walked away.

After hiking for most of the day, a huge rain storm appeared and I ran back down to the monastery. Brother Ivan told me that it was dinnertime and urged me to join him. I told him that I had decided to fast that day, but he said that when Brother Todor had learned that I was leaving the next day, he made a special dish for me. I told Ivan that I was resolved to continue my fast, but I would join them in the dining room since it was my last night.

Brother Ivan and I sat down with Brother Petár and Ana as Brother Todor appeared from the kitchen with his wooden tray. This time, though, he was not solemn like the previous times. He wore a huge smile and exclaimed with great gaiety, "Tonight, since it is your last, Brother David, I have made my specialty, sirene po shopski."

I told Brother Todor about my vow to fast that day, and he said that he understood but placed the earthenware bowl in front of me in case I changed my mind. I watched the four of them gleefully gobble up their entrée of baked cheese, eggs, and tomatoes as I steadfastly sat. Ana and the others urged me to break my fast and do it another day, but I did not cave in to their persuasions.

Brother Todor brought out a bottle of plum brandy and poured drinks for all five of us, although I declined to drink. He made a toast to the strength of my convictions and they all said, "Nasdrave" which brought back the unpleasant dream that I had two nights earlier. However, in reality, I did not sweep up their brandy spills. No brandy was spilt and Todor said, "Tonight I will do the sweeping and you may go back to the room and rest."

I lay in bed and wondered why Todor had behaved so differently that night. What were his plans for me? Was there some ulterior motive behind his actions? Would Ana join me on the bus? Would I ever get on the bus?

I fell asleep and had three dreams again, although they were quite different from the ones that I had the previous night. In the first dream, I am a student at a high school in some foreign country. The principal of the school, Brother Todor, tells me that I must open up my locker for an inspection. I walk with him and the police officers in front of the entire school population. I feel confident as I dial the combination on my locker because I know that I am innocent and that my locker holds nothing bad.

In the second dream I am the American actor, Tim Robbins. I am jogging around the city when I pass a house where two little black girls are playing in the front yard. There is also a baby crib there and I see a small black baby boy falling from the crib. I reach out my hand and catch the baby just before he is about to crash to the ground. The mother comes out of the house and looks at me as if I am a baby thief. I tell the two girls to tell her that I saved their brother from falling. The mother seems unmoved by my act and tells me to put the baby back in the crib. I try to do that, but the baby won't let go of me. Finally, the mother grabs the baby from me and carelessly throws him down, then goes back into the house.

The next day I, Tim Robbins, am doing my daily run around the city when I pass this house again and see the two girls playing outside. I ask them if their mother is always so unfriendly. They say, "No, she is very happy when she has fruits and vegetables with sugar icing on top." So the next day when I, Tim Robbins, run around the city, I take a bag of fruits and vegetables with sugar icing and present it to the mother. She becomes very warm and friendly and invites me into the house. The baby boy has now grown into a young man who is an electronics genius, with a thick, dark beard. I find out that he's being bullied by some skinheads at the school and he tries to befriend them by doing crimes for them. I think about confronting the bullies, but the dream ends abruptly.

In the third dream, I am Rupert Murdoch, the billionaire who owns newspapers and television stations. I come out of my house and am being hounded by reporters and television cameras. I cry to them, "Show me some mercy! Please leave me alone! Let me live in peace!" I escape from them and walk along a vacant road lined by trees. I look back and see in the distance a hooded solitary person following me. I don't know whether this person is my bodyguard or my nemesis. I scream, "Show me mercy!" as the hooded figure catches up to me and raises a large knife in the air and directs it toward me.

I awoke and looked at my portable clock and saw that it was 5 o'clock. Brother Todor was sleeping silently in his bed on the other side. I lay on my back and analyzed these three new dreams. The first dream seemed to be about justice. I knew that I was innocent, so I had no fear in opening my locker. I thought that probably my locker represented my inner self and Brother Todor thought that there was evil lurking there. He wanted me to open myself up, express my feelings, and let the evil escape.

The second dream seemed related to Jacob and love. I think that I appeared as Tim Robbins because I recalled that he made a prison film called 'Jacob's Ladder.' I thought that possibly the black woman in the dream was Ana because the sugar icing on the fruits and vegetables was like the icing that she is so fond of on her croissants. I felt a familial type of love growing between me and the black family. When the little boy grew up with the beard, he looked sort of like a negative image of Brother Petár.

The third dream was obviously about mercy. My character, Rupert Murdoch, was unsure about the hooded figure following him until the very end when he recognized him as a murderer. Although I never saw the face of the murderer, I had a very strong feeling that it was Brother Ivan. I had trusted Brother Ivan the most of the three brothers and now suddenly I felt that he was probably the most dangerous. I felt guilty about helping him administer the 'medical care' to the busload of people. But how was I to know and what proof did I now have that there was any foul play involved? Afterall, it was only a dream.

I quietly carried my things outside of the room without waking Brother Todor and went to the bus stop. There was Ana waiting for me with a bright smile on her face. She kissed me and told me how much she had missed me during these past few days. The bus arrived, we loaded our things onto it, and sat in the back seat; I felt like Benjamin Braddock in the final scene of the movie, 'The Graduate'.

It took us two bus rides and a taxi to get to the Sofia train station. We bought our tickets for Bucharest but needed to wait for seven hours until the train would depart. One man in a full length blue jump suit kept following us around and offering to carry our luggage for us. We shook our heads vigorously at him whenever he offered any assistance, but he kept grabbing at our bags. Finally, we recalled from our guidebooks that shaking one's head in Bulgaria meant 'yes' so we started nodding our heads to indicate 'no'. Unfortunately, he thought that we now meant 'yes,' so he became more excited and grabbed for our bags some more. Finally, we relented and let him carry our very heavy bags up the stairs to the café and rewarded him with a few coins. He looked at his hand and then begged us for more. We shook our heads, which brought a big smile upon his face. Then we turned away and left him with only the original 30 leva in his soiled hand. We spent our remaining leva on pizzas and coffee at the café and purchased some fruit, biscuits, and juice for the train ride.

With still a few hours to burn, we walked with our luggage to a park area outside of the train station. Numerous gypsies were gathered there, but they were not the romanticized kind that you would find in Hollywood movies. Instead of playing passionate music and performing feats of magic, they screamed obnoxiously at each other, obviously under the influence of drugs and alcohol, and kept walking past our bags waiting for a momentary lapse of our alertness. Ana was very disappointed with our first encounter with gypsies and menacing dark clouds appeared in the sky, so we walked back inside.

I needed to take a pee so I went to the men's room but as I exited, I noticed a sign that said that I needed to pay thirty leva. The woman at the desk screamed at me, but I acted as if I did not understand and kept walking. A man grabbed my shoulder and said that I needed to pay. I told him that I did not have any more leva. He told me that I must pay in Euros then. I had only a twenty Euro bill, but I was not going to waste it on a piss so I refused and kept on walking. When I got to Ana, I told her about the encounter and suggested that we get on the train before the toilet police came after us.

As we were looking at the departure sign to see where to go, the man in the blue jump suit came up to us and told us that he would show us where our train was. The man had very ugly brown and yellow rotted teeth and bloodshot shifty eyes but Ana said, "I trust this man. Let's go with him," and so we did. He offered to carry our luggage for us, but we refused as we followed him down a long flight of stairs and then immediately up another long flight of stairs. When we got to the top we saw that we were just outside the door from where we had first met him. We could have been in the exact same spot by simply opening the door and walking outside, but the man took us on this wild goose chase in order to secure a tip. Ana became very upset with him and indicated with grand gestures the lunacy that we had just been through. We easily found our train by ourselves and settled into our cabin.

Ana became visibly upset because there were three beds in our cabin. She said, "I just know that the Asian guy that was at the ticket counter is going to join us."

I tried to reassure her that it wouldn't happen. "If we were two guys possibly it might happen," I said, "but since we're a mixed couple, they won't throw another person in here with us. The train won't be very crowded."

"You're wrong," she shot back, "I can feel it. What I say is what is going to happen." We watched the Asian guy climb onto our car. Ana looked at me and raised her chin indicating that she had been right. Her gesture indicated pride, but her eyes showed disappointment and distress. The Asian guy, a lanky, effeminate lad with a pony-tail extending from the top of his head, peaked into our cabin, looked at the number on our bunks, then turned around and headed further down the car. I raised my chin in an exaggerated pose, then closed the cabin door as the train started to pull out.

The train picked up speed as Ana lay down with me and I watched the rocky cliffs flash by. Faces appeared on the cliffs before me. First there was Hermina, then Izmael, then Freddie, then George, then Eddie, then Constanza. Suddenly, Ana's face lifted up and replaced the stone image of Constanza. I jumped back because I thought at first that Constanza had magically turned into Ana.

I regained my composure and asked, "What is today's date?" although I already knew the answer.

"The 14th, I think," she answered with a mischievous grin.

"Happy Anniversary, honey," I said as we kissed to celebrate the four months since we had first met. The number 14 was always a special number for me and on this date in April, we both instinctively knew that something very special had just happened.

We fell asleep in each other's arms and I dreamed that we were each riding horses. Our eldest daughter sat behind me and our second daughter sat in front of me. Ana rode her horse with a baby boy harnessed alongside her breast as we slowly galloped into the sunset.

Upon our arrival into Bucharest we immediately caught another train, which took us into the heart of Transylvania; the popular medieval town, Brasov. A pasty-skinned thin man of about 30 with spooky, deeply-set bloodshot eyes and golden painted hair that matched his numerous golden teeth met us as we got off of the train in the early evening.

He introduced himself as Vladam and requested that we rent an apartment from him. I tried to ignore him because he seemed awfully sleazy and untrustworthy to me, but when he mentioned that the apartment had a wonderful kitchen, Ana's ears shot up and she insisted that we at least have a look at it. I asked him if it was in the central old part of town and he promised me that it was, so we took a cab with him.

The cab stopped beside an ugly Communist-era apartment house in a traffic-congested industrial area of town. "This is not the central old part of town," I said.

"Oh, it's very close," said Vladam.

"You said that it was <u>in</u> the central part. I'm not even going to look at this. Cab driver, please take us to the Hotel Postăvarul."

"No," Vladam persisted, "we have other apartments in the center. I just need to call my cousin."

"No," I answered doggedly. "We're tired and we're going to get a hotel. Driver, the Hotel Postavarul." Vladam tried to open the door, but I held it shut and the cab drove away.

I thought that Ana would be happy with my decision not to look at the apartment, but she sat there looking very upset. "You didn't want to look at that pit, did you?" I asked. Usually you like to stay in the old parts of town, which have ambiance."

"I wanted a place with a kitchen. We should have looked at it," she answered with a childish pout.

"'He lied to us about its location. He looked to me like a sleazy, rip-off artist."

"Now, this place looks nice," I remarked as we pulled up alongside the Hotel Postavarul. The hotel was dripping with ambiance. It was a beautiful old building, which stood alongside a tree-lined pedestrian walkway, where musicians performed throughout the day and night.

There was a double room available at a very cheap price, 42,000 lei per night (about $18). The hotel had everything we wanted, except a kitchen. It had atmosphere, an elevator so that we didn't have to carry our heavy luggage, a large double bed, a private bathroom, and even free breakfast, but Ana was still unhappy.

We went to a nearby restaurant and ordered some pasta and pizza. I wanted some red wine to wash down the pasta so I ordered a bottle because they didn't serve it in individual glasses and the bottles were very inexpensive. I was hoping that Ana would help me drink some so that she would loosen up, but she refused. I thought that I'd drink only half of the bottle but each time that I poured some into my glass, Ana started to complain, which motivated me to drink more. By the end of the meal, I was feeling pretty tipsy and Ana was fuming with rage.

As we walked along the central square, Pinta Sfatului, we began to have another of our 'discussions'. Ana complained to me that I didn't show her proper respect.

"I'm not feeling well," she groused, "but instead of showing me tenderness, you get drunk and laugh at my pain."

"I wasn't laughing at your pain," I countered, "I laughed because I was feeling good and I was happy to be finished with a long journey. I'm in a good mood. I'm sorry that you're not. Ever since we arrived into town, you've been intent on bitchin'. First about no kitchen, then about the walk to the restaurant, then about the pasta, then lastly but more repeatedly about the wine. I'm in a new town in a new country and I feel good. It's too bad that you don't, but baby don't bring me down 'cause I don't wanna go there. The more you bitch, the more you make me wanna drink!"

Ana complained, "I don't understand why men feel that they need to drink alcohol in order to feel good. Why is it that you always drink?"

"I don't always drink, honey, love-of-my-life, sweet angel," I replied sarcastically and was about ready to blow up into another tirade, when a gypsy boy interrupted and began to whine at us to give him money. The boy persisted even though we answered, "No" and shook our heads expressively many times over. Finally I said, "F*!k off," and he understood me immediately. He stopped and pointed his middle finger at me. Ana and I both laughed that he didn't seem to understand the Romanian word for 'no', but he immediately understood the expression that knows no boundaries.

The tension between us dissipated and we walked back to the hotel with our arms around each other. Ana said, "That's what we need when we get into one of our discussions. We just need someone else to direct our anger at, and then everything between us becomes okay."

"Well, fortunately, it looks as if there are plenty of gypsy beggars here in Romania," I added, "so our stay here should be one of incessant bliss," and we kissed in front of the hotel as the Andean quartet blew their flautas and strummed their guitars beneath the softly lit dusky sky. Once again everything was alright with the world.

We went to bed and fell asleep immediately from sheer exhaustion. I dreamed that I had become seriously ill with a cold. I lay in bed in my dingy apartment and wheezed and coughed over my sweat-stained sheets. My mouth was very dry and I decided to get up the energy to stagger to my kitchen to try and make myself a cup of peppermint tea. I walked across the kitchen floor splattered with rotting fruit and opened the cupboard above the dish-filled sink and discovered that I was out of tea. I grabbed a dirty glass from the sink and tried to fill it with water from the faucet but discovered that there wasn't any.

I gathered my strength and decided to climb up the steep and winding stairs, which led up to Ana's flat on the top floor. I stumbled many times as I ascended and continually sat down on the icy cold stairs while struggling for breath. Finally I reached her flat and banged on her door with the little strength that I had left, but there was no answer. I turned the doorknob and pushed on the heavy iron door. There she appeared at her kitchen table sipping on a steaming cup of peppermint tea and reading a newspaper. I asked, "May I have a cup of peppermint tea, please. I'm very sick."

She replied without looking up from her paper, "Sure go ahead. Help yourself."

I looked through all of the cupboards in the kitchen but couldn't find any mint tea. I repeatedly asked her for assistance but was ignored. I collapsed to the floor and screamed hysterically, "I need mint tea now!"

She calmly looked up and opened the small cardboard box that was on the table and answered with a smile, "Oh, I guess I'm all out. Sorry." She then gulped down the remaining tea from her cup and threw the tea bag out of the window.

I rushed to the window and screamed, "Stop this insanity!"

Suddenly, I woke up and found myself standing on my bed and looking out of the window. In the street below, the Andean musicians were looking up at me with their middle fingers extended. They shouted up to me in unison, "F*!k off!"

I reacted by screaming back at them in rage, "You f*!kin' wankers play that same damn Condor song over and over again. Don't you know any other songs? And you're everywhere. Every damn city I go to, you're there. Why don't you go back to the Andes where you belong?"

"Go f*!k yourself," one of them replied and the crowd applauded.

I slammed the window shut and looked down at Ana, who was sitting on the bed with an incensed look on her face. "What the hell is wrong with you?" she said in a very snooty way, "You used to love music. You listened to your CDs all of the time, you went out to see bands, you played guitar, and wrote songs. Now you don't do any of those things. Now you scream like a blathering fool at those poor musicians. What has happened to you?"

I replied as my vision became blurred and I collapsed on the bed, "The music just ain't... no... good...with...out...you....babyyy." I think that I then passed out, because the next thing I remember, I was lying in bed and the sun was shining brightly through the windows.

Ana had left me a note that said, "I went out. I'll be back tonight. I've left you some water." I anxiously grabbed for the 1.5 liter bottle because I was feeling very dehydrated but spilled it over the floor and watched it soak into the carpeting. Although I could have saved some of it from spilling out of the bottle, I lay there paralyzed with my mouth hanging open as the moistened circle of carpeting grew larger and larger. I could hear that same damn song being played by the Andean musicians, but this time it did not annoy me. This time I found the music soothing as I rolled over on my stomach and fell back asleep. Then I had this dream...I think I was lying on my back in a darkly-lit room, which looked like the hotel room, although it felt like an operating room. Vladam and Ana were standing beside my body, which appeared to be without life. My spirit appeared to be hovering above the three of us and watching the events that took place. Ana asked, "Is he dead yet?"

Vladam answered, "Yes, without a doubt."

"When will he live again?" she asked.

"When the clock strikes twelve," he answered.

"Are you sure? I still need him," she said.

"Do not worry," he answered, "you will have him." Their faces glowed in the darkness and then everything turned black. The next thing I remember was hearing the clangs from the bell of the nearby Black Church. I silently counted as I lay there perfectly still with my eyes closed. One, two, three, four, five...On the twelfth clang, my eyes opened wide and my back sprang up from the mattress.

Then I awoke. The sun was shining through the windows again and Ana was standing beside the bed, getting dressed. I asked, "Where are you going?"

She answered, "I'm going to visit the castles in Bran and Rasnov. You stay here and rest, honey."

I replied, "I want to go too," and rose from the bed. Although I had a terrible headache, I felt much stronger and thought that I would be okay for a short excursion.

"No, you stay here, honey," said Ana, "You need your rest."

"No, I'm going," I remonstrated as I put on my pants and acted as if I was perfectly well.

"Okay, but take it easy. You were very ill."

"I know, I'll be careful."

As we walked along Strada 13 Decembrie to Fara Brasov, the main bus station, I feigned as if I were strong and healthy by walking at a rapid pace and urging Ana to catch up with me. At times I started to feel dizzy and thought that I was going to pass out, but I hid my lack of equilibrium, and turned forward and trudged on. The buildings beside the sidewalk seemed to be swaying forward and then back. At first I thought that it was an acid flashback; then suddenly I was back in San Francisco on October 12, 1989 at 5:04 pm. At that time I was looking for a television to watch my San Francisco Giants play their Bay Area rivals, the Oakland A's, in game 3 of the World Series of baseball. I had just finished work for the day and I raced on my motorcycle to Bloom's bar to catch the pivotal game on television. The Giants were down two games to nothing, but now the Series would be played for the next three games at Candlestick Park in San Francisco. I was confident that the Giants would sweep the A's at home and eventually win the whole shebang.

I entered Bloom's eager with anticipation for the game's first pitch but quickly became disappointed to see that all of the barstools and chairs were filled. I could not envision myself standing throughout the entire game after a full day of work, so I exited and got back on my bike and waited for Craig, my buddy from work, to appear on his motorcycle so that we could find a bar with available seating.

I started the engine of my 1978 Honda CB750K, when suddenly I felt a strange tugging near the back wheel. I thought, "Now, what's wrong with this piece of shit?" Almost every day I had to deal with some type of mechanical problem, but I was not yet ready to remedy the problem by doing what my mechanic buddy Morty would advise, "Drive it straight into the bay."

On this day, though, the problem was not my bike. As I turned to look at the back wheel, I heard an explosion and my bike abruptly fell on its left and almost crushed my leg. I gathered my strength and pulled the bike upright and looked across the street at the buildings that were swaying to and fro. And that's at the moment that I found myself on this sunny April afternoon in Brasov, Romania. I looked back at Ana and saw my buddy, Craig, approaching on his motorcycle. I said, "We have to hurry and get a seat," as I turned forward and picked up the pace. I was back in Bloom's Bar and now there was plenty of available seating because the patrons had run onto the street after the explosion, but the electricity was out and the T.V.

was no longer working. "There's no energy!" I yelled back to Ana, "We've got to find some!" and I started to run. Craig and I rode throughout San Francisco and noticed that the traffic lights were out everywhere. We then realized that this was not your average San Francisco earthquake but one with very serious implications. I yelled, "I'm worried about my home. I better get there." He replied, "Me too," and we set off in opposite directions driving past swarms of people, who seemed to be in a state of shock. Some seemed to be walking with a purpose such as acquiring supplies of bottled water, flashlights, batteries, and candles – but most of the people seemed to be wandering aimlessly as if they were creatures from the film, 'The Day of the Dead.' "Oh my God, the stairs!" I exclaimed as I rode up to my flat in the Lower Haight and saw a two foot gap between the front stairs and the building with a fresh jagged crack across its front exterior. I jumped across the space and entered the building.

Inside my flat I saw that lamps, shelves, and my television were thrown to the floor and damaged from the eruption, but I did not become upset until I entered my study. I ran to my desk and was horrified at the sight of the worst possible damage that could have happened in my unoccupied flat.

On the top of my desk was my almost finished screenplay that I had written in long-hand and labored with for the past 2 ½ years. I thought of myself as an artist back then and did not want to make any copies of it until it was completely finished. I would have finished it the week earlier but I, like most Bay Areans, got caught up with baseball fever and let it sit unattended. Also unattended were the bottles of red wine that were stored on the shelves above my desk. Red wine seemed to complement my writing, so I bought bottles by the caseload and sampled a different bottle each day.

Well, you know what happened to those bottles during the 7.0 on the Richter scale earthquake. Of course, they fell upon my desk and shattered and the cabernet sauvignon, merlot, pinot noir, and 2 ½ years of perspiration amalgamated into what some in the contemporary art world would call 'a great work of abstract art'; for me, though, it was now a useless piece of bloody shit. The pages were stuck together and when I tried to separate them, they tore away like cheap, generic one-ply toilet paper over an anus festooned with blood-capped hemorrhoidal hillocks. I screamed out with tears streaming down my cheeks, "It's completely ruined!"

A voice said, "What's ruined, David? What's wrong, David?"

My eyes turned to the face from where the voice emanated and they slowly came into focus 'til I could see that the voice belonged to Ana, who was sitting next to me on the bus. "Nothing. Nothing's wrong," I answered.

"You're not well, David," she said, "You've been acting very strangely. That was very weird when we boarded the bus."

"What happened?" I asked because I had no memory of the incident.

"You screamed, 'Oh my God, the stairs!' and then jumped past the driver without paying. He was very upset, but I calmed him down by giving some extra money. But look at him now looking at us through the mirror. He's going to throw us off unless you behave yourself."

"Okay, I'll be a good boy now, Mommy," I said in a silly voice with my back upright and my hands folded.

The bus continued on without incident until a gypsy family boarded the bus carrying their blankets, rugs, and baskets containing who-knows-what. The four of them took over nearly all of the back third of the bus as the mother and two children lay on their seats and fell asleep while the father stood in the aisle with one foot upon a seat while he surveyed the belongings of the other passengers.

I was watching the man's dark beady eyes darting across the bus in all directions, when I suddenly noticed that Vladam was sitting in the seat directly behind him. I said to Ana, "Vladam's on the bus with us."

"Who's Vladam?" she asked.

"The creep who tried to rent that crummy apartment to us," I answered.

"Where is he?" she asked eagerly.

"Behind the standing gypsy," I replied.

She looked back and then quickly turned to me and said, "He's not here."

"He's sitting right behind the standing gypsy," I repeated as I looked back and he flashed his gold-toothed smile at me.

She looked back again, then turned to me and said, "You need to rest. You're seeing things. Nobody's behind the gypsies."

I looked back again and this time Vladam was waving to me with an even brighter smile, but I replied, "Yeah, you're right, Ana. I guess I just need more rest," and I put my head upon her shoulder and fell asleep.

A few minutes later, Ana awoke me, "Honey, we're here. It's Dracula's Castle!" I opened my eyes and we got off of the bus and looked at the famous castle perched on top of a hill with its white majestic towers beneath red cone-shaped rooftops. We walked past numerous souvenir shops where barkers tried to convince me that I could not leave Bran without first purchasing a Dracula toothbrush set in its miniature coffin. Somehow I found the strength to pass on such a once-in-a-lifetime opportunity and made my way up the hill to the castle with Ana at my side.

Inside the castle Ana and I wandered throughout its 57 rooms and twisting narrow stairwells. At one point I became very tired and sat down on a bench to rest and let Ana walk on ahead. A few minutes later, I stood up and tried to catch up with her but to no avail. I entered the Gothic Room, which held statues of hooded, devious-looking figures that frightened me in my weakened state and sent me out of there in a panic. I then stumbled into the Council Room, where I leaned against a wall, which opened up into a hidden stairwell. I climbed up the dark steep stairs until I came to another wall at the top and pushed on it and found myself in what looked like a study. I heard sounds coming from the neighboring room and softly opened the heavy wooden door and peeked inside and saw Ana. She said, "Isn't this bed magnificent? It belonged to King Ferdinand. Look at the woodwork on the bedposts. It shows Christ's birth."

"Yeah, it's magnificent," I replied.

A woman entered the room and invited us to see a room that was not on the usual tourist route. She said, "This room I will show you because I can tell that you are not like the others. This room is very special." Ana and I smiled at each other for our good fortune and followed the woman up the dark and narrow winding stairs. The woman looked back at us with an expectant smile before unlocking the heavy wooden door and then showed us the sweaters and doilies that she was selling for "next to nothing." Also in the room were Dracula toothbrushes set in their miniature coffins.

We got onto another bus which took us to Rasnov, where the ruins of the 13th century castle stood on top of a gigantic hill just beyond the village. Ana and I were both hungry and tired so we decided to have lunch at a village restaurant before ascending up to the castle. I ordered a typical Romanian dish called cabanos prajit (fried sausages) and mămăligă (corn polenta) while Ana went a safer route by ordering chicken breast and fried potatoes. The sausages had an unusual taste unlike any meat that I had ever sampled before and I consumed them with gusto although I had trouble with the neon yellow polenta, which tasted like regurgitated tennis balls.

The cabanos prajit gave me strength as I led Ana up the rocky path that led to the castle. Several times we passed schoolchildren, who were sneaking in a mid-afternoon smoke away from their parents and teachers. Ana and I related to each other that we were glad that we had given up cigarettes otherwise the hike would have been much more strenuous.

Finally, we reached the top and paid the fee to enter into the castle's ruins. However, we were both too exhausted to enter the museum or even walk around the surroundings, so we found a bench and sat down. We sat in silence for close to an hour.

Looking at the collapsed walls of the fortress, I felt as if I could see the spirits of the people, who had lived there eight centuries before. I envisioned women walking past me with large containers of water upon their heads and men carrying in the hunt from the day. I watched bodies fall from the top of the walls as the Turks with their large armies overtook the fortress.

I stared at a large crucifix that stood on the top of a hill in the courtyard. Christ was hanging from the cross with blood dripping down his face from his crown of thorns and his hands and feet bleeding from the large spikes that were driven into them. All of a sudden, Christ raised his head and opened his mouth, which revealed his golden teeth. His hair turned to gold and his hands began waving at me although the iron spikes still protruded from the palms. Christ had turned into Vladam and I let out a shriek.

Ana held me in her arms and said, "Don't worry, David, it's all over. We're home now." I looked into her soothing blue eyes with the small luminescent moons surrounding her pupils and felt at peace again, until I realized that she was not next to me on the bench at the fortress, but was sitting beside me on the bus with the same angry bus driver.

"How did we get back on this same bus?" I asked confused. "I thought we were in Rasnov."

"We never got off the bus," Ana answered. "I thought that it would be better if you slept. We're back in Brasov now."

"Did we climb up to the Rasnov Castle?"

"No, honey."

"How about Bran? We were in Bran Castle. Remember King Ferdinand's bed?"

"No, honey, No Bran, either. We never got off the bus." She helped me off of the bus past the sneering driver at Gara Brasov and then flagged down a cab, which took us back to the Hotel Postavarul, where I stayed in bed for I don't know how long because the thick curtains were always closed and the room was completely dark.

The clock struck twelve from the nearby Black Church. I awoke and heard the window being pelted with what sounded like large lumps of hail. I stood upon the bed and opened the curtains as the sky thundered and I beheld a night time sky unlike any that I had ever seen before. The sky was filled with stars although they appeared to be flickering on and off in random succession. Lightning flashed across the sky and revealed flocks of black birds swirling in the air.

Ana was standing outside in front of the church tower. She stared at the mural at the top of the tower that showed the writer from young to old accompanied by the ox, lion, man and eagle just like we had observed at the Sila Monastery. The characters on the mural began to swirl like the birds in the sky and appeared to become animated and alive. The writer smiled and frowned, the lion roared, and the ox wailed. The swirling continued as the different ages of the writer were matched and then changed with the four creatures. All at once the lightning and thunder abated, the birds vanished, and the stars glowed unceasingly. The mural was now stationary although the ages of the writer were now matched with the creatures in the opposite way of what they had been before. The young writer was now with the eagle, the middle-aged writer was with the man, the older writer was with the lion, and the eldest writer was with the ox. Ana stood below and smiled with an expression that showed that she was very proud of her handiwork. A new world order had been established.

The next day we decided to set off for Budapest, Hungary. On the way we decided to stay for one night in Sighisoara, the birthplace of Vlad Tepes. We got off the train and found a room at the nearby Hotel Chic. The room seemed a great bargain. It had a double bed, hardwood floors, and a large television, which showed MTV that made Ana very happy. It cost us only 30,000 lei (about 13 US dollars) per night and we thought that perhaps we might take profit with the good deal and extend our stay.

We exited the hotel to go for a walk and were met by a large group of gypsies, who implored us for money. A child of about twelve years wearing a red and white striped stocking cap like the character from 'Where's Waldo?' tried to communicate with us in various languages, "Sprechen Sie Deutsch? Parlez-vous Frances? Do you speak English?" but we continued to ignore her and walked ahead.

We hiked up to the cobblestone streets past the 16th century Burghen houses and entered the old part of town at Piata Muzeului. Above us stood an immense 14th century clock tower. We thought that we'd wait for the clock to strike six, so that we could witness the little blue-skirted characters on the tower do their dance or whatever, but the band of gypsies started to approach us, so we snuck into a restaurant that supposedly was once the home to Vlad Tepes, the Prince of Darkness.

Although the food was reasonably priced and rather tasty, Ana became uncomfortable with the formal atmosphere of the restaurant and got upset with me when I grabbed a chicken wing from my soup and started to eat it straight from my hands. I had fumbled with it earlier using a fork and knife but was unable to clean the bone to my satisfaction, so without shame I picked it up and sucked up the remaining meat. I tried to do a comical impression of Count Dracula sucking up blood but Ana was not amused and said, "I hate to come to fancy restaurants like this. I become very uncomfortable. I'm sorry but I must leave." She grabbed her coat and ran down the stairs. I tried to quickly pay the bill, but the waiter was very deliberate in his formality, so by the time that I got outside, Ana was nowhere in sight.

The gypsies crowded around me and I suspected that they were trying to pickpocket me, so I yelled, "Keep your grubby hands away from me!" and they all backed away. The girl in the 'Where's Waldo?' hat said something about me being an American and they started to swarm around me again. I swung my arms around to provide space for myself and then ran down the hill with the gypsies in hot pursuit. The children stayed on top and pelted me with stones. One stone hit me on top of my head and blood gushed out over my face and onto my clothing. Although I was feeling very weak and dizzy, I made it back to the hotel and went to the bathroom to bandage my wound.

The cut was not serious although it was in the exact same place as my last travel injury that I had received in India 1 ½ years before. I was in Jaisalmer at that time staying in the fortress of the Rajasthan region near the Pakistani border. It was my first day there and I was very excited about staying inside a fortress, so I grabbed my video camera and walked along the narrow paths. Along the way an elderly Indian man dressed in white asked me to sit down with him. I introduced myself as hanumanji and he let out a big laugh and told his friends my name and then introduced himself as Krishna. They all started laughing and I began to feel uncomfortable, so I excused myself and said that we would talk again and set off on my way.

I turned a corner and the path seemed to branch off into two different directions. The branch on the right led to a tunnel but there was a large cow standing in front of its entrance, so I took the branch to the left. However, that branch led to what appeared to be the front yard of someone's private property so I turned back around and returned to the tunnel. The cow was no longer there, so I decided to go through the tunnel.

Inside the tunnel, it was dark and rather smelly so I walked quickly through it and then found myself on the outer edge of the fortress. There was a small area to walk there but I saw that the ground was strewn with feces. At first I thought that this must be the area where the cows go to shit, but upon closer observation I noticed that the dung was of human origin. I decided to get the hell out of there and set back forth through the tunnel.

As I went through the tunnel this time, I noticed that the smell was very strong and also that it was populated with a dense mass of flies. I ran through the tunnel with my head lowered and my hands over my nose and mouth. I thought that I had cleared the tunnel so I raised my head but it hit the sharp outer edge of the tunnel and I fell back onto the dirty ground. I raised myself up and saw a couple of German tourists and some local villagers staring at me with horrified expressions.

I lifted my hat from my head and asked, "Does it look like I am hurt?"

The German man replied, "There is blood everywhere," and suddenly blood began to gush out over my face and body. The villagers shielded their eyes from the horror.

Krishna appeared and took me to his home. He instructed his daughter to bring clean water from the kitchen. Then his wife brought some type of ointment that Krishna applied to my head to stop the bleeding. Throughout all of this, I laughed at the stupidity of my actions and videotaped myself in my grisly state. Krishna washed and bandaged me and said that I would be fine temporarily but I needed to go immediately to the hospital. I exited the fortress to the taxi stand as beggars approached me and then fled away when they saw my blood-drenched clothing.

At the hospital I was given immediate care. The doctor was amused by my story and my Indian name as he stitched my head. Young beautiful Indian nurses in their light blue uniforms surrounded me as the doctor worked. One nurse held a gigantic scissors about three feet long, which she used to cut the tape that fastened the bandages to my head. The doctor remarked, "The nurses are all fascinated by you, hanumanji. They are like moths to your flame." I felt remarkably powerful at that moment and was gladdened when the doctor suggested that I come back to the hospital each day for a new dressing.

This time, however, in Sighisoara, Romania, I would need no stitches. I cleaned the cut with mineral water and attached a band aid from my first aid kit. I had hoped that Ana would be at the hotel to help me, but she had not shown up there. I worried about where she was but figured that it would be best for me to remain in the hotel and wait for her to return since I had the only key and I was beginning to feel very ill again.

Each time that I crossed from our hotel room to the common bathroom at the opposite end of the hall, a door would slightly open from one of the neighboring rooms, although I was never able to see who the person was. I lay in bed, turned on some MTV, and waited for Ana to return as the sky became dark.

She entered the room at half past nine and explained that she had turned the wrong direction and had gotten lost. Knowing her sense of direction, I believed her and requested that she never leave me like that again. She assented and we lay in bed and I told her about my clash with the gypsies. We looked out of the window through the transparent curtain and saw them huddled up on a hill near the train station. They stared at us through the gauze curtain and mimicked our movements even though the lights in our room were turned off. I sat down on the bed and complained about my headache and Ana massaged the temples along the sides of my head and the gypsies did the same thing to themselves. "How can they see what we're doing?" I said perplexed. "The room is dark."

"They are gypsies," replied Ana. "Don't try to apply logic to them."

"I wish that I had thrown them a few thousand lei before. They're starting to really freak me out."

"Just lie down and relax," she said. "I'll get you a hot water towel to help you with your headache."

I lay back onto the bed but as soon as Ana left the room, I jumped up and opened the door slightly and spied on her as she walked to the bathroom. The door from the neighboring room opened again and I caught a brief glimpse of the man behind it. It was Mats, the Swiss guy that we had first met on the train to Nimes and that I later saw in disguise near the Italian border. But that was back in February about three months ago. How did he catch up with us? Or was he always with us?

Ana returned with the hot towel and I was back in bed underneath the covers. She placed the towel upon my forehead and lay beside me as we tried to fall asleep. For Ana, it was easy. She was sleeping within moments of her head touching the pillow. But for me, it was an entirely different experience.

First, the hardwood floors outside of our room would squeak as if there were a dozen people walking. I suspected that it was the gypsies, so I rose from the bed and peeked out of the door, but found no one. I locked the door from the inside and lay back down. The squeaking of the floor commenced again and then doors appeared to be opening and closing very rapidly and very loudly. I knelt on the bed and looked out of the window and saw that the gypsies were kneeling and staring back at me.

I lay back down and rested my head against my pillow and thought of a time many years ago when a similar supernatural appearance occurred in my life. I was fifteen years old and had just completed my freshman year in high school. Three friends and I had decided to take a bicycle trip up to Door County, which is in the northern part of the peninsula or thumb of the state of Wisconsin. We were not experienced bicyclist tourists and we did not have the panniers (bags that sit along the wheels) that the more experienced bicyclists used. We carried everything on our backs in huge, cumbersome canvas sacks. The sacks were filled with heavy metal pots and pans and other things that only a greenhorn would dare bring on such an excursion.

Along the way I noticed some small thing shining on the road and I stopped to investigate. It was a beaded Indian bracelet. I grabbed it and tied it onto my wrist and continued on. The beads of blue, yellow, orange, and red glowed in the afternoon sunshine and I felt very fortunate to have made such a find.

Soon thereafter, we took a break along a lake and rested our bikes against some trees in a picnic area. I entered an outhouse and sat on the toilet when suddenly I heard two voices that appeared to have come from just outside. A boy asked, "You think he's got it?" and a man replied, "Oh yeah, he's got it." I quickly zipped up my blue jean shorts and looked outside the outhouse to see who was talking. No one was there but across the lake I saw a man and small boy watching a fisherman reel in his catch. I assumed that their voices had carried over the lake and dismissed the previous idea that the voices came from a nearby source. However, I turned around and looked up a stony cliff and saw at the top, a silver-haired man wearing dark sunglasses standing beside a sitting silver-haired German shepherd. They both appeared to be staring at me and smiling, and for some reason I felt that the voices that I had heard came from them and not from the man and the boy on the other side of the lake. They weren't talking about the fish; they were talking about the bracelet.

We continued our ride although now I wasn't having fun anymore. All I could think about were the silver-haired man and dog and what they wanted with me. Day turned to night and we pitched our tents and lay down in our sleeping bags. We were all exhausted after the strenuous workout of the day and my three pals immediately fell asleep, but not me. I lay in my bag and started crying for reasons that I did not know. The image of the man and dog stayed transfixed in my mind as if they were right beside me. I knew that something very bad was going to happen to me unless I did something.

I knew that the Indian bracelet was the cause for all of my distress, so I put on my shoes and crawled out of the tent. The moon was full and I could see a huge field of tall grass that stretched out until it was met with a wooded area. I walked into the center of the field, removed the bracelet from my wrist, and spoke to the silver moon. I apologized for taking the bracelet; it did not belong to me, and asked the spirit to forgive me for being so selfish. I said solemnly, "This bracelet and its magic, I return to you," and I threw it up into the air and then turned around and headed back to my tent, never seeing where or if it had landed. At once I felt at peace again and climbed into my sleeping bag and fell asleep and everything was good after that.

As I lay in bed in the Hotel Chic, I thought, "That's what I must do now. I must remove the curse." I wadded together 60,000 lei (about $20) and opened the window and said, "This money belongs to you. Please accept it with my humble apologies." I threw it toward the gypsies and then turned back to my bed and heard them scrambling for it. However, the curse did not disappear, it only got worse.

The squeaking footsteps on the hardwood floors increased as did the opening and closing of the doors. Also, the pipes started to rattle and the noise grew louder and louder. At first the rattling seemed to resound in a rhythmical pattern but as soon as I got used to the pattern, the rhythm would slightly change which made sleep for me impossible. I looked at Ana and envied the way that she could sleep through all of this racket. I was tempted to awaken her because I felt so alone, but I decided against that action. It would only put another person in the opposite corner from me. I would need to ride out this agonizing evening alone.

The next morning the sun glared into my face and I was surprised to see that I had fallen asleep. I had slept probably only a few moments, but I was glad that I had been given some respite. Ana woke up a couple of minutes later and exclaimed, "That's the best sleep that I've had in a long time! I love this bed! Let's stay here longer."

I replied rather grouchily, "We're leaving today. I couldn't sleep. I can't stand this place. It freaks me out." Ana looked at me as if I was nuts, but she could tell from my manner that it would do no good to argue with me. We showered, packed our bags, and walked across the street to the train station.

I was surprised to see that no gypsies were around. Perhaps the wad of lei had worked after all. And Mats, the Swiss spy guy, didn't open his door when we had used the bathroom earlier. He always looked like a late sleeper, I thought.

At the ticket window we found that we could only purchase tickets to the Hungarian border and would have to purchase separate tickets for Budapest when we reached the border. We were shocked by this revelation because we were told the opposite thing the day before. We bought the tickets and hoped that we would not have problems when we got to the border.

We waited for our train to arrive on the 3rd rail, when a girl approached us selling a used Romanian newspaper. She seemed very bright and spoke excellent English as she inquired where we were going and where we were from. Ana replied that she was from Spain and I added that I was Canadian. Sometimes, I found it's easier to lie and say that I'm Canadian because the dollar signs do not flash in people's heads when I reply that way.

The girl said that her name was Daniella, she was twelve years old, and she was an orphan. "My mother abused alcohol and became very violent toward me," she said, "so now I stay with a friend and support myself by selling newspapers."

"How many newspapers do you sell per day?" asked Ana.

"Hardly any," Daniella answered, "But two days ago an American couple gave me 100 Euro for only one newspaper. How many lei is 100 Euro?"

"That's about 3,000,000 lei," I answered.

"My papers cost only 30,000 lei but they didn't want any change from me. Why would they do that?" she asked.

"They were probably touched by your story and wanted to help you," Ana replied.

"Why would they want to do that?" Daniella asked as she feigned innocence.

"Some people are like that," I answered as I smiled at Ana and she reciprocated. We both knew that we were being set up as easy marks by this young con-artist, but we did not cave in.

"I have no family now," Daniella continued, "Sometimes I feel like ending it all and stopping the pain."

Ana advised, "I've learned in my life that people have many different families and sometimes the families that you create through friendships are better than the families that you are born into."

"I like that idea," Daniella smiled at us, "I hope that I can make friends that will be like my family."

"I'm sure you will," Ana assured her and I agreed as I looked the girl over. It was obvious to me that she was lying. Her clothing was too neatly pressed and she seemed to be well educated, although she had said that she stopped going to school after she had turned eight. Her face looked familiar to me and I thought that, perhaps, she was the gypsy who yesterday had worn the red and white striped cap.

"Do you have a sister?" I asked.

"No," she answered, "there's only me."

The train arrived and we boarded it as did Daniella and her friend, who walked up and down the aisles trying to sell their newspapers. Before we reached the border, we asked the conductor if we could extend our tickets into Budapest, but he said that we'd have to go to the ticket office to buy our tickets. "Will the train stay there long enough for us to get back on it?" I asked.

"I doubt it," he replied. "It's a short stop."

"Is there another train that goes onto Budapest later?" I asked.

"No, this is the last train today," he answered. "It's Sunday," and then left.

Ana turned to me and asked, "What can we do?"

I shrugged my shoulders and a young voice shot up behind us, "I can get the tickets for you." The voice belonged to Daniella and Ana and I looked at each other with skepticism.

I said quietly to Ana, "The conductor said that the additional tickets to Budapest would cost us about 1,500,000 lei and that's exactly what we have left. I can try running to the ticket office, but what if the train leaves before I'm able to get back? He said that the ticket office is downstairs. I doubt whether I'll make it back in time. We should probably get off the train with our bags and then you stay with them while I go."

Daniella suggested again, "I'll get the tickets for you. I know right where the ticket office is. I swear I can make it and return in time. I know that you don't trust me, but I will not steal your money. I swear."

The train slowed down as it approached the border town and I suspected that in my weak condition, I would never return in time. Ana realized this as well and said, "We have to trust someone sometime." I nodded and reluctantly handed over the money to Daniella who jumped off the train, as soon as it stopped, and darted down the stairs.

"Do you think we'll ever see her again?" I asked Ana.

She could only shrug her shoulders and reply, "We must have faith."

The Romanian border agents entered our car, inspected our passports, stamped them, and proceeded to the next car. We stood up and looked out of the window for Daniella, but there was still no sight of her. The doors in the rear of our coach opened and down the aisle the new Hungarian conductor approached us followed by two Hungarian border agents. The conductor asked us for our tickets and I tried to explain the situation to them although it was obvious from their facial expressions and body language that they didn't believe me and were ready to physically throw us off. I stood up and said meekly, "We'll leave," and began to grab my backpack when suddenly the front door of the coach opened and Daniella appeared holding our tickets.

She was out of breath but still managed to smile as she said, "Here are your tickets and your change."

"Keep the change, and thanks," I said although she was already out of the car. She seemed to have been frightened by the border agents. The conductor inspected our tickets very carefully as did the border agents, our passports, but we passed muster and they continued on to the next coach.

The train started to pull out and Ana and I looked out of the window and saw Daniella waiting for the next train to take her back to Sighisoara. We thanked her and wished her a happy life and I took off my belt and threw it out of the window at her. She picked it up with a confused look on her face and I shouted over the sound of the train, "Look inside!" She looked at us again incomprehensively. "Look inside the belt!" I shouted as the train accelerated and the figure of Daniella disappeared from our sight. "I hope she found it," I said to Ana as we sat back down.

"Found what?" Ana asked.

"The $100 bill in my money belt. I kept it there for an emergency."

"This was an emergency," Ana said with a reassuring smile.

"Not just an emergency, this was a miracle," I replied as we smiled and reflected upon the events that had taken place.

We both had acted in a most unusual fashion. We had entrusted 1,500,000 lei to a stranger that we both did not trust. We could have easily gotten off the train, found a hotel for the night, and entered Budapest the next day. That would have been the logical thing to do. But we chose illogic over logic. We chose faith. We chose to have faith when all logic told us that we were acting like foolish dupes. Ana and I looked at each other with wide foolish grins and saw that the cynicism had disappeared from our eyes like the little girl that had been standing at the train station.

I was feeling very ill again when our train arrived into Budapest, so Ana suggested that I wait at a café with our luggage while she looked for a place for us to stay. I suggested that she look at my guidebook for recommended hotels, but she only smiled and said, "Don't worry, honey, I'll find a nice place for us," and left without even glancing at the book. Ana never really liked my guidebook and showed displeasure whenever I seemed to be relying on it too much. She preferred the method of wandering around and letting fate intervene by stumbling upon a hotel or a person offering a place to stay. I felt her method to be impractical, but I was too weak to argue and said that I would be happy with anything that she found.

She returned an hour later and said, "I have found a wonderful place for us. It's an apartment that we'll share with this beautiful grandmother. We have our own spacious bedroom and we can use the kitchen! I checked out some hotels, including those in your silly book, but they were much too expensive. This apartment is really cheap. You'll love it."

"How cheap, baby?" I asked.

"Only ten dollars a night."

"I love it," I replied, "Let's go," and we went.

The apartment was beautiful. It had an elevator, which I really appreciated in my weakened state, and our bedroom was huge with a king-size bed, a couch, two reclining chairs, a dining table, a wash basin, and a large T.V. with cable and a remote control. I felt as if Peter had unlocked the Pearly Gates.

The grandmother welcomed us into her home with a charming smile. She showed us the common areas and supplied us with soap, fresh towels, and bottled water. She even offered to make coffee for us, but we politely declined and made ourselves comfortable in our bedroom. I went straight to the bed and collapsed upon it while Ana unpacked her things. She said, "I noticed a library nearby here. I'd like to check it out. You'll be okay here, won't you? You probably will want to sleep."

"Yeah, baby, you go ahead and have fun. I'll be f...," I replied and fell asleep.

I dreamed that Ana and I were back at that Dracula restaurant in Sighisoara. The waiter asked me if I'd like any more blood. I replied, "Yes, that would be nice," and looked up at him and recognized that he was Vladam in a Count Dracula outfit. He bent down to Ana and bit into her neck. She sat impassive as I fumbled through my backpack looking for that bottle of water from the Sila Monastery. Finally I found it and poured the contents onto Vladam, who melted like the Wicked Witch from 'The Wizard of Oz'.

I awoke and wondered what had happened to the bottled water that I was given from Brother Petár at the Sila Monastery. I searched through my bags but it was not there. I remembered packing it before I had left the monastery. When did I see it next? 'Let's see, we went to Sofia, then Bucharest, then Brasov. We unpacked in Brasov. I don't remember seeing the bottle, but I drank a lot of water there because that's where I first became ill. I don't remember much in Brasov except for all of those weird dreams. Well, to hell with it, I don't need that bottle. It looks as if the sweet grandmother has supplied us with plenty of water.' I grabbed one of the bottles and took a long swig and then lay back down in bed and slept some more.

I pretty much stayed in bed and slept for an entire week. Every once in a while I saw Ana and talked with her a bit, but it was very seldom. She told me that she was spending her time at the library doing research on the Kabbalah. She had missed doing that when we were in Bulgaria and Romania because there weren't books available in our languages. "In Budapest," she said, "There are many interesting books on the subject. The book that I read this afternoon concentrated on the Sephirot; justice and mercy. The author stated that mercy was a sign of weakness, an illusion, and that the state of true reality, or truth as he calls it, can only be attained when justice is served. What do you think, honey?"

"That sounds about right to me," I answered although I only had a vague idea what she was talking about. I rolled over and fell back asleep.

Although Ana was rarely around, I was well taken care of by the grandmother. She fixed me meals, changed my sweaty sheets, and even did my laundry on a regular basis so that I never smelled too ripe. One day she drew a bath for me and stood beside the tub waiting for me to unclothe and get in. I think that she was planning to scrub me. I thanked her for her help but told her that there were some things that I would prefer to do on my own.

'Grandma' was almost always around and she watched me like a hawk. Sometimes I would feel a little stronger and wish to have a change of scenery, but I would need to wait until I heard her leave, because if I would try to leave while she was around, she would always grab me by the arm and guide me back to the bed.

It was always very difficult to say 'no' to Grandma. It was also very difficult to enter or leave the apartment due to the large number of locks that Grandma had at the entrance. After punching in the secret code in order to get access to the elevator, Grandma had two locks on the gate that stood before the door that had two other locks. Each time that you wanted to go out, you needed to unlock the four locks and then re-lock them. It got rather exhausting. Was she just a frightened old lady or was there another reason for such a high level of security?

When I did get past Grandma and the conundrum at the doorway, I would usually go just downstairs to Stex Ház, a bar and restaurant that had a killer vegetarian lasagna. It was nice being in a country again where there were other vegetables besides tomatoes and cucumbers. Sometimes when I was feeling unusually strong, I would hike all the way to Andrassy Street and indulge myself at Café Eckermann with a Café Au Lait that was served in a large bowl and decorated with powdered chocolate on top in the design of a flower, or a star, or a peace sign.

Every once in a while I would watch the news on the television although it was usually the same old story; Suicidal Palestinian terrorist kills Jews, Jews retaliate and kill Palestinians. One day, however, the banner at the bottom of the television screen reported that there was a mysterious virus on Crete that had killed three people and infected at least 29 others in less than a week. Strange, I thought, how newsworthy events seemed to keep occurring wherever we traveled. I tried to find more information about it because I thought that perhaps my illness may have been related to it, but I couldn't find any further information and Ana and Grandma scoffed at my suspicions.

Most of the time, though, was spent in bed sleeping or reading the Irving Stone biography on Vincent Van Gogh entitled, 'Lust for Life'. Vincent never really had much luck in his relationships with women and it was the same story with me until I had met Ana. Sure, we had our rough moments, but our love was strong enough to withstand all the difficulties that would come our way.

The part in the book that most interested me was during Vincent's later years when he moved down to Arles in southern France. (I had hoped to visit there when we were in the area but Ana seemed to be in a hurry to get into Italy, so I scrapped that plan.) Arles was known as the place where Van Gogh painted some of his most famous paintings and also went mad and cut part of his ear with a razor. The fierce, blinding sun in Arles led to this condition in Van Gogh and I began to feel as if I was going mad as well because the heat in Budapest at this time was insufferable. Grandma tried to make me comfortable with lots of bottled water and an electric fan, but the sun shone through the light curtains and fried my brain like it had done to Vincent so many years before.

In Stone's story, Vincent meets a woman named Maya who is the essence of perfection and proclaims her everlasting love to him. However, she is only a figment of Vincent's sun-drenched hallucinating imagination. I set down the book and wondered whether Ana, like Maya, was only an illusion. Impossible. Her clothes were hanging in the closet and there were photographs of us at the various places that we had visited. But it was strange, I thought, how whenever we met anyone, they always asked me and not Ana where I was from. It was as if they were only talking to me. Were they? Was I actually traveling alone? Impossible.

My doubts about the reality of Ana were further reinforced when I convinced her to go with me to a movie theater that evening and see 'A Beautiful Mind'. The movie was about a math genius who suffered from schizophrenia and had hallucinations. He was convinced that he had this wild roommate, who liked to party a lot when in reality he lived alone. Was this what was happening to me? I held Ana's hand as I always did at movies and kissed it. It felt real. Unlike the roommate and his imaginary niece in the movie, Ana's appearance changed from day to day; sometimes pimples appeared on her face or her hairstyle would change, so she must be real. Or was my schizophrenia in a more advanced state than that of the character in the movie?

The second week of our stay in Budapest I was feeling healthier and Ana was finding more time to spend with me, so we did some sightseeing. We crossed the Danube River along the majestic Szabadsag Bridge and entered the castle district of Buda, where we visited the Hungarian National Gallery of Art. The painting that moved me the most showed a woman who had just murdered a man, who lay dead in the background. In the foreground the woman held a bloodied knife and her dark eyes looked truly mad. It reminded me of that dream that I had back in Rethymno when Ana was stabbed by that man in grey. His eyes, though, were not mad like the woman's in the painting; they were steely, cold, and blue like mine. But he wasn't me, I tried to convince myself.

Ana's favorite painting was an abstract showing the bloodied figure of Jesus crucified on the cross. She remarked with Pontius Pilate arrogance, "Jesus of Nazareth, King of the Jews."

"What?" I asked, but she only turned to me with a devious smile and then continued on to the next painting.

Later we visited the nearby underground labyrinth, but it was rather hokey with the sound effects and stage props that, I guess, were intended to elicit terror and mystery. The dampness of the caves was no good for my recovery from illness, so we quickly found the exit and got back into the sunshine.

On another day we visited the Great Synagogue on Dohány Street and were surprised when we saw that the little bronze plaque, that was posted in the pew where we sat, displayed the name, Endre Geiger. Perhaps, I was Jewish after all. Later we searched for information about him on the internet and found that he was the son of Samuel Geiger, who had died in the Holocaust as an elderly man. The Holocaust list included a rather substantial number of Geigers.

I never knew anything about my family history. Was this coincidence of sitting by the nameplate going to answer some questions for me about my ancestry? I had always felt that I had some Jewish blood even if my blue eyes and blonde hair indicated otherwise. I once told my friends that I thought that I was Jewish, but they said that it was absurd. "The only Jewish features that you have," they said, "is your tightness with the wallet."

But my relatives on my father's side of the family had darker features. Endre was probably the Hungarian form of Andrew and I thought that my grandfather, Joseph, had an older brother named Andrew. Perhaps Endre was their father and he had come to America as a young man and became a Christian, while his father, Samuel, stayed in the old country and suffered the consequences of being a Jew in crazy times. Perhaps I would find out more about myself as we continued our travels. Ana seemed intrigued with the idea of me being Jewish. She said that she had always dreamed of marrying a Jewish man.

It was Ana's birthday the day that we visited the Great Synagogue so I bought for her a Star of David necklace similar to the one that I wore. We also found tarot cards that were based upon the Sephirath to help her with her research.

Statue Park was probably the least memorable sight that we visited. It was described in a pamphlet as "the most exciting outdoor museum in Eastern Europe." In actuality, it was a bore. It took us a good part of the day to reach it by buses and when we arrived there, the Communist statues that were removed from the streets of Budapest were placed alongside another road outside of town. It wasn't a park, it wasn't exciting, it wasn't educational; it was another wasted day.

I looked in my guidebook to see if there were any other sights that we should visit and I was surprised when I read that Budapest's tap water was considered some of the healthiest in all of Europe. Why was Grandma always supplying me with bottled water? Didn't she realize that she was only wasting her money?

On our final full day in Budapest, Ana and I went to Sunday church service at St. Stephen's Basilica. Ana didn't seem very interested in going there since she had already visited it the previous week, but I convinced her to join me. "It's been a long time, honey, since we've been to church. We really should go."

"Alright," she agreed, "as long as we sit in the very back."

We entered the Basilica, which was named after Hungary's first king and patron saint and sat in the back pew as Ana had requested. I looked up at the ceiling high above us and saw in the center a silver-haired, bearded man with outstretched hands who must have been God. In the four corners surrounding God were the writers again at four different ages along with the eagle, lion, and ox. Also, there were the names of the four gospel writers, Matthew, Mark, Luke, and John. I tried to point this out to Ana, but she gave me that Harry Potter girl expression, "Yeah, I know," just by raising her eyebrows.

The mass was a traditional Catholic mass and reminded me very much of the services that I had attended in Palma. There was a lot of burning incense and I was glad that Ana had requested that we sit in the back. Ana excused herself to go to the bathroom and missed nearly all of the service. She returned just before Communion time and said that she needed to talk to me immediately, so I followed her out the back door while the other parishioners lined up to receive the body of Christ.

Once we got outside, I said facetiously to Ana, "This better be important, honey, because I was really dying to have that heavenly host."

She replied very seriously, "I took the test, I'm pregnant," and waited for my response. I was shocked because I never thought that I would be capable of producing a swimmer, or fertile seed. I thought that my many years of pot smoking had cancelled out that possibility. I was stunned, but I was proud, and I was happy. "That's great," I said as we hugged each other.

Poland was my idea. There were four reasons why I wanted to visit it: 1. My grandmother on my father's side of the family was Polish so I was hoping that I could learn more about my ancestry from a visit there. 2. Before leaving San Francisco some friends had told me that they were convinced that the most beautiful women in all of Europe came from Poland. I was now involved with Ana and very much in love with her, but I was still curious to see whether or not I would agree with my friends on this matter. 3. I wanted to visit Auschwitz and witness the remnants of one of the most ignominious atrocities of the twentieth century. And 4. My guidebook described it as one of Europe's last bargains.

My plan was to spend one week in Poland and then about another week in Prague in the Czech Republic. I had a feeling that Prague was going to be something very special for Ana and myself. We had met each other in Palma last December when we sat in the balcony at the Sa Nostra Cultural Centre and listened to a quartet from Prague play classical music. Ana had once said that she thought that she had ancestors from Prague.

Ana didn't seem to care whether or not we visited Poland and Prague. The only thing that seemed to matter to her was that we be in Berlin in two weeks. "Why do you want to be in Berlin then?" I once asked.

"I want to make sure that you can get back into the European Union, so that you can be with me when I see my doctor for the tests of the baby."

"But why Berlin and why then?" I asked with puzzlement. Her eyebrows raised and she gave me that Harry Potter girl expression that told me that I was an ignorant fool and that she had already explained the reasons many times before, so I didn't press the matter. "Don't worry, baby. We'll be in Berlin in two weeks, come hell or high water."

"What does that mean?" she asked.

I thought for a moment and then replied, "I haven't the slightest idea." Again she gave me that Harry Potter girl expression and I felt like the stupid red-haired boy from the movie once again.

We were hoping to go directly north from Budapest through Slovakia and then spend a couple of nights in Zakopane, which is in the Carpathian Mountains near Poland's most southern point. However, there

151

were no direct trains that went there; they all went further north to Krakow first, so we decided to visit Krakow and then maybe later get down to Zakopane.

When looking at the map, it seemed as if the journey to Krakow would not be very long, but we were basing our assumption on the way that birds would fly. The train from Budapest to Krakow was an entirely different matter. Rather than going north we went west into Slovakia, then Austria, then east back into Slovakia, then west again into the Czech Republic, and then east as we entered Poland from its western border. We continued east for many hours until we finally made it to Krakow.

We were very tired from the long journey and from dealing with so many border agents along the way. Also, we were very hungry because we had assumed that there would be a food bar car on the train, but there wasn't. So all that we had along the circuitous journey was a limited amount of water and some crackers.

Since we had such good luck renting a private room with Grandma in Hungary, we decided to try the same thing in Krakow. We walked into a tourist office nearby the train station and looked through the binder at pictures and descriptions of the accommodations that were available. One place, that looked pretty nice from the photograph and was within our price range, was located nearby Rynek Główny (supposedly the largest medieval town square in Europe). The photograph showed a large bed beside an entire wall of glass that supposedly looked onto the square and it had a television too. We asked whether the bathroom was private or shared with others and the man at the tourist office replied, "You will share it with the family that lives there. All of our places are like that." Hungry and exhausted from the long trip, we paid in advance for three nights and plodded down Szpitana Street until we reached the apartment.

We crammed into the elevator, which was without safety doors, and ascended to the second floor, where we expected to be greeted warmly as we had by our Hungarian grandma. Instead, an ornery-looking hag with a short cigarette butt hanging from her gnarled lip opened the door and gestured with her head that we should follow her. She opened the door to our bedroom as cigarette ashes fell to the floor and then grunted towards the door opposite our room, which we took as an indication that the bathroom was there. She dropped the keys into my hand and then sluggishly disappeared behind another door which was immediately bolted with locks. I turned to Ana and asked, "Do you suppose that this grandma is going to do my laundry for me?" Ana raised her eyebrows at the foolishness of my question and did not reply because an answer was totally superfluous.

We dropped onto the bed and sank into the quagmire, that was once a mattress and jumped back up simultaneously when we felt something sticky oozing through the sheet. I turned on the television and monkeyed with the antenna but was unable to get any semblance of the characters, whose voices chattered incomprehensibly to us. I dusted off the television screen that was thick with grit, but that did not help either.

The windows were covered with transparent curtains, but we dared not open them because the view was of an abandoned building which looked as if it had been taken over by a band of skin-headed squatters. There was an extra blanket that we thought about putting over the window for added privacy, but we chose to use it on top of the bed to absorb the mysterious ooze. Our long coats, we decided, would need to serve as blankets.

We went out for pizza and then headed back to the apartment for what we had hoped would be a night of much needed sleep. Ana and I both dreaded going back to that bed, but we were so tired that we thought that sleep would not be difficult. As we opened the door to the apartment, a small yelping dog greeted us. It looked as if it was going to attack us if we tried to enter further, but then a shirtless man with an enormous stomach and very ratty-looking underwear appeared and kicked the dog, which crashed against the wall. The man mumbled something to either us or the wounded beast, scratched his ass, and then went into the room next to the bathroom as the dog followed. Many loud voices – male and female, young and old – came from that room, which was muffled after somebody very loudly slammed the door shut. "It looks as if it's not only us and Grandma," I whispered to Ana as we headed into our room.

Trying to sleep that night was not easy. The blanket that we placed upon the mattress kept the sticky substance from reaching us, but we now noticed a very strange smell that permeated throughout the room as if someone or something had died there recently. It did not help, as well, that members of the neighboring family kept going to and from the bathroom; many times they didn't even bother to close the bathroom door as they relieved themselves. Also, I had a strange feeling that someone was watching us. I peeked underneath the curtain at the squatters abode, but I didn't see any sign of the skinheads.

As we lay in bed trying to fall asleep, we were alerted to the time each hour. From the nearby St. Mary's Church, the sound of a trumpet would blare every sixty minutes. This served as a remembrance to the 13th Century trumpeter who was killed by a Tatar arrow while sounding a warning of invasion. 'Just make a damn statue of the guy,' I thought as I rolled around restlessly in the bed.

We rose early the next morning and Ana went to use the bathroom, but it was already occupied. We waited for over an hour but members of the family kept getting into the bathroom before we were able to use it. Unable to wait any longer, Ana cut open the top of a water bottle and pissed into it. She then returned to bed and cried her eyes out while I tried to comfort her. I said, "Don't worry, honey, we'll find another place to stay. It's going to be alright."

After having breakfast and using the bathroom at a nearby café, we returned to the tourist office but found that it was closed for the day. We searched for an available hotel room for the next four hours but came up empty-handed. Frustrated and tired from walking around under the scorching sun, we resigned ourselves that we would stay in the apartment from hell for another two nights. It wouldn't be so hard, we reasoned. Today we would visit Wawel Castle and Kazimierz, the Jewish quarter, and tomorrow we would go on an excursion to Auschwitz. We could use the bathrooms at cafes whenever the need arose. We had already paid for those nights so we might as well use them. It wasn't such a bargain either (about $30 per night).

We decided to visit the Jewish quarter first and then check out Wawel Castle afterwards. But we never made it to the castle. In fact, we didn't even visit any synagogues in the Jewish quarter. We went to the old Jewish cemetery along Sledleckiego Street and fell asleep in the tall grass among the deteriorating gravestones.

In my dream Ana and I were trying to move into my grandparents Geiger's old house in Neenah, Wisconsin. We stood before my Aunt Peggy, who was sitting on the stairs that led to the second level of the house. I asked Aunt Peggy, "Do you think it would be possible for us to live here?"

She answered, "You'll have to look at this document from the lawyer," and handed it over to me.

The document stated, "You can live here if you want," and had the signature, "Jeff Greene, lawyer."

I said, "This is a strange document...and that lawyer's name, Jeff Greene. I know that name from somewhere." Suddenly I remembered. I asked Aunt Peggy, "Was the lawyer a big, fat guy with dark hair?"

She looked surprised and answered, "Yes!" and suddenly Jeff Greene appeared before us. (Jeff Greene is a character from Larry David's HBO series, 'Curb Your Enthusiasm.' He is Larry David's agent in the series. Larry David was the co-creator of Seinfeld, the hit television series).

I said to Jeff, "You're not a lawyer, you're an agent," and Jeff replied, "You're not David, you're Larry." I looked into the mirror that was hanging on the wall beside me and, sure enough, he was right. I was Larry.

Jeff said to me, "Larry, do you really think that you can move into this house?"

And I replied, "Hey Jeff, I can do anything I want. I'm like the Rainman."

Suddenly Ana and I (not Larry) were underneath the house, where there was a bridge that was decorated with bright yellow graffiti. Most of the graffiti said, 'NEW YORK, NEW YORK' in many different shapes and sizes. Ana and I both feared that there were neo-Nazi skinheads lurking around. We looked across the misty pond and saw poverty-stricken young women clad in rags and carrying buckets. They pleaded, "Don't leave us. We won't hurt you. All we want is a chance."

Suddenly water splashed across my face and I woke up in the graveyard. An elderly Polish woman stood before us holding a bucket that previously held the water that was all over Ana and me. We did not understand the words that she was saying but it was obvious to us that she did not approve of us sleeping there and that we'd better leave.

I glanced at the tombstone that my head had been resting on and although most of the inscription was withered away, I thought that I could make out a capital W. 'Wisinske?' I thought. That was my Polish Grandmother Geiger's maiden name.

We had dinner, brushed our teeth, and used the toilet at a restaurant and then returned to the apartment. The family and the dog appeared to be asleep. We entered the bedroom and the smell was not as repulsive as before because we had left the windows open the entire day.

The next morning Ana and I woke up very early and took a shower together before the family could begin their monopoly of the bathroom. We had breakfast at a restaurant and then took a bus to Auschwitz about 1 ½ hours away. It was a good thing that the trip wasn't any longer than that because during the last thirty minutes of the ride, Ana complained that she needed to pee and became very cranky. Fortunately, we found a toilet immediately after the journey and she was able to relieve herself.

Above the main gate to Auschwitz was inscribed in large lettering the phrase: "ARBEIT MACHT FREI" (work brings freedom). Prisoners were brought to the camp under the misconception that they were going to be resettled there. The Nazis sold them non-existent plots of land and offered them work in fictitious factories, but this was all a great deception. Work did not bring freedom; it only prolonged suffering.

The prison blocks in Auschwitz were now set up as a museum exhibit to remind people of the horrors that had taken place there some sixty years ago. One room displayed bales of hair that were shorn from the prisoners to be reused as textiles or fuses for their explosives. In another room were sorted thousands of shoes and artificial legs as well as hairbrushes, toothbrushes, and pots and pans. Ana turned to me and said with a wry smile, "We hear so much today about the importance of recycling for the environment. The Nazis were many years ahead of their time, weren't they?" I looked at her and was too shocked to reply. I imagined that she was being facetious, but I really wasn't in the mood for any jokes at that time.

We entered another room and suitcases with the names and addresses of the prisoners were stacked on top of each other. Immediately my mind shot back to that image of the Graffitied Bridge in my dream yesterday. I think that it was the lettering that looked the same.

Photographs of prisoners were displayed along the walls in three different poses – front view, side view, and three quarter view with headwear. The Nazis were so organized and efficient. I looked along the walls to see whether I could spot Samuel Geiger, but I did not. He was probably so elderly that they didn't bother with photographs of him; he went straight to the gas chamber.

The exhibits of Auschwitz were terrifying but the horror did not really hit home for me until we visited the second concentration camp some three kilometers away in Birkenau. Here the Nazis were able to perform their art of extermination with greater efficiency. The gas chambers, which the prisoners were deceived into believing were showers, could accommodate up to 2000 people. Shower fixtures were fastened to the ceiling to aid in the deception, but they were not connected to any water lines. Instead, the S.S. men would pour the poisonous substance, Zyclon B, into the chamber through special openings in the ceiling and within 15 to 20 minutes, the occupants would be dead. Gold tooth fillings, jewelry, and hair would be removed and then the bodies would be incinerated.

Ana and I walked through the prisoners' living quarters in Birkenau and got a better sense of the deplorable conditions through which the prisoners persevered from day to day. At Auschwitz, the buildings appeared to be renovated and everything was neat and tidy, but here in Birkenau, the quarters were preserved in their original state and it was eerie. The ghosts of those who were crammed in the bunks and who walked along the swampy ground, that was the floor, were very present.

We walked out to a pond where human ashes had been deposited and saw multitudes of frogs staring up at us. The final part of yesterday's dream appeared in my mind again and the voices pleaded, "All we want is a chance."

Ana and I got on the bus to take us back to Krakow and within thirty minutes, she needed to pee again. I advised her to read the book that we had purchased at Auschwitz, 'I was Doctor Mengele's Assistant,' by Miklos Nyiszli. I wanted her to think about something else, but she ignored my advice and continued to complain. I tried to help her relax by placing my hand lightly over her and transferring strength and positive energy (a Reiki technique of which she was very fond) but it didn't work.

Twenty minutes passed and Ana could stand it no longer. She arose from her seat and said, "I'm getting off here," as the bus pulled into the next stop.

I said, "Well, you're not going alone. Where's your sketch pad?"

"I have no idea," she answered as she ran to the exit. I searched for the sketch pad below the seat and in the overhead luggage space, but was unsuccessful in finding it, so I jumped off of the bus as it was ready to pull out again.

Ana searched frantically for a place to pee and screamed hysterically as tears streamed down her face, "I hate cities! There are no private places to pee! All I need is a small space where I can go!" I saw a sign in the distance across the street that looked like a beer advertisement, perhaps a bar, so I calmly told Ana to follow me. Fortunately, it was a bar and it was open so Ana was able to relieve herself. Unfortunately, we waited for the next bus but it never came and no taxis were sighted, so we walked back to Krakow throughout the night.

We finally reached familiar territory and lumbered down Sepitana Street to our abode. A scrawny girl with a heavy accent played guitar and sang Dylan's 'Blowin' in the Wind.' I recognized the skinhead squatters who lived across the street from us forcing people who passed by to contribute money for the music, although I was sure that it was for their own addicted aid. I pulled Ana to the other side of the street, but it was too late; they had already spotted us. They swarmed upon us with their empty beer glasses and forcibly exhorted us to contribute. I reached into my pocket and tossed some zloty into the glass. But we had not yet passed Go. The skinheads tugged at the Star of David medallions that hung across our necks and joked at our expense. I said, "I've given you money, please let us go."

One of the skinheads said, "Oh, they're American Jews," and our personal space became less.

The skinhead that spoke English said, "Do you think, Jewboy, that some measly zloty will accommodate us?"

I replied, "What do you want?"

"Well, for a start," he replied, "we'll take your girl." He translated to his cronies what he had just said and they laughed like slobbering hyenas in heat.

I shouted in Lear-like Shakespearian eloquence that I'm sure reverberated throughout all of the old town, "Stop this madness!" The skinheads backed away slightly and I grabbed Ana as we continued on our way. But the skinheads persisted and continued to taunt us.

Just before we reached the entrance to our building, they jumped ahead and blocked our way. I thought about the possibility of fighting them but it seemed futile; there were three of them and they were all younger and stronger than me. Ana calmly said something to them in a foreign tongue and they laughed uncomfortably, shrugged their shoulders, and let us pass.

As we rode up the elevator to our apartment, I asked Ana what it was that she had said. She replied, "I said to them in Polish, 'What would your mothers think about your behavior?'"

"That's what you said?" I questioned with disbelief.

"That's what I said," she replied with a smirk that came either from her pride in convincing the skinheads or her pride in convincing me.

Ana went to the bedroom and I headed to the bathroom to relieve myself. I closed the door and turned to the toilet and jumped back when I saw the man with the enormous stomach sitting on the toilet with his ratty underwear hanging around his ankles. He grunted and I scooted off to bed.

We decided to scratch our plans about going down to Zakopane. Trying to find a hotel room in Krakow was so difficult and we figured that Zakopane, being Poland's number one resort area, would be equally if not more demanding. Also, buses seemed to be the most practical way to get there and with Ana's current weak bladder, we did not want to experience a reoccurrence of yesterday's problems. So we chose to take a train to Wroclaw for two reasons: 1. Because it was on the way to Prague, and 2. We figured that it wouldn't be as touristy as Krakow and thus we could find a hotel room much more easily.

We arrived into Wroclaw and took a taxi to a teacher's hostel that my guidebook had recommended. It was located nearby Rynek Square and the price seemed very reasonable, but unfortunately there were no vacancies. So we walked down to Rynek Square, where Ana sat with our things at a café while I went searching for accommodations.

I started with the municipal tourist office, but the women there did not seem very eager to be helpful. They gave me a sheet of paper that listed some hotels and then went back to reading their magazines and chatting about women's fashion. I interrupted them by asking, "Can you recommend any of these? Are they nearby?" They raised their eyebrows at me (three Harry Potter girls at once), pointed to the sheet of paper, and then continued their chatter.

I set off first checking out the hotels that were listed in my guidebook, but they were all full. Numerous other hotels followed, but the result was always the same; No Vacancies. I headed back toward the train station to find a tourist office that my guidebook said would accommodate you in private rooms with Polish families, but the office no longer existed. I went back to the train station and sat in the lobby trying to figure out the locations of the hotels that were listed on the paper and hoping that someone would come along and offer me a private room. No one came. They're like police officers, I thought, they're never around when you need them. I thought about Ana sitting alone at the café with her weak bladder and decided that I should get back there. On the way, I visited many other hotels and finally found a shabby room that was located above a youth center, and booked it. The room was very small and dilapidated, but the price was very cheap. Unfortunately, it was only available for one night.

I returned to the café and found Ana in a rather unpleasant state. She complained that I had deserted her. I apologized but my patience was wearing thin and another one of our unpleasant discussions ensued. Finally, we calmed down and began to behave like rational adults and took a taxi to our new love nest.

The room was rather run-down and the twin beds were very short and uncomfortable, but there was also something very nice about the place. Perhaps it was the sound of small children playing in the playground below or the view through our lace curtains to the attractive red brick building across from us. Whatever it was, we felt at peace again. We hoped that, perhaps, there would be a cancellation so that we could stay more nights, but that was not to be.

The next morning we left our bags in the lobby of the hostel and decided to try one more hotel that I had seen nearby. If it was full, we decided that we would take a train to any small town on the way to Prague and try to find some accommodation there. If there wasn't any, we'd sleep in the open air.

We walked to the nearby hotel, The Saigon, and were amazed when the receptionist told us that there had just been a cancellation and a room was available. We booked it for the weekend. Even though it was quite a bit over our budget (about $60 per night) we felt very fortunate and enjoyed the comfort of a large king-size bed and a private bathroom again.

Over the next two days I spent much of the time in the hotel room reading the book, 'I was Doctor Mengele's Assistant'. The weather was very hot outside and most of the city seemed to be swamped with tourists, so resting my ass on a luxurious stuffed chair with my feet propped up on the bed, seemed like a much better option than baking in the sun. (Besides, we were paying a lot of dough for this hotel room and I was going to get my money's worth).

Ana, however, did not see it that way and grew restless sitting in the room. I urged her to go off on her own if she wished, which she took as a sign that I was angry with her.

I replied, "I'm not angry with you. I'm reading a book in which thousands of Jews are being stuffed into gas chambers. The youngest and the eldest die first, so the others climb upon them to escape the gas. Then the women die and the men climb upon them. The strongest of those, that were once filled with vital life, lie on top of their children, parents, brothers, sisters, wives, on this hill of human carnage. So I'm sorry that I'm not in a real happy-go-lucky mood right now, but I'm not angry at you."

"Yes, you are," she disagreed, "you say that you're not angry with me but in your sub-conscious, you are."

And that set me off again. "You and your psycho-babble!" I screamed, "I can't stand it when you do that! I wasn't angry at you before, but now I am. Why can't you believe what people tell you? Why do you feel that there must be some other ulterior thing going on in one's subconscious? Why can't you trust me?"

"Because I know that you're not telling me the truth," she answered.

"I think that we should spend the day apart," I said. "We've been together for so long with rarely a break. I think that we each need some time alone."

"Good idea," she said as she slammed the door behind her.

I resettled into my comfortable chair and continued to read the book. It told about a girl, who had survived the gas chamber. She had fainted immediately when the Zyclon B had entered the room. Her face had apparently landed on a damp part of the floor. The poison was not as effective under wet conditions, so she survived. However, when the S.S. officer discovered that she was still alive, he put a bullet through her head.

I closed the book and thought about what Ana had said. Was there justification for her suspicions about me? Sure, I was not very anxious to go sightseeing with her because she was becoming easily tired and then irritable whenever we did that. But I understood that she was pregnant, and that was one of the side effects of being in that condition. I thought that I was taking it in stride and handling it rather well. But I was not angry. I just wanted some of my independence back. We had been sharing one room for over three months now and had been rarely apart from each other. It did not seem like a healthy condition to me. I loved that we were both free spirits when we had met, but now it seemed as if we were becoming too dependent upon each other. I loved being with her and she being with me, but too much of a good thing was not a good thing. We needed to find the middle way, like the Buddha.

I thought that Ana was probably right and that I was spending too much time inside, so I decided to go for a walk. I went across the Odra River and visited the Cathedral of St. John the Baptist and prayed that the love that Ana and I had for each other would remain strong in good times and in bad. I cried as I knelt in the pew and recalled a similar experience to this, many years before. I was ten years old and my mom and stepdad, Jed Modine, had gotten into a terrible argument and he stormed out of the house and I thought that he was gone for good. I went to St. Mary's Church in Menasha and tearfully prayed to God for their reconciliation. When I returned home, he was reclining in his lazy boy, eating chocolate kisses, and reading his horse magazine like he usually did. All was well again.

I walked along the river and saw couples pushing baby carriages and thought, "What a strange child our kid is going to be, coming from the likes of Ana and myself. Paranoid, depressed, immature we were; the baby would probably have to parent us."

I walked to Slowachiego Park and sat nearby the Panorama of Raclawice, which depicted a battle on a gigantic, circular canvas. As I ate my sandwich, a young couple sat on the park bench opposite from me. The man stared straight ahead with an angry glare while tears streamed down the woman's face. They did not talk, they did not embrace.

I tried to hypothesize about their problem. 'Was she pregnant? Were they breaking up? Could they not find a hotel room? Was he angry because she could see into his subconscious when he could only see things on the surface?' I wanted to say to them, "Don't worry. Talk it over and give each other love and everything will turn out alright. Love is the answer, love is the key. All you need is love." Then I thought that rather than intruding upon their privacy and sticking my nose into their business, of which I didn't have a clue, I should take my own advice and talk with Ana and express my love to her and be patient.

When I returned to the room, Ana was there and we talked. She said that past lovers had complained to her when she tried to read into their subconscious, and that she would try to keep those feelings to herself. I said that I would try to communicate my feelings better and try not to lose my cool. We both decided that we should try to do some things independently. We called ahead in Prague and reserved an apartment there. Besides having a kitchen and a bathroom, the apartment had two bedrooms, which would provide for us a little more independence. If I, the nighthawk, wanted to write or read until very late, it would be easier to do that under those conditions.

On our final day in Wroclaw, we took a walk together and visited the Jewish cemetery on Slezna Street. At the cemetery's entrance, were photographs of some of the people that were buried there. Ana said, "Oh my God, he looks like you," and pointed at a photograph of Rabbi Abraham Geiger, who lived from 1808 to 1860. I didn't notice any resemblance, but Ana said that the Rabbi "has deep lines from his nose to outer mouth just like you and Bruce Willis."

I looked more closely at the photo and began to wonder what Bruce Willis' original name was. Perhaps it was Geiger and he was a brother that I never knew I had. 'No,' I reasoned, 'no actor would ever change his name from Geiger to Willis. Bruce was not my brother, but perhaps there could be a family connection with the rabbi.' We visited the Geiger family plot and made out from the booklet written in Polish, that the family was involved in literature and the study of history, much like me, the teacher of those subjects.

We made it to our apartment in the Yinohrady district of Prague, after getting ripped off by the taxi driver at the train station and paying four times what a local would pay. "You actually did quite well," said Yosef, the man whom we met at the apartment. "Most people end up paying ten times the correct amount. Those drivers from the train station are terrible thieves. Beware of any that don't have a meter."

The apartment was lacking in proper maintenance and was very filthy, but it was very roomy. We moved some of the mattresses from one of the rooms to the master bedroom to make a gigantic bed. We planned to use the other room as a late night study for me, but discovered later that the lights in that room did not work. However, I was rather low in energy and did not feel like staying up late, so we used that room instead to hang our wet laundry.

The neighborhood was quite nice. Ana said that it reminded her of Paris, with earth-toned buildings on top of grassy hills and tree-lined streets running along numerous parks. Vinohrady was once the location of numerous vineyards and the fertile soil was still very evident.

We were quite a substantial distance from the old town, Staré Město, where we figured we would want to spend most of our time. But a streetcar line was on our street and we were told that the public transit system was exceptional. There was no elevator in this very tall building though, and the walk up and down the stairs was very exhausting. Thus, we chose very carefully when we would leave or enter the building to avoid unnecessary trips up these mammoth stairs.

The apartment was only available for four nights, so we spent part of the first two days looking for a future accommodation. But we could not find any other places to stay. However, as we got to see more of the city, we decided that four nights would be enough for three reasons: 1.There were too many damn tourists 2. It was rather expensive, and 3. There were too many damn tourists.

We thought that the crowds of tourists were bad in Krakow and Wroclaw, but it did not at all compare to the throngs of obnoxious camera-toting holiday-makers in Prague. They were everywhere and always in large packs like wolves ready to devour anyone that wanted to occupy a small piece of the sidewalk. If we were in a restaurant, they would swarm in after us and monopolize the waiter's attention. And forget about trying to get information at a tourist office if they would happen upon the place. They would enter the office and step right in front of me as if I were invisible. I never cared for large groups of tourists, but in Prague I was beginning to hate them with a passion.

Prague was also rather expensive. It offered many cultural events such as classical music, but the price was rather steep. Ana and I were probably spoiled from our free shows in Palma, but here in Prague nothing came without a price. There was no street entertainment and visits to simple sights such as churches, synagogues, or cemeteries were outrageously priced.

We did splurge one night on a black light theatre show, which seemed to be an art form uniquely Prague. We were curious as to what it would be like so we bought two tickets to see a musical version of the classic tale, Faust. We were herded into the small theatre after first getting the hard-sell treatment to buy a program. The audience was exclusively tourists from all parts of the world, which I took as a bad sign for the production value of the show.

The black light effects were interesting, which made it look as if the characters and objects were flying through the air or vanishing instantly but the entire sound of the show was dubbed. The actors mouthed their dialogue to the pre-recorded tape and I felt as if I were at a Milli Vanilli concert.

Most of the production was incomprehensible to me due to the bad acting and little use of English. However, I was able to gather that Faust had sold his soul to the devil and as a result, he would receive great success. I thought about that strange character that I had met in that bar in Pollensa on Mallorca after my road trip with Eddie. He seemed to be convinced that he was the devil and he kept trying to make me bet on my soul as he flipped a coin. I was too wise, though, and I never gave in. I remembered saying to him, "I will never make any bet, if it means that I might lose my soul." 'The devil comes in many forms, though,' I thought. 'Could I have sold my soul to the devil and not even have realized it?' I looked at Ana and she smiled sweetly at me. 'How lucky I am,' I thought, 'to have found love when I thought that it would have been impossible. And to have a child on its way. All my dreams have come true.' I sat back and daydreamed about my change in life from a lonely loser to a future husband and father in less than a year. 'What a lucky man I am,' I thought as the actors lip-synched another interminably long song that seemed never to reach its end.

For our final night in Prague, Ana and I visited the Prague Castle in the Hradčany district and then walked across the Vitanva River along the Mánisuv Bridge. To our surprise, we found a little outdoor café alongside the river, where there were no tourists, and we had a romantic candle-lit dinner. The view of the castle from across the bridge was breathtaking at night and Ana and I kissed between bites of our salads.

The next morning as we stood outside and waited for a taxi with a meter to take us to the train station, we noticed that we were standing in front of a jewelry store. We were both still filled with romance from the night before and we simultaneously thought about looking in the shop for our wedding rings. Prague would be the ideal place to get them, we reasoned, because we had met at the concert of the quartet from Prague. We walked into the shop and asked the woman if she had any wedding rings. "Just one pair," she replied and showed them to us. We liked the simple rounded design and the non-glossy finish, so we tried them on and they fit each of us perfectly. Within a couple of minutes, we had bought our wedding rings. Our romance and relationship had evolved so quickly, why not our wedding rings.

I was very nervous about trying to get back into the European Union and thought that my chances were very slim on being re-admitted. We decided to buy tickets for Dresdan, since it was just a little way across the border. No use wasting money on tickets to Berlin, I figured, if they wouldn't let me cross the border.

At the ticket office I struggled to comprehend what the ticket agent was saying to me. I kept asking him to repeat what he said because he had a very strong accent, a thick glass window stood between us, and some punks sat nearby playing loud, irritating music from their boombox. I believe that he told me that the train was already sold out, but I could buy tickets without any seat reservations. I nodded yes and he gave me two tickets. We took our bags to the track and waited for the train to arrive. I was drenched in sweat due to the difficult conversation with the ticket agent, the hot weather, and the fact that I was very nervous.

If I did not get back into the E.U., I figured that I would check out Lithuania and some of the other Baltic States and try to get back to San Francisco from there. I would probably have to buy an entirely new ticket since my original return ticket specified that re-routing was not allowed. I really did not want to spend the final month and a half without Ana. Even though at times I wished for more independence, I didn't want to go back to being a solitary traveler like I had been most of my life. I knew that I would become very lonely.

The train arrived and we squeezed ahead of a large group of tourists and felt that justice had been served. We found some open seats in a cabin and sat down. It looked as if nobody had reserved seats; perhaps that was what the ticket agent was trying to say to me.

Our cabin filled up quickly with six people and many more stood just outside in the aisle. Ana whispered to me, "With the train being so crowded, we'll probably have a good chance at getting across." I nodded back nervously to her and looked at the other four people in our cabin to detect whether they heard what she had said. The two women next to us seemed to be reading, the business man was messing with his laptop computer, but the strange-looking thin man, who smelled like cigarettes and looked like a drunkard, was staring at us. I had no idea whether he understood English, but I silently prayed that Ana would not mention any more of these thoughts out loud.

The Czech Republic border agents entered our cabin and inspected our passports. The tall agent looked repeatedly at my passport and my face and tried to detect whether or not the passport was phony. Finally, he handed it back to me and said very harshly, "Next time, you have a new passport."

I replied, "Yes, sir," and the women next to us smiled at me, who looked like a little boy that had just been scolded.

When we were nearly at the German border, Ana asked me, "Was it Manhattan where those planes crashed into the towers?"

I nervously replied, "Yes."

Then she started singing the Leonard Cohen song, "First We Take Manhattan'. Everyone in the cabin looked up. I was flabbergasted, I couldn't believe it. I was trying to cross the border illegally on a train heading to Berlin. We're just before the border and Ana started singing a song that made us look like terrorists going to attack Berlin.

The strange thin man stood up and left the cabin. I was afraid that he was going to alert the authorities of his suspicions about us. I stood up and walked up the aisle in the opposite direction from him. I went into the W.C. and locked the door when suddenly someone knocked on it. I immediately opened the door because if it was a border guard, I did not want it to look as if I were trying to hide.

Outside of the W.C., stood a small friendly-looking border agent with a beard. He asked me for my passport and I immediately produced it for him and said, "Yes, of course," so that he would recognize my American accent. He looked at it briefly, looked at my face, handed it back to me, smiled and said, "Thank you," and went on his way. I could not believe my luck. I had expected a rigid, by-the-book agent like the Czech guy, but even more anal since he was German. Instead, I got a man who looked like a combination of Kris Kringle and Mahatma Gandhi.

I went back into the W.C. and waited a while until I felt that the border agent had passed our cabin. I wondered whether Ana was going to blow my cover; she was acting so strangely. Was she purposefully making it difficult for me to get across? What the hell was going on?

I walked back into the aisle of the coach and saw the border agent standing in front of our cabin. He turned and spotted me so I continued walking there. 'Ana spilled the beans,' I thought to myself, 'He knows that I'm entering illegally. He wants to see my passport again.'

Just before I arrived to the cabin, the agent smiled at me again and then continued down the aisle. I told Ana that I had passed the inspection and she seemed pleased. Shortly, thereafter, we got off of the train at Dresden.

I said to Ana, "What in God's name prompted you to sing that song at the border? Do you know how that looked?"

She answered, "I know. I'm sorry. I was nervous and being pregnant, my hormones were making me act bizarrely. Sorry." She smiled sweetly back at me and I shook my head and wagged my tongue like a madman, who was blissfully exasperated.

We looked through my guidebook and Ana convinced me that Dresden was not worth a visit and we should take the next train to Berlin. I was skeptical since it was the beginning of a weekend and my book recommended that for Berlin, like Prague, you should reserve a hotel room at least two weeks in advance. "Don't worry, honey," she said as she massaged my neck, "I'll find us a place."

We arrived into Berlin and Ana said that she needed to use a payphone to check about a hotel that was nearby. I asked her how she knew about the place and she said that it was recommended in my guidebook. "Good!" I exclaimed, "I'm glad that you're starting to see the value of this book."

I stood nearby while she talked in German to the person at the other end of the line. She hung up and said to me, "We have a room. Follow me." Follow her I did; I was most impressed with Ana and gladdened that my guidebook had been useful once again.

We walked a short distance and arrived at the Hotel Morbina, where a large, comical woman showed us to our room. The room was nice although it did not have a private bathroom. However, the bathroom outside of our room would be shared with only one other room, which was occupied by an English couple that we had met when we entered the hotel. Fortunately, the bathroom was close by and the English couple was not monopolizing it because Ana needed to use it a great deal.

While Ana was in the bathroom, I looked through my guidebook to see what it said about the Hotel Morbina. I checked the entire section of Berlin, but there was no mention of the hotel. When she returned, I mentioned it to her and asked, "Where did you get the name and phone number?"

She thought for a little while and then replied with a bright smile, "Oh, yes, I remember. There was a pamphlet at the tourist office in Prague. That's where I got the information."

"Oh, okay," I replied. I remembered being so upset at the tourist that had butted in front of me that day that I didn't notice what Ana was doing.

The next day we decided to do some sightseeing and check out some of the culture in Berlin. We felt as if we hadn't done enough of that in our travels, so we thought that we'd try to make up for it here, since it was so well-known for its museums and historical buildings. I suggested that we first visit the New National Gallery because my guidebook had recommended it. The artwork was displayed in the underground floor of a modern building of glass and shell. Actually, the word, 'artwork' is probably not appropriate because I did not consider most of what I saw art and it looked as if there was very little work put into it. Sure, I loved the elongated figures with green faces in the painting by Ernst Kirchner entitled 'Der Potsdamer Platc' as well as the half-bodies of maniacal German officers playing poker by Otto Dix. The German Expressionism was great, but most of the other things were in my humble opinion, pretentious masturbation.

First there were these old radios that some clown named Kienholz thought was art. Then this bozo name Beuys made some scratches on canvases and expected us to find some great significance into what any four year old child could do. There was also a basket of eggshells by Whogivesaf*!k and florescent light fixtures by Getajob.

And then we entered this room where there was this huge canvas by Barnett Newman with a red square on the left, a yellow square on the right, and a black or dark blue rectangle in between. Ana and I sat on a couch in the back of the room and watched a young woman kneeling on the floor in front of this thing for about twenty minutes. "What is it that she sees in this painting that a mere mortal like I cannot?" I asked Ana. She tried to rationalize an answer when suddenly I saw a large canvas in the next room painted only in the color pink. I walked toward it and said, "Now this guy must have spent half of his life doing this. Who is this wanker?" I nearly passed out from shock and humiliation when I saw that the artist's name was Rupprecht Geiger. "Rupprecht," I scolded, "you have brought great dishonor to the family name. Get a life, dear boy."

The next day we went to the Old National Gallery on Museum Island and were much more impressed. There were works by impressionists such as Renoir, Manet, and Monet and many 19th century German artists. In these paintings, I could actually see some talent and effort involved and the fact that we were given headphones, which explained the paintings and artists, helped us as well. "I would have loved to have had headphones to explain the crap that we saw yesterday," I said to Ana. "The eggshells signify our fragile existence and the basket is God, who holds it all together, wank, wank, wank."

On Monday we visited the New Jewish Museum, which looked like a smashed Star of David from the outside. Inside the museum were displays which showed truly trivial facts about every German Jew that ever existed. It seemed like an endless journey through 2000 years of very boring information. Security was very high there; we weren't even allowed to wear our coats, although it was very chilly inside. After seeing that there were very few things of interest for us there, Ana and I rushed through the rest of the icy maze, retrieved our coats, and exited. I said, "Let's avoid any places that have the word 'new' in the title." Ana agreed.

Next we checked out a bit of the Berlin Wall that was still standing and walked up Friedrich Street to Checkpoint Charlie, which was the entry point into the American section, when Berlin was divided between the English, French, Americans, and Russians.

Then we went to Potdamer Platz, which is a cluster of high-rise buildings that serve as the European headquarters for such corporations as Daimier Chrysler and Sony Entertainment. For 3 ½ Euros you can ride up Europe's fastest elevator to the Panoramapunkt, which is on top of the glitzy Kollhoff building. I joked to Ana, "If I were a terrorist, I'd probably want to crash my plane here." She turned to me with wide eyes, then smiled, and nodded in agreement.

The next morning Ana came back from the bathroom and announced, "In Wroclaw we decided that we would do things more independently. We haven't been doing that. Today I think that we should do things on our own."

"Okay, honey," I agreed, "What are you going to do?"

"I don't know. First, I'll go for a walk. I'm sure that you'll want to stay in bed longer. So I'll see you later and we can share our experiences at dinnertime," she said with a kiss and was gone. I lay down in bed and enjoyed the luxury of not having to rush off anywhere. I snuggled under the covers, rested my eyes, and just chilled.

Some time passed, I'm not sure how much, and I decided to walk inside the Piergarten, which is Berlin's huge public park. I lay down in the shade of some trees and then walked up Strasse des 17 Juni, which was named for the 1953 workers' uprising. In the center of the street stood Siegessäule (Victory Column), which was built in commemoration of 19th century Prussian military triumphs.

I turned left on a path called Bellevueallee, which led me to a most unusual sight. Clustered on both sides of the path were about a hundred Arab families barbecuing and picnicking. At each family site there stood a large hookah, from which the men smoked. I thought, 'This is really wild. I didn't realize that there were so many Arabs here in Berlin. Everywhere I look, that's all I see.'

Everywhere, that is, except at one gathering beside some trees. This gathering did not look like a family and they didn't all look Arabic. There were two Arabic men whose faces I had never seen before, but the rest of the people at that gathering were very familiar to me. There were Ana, the English couple from the hotel, Ana's former roommate, Andreu, his German boyfriend, Klaus, and my old girlfriend, Constanza, who seemed to be doing most of the talking.

I walked further up the trail and then hid among some trees so that I would have a better vantage point and not be so conspicuous. Constanza continued to talk although I did not understand what she was saying. Then Ana talked and I could not understand her either, although I knew that she was not happy. Andreu and Klaus, however, sat with huge grins and laughed loudly, the more that Ana became enraged. Constanza seemed to give some final instructions and then they all dispersed.

I tried to follow Ana in the direction that she left, but I lost her immediately. So I went back to the hotel. I felt pretty exhausted after the long walk, so I lay back on the bed and rested my feet. Ana burst through the door and appeared startled to see me there. She said, "Are you going to spend the whole day sleeping?"

I answered, "I wasn't sleeping. I just got back from a walk. What did you do?"

She replied, "I need to use the bathroom," and exited.

I jumped up from the bed and watched Ana from the peek-hole in our door. She didn't go into the bathroom, but knocked on the door of the English couple and then entered their room. I grabbed a glass and went into the bathroom, which was right next to the room of the English couple. I placed the glass against the wall and heard fragments of the conversation that took place in the next room.

Ana said, "I can't believe it. We've been planning this for months and now at the last minute, she announces a major change."

The English woman replied, "I don't think that it's such a big change."

Ana – "Oh, it's big. We have planned for months to use remote control to detonate the RDD and now these two hyenas have convinced her that it should be a suicide mission instead."

Englishman – "I think that it should work. We're not sure how reliable the remote control system is under these conditions."

Ana – "It's more reliable than those two."

English woman – "That's the beauty of the change. If the two of them chicken out, we can always use the remote control as a backup."

Ana – "I don't like it. I better go."

I rushed out of the bathroom, re-entered the bedroom, and jumped onto the bed just before Ana came back. She screamed, "Are you going to sleep the rest of your life away?"

"I wasn't sleeping," I replied, "I was just resting my eyes."

The next morning Ana and I visited the Reichstag; the German Federal Parliament building. At the entrance a sign said that visitors could enter after making written reservations. I turned to Ana and said, "Well, I guess we can't see the inside."

She produced from her pocket two tickets and said, "Oh yes, we can." I looked at the tickets and they were good for admittance on that day.

"How'd you get these?"

"I wanted it to be a surprise for you since it's your birthday soon. That's why I wanted to be in Berlin at this time."

Just before we entered, I noticed the two Arabic men from yesterday at the park, and they were followed shortly thereafter by the English couple, who nodded at us and then continued on. "It's strange to see them here, don't you think?" I asked.

"Not at all," she answered, "this is a very popular sight."

I figured that this was probably the target for the terrorist act and I tried to hypothesize why. Capitalism was readily visible throughout all of Berlin, but Potsdamer Platz was the symbol of capitalistic greed. Why not there rather than here? The song, 'First We Take Manhattan' kept running through my head.

Security was very high throughout the building. First we went through a metal detector, then our bags and clothing were inspected individually by security guards. And there were other guards stationed practically everywhere. "If I were a terrorist," I said quietly to Ana, "this is the last place that I would want to be." I looked for a reaction but got none.

The public was able to visit only the glass dome area that sits in the center of the building. This dome, which was reconstructed in the 1990's and designed by the architect, Lord Norman Foster, was stunning, to say the least. We walked along spiral walkways of glass, sparkling tiles, and gleaming silver railings, which encircled an enormous funnel made from mirrors, which were used to generate solar energy.

At the top of the funnel was a very fancy restaurant, where Ana surprised me again by having reservations. We sat at a table overlooking the city and ordered the lunch special, which consisted of bratwurst (spiced sausage), weisswurst (veal sausage), and blutwurst (blood sausage) with some bratkartoffeln (fried potatoes) on the side.

Ana excused herself to go to the bathroom, but I noticed that she walked right past the ladies' room and exited the restaurant. I got up from the table and walked to the door to see what she was doing. She appeared to have passed out and was lying on the floor. I saw security guards rushing towards her and I was ready to join them when I suddenly saw Andreu and Klaus sneak into a silver panel that looked as though it led to the inside of the mirrored funnel.

Ana became 'conscious' again and I ran to her. I explained to the guards that she was pregnant and that she did this often. I assured them that the luncheon special would give her the strength that she needed and that a doctor was unnecessary. I walked her back into the restaurant and showed her the door to the ladies' room. She said, "Oh, I walked right by it. I need to use it."

"Later, honey," I said. "We need to talk first."

We sat back down at the table and I told her what I had witnessed. She denied everything and said that I was imagining it. She tried to convince me that everything that I saw in the park yesterday and the conversation that I had heard with the English couple was only a dream. "You were sleeping the whole day," she said, "and now you're letting your imagination get the best of you." I told her that I would tell everything to the authorities unless she 'fessed up, but she remained resolute in her denial. She asked, "Can I go to the bathroom now?"

I answered, "Sure, but don't miss the door this time."

While she was gone, I thought about what she had said. Perhaps it was all a dream yesterday. I was in bed a great deal of time. And perhaps I did imagine seeing Andreu and Klaus go through that silver panel because that's what I was expecting to see. "Maybe I need this luncheon special more than Ana," I said aloud to myself as I bit into a blood sausage and juice squirted onto my shirt.

On the way back to the hotel, Ana tried to convince me that we should fly directly to Palma rather than taking the train to Amsterdam and Paris first. I admitted to her that I was tired of traveling and that I'd like to just hang out in Palma for the rest of my sabbatical but I was afraid that if I'd try to fly in Europe, the authorities would notice that I had over-extended my visa and I'd be in trouble.

"They won't even look at your passport," she said, "We're in the E.U. It's like flying from state to state in the U.S."

"And need I remind you," I said, "The planes that crashed on September 11th were domestic flights. Security is much tighter now."

"Not in Europe," she remarked. I agreed that we'd check at the train station and see what it would cost us to take trains and then we'd visit the tourist office and see what a one-way flight to Palma would cost. "It'll cost hardly anything to fly to Palma," she promised me. And she was right. The train tickets were extremely expensive. (It would have cost us about 1000 euros to get back to Spain), whereas two tickets to Palma would cost us only 140 euros. There was a flight available the next day and we bought the tickets immediately.

We were both very excited about getting back to Palma. We decided that we'd rent an apartment there and just relax. No more running around with our backpacks. No more one-room hotels. Things were going to get back to normal again. I was going back to that beautiful, magical island, Mallorca. I clicked my heels together like Dorothy from 'The Wizard of Oz' and chanted, "There's no place like home, there's no place like home..."

We checked in at the airport without any trouble. They never bothered to ask for my passport. We had some extra time so I went to the Lufthansa ticket office and cancelled my return flight from Amsterdam to Frankfurt while keeping my Frankfurt to San Francisco flight. I figured that the Amsterdam connection would be useless since Ana and I were going to stay in Palma. "Are you sure that you want to cancel this, because once it goes into the computer, it can't be changed back?" the ticket agent asked me.

"Yes, I'm sure," I answered back immediately, "cancel it," and she did.

We boarded the plane and after it took off, the stewardesses came around with complimentary copies of German newspapers. The man sitting next to me took one and I looked at the top headline. Even though I could understand very little German, I was able to make out what the headline said. It said that U.S. President Bush was arriving into Berlin today and he was going to give a speech at the Reichstag. Should I scream right now? – "Stop the plane! My fiancée's a terrorist! She and her gay roommate and his lover, and my former lover (a girl) are going to assassinate the president." No, I thought, I better just keep quiet. It all will pass.

Part III   Death

We called ahead from Berlin and reserved a room at the Hotel Havana in Palma so that we would have a place to stay until we found an apartment. The manager promised us that we would have a room with a large bed and a view overlooking the Cathedral. However, when we arrived there, we were given a room with two very uncomfortable single beds and a window that did look out to the Cathedral, but it was very small with large iron bars that went across from top to bottom. I felt as if I was in a prison cell.

I wondered whether the magic that I had felt on my first trip to Palma would come back to me; this room was not an optimistic sign. I took a shower to freshen up and the shower curtain was not long enough, so water splashed out onto the floor. It streamed out of the bathroom and collected in a large puddle beside my bed. Memories of the ash-filled pond at Birkenau came back to me and I became more depressed. I grabbed the bars of the window and said to Ana, "We've got to get out of here."

She replied, "Let's walk around and see if we can find an apartment."

We visited many real estate agencies and used our cellular phones to call numbers that advertised 'Se Alquila' on the outside of buildings, but came up empty-handed. The real estate agencies only had places that were located outside of Palma and the numbers that we called only had places available for one-year minimum. Exhausted and hungry, we labored back to the Havana until we came upon Lucia and her boyfriend, Marcos, sitting at an outdoor café along the Passeig de Born. They invited us to sit down and we ordered some sandwiches and told them about our travels and our most recent task: trying to find an apartment.

Lucia turned to Marcos and they spoke to each other in Castilian for a lengthy time. Marcos then turned to me and said, "I think that we can help you. We have a friend." He brought out his cell phone and talked to someone in German while I tried to decipher from his facial expressions whether or not he was having success. Marcos said that there was a place available until the end of June and that we could meet with the agent immediately if we wanted. Ana and I simultaneously answered, "Yes!" paid our bill, and dashed off to the Plaza Frederic Chopin, where the apartment was located.

The real estate agent, Dante, was an odd-looking fellow with red, large-framed glasses and a matching scarf that he wore around his neck. Although he had darker Mediterranean features, he spoke with a German accent to which an effeminate lisp was attached. We squeezed into the small elevator and rode up to the 4th floor. The scent of Dante's cologne was intoxicating in such a small space. He turned to me and said, "Thisth lift isth a necthessthity on sthultry daysth sthuch asth thisth."

I unintentionally replied, "Yesth, it isth," and Ana elbowed me in the ribs and gave me a dirty look. I tried to gesture with my face and hands that my reply was merely accidental, but she was not amused. Dante, meanwhile, didn't notice anything; he was busy dabbing his forehead with his matching red handkerchief.

The apartment was wonderful. The kitchen was well equipped so that Ana could fix her meals. The bathroom had a large bathtub for Ana and a shower for me. There was a laundry room with both a washer and dryer. A dining area was adjoined to the living room that had a loveseat, a chaise lounge, and a television. And the bedroom contained a very comfortable queen size bed.

There were three terraces with three spectacular views. One faced east where we could watch the sun rise behind the St. Eulalia Church tower. Another terrace faced west, from where we could watch magnificent sunsets. And the third terrace overlooked Plaza Frederic Chopin and St. Nicholas Church.

The cost was much more than I was expecting to pay but Ana was so excited about us having our own apartment that I brought out my credit card and paid for the monthly rent plus a hefty security deposit on the spot. Dante said that we could move in right away, so we went back to the Hotel Havana and gathered our things and checked out. Ana fixed some pasta and we had a candlelit dinner before retiring for the night. Once again, all was right with the world.

The next morning I awoke around 10:30 and found a note from Ana saying that she had gone for a walk. I threw on some clothes and walked down to the newsstand to pick up a morning paper. The headlines were plastered on all of the newspapers in many different languages. Basically, they all said the same thing, "Assassination Attempt on President Bush Fails in Berlin." I felt as if my heart had sunk into my stomach. I bought three different English language newspapers and ran back to the apartment, both eager and frightened about reading the contents.

The articles stated, "An assassination attempt upon United States President George W. Bush was averted when Reichstag security guards discovered two unnamed terrorists inside the gigantic mirrored funnel, which stands in the center of the Parliament building. A security sweep was done hours before Bush was to speak and guards noticed a peculiar high-pitched squeal of laughter emanating from inside the funnel. A special anti-terrorism unit consisting of both American and German forces burst inside the funnel and surprised the two male terrorists, who were caught with their pants down, literally.

"This terrorist attempt appeared to be a suicide mission, in which the funnel was loaded with enough explosives to destroy most of the building. The explosives were efficiently dismantled and carried away by the special bombs unit. Inspectors feel that the two terrorists, one German and one Spaniard, were in the funnel to activate the explosives, although evidence was also found that the explosives could have been set off by remote control as well. Said the security spokesman, 'This was obviously not a two man operation.' A full scale investigation and search for the accomplices involved in this act of terror is underway.

"Hours later," the article stated, "President Bush stood in the well under the spectacular glass dome on the Bundestage and stated, 'The terrorists are defended by their hatreds. They hate democracy and tolerance and free expression and women and Jews and Christians and all Muslims who disagree with them.' Alluding to the Nazis of Germany's past, Bush continued, 'Others killed in the name of racial purity. These enemies kill in the name of a false religious purity.'

" 'Call this a strategic challenge,' Bush continued, 'Call it, as I do, the axis of evil. Call it by any name you choose, but let us speak the truth. We must confront this conspiracy against our liberty and against our lives.' Said Bush about Iraqi leader, Saddam Hussein, who is on Bush's axis of evil, 'He's a dictator who gassed his own people.'

After the speech when the President was asked about the day's terrorist attempt, Bush told reporters, 'That's life in the bubble of security that surrounds a president.' "

I decided to go for a walk and try to decide how to deal with this matter. I was torn between alerting the authorities about all that I had witnessed and keeping my mouth shut. After all, Ana was carrying my child, or so I thought.

I ran into Marcos who had helped us find our current living arrangement. He invited me into his apartment where he offered me a tall glass of water and rolled some spliff that of which we immediately partook. It had been about a half a year since I had last gotten stoned and it affected me to great measure. I asked, "Do you think that it's possible for human beings such as us to understand God?

He seemed mildly surprised by my query and then replied something about all beings being iron that gets formed into energy. "Your nerves can feel frequency, your eyes can see frequency. A newborn child's receptors are at zero but as she ages, she begins to notice things beyond herself."

"But does she understand them?" I asked. "Over time as she develops, yes," I answered my own question.

Marcos replied, "Perhaps, but I think not. One needs to be on the outside in order to understand it."

"Huh?" I inquired as the smoke saturated the sponge that was my brain.

"It's like a fish in a fish tank," he continued. "It does not understand anything beyond its tank."

"I am its God," I replied excitedly. "I feed it and I clean its water, but it doesn't understand me."

"No, it doesn't understand you. Its receptors are not capable of that," Marcos said. "An orange has receptors, but it doesn't understand you."

"How do you know that?" I challenged him. "How do you know that an orange does not understand me?"

"Because it is not beyond your universe. Go to a Greek Orthodox church sometime," he suggested.

"I have been to many," I boasted.

"What did you see there? When Moses climbed up Mount Sinai to speak with God, what did you see?"

I toked, exhaled and joked, "All that I see is smoke."

"Exactly," answered Marcos with a wide grin. "Smoke, vapors, clouds. Why?"

"Cuz I'm high," replied I.

"Because God cannot be seen, cannot be understood. Moses, at the burning bush, asked his God, 'What is your name?' And what did his God reply?"

"Yahweh," I proudly answered back.

"Well, no, David, supposedly Moses' God said, 'Ehyeh Asher Ehyeh,' which many years later somehow became Yahweh in the Hebrew Bible. Do you know what Ehyeh Asher Ehyeh means?"

Stupefied I replied, "It's beyond me."

"That's correct," said Marcos, "It is beyond you and it was beyond Moses, too. Ehyeh Asher Ehyeh means I am what I am, or in more straightforward way, piss off, it's none of your business."

"That reminds me of something that happened to me about twenty years ago," I said.

"Tell me about it."

"I had returned from Alaska and moved into this big house in Minneapolis with a bunch of derelicts."

"Sounds delightful."

"No, it wasn't. This was a big, old house full of a bunch of guys, I don't know how many. A few of them went to the University, but most of them were just slackers and drug fiends. My bedroom was in the basement and I was very poor then; I didn't have a bed so I laid my clothes upon the floor and slept on them. There was also this freezing cold draft coming through the broken window of the room, so I also had to use some of my clothes to stifle that.

"It was in the middle of winter in Minneapolis, Minnesota, one of the coldest places in the world and the house had no heat because we were all a bunch of derelicts and could not afford it. I lay on my back in my sleeping bag on top of my clothes and just shivered as I listened to the wind howling outside.

"After a few hours I felt as if I was in a sleep-like state even though I think that I was still awake. Suddenly I heard a voice although the voice wasn't heard through my ears but it was felt throughout my entire being. The voice said very slowly and very softly, "Ooroo, ooroo, U-R-U."

"Interesting," replied Marcos, "what did you do?"

"I lay there thinking about what had just happened. I contemplated whether the voice had really appeared before me or whether I had just imagined it."

"Imagination is the accumulation of sensation," said Marcos.

"Yes," I replied, "I felt as if I had just experienced a revelation with God, like Moses or Muhammad. God had appeared before me and he gave me a new name and a message. He said U-R-U, you are you. The message was I am what I am and I must accept that. One cannot move forward and improve upon oneself until one recognizes what one is."

"And what are you, dear David?" asked Marcos.

"I am a fish in a tank of water. I have no understanding of He that feeds me, but I don't care. I am URU (oo roo), I am what I am, I'm URU, the banana man," I answered musically back, and we both laughed hysterically.

I said, "You know my initials spell God backwards."

"D-O-G. What's the O stand for, Dog?

"Oddfellow."

"Oddfellow? That's odd. Explain."

"When I was born, the top of my right ear did not curve down but stood straight up. The doctor said, 'Look at this odd fellow,' and he and the nurses all laughed. My right hand was cupped under my chin like Rodin's 'The Thinker' and my mother confused that statue with Michelangelo's 'David' and named me David Oddfellow Geiger."

"The name fits you, Dog, the name fits you."

Marcos looked at his watch and said that he must do his work. I said that I had a lot of fun and suggested that we soon get together again.

He replied, "Yes, I'd like that, but I'll be out of town for a week. I'm leaving for Barcelona tomorrow."

"Barcelona, why there?"

"There's an exciting media conference there. That's why I need to finish this program. I'm going to present it there."

"Are you taking the ferry?"

"No, an airplane. Lucia's getting the tickets as we speak."

"Lucia's going as well?"

"Oh, yes, of course. We are a team."

An uncomfortable feeling came over me and I awkwardly dismissed myself as Marcos worked at his computer. In the elevator the high feelings of elation were replaced by feelings of uncertainty, suspicion, and fear. I knew that I needed to talk with Ana, but I dreaded it.

As I was walking home, I saw my old nemesis, Pere, Ana's suitor. Pere was now dressed in a black Jewish cap and a long blue coat and he wore a goatee almost exactly like me. Around his neck he wore a garish medallion depicting Hanuman. He was looking up at the sky. I stood beside him for a minute, but he didn't seem to notice me. I said, "Hi Pere, what are you looking at?"

"A bird shit on me and I'm trying to find the f*!ker."

"The f*!ker probably flew away after he hit his target."

"No, the f*!ker's still there. I feel his presence."

"What will you do when you see the f*!ker?"

"I will stare at the f*!ker with an evil, mother-f*!king stare and wish him to have a terrible, mother-f*!king existence in his next mother-f*!king life.

I continued walking back to the apartment as I thought, 'Pere has grasped the concepts of reincarnation, karma, and dvesha (hatred), but perhaps he needs to learn more about yama (refraining from actions, words, and thoughts which bring harm to others.' Before I turned the corner, I looked back and Pere was still standing in the same spot looking up at the sky with his evil mother-f*!king stare.

I got back to our apartment but Ana was not there. Dazed and confused I took off my shoes and lay down on our bed. The line that Marcos had said kept repeating in my head, 'Imagination is the accumulation of sensation.' Was everything that I had witnessed in Berlin just a figment of my imagination? Reality and illusion seemed so blurred now. What was real? Who was Ana? Who was I?

I think that I fell asleep. The angel Gabriel appeared before me. He said, "Uru, Uru, U-R-U." I tried to speak, but he stopped me and said, "Be silent and listen to the in-between." I tried to listen, but he said, "Do not listen with your ears. Listen with all of your senses, all of your being. What do you feel?"

"I feel love," I telepathically answered him.

"Yes, love is the answer," he replied, "never forget that. Never forget what you have learned and from whom you have learned it."

The angel Gabriel transformed into Ana and she said, "My love, I must go now."

"Where? Why?" I asked.

"I need to go to Barcelona. I talked to my mother and she needs me to work in the wine shop because my sister is going to be in the hospital. I promised her that I would go."

"But what about us and our apartment?"

"I'll be back in one week, two weeks maximum. Don't worry; this will give you more time to do your writing. That's what you do and who you are. You are you and I am I. Now I must fly, so goodbye, my love, goodbye." And she vanished into a mist.

Some time later I awoke and saw not a trace of her belongings. She was gone. It was as if she had never been there. Was she just a figment of my imagination?

I tried calling Ana on her cellular phone, but there was no answer; she was probably still on the airplane and had the phone turned off. I searched throughout the apartment again for any trace that would prove to me that Ana had existed, but I came up empty. I found some photographs of our travels across Europe, but there were none of her. All of the receipts from the hotels where we had stayed had only my signature. I ran to Ana's former workplace, the flower shop, but a sign in the window said that they were closed for a week. 'Were they in Barcelona as well?' I wondered.

I sat outside on the terrace at Bar Bosch and consumed a large number of café con leches and cigarettes. This was the first time that I had smoked cigarettes since Crete and the nicotine rushed to my head and paralyzed my body while the caffeine from the coffees gave me the shakes. People around the tables were staring at me with horrified expressions, when Danté, our apartment landlord, appeared before me dressed in red again and asked, "Isth everything alright, David? Are you sthick?"

"No, I'm fine, Danté," I replied, "Too much coffee, I think."

"Where isth Ana?" he asked.

"Ana? You know Ana?" I excitedly shot back.

"Of course, I do. Where isth she?"

"She's gone, Danté," I replied, "she's gone."

"I'm sthorry. Where isth she?"

"Barthelona," I answered back, "with family. They need her."

"It looksth asth if you do asth well. Are you lonely?"

"Yesth," I replied, "but it'sth only temporary. She'll be back sthoon."

"That'sth niceth, David, but if you get lonesthome, pleasthe give me a call," he said as he handed me his card, kissed me on the cheek and then disappeared.

I looked down at the red-lettered business card, and then I shrieked as the red ball of the cigarette burned the index and middle fingers of my right hand. Instinctively, I threw the cigarette up in the air, which landed into a salad bowl of a fat German tourist at the table next to me. Everybody in the terrace shot me dirty looks and mumbled about me. I apologized to the tourist and put a twenty-euro bill on her table, threw another twenty on my table, and sheepishly exited amid murmurs of condemnation.

A weariness came over me and I trudged back to the apartment via Plaza Frederic Chopin. As I crossed the plaza, I heard the familiar phrasings of the Marvin Gaye song, "Let's Get It On." I followed the music to a small women's clothing shop. The walls of the shop were covered with billowy white satin sheets that hung from the high white ceiling.

Inside the entrance to the shop danced a slender, long-haired blonde dressed in white. Her arms extended toward the ceiling and swung seductively in complement to her willowy alabaster torso. I stopped walking and gawked at her. Instantly her face turned toward me and enraptured me with the slightest lift of her chin. The left edge of her thin, rich lips turned upward and invited me into the shop although my legs, I could not move. Her milky blue eyes suggested appetite and animal desideratum. My tongue hung as she continued to sing the song, 'Let's Get It On'.

Somehow, I managed to get inside of the shop and I found myself standing beside her. I wrapped my arms around her and leaned in for a kiss. The temptress slapped me harshly across my face and chastised me, "What are you doing? Where is your wife?" She grabbed my left hand and twisted my wrist so that my wedding ring was planted squarely between my eyes. "You think that you're a player?" she said, "You're a fool, old man. Go back to your wife and be thankful that she will have you."

She let go of me and I fled from the shop like a wounded animal. I fell onto the sidewalk and felt the sensation of having been castrated. I looked down to my groin area but saw no evidence of any damage. Relieved, I lifted myself up using the Chopin mantel as my crutch and dragged myself back to the apartment.

In the elevator, I looked at myself in the mirror and saw humiliation personified. I said, "I'll change my name. Hugh Miliation. That's me, you old fool. Hugh Miliation."

"Thstop the jokesth," Danté's image reprimanded me. "Thisth isthn't funny." I planted my lips against the mirror and kissed Danté as the elevator door opened. There stood my next-door neighbor and her little rat dog. Their usually smug attitude was replaced with shock as both of their open mouths hung aghast.

"Going down? Enjoy the ride," I said to them as I stepped aside and opened the door to my apartment. Once inside, as I was closing my door I saw that the two were still standing in front of the now closed elevator with the same dumb-founded expressions.

I lay upon the red settee and tried to call Ana again, but again there was no answer. The phone fell from my hand and continued to ring from the floor until the recorded voice was followed by the repeated beeping of a disconnected line. And then the phone went dead. I had expected the beeping of the disconnected line to be transformed into a gigantic street cleaner that would wash away the filthy secrets in my subconscious, but that did not happen. The phone went dead. I had expected to dream, but I did not. I lay awake on the red settee and watched the birds swarm above me as day became night and night became day.

The familiar sound of the hand-held sidewalk cleaner that blew garbage into the street told me that it was morning again. I heard this sound each morning since I had moved into this apartment and it always irritated me immensely. Was it really worth being awoken each morning by this obnoxious noise for the sake of a clean sidewalk? The sound of a broom sweeping across the pavement seemed much more soothing and practical. Was I the only one who felt this way?

Palma seemed to have lost the magic that I had felt on my first visit there. Coincidences seemed to be continuous then and my daily horoscopes seemed to always be talking directly to me and guiding me. Now, the horoscopes did not seem to apply to me at all.

The clubs no longer appealed to me either. At Bluesville, different bands were advertised nightly but usually these bands had the same musicians plus or minus one. And they seemed to have lost their passion that I had felt during my winter visit.

The house at 86 Joan Míro, that I had planned to make into a youth center, was now over-run by anarchist squatters, who spray painted in red their symbols across the entire building. In the front yard a vulgar sculpture stood of a headless woman humping a gigantic snail surrounded by hundreds of baby snails. A sign on the gate notified me that the building was to be demolished.

All of the Catholic churches were practically empty during the services. There was never any singing anymore. The messages that I seemed to have gotten from the sermons or incidents before were now non-existent.

Although it was not the peak summer season, tourism seemed to have dropped off dramatically. Gypsy beggars and thieves were now much more prevalent. It reminded me of the scene in the Jimmy Stewart movie, 'It's a Wonderful Life' where Bedford Falls had turned into Pottersville. This time, however, there was no Clarence the Angel to make all things right.

My cellular phone rang as it lay on the floor beside me and I saw that it was Ana, but I decided not to answer it. What good would it do for me to talk to her? I would only suspect, whether it was real or imagined, that Lucia was standing behind her and plotting, as she explained to me how boring Barcelona was and how she missed me so.

The phone rang many times over the next few days and I never answered it. I didn't even bother to look at the number; I knew that it was Ana. I sensed her within me and I could predict accurately whenever the phone was about to ring.

It wasn't so much these paranoiac suspicions that I had about her being with Lucia that kept me from answering the phone, I decided. It was more of an acceptance of the inevitable that I now felt. I knew that Ana was involved in a terrorist network and I too was entangled in its web. I could try to fight my way out of it, but I knew that it would be useless. I was already too deeply involved and aware of incidents, such as the plot to assassinate President Bush to try to claim my innocence now.

Ana returning to Mallorca and to me was inevitable; our marriage in the States was inevitable; our life together in San Francisco was inevitable. Why fight destiny? Accept what is and set yourself free, I thought as I watched another episode of 'Married With Children' dubbed in Castilian on the television.

I would become Al Bundy. My wife and children would take what was once mine and would drain me until I was dead and dry. That was my fate, I decided as I lay on the sweat-stained red settee and added another cigarette butt to the already over-flowing ashtray.

There were times that I removed myself from the red settee, I remember. One night I walked down to Parc de la Mar for the St. Joan Festival. There were bonfires and smoke and people dressed up as devils everywhere. The traditional St. Joan food was being eaten by everyone – Coca de Llardons, consisting of pigskin covered with a white, acidic powder. But usually, I just stayed home.

Once I went to the bathroom and peed toward the toilet and then stood before the mirror that hung upon the wall above the washbasin. I saw that my face had aged dramatically since I had last studied myself. The circles that had always been beneath my eyes since my early twenties were now deeply set like the tires of a monster truck at one of those events that I could never envision myself attending.

I saw a bottle of Ana's bath soap, Mandarine I think it was, that I had bought for her on one of her moody days and I decided that I deserved for myself a long and luxurious bath. I poured more than an ample amount of the contents into the tub and sat on the toilet as the water poured and the bubbles grew.

Dylan sang to me from the CD player. "It feels good, Bobby, that's how it feels, all alone," I said as I lowered my back into the seething agua that did not discomfort me in any way, although it turned my normally pale skin into an abnormally pinkish glee.

I sat for hours listening to Dylan's Highway 61 Revisited and pressing the play button with my wet and bubbled index finger and kept thinking about Ana and wondering why I was not happier. She was young, I was old, she was beautiful, I was not so…anymore…

At one point I remember not thinking about her anymore and began to relax. It was during 'Desolation Row' when I crossed my leg in the tub that the image appeared before me that I now share with you.

My kneecap was his head, the scar from my Philippine motorcycle accident was his face, and the soap bubbles that attached to my thigh was his long, white beard. He was Mr. Natural, that comic book character that R. Crumb had created in the 60's.

"Mr. Natural!" I gasped, "What are you doing here?"

"I've come to provide for you some enlightenment, free of charge."

"Wow," I replied, "Lay it on me, I'm ready."

"You, sir, are a fool," he said, "You, sir, need to be who you are. Do not deviate; do not compromise. If to thyself be true, all will be well."

I stared at Mr. Bubble…Mr. Natural for an exceedingly long period of time and tried to figure out what exactly he was trying to tell me. I asked, "What should I do? What is the meaning…of life?"

He replied, "Love it or leave it."

I must have then uncrossed my legs because Mr. Natural suddenly disappeared into the bath water. I tried to follow him by lowering myself. My face became submerged in the frothy water. I don't know for how long I stayed this way. It seemed as if bits of my life played out before me. But it was not like the brief flashes that I had read that people experience during death. It was very slow and very drawn-out.

It began with drawings done in black, brown, and gray. They were held by my kindergarten teacher, Mrs. Bell and they were shown to my mother sitting with her hands crossed as she tried to conceal her anxiety. "These drawings are David's," said Mrs. Bell. "Notice that each of them are done with the same dark colors. Psychologists feel that children who do such art are deeply disturbed. I think that David is a very depressed little boy."

My mother came home and asked me why I had used such colors. I explained, "We have to stand in line to pick crayons from the teacher's basket. I'm always last in line. By the time I get to the basket, those are the only colors that are left." My answer seemed to have given solace to my mother, although I'm not now convinced that I would not have picked the same colors even if I was in front of the line.

In the next episode that played before me, Brady Ballbock, a neighbor boy, and I were in the field across the street from my house. We were nine years old and we were playing with matches that I had stolen from my mother's purse. We would take turns lighting the matches and burning pieces of paper. As we continued to play this game, the papers that we burned kept getting bigger and bigger. We would throw them onto the dirt ground in front of us and laugh uncontrollably.

During one of these laughing fits, a piece of burning paper must have blown from the dirt area and ignited a patch of the long, dry weeds that covered most of the field. We made a feeble attempt to pat the fire out and saw that it was beyond repair; so we bolted the scene.

We found ourselves in front of the neighborhood elementary school. It was summer and school was not in session, but I knew that the library was open so I suggested to Brady Ballbock that we sit in the library and check out some books so that we would have a good alibi for our whereabouts.

I came home from the library with a stack of books underneath my arm, as I saw my mother and our neighbors watching the firemen putting the hoses back on the fire trucks after extinguishing the fire. The field was now scorched black and the fire had come within a few yards of reaching the Bangles' house, which was across the street from ours.

My mother grabbed my arm and said that Mrs. Bangle had seen me playing in the field moments before the fire had started. I looked straight into my mother's eyes and said that I had been at the library all afternoon and held up the books as proof. I think that I convinced her; I don't remember hearing about the incident again.

In the next episode, I had just completed my final day in the 7th grade and I was walking sheepishly home with my report card in my hand. I was mortified because I had just received my first D ever in my scholastic career. It was printed in black ink by my math teacher, Mrs. Hutter. Every half a block, I would stop walking and would look at the report card and would hope that the D was only an apparition. But each time the D shouted back to me, "Dunce!" I thought of the times in kindergarten when I needed to sit on a tall chair with a pointed cone-shaped dunce cap because the teacher thought that I was goofing off, when the class was required to skip in a circle around the classroom. The teacher thought that I was purposely trying to create a disturbance, but in truth, I was doing my best to skip properly.

It's just that I was so damn uncoordinated. The right side of my body was under-developed. Whenever I crawled as a baby, I would drag my right leg as my left leg did all of the work. When I began to walk, I dragged my right leg, Quasi Moto style and even today it is only through a concentrated effort that I walk without my right toes pointing to the side.

Thus, the dunce cap.

Anyways, back to that day in June in the 7th grade; I was staring at the D when suddenly my eyes unfocused and it became a B. I thought at first that it had miraculously transformed into a B, but when my eyes became focused again, the D stared back at me.

But being the clever juvenile delinquent that I was in those days, I immediately thought that my problem could be solved by placing another D above the one already recorded by Mrs. Hutter; thus creating a Brilliant B.

I went into Stan's Market and swiped a pen like the one that Mrs. Hutter had used. Shoplifting in the 7th grade was very commonplace for me. I hung out with the bad kids in my class that year and we boys, known as the Hart Park Gang, each had our own shoplifting specialty.

Paul McKey, our leader, stole pocket t-shirts. I never saw him in anything but a pocket t-shirt and usually the pocket held a red box of Marlboro cigarettes. Peter Wonciski stole 8 track tapes. My specialty-Swisher Sweet cigars.

These smallish cigars became my specialty quite by accident. One wintry day, I stepped into the walk-in cooler at Shron's Beverage Market to get a coke when I noticed that Swisher Sweets were also stored there. I discreetly placed a pack into the hip pocket of my coat, then walked out of the cooler, and paid for my coke. Mr. Shron and his sons looked at me suspiciously. One of the sons walked into the cooler and then briefly returned and whispered into his father's ear.

Mr. Shron demanded that I empty my pockets. I first emptied my pants pockets and tried to act as if I had already emptied the pockets of my coat. Mr. Shron said, "Now your coat." When I reached into those pockets, I did not feel the package of Swisher Sweets. I grabbed the white lining of those pockets and extended them like elephant ears. Mr. Shron apologized to me although his sons, who used to be my friends during my more innocent years, continued to look at me with suspicion.

I walked to Hart Park and then inspected my coat. I discovered that there was a rip in the lining of my left hip pocket and thus the cigars had slid to the back of my coat. From that day onward, I used that jacket for shoplifting and even cut slits into the linings of other jackets for less frigid days.

So anyways back to that day in June; I changed the D into a B and displayed my report card to my mother and she looked relieved because she had expected my grades to be much worse. The report card was displayed on the refrigerator for a few days and was then tucked away into a cardboard box that was stuffed with other documents and memorabilia.

Mr. Natural put me in the passenger seat of my mother's car in the next episode. I'm now in my early twenties and she has just picked me up from the Greyhound bus station in Appleton, Wisconsin.

I'm shivering, not because I have a cold; it's a warm September day, but because I am scared. Things have been changing much too quickly for me. I had pretended to be someone else and as a result I had lost sight of whom I really was. This loss is what scared me so on this day. Let's go back a few months to June to help explain this scene in the car, before we return there again.

I have just graduated with a B.A. in Speech from the University of Wisconsin-Eau Claire. I have decided to travel to Alaska, known then as the Final Frontier, to seek adventure before returning to the Midwest to begin my career in whatever would befit a graduate with a degree in Speech.

This degree took a circuitous route. I started my college career with a comprehensive major in Business Management, although I never took any high school courses in Business and never showed any interest in it, whatsoever. I did it because that's what most of my friends were doing. Almost immediately, I became disenchanted with this choice of major so I switched to a non-comprehensive major in Business Administration with a minor in Psychology, which quickly changed to a major in Psychology with a minor in Business Administration.

Being a Psychology major did not please me either. In lab classes, I was frightened of handling tiny mice. In other Psych classes, I was frightened of the truth. I remember being interviewed on videotape by a graduate student. She asked me questions about my life and there was not one thing that I replied truthfully. Even simple questions such as, "Number of brothers and sisters?" was answered with a lie. She started by asking me my age and I immediately lied. Once I started, the ball got rolling and everything became a fabrication. She looked totally confused at my answers and I began to think that she was suspecting their legitimacy, but what else was I to do. I couldn't stop; it had become a mammoth snowball.

Next, I became a Criminal Justice major; I envisioned myself changing the laws so that pot and other drugs would become legal. I soon saw that nothing in these classes would lead me to actualizing this pipedream.

One day I saw an advertisement for an audition of a college theatrical production of 'One Flew Over the Cuckoo's Nest.' I thought, "Yes, that's what I'll do. I'll become a theater major." I had acted in productions in high school and had received awards and notoriety. I walked down the long hall in the Fine Arts building trying to find the location where the auditions were being held. From the other side of each door that I passed, I heard operatic voices or classical piano concertos emanating from the rehearsal rooms. I became scared because I knew that I could not sing or play like those students on the other sides of the doors, so I bolted. I skipped the audition and missed a chance at being in a production that would have showcased my talent of being a nutcase.

But the next semester, I took a couple of theatre classes and felt for the first time that I now belonged. I switched my major to Speech with an emphasis in Theatre; a comprehensive major in Theatre would have been too time-consuming. Since I had accumulated so many credits in Psychology and Business, I decided to get minors in those fields. During my final semester, I needed to take one more class, a second accounting class, to achieve my minor in business. That class, I took on a pass/fail basis, and passed. It was up to that time, one of the most painful experiences in my lifetime.

Anyways, I had just graduated from college and I was seeking adventure in Alaska. A college buddy and I found employment working in a fish factory in Anchorage. However, Bill, my buddy, got homesick for his girlfriend back in Wisconsin so he flew back within a couple of weeks. His exodus created for me the inspiration that I had been desiring. Now as a solo act, I didn't need to worry about the concerns of others, I needed to worry only about myself and my actions became more spontaneous.

I began to write poetry non-stop. The paper towels from the fish factory were my stationary. My sleeping accommodations were under bridges or wherever I decided to throw down my sleeping bag that night.

I read Walt Whitman and Jack Kerouac religiously and discovered Robert W. Service, whose poem, 'A Rolling Stone,' became my mantra. I hitchhiked to bluegrass festivals throughout the state and sang my ever-popular, 'Livin' like a Bum'. I felt a freedom unlike any that I had ever experienced before. I'm quite sure that I was mad during this period but it was such a euphoric madness, that neither I nor the people that I met were bothered in the least.

The crew at the fish factory was an odd assortment of characters: Don was a good-natured, always smiling Aleutian, Big Joe was a burley and boastful redheaded teenager who came from the state of Washington with his sidekick, Loveable Lenny. There were three Lutheran ministers-to-be and Snake, the forklift driver, who would pass me a pipe containing Matanuska Thunderstick pot before taking the stack of freshly, laid racks of salmon to the glazing station.

My first job at the fish factory was as a slimer. I would grab the freshly gutted salmon from the conveyer belt and grab the heart and slime that ran along the fish's spine. Then I would throw the heart and slime across the conveyor belt at the slimer standing on the opposite side from me. The slime would be wiped from our faces if it was a direct hit and would slide down our yellow rubber aprons and collect in a slippery mess alongside our tall rubber boats.

Then the salmon would proceed further down the conveyor belt to the grading station where the graders would check the weight and quality of each fish. There was a scale at this station but Don the Aleutian, never used it. He knew instantly the fish's weight; at times I tested his accuracy by weighing his fish myself and he was always right on the mark.

From the grading station, the fish were placed on their appropriate sides of the next conveyor belt where they would meet up with the racker at the end. This job became my favorite not only because that's where Snake provided me with the Thunderstick but also because Big Joe usually stood on the opposite side from me and we would compete to see who could complete the stacks of racks first. Big Joe was clearly the stronger and taller of us two, but the inspiration that I would receive from Snake seemed to make me the Dr. J of racking. I was swift and smooth as I laid the salmon down always keeping the heads on the outside and the stomach cuts in. Big Joe slapped the racks down with authority like a Shaquille O'Neil but my racks stacked up with the finesse of a Connie Hawkins' finger roll. When I was in my groove, there was no stopping me and Big Joe would become clearly agitated and would begin to make mistakes and mishandle the fish or racks.

Each Wednesday night the entire crew would head downtown to McDonald's for the 'All You Can Eat Flapjack Special.' This event again became a showcase for Big Joe's and my talents. The others would usually stop somewhere in the teens but Big Joe and I would never consider stopping until we had reached at least 30. Don, the Aleutian, and Loveable Lenny would keep count for each of us by announcing to the other patrons whether we were close to breaking another record. Afterwards, I would usually swaddle back to the fish factory and sneak into a room filled with stacks of flattened cardboard boxes. Snake had made a secret tunnel between the stacks that led to a small open area where my sleeping bag awaited me.

From the fish factory, I would stare across the city to the Cheynuga Mountain Range. The mountains, which would continually change colors due to the sun or cloud cover, seemed to be calling me to enter. It frustrated me that I had come to Alaska to seek adventure, but I had not yet hiked up even a foothill. I decided that on the following weekend, I would be in the mountains.

I took a bus to what I thought would be my best place to begin my ascent. When I got off the bus, I discovered that a barbed wire fence kept me from hiking inward. Signs were along the fence that said, "Keep Out! Restricted Area. Military Maneuvers." I walked for a very long time along the fence, but could see no end in sight. Meanwhile, the mountains kept beckoning me to enter. They were so close and yet so far away. In a fit of frustration and reckless what the heckedness, I threw my backpack over the fence and then scaled it myself.

I boldly hiked through the restricted area, but became much more cautious when I began to hear artillery fire nearby. Each time that I heard shots, I would duck undercover. Finally, I reached another fence and quickly climbed over it to get out of harm's way. I now found myself at the base of the mountain.

With my first step upward, the sky suddenly opened and rain poured down upon me. I kept trudging onward although the muddy path became very slippery. I fell a few times but got right back up. I was determined to reach the top although my clothing and boots were now drenched with rainfall and wet clay. As I hiked, I wrote the first of my songs in the "I Want" series.

"I want to live a good life.

I want to be real kind.

I want to have that peaceful, easy feelin'.

Everything bad behind.

No more headaches

My body's running fine

My eyes are glowin',

The water is flowin',

The sky so high is mine.

A bird flies over yonder.

She whistles as she flies

My feet in mud.

A swishin' in crud.

Won't fly 'til I die.

I want to live a good life.

I want to be real kind.

I want to have that peaceful, easy feelin',

Everything bad behind.

After a few hours I became exhausted and saw that the summit was beyond my reach. I found an open area nearby some trees that I had hoped would serve as an umbrella while I pitched my tent, but they did not. The rain turned into hail as I set up my tent and drove the stakes into the ground. Once complete, I threw my backpack into the tent and then tried to find an area inside that was not already soaked. Fortunately, I had put my sleeping bag and an extra set of clothing into plastic bags, so I tore off my wet clothing, threw them into a corner of the tent, put on my dry clothing, and then immediately lay inside my sleeping bag. Now relatively content, I decided that I would stay in this position on my back so as not to roll into the surrounding wet areas of the tent.

All was well until I began to smell. My clothes were, of course, the clothes that I had worn when I was working at the fish factory. Now inside this small pup tent, the smell of salmon overwhelmed me. I thought about the area that I had just pitched my tent and I realized from the growth of trees that I was most likely in bear country. I smelled like a gigantic king salmon and I was lying in my tomb-like tent in the habitat of the grizzly. Although I was exhausted beyond reproach, I decided that I needed to immediately pack up my tent again or I would soon become the main entrée for a lucky Yogi. I made it back down the mountain and found a way to the bus stop that avoided the military maneuvers and maneuvered my way through the stacks of cardboard in the box room, lay down in my damp sleeping bag, and slept soundly throughout the night with no fear of bears attacking me.

Some days later it was payday, so I decided to head down to the bank and cash my check. As I stood in line I noticed that there were still fish guts on my clothing and I must have smelled pretty bad because the people waiting in line behind me were a good six feet away.

With money in hand, I walked to a thrift sale that was taking place by the rescue mission where I had spent a night when I had no money or food. At the sale I purchased a bright blue plaid sportscoat; brand name Botany 500, a touch of class. Also, I threw in a buck for a chain, which I wore around my neck to complement the string of beads that I had acquired at the Talkeetna Bluegrass Festival. To me, the beads signified good times and the chain signified charity. The only comment that I was ever given about this chain was from an Anchorage woman, who allowed me to spend some time in her apartment, feeding me rum and steamed broccoli with seasoned croutons. She said, "That's a really ugly chain."

The final item that I purchased was a beautifully constructed black, balloon-tired bicycle for a mere twenty bucks. Off I went on my bicycle wearing my new sportscoat and my really ugly chain through the streets of downtown Anchorage. After participating in my daily ritual of a 25 cent ice cream cone from the Golden Arches, I pedaled into the seedy section of town and was suddenly overcome with the harsh realization that there was nobody within a great distance of me that gave a roarin' shit about my existence. I was alone in this big stinkin' city without anyone to love or to love me.

Pedaling blindly with this ugly thought, I passed a blurred figure on the corner whose words hit my ears, "Wanna date?" Pedaling forward about ten yards, it finally hit me that I was the one being addressed. I maneuvered a U-turn and braked along this now focused figure, who wore a pretty dress and had an okay face of about 21.

"What's that you said?" I asked.

"Ya wanna date?" she replied.

"Yeah, that sounds like a real good idea."

"How much money you got?"

"Oh, quite a bit."

"Enough for a motel room?"

"Oh, I got enough for a decent meal and a couple of drinks."

"Forget it."

"You sure?"

"Yeah, forget it. Get lost."

"Okay, happy hunting," I replied and pedaled away now even lonelier than I was before. I said aloud to myself, "I need to find a friend now," and turned the corner and saw a large wooden sign on a shop that said, "PETS – MAN'S BEST FRIEND." Instantly, I knew that this would cure my blues.

I took off the rope that I used to hold my pants up and tied up my black stallion outside of the shop. Inside the pet store, I was greeted by a pretty teenager named Mary who offered to help me find the perfect travel companion. She first took me to the birds where I saw a brightly colored parrot stoically standing in its private cage. Instantly, images of me standing alongside the road with my thumb out and the parrot on my shoulder came to my mind. I thought that perhaps he would be too big and require too much maintenance, so Mary took me to a cage full of black mice. I had always had a fear of mice dating back to my college days when I was required to handle them in my psychology lab classes. But I needed a friend badly so I grabbed one and he started digging into my hand. I got scared and threw him back into the cage. Feeling desperation for friendship, I held out my hand in the cage again and waited for a mouse to come. But no more came, so I grabbed one and threw him into a shoebox and gave him a name. His name was Buddy. Buddy Boo Boo. Buddy Boo Boo Booper.

It took a while for each of us to get used to each other, but within days we were good friends and Buddy would stand up and peek out of the breast pocket of my plaid sportscoat as we bicycled throughout the city. We would usually end up at a park where I would lay on the grass and bask in the sun while Buddy would curl up next to me in the shadow that my stomach made. Later, however, Buddy would discover that there was a bigger world beyond my shadow and he wanted to explore it. I didn't want to lose my buddy so I started keeping him in a cage which seemed to piss him off. He was continually trying to escape and it became a constant battle between him, the inmate, and me, the warden.

Around this time the three Lutheran ministers-to-be decided that they were going to head back down to Wisconsin to continue their religious training and they offered me a ride in their van. It was late August and the salmon season was coming to a close, but I decided to stick around longer and experience the shrimp season.

I decided that I had enough of living in box rooms, on beach strips, under bridges, and in rescue missions so I decided to find a more normal place to live. I posted ads on the break room bulletin board. The first one said, "Need help with rent? Washed-out beach dweller seeks shelter. Bedroom unnecessary. Floor is fine. Contact Slimer Dave." I didn't get any replies. The second one was painted with a simple Japanese background and said, "Aspiring Zen Lunatic seeks Bodhisattva equipped with temple to share in cosmic quest for The Eternal Truth. Inquire within. Dharma Dave." No reply. The third message said, "Live with primitive man. Study anthropology firsthand. Contact Hairy Dave." From this ad I got an offer to sleep on the floor of an apartment rented by two workers. For a small fee, I also had bathroom and kitchen privileges.

The crews changed for the shrimp season and I became attracted to a pretty co-worker. I invited her over to my place for dinner and spent the afternoon preparing a shrimp salad and baking an apple pie. When she accepted my invitation, I was delighted although a bit surprised, but as the time passed and I saw that she was 15 minutes, then 30, then 45, then an hour late, I realized that she had interpreted my invitation as a joke and had never really intended to meet with me.

I went back to work the next day and acted as if nothing had happened although I felt deeply embarrassed and hurt. I pulled out a month old letter from my girlfriend in Wisconsin and decided that I would hitchhike back to Wisconsin to marry her. Buddy Boo Boo Booper, I decided, would not make the trip. He was constantly fighting with me for his freedom, so I decided to give it to him. I bought a huge bag of birdseed for him and we rode together on my bicycle to the park where we used to hang out. I found a comfortable wooded area that I thought that he would like, opened the bag of birdseed, and set him down beside it. He looked excitedly around and then stared at me with a quizzical look of "What's up?"

I replied, "Buddy, for weeks now you have been seeking your freedom. Well today, my friend, you are going to get it. This is your new home if you decide to stay here. There's plenty of food for you and this looks like a nice, safe spot. I'll just sit here for a little while to make sure that you'll be okay." Buddy looked at me as if he was trying to decide whether or not I was joking, then tried a little sampling of the birdseed, and disappeared in the underbrush never to be seen by me again.

Over the years many a time have I thought about my buddy, Buddy, and wondered what he did with his freedom. Did he stay with the birdseed or did he forge ahead and begin his new life without any of my assistance? Was the birdseed a bad idea? Did it attract other more powerful creatures, who destroyed Buddy instantly? If Buddy had made it to the winter, how did he survive it? Did he find someone's warm home and nestle inside the wall alongside the fireplace? Perhaps he decided that he didn't like his freedom and crept out to an unsuspecting greenhorn lying in the park and made his home in the shadow of the man's stomach.

My first day of hitchhiking back to the lower 48 was not very successful. I got a short ride which put me in the middle of nowhere where no cars or people passed. I spent the entire day in this village which consisted of a bar, with a few very unfriendly and inhospitable inhabitants, and a post office. As night fell, I started to suspect that the bar hounds were plotting to kill or rape me, so I ended up hiding in the ditch by the post office. My sleeping bag became very damp during the night and I shivered throughout without a wink of sleep.

Early the next morning, my luck changed and I was picked up by a guy and his dog who were going all the way to New York in their truck. The man seemed pleased to have someone else to talk with besides Roger, his dog. I was tempted to go with him all the way to Manitoba, north of Minnesota, but as we entered Alberta I decided that I would stop in Calgary and visit some friends. Juan and Elmo were twin brothers who had gone to school in Eau Claire with me. These furry freak brothers had duo US/Canadian citizenship and I remembered before departing from Eau Claire that Elmo was moving to Calgary to study archaeology. Juan, I suspected, would be there as well, since these twins were rarely apart.

Arriving into Calgary, I found a pay phone and called directory assistance. Elmo's number was listed; I called him and he gave me directions to his house. Arriving there I found that Juan had recently come from an extended stay in Central America where he said he had lain in hammocks and smoked pot. He now sat in a corner by a sun-illumined window and was absorbed in reading a biography of Adolf Hitler. Elmo, the friendlier of the two, welcomed me into his home and rolled a joint from which we subsequently partook. With the scent of ganja in the air, a gigantic figure appeared at the front door. His name now escapes me but looking back he seems like some drug-crazed Canadian equivalent to Seinfeld's Kramer. The joint was passed to him and he bogarted it until Elmo was able to wrestle it away. Kramer then opened the window from where Juan sat and climbed outside and hung with his arms from the ledge for a good part of the rest of the afternoon.

Elmo and I talked about what each of us had done since departing Eau Claire, while Juan stayed transfixed to the Hitler book, and every once in a while Kramer would comment from beneath the 3rd floor window. This situation seemed to be a regular occurrence at Elmo's. Whenever pot was lit, Elmo remarked, Kramer would instantly appear from his attic apartment, bogart the joint, and then hang outside their window.

Kramer's behavior was certainly odd, but I began to understand it when I saw the transformation that the pot seemed to be having on me. My speech pattern changed dramatically and I found myself speaking in a heavy Russian accent using the grammar of a cave man. My posture also changed as I stood with abnormally straight posture with my arms rigidly crossed in front of my chest.

"So what did you do in Alaska, Dave?" asked Elmo.

"I work," I replied.

"What type of work, Dave?"

"Fish."

"You were a fisherman?"

"No, I slime." Then I went into a stiff pantomime performance in which I grabbed the imaginary slime from the imaginary fish's spine and threw it across the imaginary conveyor belt at the imaginary co-worker who stood opposite me. Juan looked up from his Hitler book for the first time since I had entered and he and Elmo exchanged looks that said, "Dave has flipped his lid."

Some English lasses from across the street visited and Elmo requested that I share with them my experience in Alaska.

"I eat, I work, I sleep."

"Where did you sleep, David?" the pretty blonde asked.

"I sleep in dark," I answered.

"Did you see the Aurora Borealis?"

"Yah."

"Did you see Mount Everest?"

"Yah."

"Did you see grizzly bears?"

"Yah. I smell like fish."

They were all amused at my behavior, but I was shocked because no matter how much I tried to speak normally, I could not. Juan and Elmo invited me to join them for a day-trip into the Rocky Mountains, but I declined because I wanted to try to get back my normal speech pattern. It was embarrassing for me that I couldn't have a normal conversation with the blonde girl. I sat alone in the apartment and tried to speak normally but did not have any success. I wondered whether I had been speaking that way for weeks now but had only noticed it when I had gotten together with old friends. Looking back it seemed as if I didn't have many conversations with people in Alaska; I was usually scribbling my thoughts on bar napkins or paper towels. My lack of practice in verbalizing my thoughts probably led me to this present condition rather than the pot as I had originally assumed.

As I sat alone in the apartment trying to utter one sound that came from my normal voice, I thought how a similar condition to this had happened to me many years before. As a child, I had created my own language. I had substituted the correct sounds for other sounds and my speech was incomprehensible to everyone except the two neighbor girls that I played with, Marla and Amy Smolinski. I went to speech therapy for three years and had never made a bit of progress. However, in my fourth year I worked with a new therapist. She was a young, pretty brunette who I was highly attracted toward. I felt ashamed about the way that I was speaking with her. Almost instantly, my speech pattern changed and I began to speak normally.

Perhaps this would work again, I thought. So I decided to walk across the street and pay a visit to the blonde cutie. She was alone in her apartment and invited me in for some tea. I struggled to break out of the Russian cave man spell that I was under. She suggested that I relax and uncross my arms, but I found that impossible to do. She stood behind me and massaged my shoulders, back, and arms until finally my arms relaxed and hung down beside my body and my normal speech pattern returned.

The next day I set off on the road again with my thumb pointing upward and found myself in Winnipeg by day's end where I tried to sleep underneath a slide in a children's playground in order to keep the rain from pouring down upon me.

A couple of days later, I was knocking on the front door of Grace's house in Eau Claire. As I waited for the door to open, I thought how I would propose to her. Would I bend down on one knee and ask, "Will you marry me?" or would I go into a long speech about the discovery of my love for her. The door opened and instantly this pipedream shattered. Grace stood at the door smiling at me and she looked good, but I knew that I was not ready to propose to her. It was Alaska that had created this illusion for me. Living in the land of the midnight sun does strange things to minds as vulnerable as mine.

I spent a few days back at my mom's place and then cut my long hair and beard, put on a suit and tie and set off for Minneapolis, where I decided I would try to make it in the business world. If Mary Tyler Moore could make it there, then why not me?

In Minneapolis, I stayed with some friends and tried to interview for various positions, such as a vacuum cleaner salesman and an administrative assistant but soon grew disillusioned when I discovered that I had neither the skills nor the motivation to do those types of work. Before each interview, I knew that I didn't have a chance at getting the position, but something inside kept me pressing on. Until one day, I snapped and tore off my jacket and tie and left my briefcase in the reception room of some office building and caught the next greyhound bus back to Appleton.

My mom picked me up at the bus station and my voice was trembling as I said, "I don't know what I am anymore, Mom. Things are changing too fast. I need to just slow down and rest a while. Can I stay with you for a couple of weeks?" "Of course," she replied. But I only stayed a few days and then I was off to Minneapolis again. This time, however, I had no ambition to make it in the business world. I was going to try to get work as an actor.

Still submerged in my bathtub, the next episode of my life had me standing at the lectern of the Lamira Funeral Home in my hometown, Menasha, Wisconsin delivering a eulogy for my stepdad, Jed Modine. It was the winter of '83 (I was 25) and I had just flown back to Wisconsin after having moved to San Francisco two months before. I had traveled to San Francisco in a beat-up yellow V.W. bug with a woman who was going to San Jose to study massage. She had advertised on a University of Minnesota bulletin board that she was looking for someone to share the driving. I had lied to her when I said that driving a car with standard transmission would be no problem for me. I had never mastered this technique after numerous unsuccessful attempts. My under-developed right side kept me from shifting the gears and releasing the clutch with the fluidity that was necessary to keep the car running. My driving companion learned this about me somewhere in Nebraska when I assumed my position behind the wheel. She, however, was very patient and took me through step by step and I was actually able to get the car across most of Nebraska even though we almost landed in a ditch a few times.

When we got near the Rocky Mountains she said that she would handle the driving and for the rest of the trip, I remained in the passenger seat. We entered San Francisco on Halloween night of '83. I had expected to stay there for only a couple of weeks before continuing down to Hollywood where I would become a movie star, but I never left.

Within the first week of my arrival into San Francisco, I had landed an acting job performing Shakespeare to Bay Area school children and a room in a flat in the lower Haight Street district. The flat was occupied by an odd assortment of characters like me. Luke was a gnarly under-achiever from Indiana U. who would continuously be proclaiming someone as being reactionary in his gruff staccato voice or he would hide away in his small room by the kitchen and obsessively whack off. Sleazy Randy fried the most god awful mystery meat on a regular basis. I would need to leave the flat for a few hours and then return and open up all of the windows while holding my nose, otherwise I'd puke. Arthur, who called himself Slim, would sit in his room for hours on end reading comic books that he had wrapped in plastic folders, which were stored in neatly arranged boxes. Big Frankie, a Zen lunatic guitar-playin' singer-songwriter, had an enormous head. Once he bent over to pick up a box in the hallway and his head went into and through the wall like a wrecking ball at a demolition site. And Richmond, who described himself as an industrial musician and artist although every song that he played on his guitar sounded the same and every painting that he did were simple red and black designs on white butcher paper which would be torn down and destroyed by some mysterious art critic whenever we had a party.

Later some of the boys moved out and the flat became less sleazy and more gender gentrified. There was Crazy Lidia, a beautician, who was always asking others how her butt looked and was always in search of that perfect soul-mate who was well-endowed. John and Martha, who met each other at the flat and fell in love; they then moved to Pacifica to raise a family. Cecilia, a coke-crazed French girl who was having an affair with her married Rastafarian konga teacher. Penny, who made me physically sick upon the sight of her; Big Frankie and Richmond had agreed to let her move in without my knowledge. When I met her on her first day at the flat, I was repulsed by her bad complexion, rat-like eyes, and grating voice that kept repeating, "I am one happy camper." I went immediately to the shower and tried to wash away the filth of such an odious creature. There were also a couple of teenage runaway nymphs that tried to share their rooms with their shirtless, white trash boyfriends. And then there was Billy.

Billy was a greasy-haired, very short southern man, who always wore the same grey three piece suit. Big Frankie worked with him as a messenger at a law office and brought him in to live with us. Every day, Billy would cook his hobo coffee; he would throw the coffee grounds into a large pot of boiling water and then drink the coffee, grounds included. He would obsess about a friendship with a woman, who he claimed to be Bob Dylan's first wife, Sarah, and would become violent if anyone doubted him. He was a little guy with a very short fuse.

One Halloween we went to a party at the 16th Note, a bar in the Mission. I was dressed as Zippy the Pinhead in an elaborate costume that I had made for my role in an independent film. Big Frankie was a toy keystone cop and Billy was Billy in his grey three-piece suit.

While the costumed partiers danced on the main floor to the singing of immodest underwearless Tina and her band Excessive Hilarity, Billy sat alone on an iron spiral staircase that led to nowhere. He was drinking a bottle of rotgut and building up his rage, which he later unleashed outside the bar after he was bounced out for bringing in outside liquor.

Billy was involved in an argument outside of the bar and Big Frankie pacified him by calmly saying, "It's alright, Billy," and rubbing his greasy head as they walked away.

The man who had been in the argument said, "Asshole."

Big Frankie bent down to Billy and whispered in his ear, "Go get him, Billy," and Billy's eyes lit up as if he was a prophet, who had heard the voice of God and he went and got him.

Big Frankie and I kept walking up the street for about a block, but then turned back to fetch Billy. We got back to the bar and asked a solitary guy standing outside if he had seen a short guy in a three-pieced suit.

The man's eyes widened and he replied, "Oh, you mean Billy?"

"Yeah, where's Billy?" Big Frankie asked.

"Billy's somewhere between God and the devil," the man answered and pointed in the direction of the projects a block away.

We, Zippy the Pinhead and the Toy Keystone Cop, walked through the crack-dealer-infested urban housing project in search of our Billy, but came up empty and went home as the crackheads guffawed, "Look at the pinhead, look at the pinhead."

The next day Billy wasn't home but we got a call from him in jail. He had been arrested because he tried to buy a bottle of hootch in the Safeway grocery store after the hour in which it could be sold. When the cashier refused to make the transaction, Billy got angry and smashed the bottle on the floor. The cops took him away and they found out that he was wanted in Los Angeles for jumping bail. He now was staying in the San Francisco County Jail before being sent down to Los Angeles. For the first time, he wasn't wearing his grey three-piece suit; he was wearing bright orange instead.

There were also our next door neighbors, which consisted of a continuously changing supply of Irish boys and girls and American teenage nymphs. Max Tuesday was the only consistent long-term resident in this flat. The residents of the two flats would be continuously climbing from one second floor kitchen window into the other to check out the action in the other flat – all except me. I never climbed through those windows because of my weak right side and also because I always imagined myself falling and splitting in two beginning at the groin from the picket fence below that divided the two properties. Instead I'd take the long journey up the ladder and over the roof whenever I wanted to party next door.

One night Max Tuesday and I got really high and we found some cans of spray paint on the roof and we decided to set off throughout the neighborhood beautifying it. Max was an experienced spray artist, but for me it was the first time. I focused mainly on painting shadows. Shadows of motorcycles on sidewalks or trees on houses were accentuated with bright colors and given permanency. All of our work was done without inhibitions or fear that we would get busted. We saw our work as something that everyone in the community would enjoy and appreciate.

We were in the middle of one piece of art on a house about a block away from home, when we saw a cop car creeping away up the street and then suddenly making a U-turn. Max and I dropped the cans and scurried on home and laughed as we got to our front gate 'cuz we felt that we had outrun The Man, but as we fumbled for our keys, our giggles of glee turned into shivers of shock as we saw that we were surrounded by a half a dozen police cars.

One of the cops grabbed me by my long goatee and then threw me against the car and slapped on the 'cuffs behind my back and threw me into the backseat of the car alongside my buddy, Max. As we drove to the station, Max and I tried to convince them that it was art that we were doing not graffiti, but it was to no avail.

At the police station in Golden Gate Park, I gave them my driver's license but Max said that he had no I.D. and gave them a false name. They put us together in a holding cell and handcuffed Max to a bench with both hands behind his back. I was handcuffed to the bench as well, but only with one hand.

Max whispered to me that I needed to get his driver's license out of his pocket and hide it in my sock. "Why?" I asked.

"Davey, I'm on probation. If they find out who I am, I'm up shit creek."

I then remembered that Max was on probation for stealing some Picassos and Paul Klees from the San Francisco Museum of Modern Art. He was given leniency because of his young age and because he had notified the authorities of the location of the artwork before they caught him.

I grabbed the driver's license from Max's pocket and put it inside my sock as I had been instructed to do. But it didn't feel right so I kept pushing the license down until it rested inside my sock and underneath my foot. Immediately thereafter, the police came back and searched us. Max was stripsearched and I was searched everywhere except for the insides of my socks underneath my feet.

We were put back into the holding cell and stayed there until dawn singing gospel songs in two-part harmony. Some of the cops seemed to appreciate our singing while others were very eager to get us out of there. We were given a court date and released.

I was very nervous about going to court because I knew that Max had no intention of attending and that I would have to commit perjury and tell the judge that I didn't know Max's identity. Fortunately, when I arrived at court, I found out that the case had been thrown out, so I never needed to lie.

Above Max's flat there was a Japanese reggae band called Yogi Mota. These Jap cats were constantly tripping on something and were spiritually advised by the resident Zen priest, Jahmahto, who was always grinning and always had a watchful eye for the nubiles. Toh, the leader of the band, had a beautiful Japanese wife, who also sang with the band and cooked delicious delicacies, and a small daughter. He left both of them after he became bewitched by an unattractive, poorly-coordinated dancing French woman whom we called Yoko.

For my first New Year's in San Francisco, 1984, I decided to go hang out with Deadheads outside of the Civic Center while the Grateful Dead were playing inside. I was just kind of making the scene when I looked over my left shoulder and saw what looked like a drug deal taking place. I thought, "God, wouldn't it be great if I could pick up some mushrooms tonight." I turned back forward and right in front of me nose to nose was a frizzy, red-haired, purple-clad hippie, who asked, "You want to buy some mushrooms?" Needless to say, he had a sale; he could have asked any price and I would have agreed. We made the transaction and I finished off the bag of mushrooms as if they were a bag of Cheetos.

After a while the mushrooms began to take effect and I imagined myself as the stock car driver Richard Petty winding around the curves and passing the Deadheads on the racetrack. After a few times around the track, I decided to head up to North Beach. I passed through Chinatown as old Chinese men with wide mischievous grins threw packs of firecrackers at my feet. Once in North Beach, I walked along the crowded sidewalks past the many strip joints.

I noticed that my tongue was continually waggling across my face as if I were a camel who had just ingested a wad of peanut butter. I also had the irresistible urge for a hotdog. Across Columbus Street, I noticed a little stand that looked as if it might be selling hotdogs. Unfortunately for me, the street was now moving like a gigantic escalator. Cops on their horses sped by on this moving runway. I stepped to the curb and cautiously put my left foot forward and walked across the street at a brisk pace and found that when I arrived to the other side, the escalator had transported me a block up from where I had intended to go. I finally got to the stand, but all that they served was ice cream. I ordered two scoops of strawberry but after one lick, I knew that it wasn't what I wanted, so I dropped it on the sidewalk at my feet and stared at it. The strawberry scoops became bloodshot eyes and the sugar cone was the nose that seemed to be growing like Pinocchio's.

Pinocchio suggested that I go into Vesuvio's, the bar across the alley from the City Lights Bookstore. I entered Vesuvio's and climbed the stairs to the second level and thought that I was on a train headed to Chicago. Somehow I got off the train and found myself walking along some dark streets in the middle of Chinatown. Gangs of teenage boys appeared in each alley that I walked past. I tried to get my bearing by looking at the street signs. I saw the signs okay and was familiar with the streets, but at this time I had no idea where the streets were. I stumbled along as my coat became heavier and heavier. Carloads of people kept stopping and asking me where such and such a place was and all I could reply was, "Shit."

Finally I got down to Market Street and waited at the bus stop. Suddenly the air seemed awfully quiet. A fellow ran by me and I asked him what time it was. We looked at his watch and at that precise moment the minute hand met with the hour hand at the twelve and it was exactly midnight on the button.

"Happy New Year," we said in unison as car horns began blaring across the city. I turned to my right and there seated at the bus stop was an old lady looking straight at me with tears running down her face.

The bus arrived and I sat next to a fellow who was on his way to an A.A. meeting. As the man rambled on in deadpan sarcasm about the exciting events that would take place at the meeting, an old black man in a porkpie hat continually turned around from his seat a few rows ahead of me and laughed at me while spinning one of those cranking New Year's party toys. All that I could think about was getting home and going to my room and turning off the lights and lying in bed. Finally, the bus got to my stop and I turned the key to my door and there at the top of the stairs was Slim, the comic book geek, with a bottle of wine. I had never seen him drink before, but since it was the New Year he had decided to get a bottle of wine to celebrate. He had probably been waiting all night at the top of the stairs for someone to come home and share the bottle with him. Unfortunately for me, I was the first one back. Although I told Slim that I didn't want to drink or socialize, he followed me into my room and sat down in a chair alongside my bed. I lay there on my back as Slim began to express his dissatisfaction over his life's current circumstances. He began to talk about the death of his grandfather, a topic with which he was obsessed. All that I could do was lie on my back with my eyes closed and pray that he would go away, but he didn't. Hours later he was still talking about the uselessness of his life and I turned to him and streams of tears were running down his face. Finally another roommate came home and Slim grabbed his wine bottle and went off in pursuit of him. I lay alone in the dark room as an overwhelming sense of loneliness and despair permeated my being. I grabbed a blanket and wrapped it around me and huddled in a corner of my room as I obsessed about the impossibility of myself ever having sex again. On the wall I wrote in barely legible red marker:

How does it feel

    to be all alone?

No one you'll see

    No one to phone.

Jackals and Jekyls

    Failures and Blues

Insights which often

    We never will use.

Poems never written

    Fish never snared

Fossils forgotten

    One never paired.

But that was New Year's 1984 and my Mr. Natural bathtub vision took me to a month earlier in December of '83. I was at the lectern delivering the eulogy for my stepdad. My eyes were glued to the paper as I read about his likes for chocolate kisses, horses, golf, and football and his dislike of phoniness. I began to hyperventilate but got my composure back and finished my speech. I wasn't entirely sure if my hyperventilating was real or whether I got caught up in the emotion of the scene; everyone was crying. After the speech I went back to my seat and tears started storming out of my eyes like a river. It felt good. The whole time since I heard that he had died, I had wanted to cry but the tears wouldn't come. It felt really good when they finally did.

All of my family complimented me for the speech and told me how happy my stepdad would have been since I had shaved off my long beard and had gotten a haircut for the funeral. He and I had been continually at odds with each other about my appearance.

After flying back to San Francisco, I decided to hitchhike to the northeastern tip of California because a Rainbow Gathering was happening there. Thousands of hippies were gathered there indulging in all kinds of drugs and camping out in a communal setting.

One night I hiked alone into the forest wearing my stepdad's old Green Bay Packer stocking cap. I came upon a lone campsite away from the hordes of hippies and the hermit tenant there was an old long-haired hippie named Hair. Hair invited me to sit down and share some tea. I noticed immediately that Hair's face was identical to my stepdad's. I shared this observation with Hair and told him about the torrential relationship that I had been through with my stepdad. Hair assured me, "I'm sure that he was very proud of you, David. He just didn't understand." I thanked Hair for the tea and said that I'd like to visit him again. He replied, "I'm sure that one day we will meet again."

In the moonlit night I made it back to my tent and awoke the next morning to find that my Packer cap was missing. "Perhaps I had left it back at Hair's camp," I thought and so I set off through the forest trying to find it. But although I searched numerous times, I never again found the campsite, nor its hermit Hair, nor the cap that had belonged to my stepdad.

Mr. Natural then put me in darkness. I am lying on my back and I cannot move and I am screaming, "I need help! Is anyone there? Help!" but no one comes to my rescue.

A few days before, it was Christmas Eve day and I was driving a motorcycle that I had rented on an island in the Philippines. The bike was running very poorly as I drove along the dirt paths and I found that in order to keep the engine running, I needed to drive it with a greater velocity than I was comfortable.

I came to a spot where I needed to turn left, but I knew that I was driving too fast to make the turn. I crashed and my left knee hit a sharp rock in the path. I stood up and looked down and saw that severed veins were oozing blood down my leg and onto the dirt path. I felt like I was going to pass out, so I sat down.

A family up the path saw the accident and the man drove his tuk-tuk (motorcycle with attached cabin) and loaded me onto it and drove me toward the hospital. In front of us were other tuk-tuks filled with tourists driving slowly along the path. My driver kept pounding on his horn, but the other drivers ignored him as blood kept shooting out of my leg.

Finally we reached the small hospital and the doctor, who looked like the boy that I had been playing basketball with the day before, started pouring buckets of water over my knee. He decided that there was nothing he could do for me, so the nurses wrapped my knee in towels and I was loaded back into the bloody tuk-tuk to be transported to the harbor to get on a boat to take me to another island with a bigger hospital.

The water was very choppy as I sat in the small, thin boat that was balanced by sticks of bamboo. When we reached the island, our boat nestled next to a large boat of photo-happy tourists, whose faces turned to terror when they saw me.

A very muscular Philippino walked through the water and told me to sit on his shoulders. I said, "I'm very heavy. You won't be able to carry me."

He replied, "No problem. Sit on my shoulders," and lowered himself so that I could get on him. He walked through the water and carried me with ease and placed me in another tuk-tuk, which sped down the path with my legs hanging out of the side. The path was very bumpy and each time that we hit a hole, I thought that the bottom half of my leg was going to fall off. I could see the cartilage and bone of my knee because the towels had opened up and were now drenched in blood.

The tuk-tuk stopped in front of the hospital but braked too late and my leg hit a large metal pole and I screamed loudly. I was wheeled into the emergency room and the doctor and nurses entered to work on me when the lights went out. Brown-outs, as they are called there, were a common occurrence in the Philippine Islands. I lay on the cot laughing hysterically as they set up a generator.

"He's in shock," said the doctor to the nurses. I asked them to give me some medication to relieve the pain, but the doctor said, "We must wait until we have done further analysis."

"What further analysis do you need?" I laughed. "I'm in f*!kin' pain and we need to f*!kin' kill it."

The generator turned the light back on and the doctor proceeded to put a long metal cone down my knee that extended down to my foot. The doctor explained, "The doctor at the other island performed very badly. The water that he poured on your knee has sent the dirt down to your foot. We must pump it out before we can begin to mend you." He embarked upon the pumping process and I, still without painkillers, sang Christmas carols to distract me from what was happening.

The pumping seemed to last forever and finally they gave me some painkillers before beginning to mend me. The painkillers did not help. The doctor asked me whether I drank a lot and said, "For alcoholics, painkillers have very little effect."

"I'm not an alcoholic," I protested. "I just need some stronger pills. These pills couldn't get a flea high," and I began to laugh some more. I started talking to the doctor about all of the experimentation that I had done with various drugs and then I repeated, "I am not an alcoholic."

As they packed the veins back into my leg and stitched me, I exclaimed, "Looks like a big Christmas turkey. What's your favorite part of Christmas dinner, Doc?"

He answered, "I like mashed potatoes with gravy."

A nurse said, "I like cranberry sauce."

"Cranberry sauce on potatoes?" I said. "That's disgusting."

"No," she answered, "cranberry sauce on the side with fresh cranberries."

"I like the jelloed cranberry that comes out of the can. As it slides out, it makes a funny sound, pplllopp," I onomatopoeiaed and laughed hysterically again.

"I think the drugs have taken effect," the doctor told the nurse.

I was put in the recovery room, which had swinging saloon-like doors and throughout my time there, villagers would peer into the room because a rumor was being spread around the village that Hulk Hogan was in the hospital. "I'm not that silly, phony wrestler," I proclaimed to them. "I have much more hair. I'm more handsome."

They set up a flight for me to go to a Manila hospital because my infection was very severe. I was afraid that I was going to lose my leg so I decided that I'd rather fly back to San Francisco so that I would get American medical care. Since it had already been arranged for me to go to the Manila hospital, once I got off the small plane in Manila, I was put into an ambulance and taken to the Manila hospital and checked in and then immediately checked out before I was taken back to the airport.

When I boarded the 747 destined for San Francisco, I needed to get to my seat without any assistance because invalids were not allowed to travel by themselves. For the first time, I tried to stand up by myself. It was extremely painful as I leaned against the walls and slid myself. When I came to the aisle, I used the seats as crutches and finally arrived to my seat and sat down during the entire flight. I was very stinky from sweat and excrement, and the passengers who sat near me must have had an awful flight. My normally long straight hair was twisted in dreadlocks due to the sweating and lack of care.

My friend, Richmond, met me at the airport in San Francisco and drove me to the emergency ward at a hospital. I was taken to a room and put on a cot and then was forgotten. No medical staff came to the room to attend to me. Because of the lack of movement in the room, after a while the lights automatically shut off and I lay there in the darkness shouting for someone to help me. But still no one came. I remembered that there was a stool with wheels over by a desk. I rolled off of the cot and stretched out my arms and reached for the stool. I painfully lowered myself upon it and then used my right leg to move toward the door as my left leg dragged along like my right one had done when I was very small.

I opened the door and shouted, "Help! I need Help!"

A gay male nurse walked toward me saying, "I didn't know there was anybody here." I was put back on the cot and a few minutes later, a doctor entered the room and I told him the whole story about the accident.

The doctor called in another doctor and said, "You've got to hear this story," so I told it again. They laughed and I felt like they thought that I was one of the many San Francisco delusional vagrants that would come to the ER for a bed to sleep. They took a brief look at my knee and sent me on my way.

My journey with Mr. Natural continues and now I am surrounded by stars. Bright, beautiful stars in all directions and I am their center.

Three weeks earlier, I was walking inside the fortress in Jaisalmer, India, near the Pakistani border, looking for a suitable place to stay when J-Chermi, the owner of the Oasis Inn insisted that I check out the shabby accommodations at his place. I was not impressed because dust and grime were everywhere and the filthy bathroom was to be shared with the tenant in the neighboring room. I had decided upon my entry into Jaisalmer that I was no longer going to share my toilet with another Frenchman, who had no inclination to piss straight into the toilet nor flush down his feces after he had completed his business. I told J-Chermi, "No."

I headed back down the stairs with my backpack when he grabbed me and insisted, "The bathroom will be solely for your use and my son and I will clean up your room and the toilet immediately." I shook my head, 'no' and he pleaded. "Please do not leave me. If you do, I will be shamed by the others in the community. They saw you enter and if you exit now without taking a room, it will cause me great dishonor." His bloodshot, rabid eyes bespoke the torment that my action would cause him.

I said. "Okay. But only for one night and only if the bedroom and bathroom are cleaned thoroughly and the bathroom is for my own private use."

He smiled ecstatically and shook my hand vigorously and I noticed that many of his fingers had been chopped off. He noticed me looking at his missing fingers and said, "I lost my fingers when I was a small boy and I put my hand inside of an electrical fan." I looked at his other hand, which also had diminished digits and he held both hands up and said, "Both hands, yes, both hands. I played in the fan; terrible, terrible accident."

"Yes. It must have hurt," I replied as we looked at each other in the eyes and we both knew that I knew that there was no accident, but that his fingers had been cut off for thievery.

J-Chermi and I walked down to the front desk, so that I could check in. He kicked his son, Arjun, who was sleeping on the sofa and told him. "Clean the bedroom and bathroom upstairs." Arjun opened his eyes and rolled over to sleep some more and J-Chermi kicked him harder. "Clean the rooms now!"

"I already did." protested Arjun without looking up.

"Clean them again and better this time. We have a very important guest." Arjun turned and looked at me with his barely open eyes and grudgingly grabbed the cleaning supplies and slowly headed upstairs. "That boy," said J-Chermi shaking his head, "all he wants to do is sleep and dream." "Clean it good this time. The rooms are filthy," J-Chermi yelled as Arjun`s extremely large bare feet disappeared from my sight. I sat down on Arjun`s couch and waited with my backpack while J-Chermi assured me, "The rooms will be immaculate, you`ll see." An hour later Arjun trudged back down the stairs without the cleaning supplies and I went up to my rooms. They were both in the same deplorable condition as I had last seen them except for the cleaning supplies that were left in my bathroom and the bed that looked as if it had been slept in.

I thought about going back down and telling J-Chermi, "This won't do," but instead I grabbed the cleaning supplies and did the job myself. I did not want to allow Arjun to warm up my bed anymore.

I cleaned the rooms as best that I could and hung up my Vishnu tapestry over the bed and decorated my bedroom with other knick knacks that I had acquired from Nepal and other parts of India. Pushy Tibetan saleswomen in Pokharra had convinced me that I couldn't live without prayer wheels and brass meditation bowls and decorated drug receptacles. "These are very rare, one of a kind," they assured me, although I saw the same bric-a-brac on nearly every subsequent corner.

The next morning, I arose from my bed and headed to the toilet but found that the door was locked. I knocked on the door and someone grunted. I waited outside for the intruder to exit my private bathroom and a filthy Frenchie came out, but not before leaving an unflushed torpedo of dung in my toilet. I went down to the desk and told J-Chermi what had happened and he replied, "I'm sorry. The man came in very late at night and he did not understand what I told him. But he's leaving this morning, so the toilet will again be only for you."

"That's what you said yesterday, J-Chermi. I do not like being lied to. I'm leaving today as well."

"Baba Hanuman," he implored me, "I did not lie. It was only an accident. He did not understand that the toilet was yours alone." J-Chermi suggested that I also rent the adjoining room at a very good discount, so that there would no longer be anymore misunderstandings and I complied.

The bed in the other room was more comfortable, so I used that one as my bedroom and used my original one for prayer and reflection. I would sit on my mattress in the prayer room and smoke grass, which was purchased from the police, and look out the window at the courtyard of an Islamic school below the fortress. The other window I always kept closed because I discovered that it opened into my private viewing of an outdoor toilet for the homeless.

On my first full day in Jaisalmer I purchased a Bang Lassi (smoothie with grass) from the police and then walked along the paths of the fortress. That was when the accident in the tunnel of dung occurred and I injured my head. My clothing was covered with blood and God only knows what else, so I replaced it with traditional Indian garb. I had a Krishna blue long shirt with matching pants made for me and bought a long length of pink linen that I spun into a turban. Pink was the color suggested for me by the salesman because orange signified warrior, which I was not, blue signified illness, and white- untouchable. Pink signified holy man and the salesman convinced me that I was one.

From that day until the rest of my stay in India, I always wore the same outfit. One day I was walking from the fort and I noticed how all of the Indian women were admiring my new look. I thought, "Yeah. I really look hot," as my ego inflated.

Immediately, a taxi drove by on the path and splashed mud all over me. This I accepted without distress because I knew that it was reminding me to work more diligently on the seventh spoke in my Wheel of Life - humility.

My Hanuman persona intensified with this change in my attire. Each morning in the prayer room, I would perform the ceremony of applying a fresh bindi to my forehead using makeup that I had acquired in Benares. The bindi was like the one that I had seen in pictures of Hanuman - a red vertical flame surrounded by a gold border with silver over one eyebrow and gold over the other to signify my devotion to Rama and his beloved, Sita. For me, the bindi served as a third eye and reminded me to always look at the other perspective.

I stopped introducing myself as Baba Hanuman, which I had acquired from the boatmen in Benares. They called me that because I wore a beard without a mustache and resembled the monkey god. An Indian friend told me that using that name seemed boastful, so I became hanumanji with no capital letters. But the Hanuman ideals of Trust, Devotion, Strength, and Courage, I tried to never deviate from.

Telling falsehoods, which had always been easy and pleasurable for me were no longer acceptable. Only the Truth would be told.

One day J-Chermi asked me how he could get more tenants in his inn, since I had been the only one there for many days. We walked together from one room to the next and I suggested that he decorate each room as I had done with mine. "Hang tapestries over the beds; make the rooms look more elegant," I said. "Tourists, who come here and sleep, want to feel as if they are Maharashis."

"But that will cost money, hanumanji," J-Chermi countered. "I have no money."

"You have many tapestries in your office that you try to sell. Use them as your decorations."

"Yes, hanumanji," J-Chermi said excitedly. "I will do it."

The next day there were tapestries hanging over each bed, although J-Chermi had attached to each a large price tag which said FOR SALE. I told

J-Chermi that the price tags messed up the Maharashi effect, but he never removed them. However, the rooms did fill up.

After three weeks in Jaisalmer, I informed J-Chermi that I would need to leave soon for Pushkar because the holy day of Hanuman was going to be there. I was told that I couldn't leave Jaisalmer without first taking a camel safari through the desert. I had been hounded by salesmen throughout my stay there and had never shown the slightest interest, but since it was an "opportunity of a lifetime", I couldn't resist.

I was driven by jeep to a Muslim family's abode in the desert and sat in their one-room shack as two camels were loaded up for the safari. The children stared at me as if I were an extra-terrestrial. They continually pawed at my Star of David medallion which hung around my neck and tried to remove it from me until their mother would come along and shoo them away.

My guide, Ligen, and I stopped at one oasis on the way to our destination and I was gladdened that I had chosen to stay for only one night in the desert because the wind was very fierce and pelted my face with sand throughout the night as I tried to sleep. The camel ride was excruciating although it was not nearly as bad as the pins up my ass on the elephant ride that I had endured in Nepal a couple of months earlier. I was told at the inn before leaving on the safari to be sure that I was served eggs for breakfast. But although I saw the eggs packed onto the camel, I was never given any. My guide served me coffee and dry cereal. I was told that at the completion of the safari, I should only give my guide a tip if I found the safari to be extraordinary, which it was not. I felt as if I had been cheated because I had not been given eggs, which I truly desired. So I gave Ligen no extra money. Instead I gave him one of the pens that I had purchased at Gandhi's Sabarmati Ashram. When you press on the pen's top button to write, a Gandhi saying appears such as 'The Truth is God'. Ligen looked at the pen apprehensively and replied. "I did not expect a tip from you. You are a holy man."

Before heading to Pushkar, I also decided to visit the Muslim school that I had been spying on from the window of my prayer room for the past three weeks. I was very nervous as I waited outside of the school's entrance. I had very little previous contact with Muslims and felt that I was more ignorant of that religion than any of the other major ones. A man came to the gate and I informed him that I was an American teacher who was interested in talking to someone about their school. The teachers were notified of my appearance and the students were dismissed for recess into the courtyard. The teachers and I met in a room and sat in a circle on the floor and discussed religion and drank tea. We discussed the commonalities of our faiths and laughed at the trivialities of our differences.

Classes resumed and I was given a tour of all of the classrooms. They were similar to my classes in America. Some students were well-behaved, some were not. In America the students sat in chairs at desks; here they sat on the floor at holders of the Koran. In my classes, my students were boys and girls: here, they were only boys. In one classroom that I visited, a boy was handcuffed and chained to a wall for misbehavior. I found that odd but thought how often I had wished that I could have done a similar thing to some of my students. Sure, there were differences between us, but our goals seemed to be the same - to educate our youth so that they would have a better life.

After I had visited all of the classrooms, all of the teachers and students met me in the courtyard and sang to me a song for farewell. They requested that I sing for them and so I did the Jackson Browne number, 'Our Lady of the Well'.

On the morning that I was leaving for Pushkar, I performed the bindi ceremony in my prayer room but decided to add a personal touch. Rather than the red flame in the center of my bindi, I made a circle with four colors - blue in the north, red in the south, green in the west, and yellow in the east. The significance of this bindi for me was that all four corners of the earth were united with the same goal - that of ananda or bliss.

I took a seat in the back of the bus, which filled up very quickly. There was one open seat next to me and two drunken men jumped onto the bus just as it was pulling out. They scrambled for the vacant seat and the one who was second kept trying to squeeze in between his buddy and me, although there was no room. His smelly body would sit upon my lap and then he would maneuver to press me against the wall. After seeing that he was going to continue to do this, I stood up and towered over him as he cowered beneath me. "Do you wish to have my seat?" I calmly asked him, "Take it, it's yours. I desire it no longer." He sheepishly indicated that I should sit back down and he and his buddy moved to the front of the bus and exited at the next stop. Then I took my seat again and a Muslim man dressed in immaculate white, who had been watching the proceedings, sat down next to me and we did not invade each other's space.

I found a room in a hostel that overlooked Pushkar's holy lake, where Hindu music was playing 24-7 and at night the temples were lit up like Las Vegas. I showered and applied a traditional Hanuman bindi to my forehead and set off for the Hanuman temple since this was his holy day.

As I marched along the dirt road, I felt my strength growing as I sang, "Hanuman, Hanuman, Hanuman, Hanuman" over and over again. I stood beside the towering temple and continued my song as I observed the depictions of Hanuman's roles in both the Ramayana and the Mahabharata. I decided not to enter the temple but sat cross-legged on the ground a generous distance from its entrance and meditated with my eyes closed. I could feel eyes looking at me although I devoted myself to remaining humble. The more vain that I became, the weaker that I would become. I felt my strength growing.

Two white vans pulled up alongside the temple and out of the first one stepped boys dressed in white who gawked at me and then entered the temple. Men in white stepped out of the second van and followed the boys into the temple. The last person to exit the van was a very old man with a long beard and long hair and a wooden staff. I continued to meditate with my eyes closed for a long time until I felt that there were many eyes upon me, so I opened mine. The men and boys in white had surrounded me and the old man asked me through a translator, "For how many years have you been in Pushkar?"

I answered, "Only one day. This is my first day in Pushkar." The old man raised his eyebrows in astonishment and said, "We shall meet again," and then led the others to their vans.

The translator told me as they were leaving, "He is a very important holy man. This was very special." I subtly nodded back to him because I was already aware of the information that he told me, and then the vans drove away.

I was walking back to my hostel when just before the entrance, a man approached me and asked, "Are you missing anything?" I thought about the spokes in my Wheel of Life and he held up the key to my room. He said, "I have been watching you at the Hanuman temple for a long time. You left this key at the place where you sat." He introduced himself as Maruti and said that he was a jeweler. I thanked and promised him that I would visit his shop, which was next to the Chai Guy. The next day I purchased a necklace for my mother and a ring for myself. We talked philosophy as the Chai Guy hypnotically poured chai tea from one pan to the other and droned on and on, "Chai, chai, chai…"

I went back to my room. I had been in search of this room for most of my three months in India and Nepal.

It began when I was sleeping in my hotel room in Benares on a sweltering night. I dreamed that I had gone to a hotel desk and asked the manager for the Star Room. He replied, "Follow me" and led me up winding staircases that were decorated with Stars of David. He came to the door and said, "Here it is," and began to open the door as bright light escaped.

I woke up, turned on the light in my Benares hotel room, and opened up the Nepal guidebook that was lying beside me. My eyes immediately focused upon the words, Hotel Star, which was located in Kathmandu.

A day later, I decided to leave India for Nepal because the beggars and the con men were driving me nuts. At first I had tried to politely say "no" to them but this seemed to give them the impetus to become more aggressive. So then I tried to ignore them, but I found that I was missing out on the Indian experience by simply closing myself off. Next, I tried anger, but this strategy did not suit me because I had not come to India to be an angry tourist. I had come there for spiritual enlightenment. I had not come there to buy a bunch of crap or to be continually harassed by beggars. I found that if I gave one beggar some rupees, swarms of them would be on me within seconds and they would not take "no" for an answer. I was going nuts. I had come to Benares to die like so many of the cremated corpses that floated before me on the Ganges, but that would have to wait. It was not yet my time.

So I bolted from India as fast as I could. There weren't any flights or trains available that day, so I bought a ticket for the first bus that was leaving for Nepal. I didn`t care that it was a third class bus and that I had to share my seat with chickens and that there were no shock absorbers and that my head would constantly bang against the ceiling. At least I was on my way out.

In Nepal I visited the birthplace of the Buddha and sat underneath a very old Bodha tree that I had imagined was the very same one that Siddhartha's mother grabbed onto as she gave birth to the enlightened one. A single leaf fell from the tree and rested upon my head.

From there, I visited a national park and had my prickly elephant ride and purchased some hashish that looked like a huge black candle for a mere $15. Then I stayed at the Holy Hotel in Pokharra and from there I hiked into the Himalayan Mountains and visited some villages where the residents were Tibetan refugees. As I was hiking, I noticed that on some of the rocks someone had painted the words 'Star Hotel' with an arrow pointing forward. I took this as a sign that perhaps my Benares dream would come true here rather than in Kathmandu, so I followed the signs into the next village. However, when I got to the hotel, it was very shabby, dark, and claustrophohic with no signs of any stars, so I declined and looked for another place to stay. A block away a dirty-faced girl convinced me to check out her family`s guest house and it was perfect. I was the only tenant and I had the top floor to myself with views of the mountains from all sides and Buddhist flags flapping in the wind. In the dining room below, there was a small library and that was where I discovered the autobiograhy of Mohandas K. Gandhi that I read and which formed the basis for my Wheel of Life.

The dirty-faced girl had a beautiful older sister with whom I was enraptured, but she paid no attention to me and so I focused upon the teachings of the Mahatma. I began to eat only vegetarian food because Gandhi said that the eating of meat created lust. However, when I went to the next mountain village and stayed at a family hotel with two sisters again, the elder sister was continually flirting with me and she convinced me to have a large plate of yak for dinner. I decided then that I would never be able to go to the extremes of Gandhi and that a more suitable approach would be that of the Buddha – The Middle Way.

From Pokharra, I took a bus to Kathmandu and checked in at the Hotel Star. The manager led me up Star of David decorated stairways to my room but when he opened the door, there was no bright flash of light as in the dream. The room was nice and the water pressure on the shower was much better than any I had ever encountered before. But there was not the magic there that I had expected to encounter based upon my dream.

I smoked a great deal of my hashish in that room and felt now that I was ready to return to India. I had decided that I would now react to the beggars and con men with humor and would laugh at the ridiculousness of my constant harassment. On my final night in Nepal, I felt that my mojo was working, so I went to a casino and won a great deal of money at the roulette wheel. Later I sent the money to a school in the Himalayas that I had briefly visited. Perhaps there was magic there, but it was not like I had expected.

Back in India I visited Gandhi's Sabarmati Ashram and then traveled to Rajasthan; first Jaisalmer at J-Chermi's Inn and then Pushkar along the holy lake.

And now in a Mr. Natural flashback of my life, I found myself seated in my Star Room in Pushkar on my last day in India before traveling back to San Francisco. This room along the holy lake I knew was the room that I was led to in my Benares dream. During the day the sun would shine through the numerous windows which were six and eight-pointed stars carved straight from the walls. The shadows from these windows would create other stars on the surrounding walls. The effect was magnificent.

I felt some regret about leaving this room and India but I knew that it was my time to return to my duties in America. I gathered my backpack and began to walk to the bus station when a priest from the holy lake called out, "Hanumanji, come to the lake. I must perform the ceremony Puja before you depart."

I had a little bit of time to kill so I thought, "What the heck, why not."

He went through the ceremony very quickly and then, of course, requested that I give him money, which I did with laughter. Suddenly rain started pouring down from the sky and the priest ran for cover and said, "Hanumanji, come with me. Get out of the rain." But I stayed beside the lake and watched the fish jumping out of the water over and over again. I knew that the Puja ceremony wasn't real; it was only a way for the priest to get some rupees. The rain coming from the sky was real. The fish jumping from the lake was real. The spirit, the true essence of earth, was real - not the politics, not the business, not the ceremony. But the spirit which could not be seen, nor heard, nor touched, it could only be felt in the heart and soul; that was real.

The bus was pulling out as I approached the station so I ran and jumped into the moving vehicle. It was filled to capacity and I stood in the aisle with my backpack on. People tried to convince me to put my backpack down, but I replied, "I am hanumanji. I do not feel the backpack." Pretty young Hindu women in their beautiful traditional saris reached out to touch my hands as their eyes brightened.

The bus let us off about a half a mile from the train station and a man with a very old chariot and horse offered to give me a ride. I stood in the back of the chariot with my backpack still on, as the driver stood and held the reins and the horse galloped. We passed the pretty women who had been on the bus with me and we waved to each other as Krishna steered the horse and I, Arjuna, went into battle with no more fears.

In my final bathtub flashback, I'm back in Palma six months ago in one of those public telephone booths making a call to my mom who's back in Wisconsin. I tell her that I met this girl and we've decided that we're gonna get married. My mom's excited for me as I share with her how Ana and I had met. I put Ana on the phone and she introduces herself as Anne. My mom and I simultaneously correct Ana and tell her that her name is Ana and not Anne because the name Anne is not held in high regard in my family. My mom's youngest brother, Ernie, married an Anne and she turned out to be a wicked bitch.

Ernie, whose real name was Bertrand, was a simple good-natured fellow, who helped pick up the slack after my father had died. He took us on excursions into the Wisconsin countryside and assured me that the black and white cows produced white milk while the ones that were brown produced chocolate milk. One day we returned home to Mom with four yellow ducklings. We named them John, Paul, George, and the funny-looking one that straddled behind with the longest beak was named Ringo.

Ernie was constantly bringing in furry creatures for us. Once I remember he gave us two rabbits and within days, I ran to my mom screaming that some fat caterpillars had entered the rabbit's cage. It was explained to me that those slimy creatures were not invaders but merely bunny babies. One day he came over with a crippled beagle named Molly and announced that the kids needed to have a dog. He bought the dog for me because I was ill with nephritis, a kidney disease. I could not go outside. I could only look out the window and watch as my brother and sister and our neighborhood friends played Statues, and Annie, Annie, Over and Red Rover, Red Rover. My mother feared that I was going to join my father in the Great Beyond. Molly chewed her way through my mother's shoes and furniture until she had to be returned to the country like all of the animals that had come before her. Each trip with Ernie always included a visit to the A&W where we would have root beers served in frosty mugs. I remember one day we had returned home after a rather miserable day that included a flat tire and Ernie sadly lamented, "Even the root beer didn't taste right today."

Years later Ernie met Anne and raised his own family. When I was a teenager, I remember seeing him over at a hamburger joint where my gang and I hung out and I remember being embarrassed because he was odd-looking. I remember the hurt look in his eyes as I discarded him in front of my cool teenage friends.

Ernie was a diabetic and became blind and his wife and children discarded him like I had. The last time I saw him, he was living in a dingy little apartment in downtown Menasha. I visited him once there as he struggled to read the newspaper with a large magnifying glass. I suggested that he should try smoking marijuana to help him with his cataracts, but he declined because he said that he didn't want any drugs; he wanted to see things as they truly were. He died shortly afterward and all that his wife and kids seemed to care about was his life insurance policy.

On the phone I told my Mom about our plans to be married on the little island in Menasha's Jefferson Park. I had picked this location because it was always a very special place for me. For as long as I can remember, I would go there and sit on the cannon from the Korean War and talk to the spirit of my father. When it wasn't possible for me to be there, I would carry throughout my travels a photograph of him in his Korean War uniform and his eyes and smile would give me assurance that everything would be okay.

Suddenly white light followed by white noise enveloped and bloated me although I now felt as if my body had become lighter than air and was no longer limited by space.

I could hear the Paul Simon song, 'American Tune', which was followed by a rendition of the old Monkees' number, 'I'm a Believer'. When the refrain began, I suddenly saw Ana`s face appear before me in a glowing vision of angelic purity. She sang the song, 'Nature Boy' from the opening of her favorite movie, Moulin Rouge.

She softly kissed me and I realized that she was standing over me and I was lying in a bed in a hospital room. I tried to talk to her, but I noticed that it was very difficult as my face was covered with an oxygen mask and my mind was disoriented and hazy. She held my hand which was connected to an IV tube and told me to relax and not strain myself. I asked, "What happened?" and she explained that she had returned from Barcelona and found me unconscious in the bathtub. She said that I had experienced a heart attack. I told her, "I'm not ready to die yet. I want to live. I want our child to see her daddy." I extended my hand and placed it upon her belly and felt the life of our child growing inside her. I tried to tell her about Mr. Natural, but I became weak and passed out again.

Part IV   Deliverance

When I regained consciousness, I found out that I was actually in an Amsterdam hospital. I had been there for three days. The doctor said that I was found in the Singel Canal floating and sinking nearby the Bloemengarten flower market and had gotten saddled up to the bridge at Leidestrat. He said that the snow which had fallen for the past two days seemed to have kept me afloat. "Snow?" I inquired. "What date is this?"

"December 28.....2002."

"Where am I again?"

"You`re still in Amsterdam."

"How long have I been here?"

"In this room - 3 days."

 "In Amsterdam?"

"In Amsterdam, I haven't a clue. Do you?"

"I better rest some more."

I closed my eyes and tried to work out what had happened between summer in Mallorca to winter in Amsterdam. I tried to come up with an answer, but I didn't have a clue. Is this a dream now or was it a dream before? It all seemed so real. Some other doctors came in and asked me questions. They were psychiatrists, I assume, and I gave them a highly detailed rundown of my time spent in Mallorca and my travels across Europe with Ana. However, how I got to Amsterdam and what happened to me over the past seven months remained a blank.

The next day, one of the psychiatrists, a Dr. Van Loon, informed me that they had received a confirmation from the Ritzi that I had stayed there although they knew nothing about any girls including Ana. They were not able to get any evidence of my stay at the flat at Plaza Chopin or any information about my landlord, Dante. They weren't able to contact anyone at Ana's old flower shop and I couldn`t recall the names of Ana`s family in Barcelona. In fact I couldn't even recall Ana's surname.

"Very odd," Dr. Van Loon kept repeating as he stared at me over hexagonally-shaped wire rim glasses, "very odd, your memory loss at times seems to be very selective. I`m very interested in your situation, but unfortunately you`re going to need to be released. The American consulate has been informed of your situation and is expecting your arrival at two o'clock this afternoon. They'll be able to help you get the necessary identification and means to return to your country. Your situation is very, very odd. I wish that I could stay with it." His eyes brightened and his mouth stretched into an elongated freakish grin that brought back memories of my first encounter with Izmael at the bookstore nearly a year ago.

I was given my clothes: underwear, socks, hiking boots, brown pants, flannel shirt, and the long blue wool coat that I had worn when I had toured with Ana as 'The Gypsy Angels.' "No hat?" I asked.

"No hat," replied the intern as he handed me my personal belongings, which consisted of four euros and eighty three cents, my Star of David medallion, which hung on a broken leather string, and a key which opened what? I hadn't a clue.

Dr. Van Loon gave me the address of the U.S. Consulate as well as a twenty euro bill. "This is for the taxi and a lunch," the good doctor stated. "Mr. Geiger, Mr. Geiger," he continued, "very, very odd," as his mouth again stretched into that same maniacal grin. The intern who sneered at me with disdain for interrupting his ritual nap, walked me to the exit and pointed to where the cabs waited about fifty meters away and then he re-entered the hospital.

I walked to the cabs but continued walking past them. I wasn't ready to deal with bureaucracy just yet and get sent back to the States. 'The States can wait,' I thought, 'I need to find some answers.' I stumbled upon a tourist office close to the hospital nearby the Prinsengracht Canal and received directions to get to the Bloemengarten flower market at the Singel Canal. 'That's where I was found,' I reasoned, 'perhaps memories will come back for me there.' I walked to the bridge at Leidestraat which crossed over Singel and walked up and down the canal in hopes that something would rekindle my memory; it was unfortunately to no avail. The sun seemed extremely bright and reflected off of the canal sending sharp pains into the sides of my head.

Although it was winter, bicycles sped past me with their bells ringing as I finally concluded that I must be walking in the bike lane. "Are you lost?" a non-descript fellow asked.

"I`m looking for some answers," I replied.

"What kind of answers?"

"Who I am? Why am I here? How did I get here?"

"Perhaps I can help, come inside. You look as if you could use a coffee."

I followed him inside the building along a long corridor which led to a small office on the right. I sat down in a simple wooden chair and he brought me coffee and some cookies, and then sat down in a chair beside me. We sat silently for a few minutes eating and drinking and then I asked, "Where am I, anyway?"

"This is the office for our church, our Mennonite church."

"Have I been here before? Do you know me?"

"No. I don't believe that I have ever seen you here before. I don't believe that I know you, although your face does strike me as familiar."

I asked to see the inside of the church and was overcome with a feeling of deja vu as he opened the door and I saw many more wooden chairs on the floor that encircled an elevated pulpit. Large cream-colored pillars supported two gigantic balconies with wooden benches that would have seated a congregation of over two thousand.

"This was a hidden church," my friend stated. "It's over 400 years old and there used to be a street just outside this door, but people passing by would never have noticed that there was a church."

"Was being a Mennonite outlawed?" I asked.

"In the early years such as the 1500's many in the church including the first leader, Jan Trypmaker, were beheaded for their beliefs. When the Spanish were in control here, Amsterdam became known as Moorddam, Murderdam. Later, the government council became more tolerant. There was no law against it, but it was frowned upon. It's like the coffeehouses that we now have in Amsterdam that serve marijuana and hashish. People just looked the other way." He then went into at long explanation of the history of the Mennonite religion, but I tuned out and could only think of the coffeehouses. I would nod and say, "Aha" although I had no idea what he was talking about. I remember him saying something about Mennonite protestors chanting, "The truth is naked," but that's about it.

All that I could think about was going to a coffeehouse and getting high. He paused for a moment to gather his thoughts and I took the opportunity to excuse myself, saying that I needed to get to an appointment.

"Have you found your answers?" he asked as I exited.

"Yes, thank you. I feel that I'm on the right path," and proceeded along the canal and across the bridge in the direction toward the city center.

Once again I was amazed by the number of bicycles speeding past me or chained up along the sides of the streets on this sunny winter day. Some of the bikes had handmade passenger seats constructed upon them for up to three or four children. Some of the bicycles, also tricycles, and quadcycles had large boxes in the front where the children played as their parents pumped on the pedals. There were very few cars going by in proportion to the number of bicycles. 'How very odd,' I thought and chuckled to myself as I recalled Doctor Van Loon's very odd smile.

I came upon the Freeworld Coffeehouse and ordered a cappuccino and pre-rolled marijuana joint. The bartender, a tall black man, replied with a bright smile, "Sure thing, Charlie."

"Do you have a match?"

"Sure thing, Charlie," he replied again and threw me a book of matches that advertised the coffeehouse. I presumed that this was the way he addressed all of his customers. I took my coffee and joint and sat down on a couch near the back.

I lit up my joint and slowly smoked it and noticed that the room was decorated with extra-terrestrials. The E.T.'s seemed to be imploring me to go home. A guy at a computer got up and left the bar. I noticed that there were still some minutes left on the internet, so I sat down there and tried to get to my yahoo mailbox. Unfortunately, the computer replied that I did not exist. "I do exist," I argued back at the computer, "I do." Immediately I thought about my wedding with Ana that had been scheduled for last August in Menasha's Jefferson Park. I tried to recall Ana's e-mail address but could not come up with anything as the time ran out and the screen went blank. "Where is Ana now and what did she think when I suddenly abandoned her? Did I abandon her or did she abandon me? What the hell happened?"

Suddenly, I knew that I was going to vomit. I ran down a narrow spiral staircase, crashed through the door of the men's room, and vomited into the toilet. Each time I thought that I had finished, I would turn to the wash basin and begin to wash myself, but again the lava would boil up inside of me and erupt.

"Too much smoke I toke," I spoke to my reflection in the mirror and another strong feeling of deja vu came over me. I had been here before. When I was at the computer and I realized that I needed to vomit, I knew instantly where the men's room was. There was no hesitation or looking around. I'd been here before and the bartender upstairs had seemed to know me.

I went back upstairs to the bar to get information from the bartender, but he was not there. He had been replaced by a grey-haired, wrinkly white guy with a cigarette hanging from the corner of his mouth. "What you need, Mac?" he asked.

"Do you know me?" I inquired.

"Can't say that I do," he answered.

"Why did you call me Mac?" I asked.

The bartender laughed and replied, "That's what I call everybody."

"The other bartender, the black man, where did he go?"

"Bob? Well, Bob's gone. His shift ended."

"Does Bob call everybody Charlie?" I asked.

"Charlie?" the bartender chuckled. "No, I never heard that."

I exited the smoke-filled coffeehouse and was relieved to breathe fresh air again. It looked as if the afternoon sun, which had glistened and blinded me earlier, had long since departed and the narrow streets lined with restaurants, bars, and coffeehouses seemed much more sinister and foreboding.

I came upon a metal cylinder rising from the ground that had a glowing red light attached at its top and concluded that I was about to enter Amsterdam's famous red-light district. Most of the shops advertised porn and the pedestrian street were filled with groups of perverts and curiosity seekers. When I came to a canal, I noticed red tubular lights above the windows of buildings on both sides of the canal.

As I walked by the windows, women posed in the small rooms. Some stood seductively with their bodies stretched out. Others sat demurely on their tall stools and looked at you with big sad eyes as if they were puppy dogs in a pet shop window that were never being taken home. One girl sat like this in a plaid school uniform but when she saw me, her eyes suddenly brightened and her mouth seemed to say something. I kept walking, but within seconds I heard the door open and she screamed, "Charlie!"

I stopped in my tracks, turned around, and asked, "Do you know me?"

"Of course I know you, Charlie," she replied. "Get in here." I walked into her small room as she closed the door and curtain behind me.

"How do you know me?" I asked.

"How do you think?" she replied and started to unzip my pants.

"Just a minute," I stopped her.

"What do you want tonight, Charlie?"

"I want information. What can you tell me about me? How long have I been seeing you?"

"A long time."

"How long?"

"Four, five months."

"How often?"

"Once a week, like clockwork."

"When last did we meet?"

"One week ago."

"From tonight?"

"From tonight."

"Right."

"Right. Shall we go?" she asked and tried unzipping me again.

"I ain't got no dough. I gotta go."

I exited and turned up a street walking past more red rooms. In this first block, all of the girls were black and the only guys on the sidewalk were a bunch of drunken college boys dressed in orange that threw snowballs at the windows above the rooms. In the next block, all of the curtains in the rooms were closed and the street was very dark and deserted except for a lone Chinese man who trudged along while screaming out invectives. Then the street brightened and there were more posers and pouters and pervs, oh my.

The sign outside of the Route 66 Coffeehouse beckoned me to enter and so I did and ordered a cappuccino from a cute punk-haired bartender. Beer or anything alcoholic did not appeal to me and besides I didn't have a place to sleep so I probably needed to stay awake throughout the night. I sat at a table in a dark corner and watched two guys shooting pool in the back. Both of them were smoking huge joints and neither of them came close to putting a ball in the pocket. The tall one seemed to be more concerned with checking out the bartender and the short guy, with a long pony tail extending down his entire back, was in a constant state of motion. He never set himself up to make the shot or study the possibilities for alternatives or consequences. It was always a continuous mishmash of the pool cue sweeping into the air sometimes hitting the cue ball in its first attempt but never with both of his feet planted firmly on the ground. On one of his connections with the cue ball, the white orb bounced off of each of the four banks two times without hitting any of the other fifteen balls on the table. He exclaimed, "Now that was a great shot!"

"How can that be a great shot?" the tall guy argued. "You didn't make anything."

"Exactly," replied Shorty. "I didn't make anything and I didn't hit anything. That shot could not be duplicated. Who agrees?" He turned away from the table looking for someone to reinforce his argument, then suddenly spotted me and gasped, "Charlie, where the hell have you been, my friend?"

"You tell me," I replied.

Excitedly, he sat down beside me and I told him what I knew beginning with my sabbatical, my time in Mallorca, Constanza and her friends, my meeting with Ana, our travels across Europe, our return to Palma, and then the hospital in Amsterdam.

"Perhaps you can fill in the blanks for me," I suggested.

"What?" he replied, not seeming to understand what I was saying.

"I've lost my memory," I answered. "I don't know how or when I got here. I don't remember being here. What have I been doing?"

"What have you been doing? Charlie baby, you've been with me. On the streets, in the shack. The act is back, Charlie baby, the act is back!"

"What act?" I asked.

"What act?" he echoed incredulously. "What act? Our act, Charlie, me boy. Me on the axe, you on the wheels."

"The wheels?" I asked. "What wheels?"

"We better get home," he replied. "It will all become clear."

He led me down the street for a block until we came upon another metal cylinder with a red light signifying the end of the district. Then we turned left and he stretched out his arms and said, "Ta da. Home sweet home."

I looked at the white building with the blue neon lights above the entrance and asked, "That's where we live? The Frisco Inn?"

"That we do, Charlie, me boy, that we do," he answered as we strolled toward the entrance, but as we got closer to the Inn and I headed excitedly to the front entrance, Shorty pulled at my arm and we disappeared into an alley along the side.

I began to ask, "Wha...?" but Shorty put his hand across my mouth and pointed forward, then placed his index finger across his mouth indicating that I must be silent. We tiptoed down the alley in the darkness until Shorty stopped and rotated a wooden wall that opened into our secret passage to home sweet home.

Home sweet home was a shack, nothing more, nothing less. Just enough room to lie down our bodies on our beds, which consisted of our sleeping bags atop old foam padding. Light came from some holes that Shorty said he and I had carved out some time ago. "Feel the heat," said Shorty, placing one of my hands by a hole. "On the other side of this wall are the ovens in the kitchen of the inn. It doesn't matter how cold this winter gets, we'll never freeze."

"Nobody knows that we're here?" I asked.

"Nobody," Shorty's eyes widened and glowed, "except the rats." I jumped up and looked for a place to climb although there wasn't any. "Don't worry, Charlie," he chuckled, "One thing about rats: you don't bother them, they don't bother you. Now just lie down, Charlie. I'm sure with the situation that you been in, you could use some rest. Everything's gonna be much clearer in the morning. Time heals all wounds. An apple a day keeps the doctor away. A bird in the hand is worth two in the bush. Don't fret, don't sweat, just cuz you forget..."

The next morning I was awakened by a rustling sound and opened my eyes to see Shorty rummaging through a plastic garbage bag and placing scraps of food on some plates. "Breakfast is served," he announced in a dreadful British accent. Then in his regular American voice he remarked, "It's very handy having the kitchen's trash bin right next to our shack. It's like having room service."

"What time is it?" I asked rubbing my eyes and feeling the after-effects of smoking too much ganja.

"Hells bells," Shorty replied, "I don't know. Time means nothing to those who are free."

Shorty arranged the scraps on the plates so that they actually looked presentable as breakfast entrees. We had scrambled eggs with sausages, bread, and mixed fruit.

"Does anyone else know that we're here?" I asked Shorty.

"Just the rats," he replied.

"Doesn't the Inn use this room for anything?"

"I don't think they know that it exists. This is a hidden room; like the Jews used when the Nazis were here. Some Jews were probably hidden in here back then."

"How did you find it?"

Shorty chuckled and then replied, "I didn't find it, Charlie. You did."

"I did?"

"You had been living here alone for a couple of months before you invited me to stay. You said that when you came to this place you knew that there was a hidden room here and that you knew how to enter it. It was like you had been here before. I told you that it was like the Dali Lama. A baby is born when the Dali Lama dies and he is the reincarnation. The Lamas go in search of the new Dali Lama and the child recognizes things from his past life. You've been here before in a past life, Charlie. You can't get in here unless you know how to do it. And you knew how and then you taught me." He then explained to me how one needed to press in and turn clockwise a hidden peg while simultaneously turning another one counter-clockwise and then rotating the hidden door upward. "You don't just accidentally open this door, Charlie. You had been here before."

"Did I say why I was here?"

Shorty chuckled again, "You said that you were hiding."

"Hiding from what?"

"The terror."

"The terror? What terror?"

"I don`t know, Charlie," Shorty replied. "That's all you ever said, the terror, and you would become all silent and glum. This is my axe." Shorty pulled out a battered old guitar case from beside his bed and opened it up. "We can't play it in here because the kitchen crew might hear. It may not look like much but it plays sweet, especially with your wheels."

"My wheels," I stated contemplatively trying to figure out for myself what he meant.

"You don`t know what I`m talking about, do you?" Shorty asked. I shook my head disappointedly. "I was at my usual spot at Qudekerksplein stroking my axe and singin` my songs makin' chump change like I did every day. Then I started the ol` Blood, Sweat, and Tears number, 'Spinning Wheel'. And then I went into my guitar solo. But this time I had accompaniment. Sounds came from beyond my guitar like some magical harp and I looked behind to my left and you had your bicycle turned upside down and your wheels were spinning and you were plucking at the spokes and the sounds that came from those wheels were truly inspirational and the crowd started gathering and throwing their money into my guitar case, not just coins but sometimes bills, and I knew that we had created the sound; the sound unlike any other. We were a hit, Charlie. The crowd loved us."

"I don't remember any of this."

"I changed my repertoire so that we performed songs on the wheel theme. Harry Chapin's 'Circles', the Byrds' 'Turn, Turn, Turn', 'A Bicycle Built for Two', all kinds of stuff. We were the draw on the street."

"Where`s my bike?" I asked.

"That`s what I`d like to know. I've been looking high and low for you and it. It`s not in its usual place around the corner. We'll find it Charlie if it didn`t end up in the canal like you." For the first time Shorty`s face expressed fear. "God, I hope that our bike didn`t end up in the canal. There was no other like it."

"Describe it to me."

"It was a beat-up, rusty old piece of shit. You called it 'Rusty Charlie'; some character from an old musical."

"Guys and Dolls," I answered.

"Everything was rusted especially the handlebars, but they were covered with purple tape."

"Purple tape?"

"Funky purple tape. If that bike ain't in the drink, we'll find it. There's not another one in all of Holland like it."

"Is this the key for the bike?" I asked while holding up the key that I had received at the hospital.

"That's it," replied Shorty. "If you locked him up like you always did, then Rusty Charlie's safe and sound."

The next two days we went searching throughout Amsterdam for my missing bike. A couple of times Shorty stole some other bikes and we flipped them over and I tried to play them, but nothing magical nor even musical was produced. "It's not at all the same sound," lamented Shorty. "The front wheel, especially that front rusty wheel made the most beautiful sounds imaginable. There was nothing like it, like angels singing. We gotta find your bike." And off we went searching high and low in search for the harp with the purple handle bars.

On the third day, Rusty Charlie was found. It looked different, Shorty remarked, because now it had a child's seat in the rear. But the bike was mine, no doubt about it. My key opened up my lock although my lock and chain was not being used to keep the bike safe. My chain was spun underneath the seat, but another chain and lock went through the frame and front tire and kept it safe from thieves. I tried my key with this lock, but it didn't work. "That's not your lock," remarked Shorty, "that's the thief's." I unwrapped my lock and chain and put it through the frame and back tire and secured it to a pole so that the thief could not remove it.

We waited across the street from where the bike stood at Anjeliersstraat in front of a strange-looking antique shop as the sun set and we began to lose faith that the thief would return that day. We were both cold and hungry and so we decided to pack it in and get back to the shack. Just as we were leaving, though, a man and a small child stopped in front of the bike and the man removed the front lock.

"Thief!" Shorty screamed as we crossed the street and he was almost hit by passing cyclists. The man and child turned toward us with expressions of bewilderment not guilt as we rushed toward them. "How dare you steal another man's bike," Shorty scolded. "What kind of example is this for your child?"

"Is this your bike?" the man asked Shorty. "I didn't steal it."

"It's not mine. It's his," Shorty screamed while pointing at me. "Why is your lock on his bike?"

"I didn't steal it. I found it lying on the walkway all smashed up. I stood it up along a rail for three days but nobody took it, so I brought it home and repaired it."

"What was wrong with it?" I asked.

"The front wheel was mangled beyond repair," he answered. "I needed to replace it." Shorty and I bent down toward the front wheel and for the first time noticed that it was not as rusty as the rest of the bike. "I replaced it with another wheel that I bought at a used bike shop," he continued. "That's where I bought Rebecca's bike seat as well."

For the first time the child spoke. "What are they doing to our bike, papa?" the blonde little beauty asked as Shorty turned the bike upside down.

"It's okay, honey," the papa answered her. Shorty spun the front wheel, then desperately urged me to do so as well. He brought out his guitar and nervously gestured for me to strum as he sang, with a bogus smile and too much volume, the song, 'Ezekiel Saw a Wheel'.

But the sounds that emanated from the front wheel were not angelic, nor melodic, nor soothing to the ear but the exact opposite. Shorty's smile turned into an excruciating grimace as he realized that the sound that would make us rich and famous was gone.

"Where's our wheel, what did you do with our wheel?" Shorty frantically queried.

"Where did you find the bike?" I calmly asked.

"Nearby my place," Papa answered. "I can walk you there. It's not too far away."

Papa put Rebecca on his shoulders because Shorty acted very possessive about the bike, but I said, "Rebecca should sit in her seat." We walked over three canals Prinsengracht, Keisengracht, and Herengracht until we stood on the bridge over the Singel Canal.

"This is where I found the bike," Papa said. "It lay here on the walkway by the railing and I tossed the broken wheel over there," he said pointing to a large trash bin on the other side of the canal. Shorty immediately scurried there and boosted himself up and into the bin. It was filled to the brim, but within a minute Shorty emerged triumphantly holding the wheel above his head as if it were a trophy for the world championship of midget wrestling

"I have some tools in the house," Papa said as he took Rebecca by the hand and entered a nearby red brick building. Within two minutes, he reappeared from the building with tools in hand but no child. "Rebecca was hungry, Mama's feeding her," he said which seemed plausible although I think that he probably wanted to get the little one out of harm's way. On the way to Singel, Shorty had explained to him about the musical wheel which I think he understood but did not believe. I think that he felt that he had become involved with a couple of lunatics; that conjecture I cannot dispute.

Shorty tried placing the wheel on the bicycle's fork and then frantically tried bending the wheel back to its original form, but as Papa said, it was mangled beyond repair. When Shorty finally got the wheel straight enough so that it would rotate on the fork, he tightened the nuts, brought out his guitar, directed me to play Rusty Charlie and then sang the Ike and Tina Turner song, 'Proud Mary'.

I tried to play the wheel but it was useless: it sounded terrible. But all was not lost because the song started to trigger a memory within me. I remembered myself rolling, rolling, rolling down the canal that icy Christmas night. I was riding my bike, Rusty Charlie, back to the shack. I had spent most of the day at Vondelpark watching girls ride by on their bicycles.

The streets were very slippery on this Christmas night as I rode back to the shack. They were especially slick on the bridges over the canals. I found that as I approached a bridge, I would need to accelerate a great deal because otherwise the bicycle would slide back no matter how hard I tried to pump forward. I remembered seeing that the bridge over Singel was deserted as I approached it, so I really worked at getting the bicycle moving at its top speed. This would be the last bridge until I reached home so I didn't want to mess around on this bridge like I had the previous ones.

The bicycle raced up the bridge and I knew that I would reach its apex but as the bridge descended, I lost control and the bike slid into the railing and jolted me into the canal. I remembered hitting the icy water and rolling with the current. I was approaching a big boat - the same one that was still there that day with Shorty and Papa, the Ave' Maria, and I must have slammed into it and became unconscious because that's all that I could remember.

The next thing that I remember was being in the hospital and suspecting that I had probably tried to commit suicide as Dr. Van Loon and all of the other doctors had probably suspected. But I had not tried to commit suicide: it was merely a stupid accident like my motorcycle accident in the Philippines years earlier.

I now saw clearly that Ana was merely a deluded figment of my imagination. I had traveled across Europe alone and had arrived in Amsterdam in June as scheduled for my departure back to San Francisco, but I had gotten caught up in the party scene in Amsterdam and became a Good Time Charlie. I had plenty of cash in my bank account from my frugal living and I over-indulged in the pleasures of the world. I knew that I had missed my scheduled flight back to the States, but I didn't care.

I remembered staying in a room inside the Frisco Inn. But then one night after an exceptionally high night of partying, I accidentally turned up the alley and discovered the shack. Somehow I instinctively knew how to open the secret door. I spent the night there and checked out of my room at the Inn the next day. During the days I spent most of my time writing or sleeping and during the night, I went carousing. I think that some drug psychosis set in and I began to feel more and more paranoid about going outside. I imagined that there was some evil force plotting against me. I became like so many others before and after me here in Amsterdam, a drug casualty. I freaked out.

Then I met Shorty who for some odd reason I connected with and trusted. I think that it was the weird expressions that his face would make when he would try to sell a song to his audiences. Instinctively, I flipped over my bike, Rusty Charlie, and began to play with him. I had never done that with a bicycle before; it just happened.

I told Papa that I didn't want the bike, that it was his and Rebecca's amid protests from Shorty. "No Charlie, I can fix the wheel, I can make it work, don't break up the band!"

"I'm sorry, Shorty, but this act is over. I'm going home."

"That's right, Charlie, we'll get back to the shack and sleep on it. You're tired. Everything's gonna be much clearer in the morning. We'll take Rusty Charlie with us now."

"The bike stays with Papa and Rebecca. I don't want it. I'm going back to San Francisco."

"Yeah, back to the Frisco, back to the shack."

"No, not the Frisco, Shorty. San Francisco. I'm going back to the States."

But Shorty was right. I did go back to the Frisco before flying back to the States. I needed to go back to the shack to get my stuff: my passport, my wallet with my Bankcards, my California driver's license, and other forms of I.D., and my writings. All of these things were hidden behind another secret door inside of the shack. Shorty never knew about this one. I trusted Shorty, but you can only trust anyone so far.

On my flight back to San Francisco I took some sleeping pills, reclined in my window seat, and dreamed that I was riding a bicycle. I was going in and out of buildings and up and down hills and around corners and passing by people as I sang in a very loud Gospel-preaching voice, "Nobody knows the trouble I've seen. You need to do the time for having done the crime."

I sang something else but it was incomprehensible to me. Suddenly, Constanza who was standing with Freddy, George, and Izmael grabbed me by the arm and stopped my motion on the bike. She pleaded, "What was that you sang? Those words were for me."

And I replied. "I don't listen to the message, I only sing it. It comes out of me but not into me." Then I pedaled away and sang again, "Nobody knows the trouble I've seen. You need to do the time for having done the crime," followed by more incomprehensible singing, followed by another person stopping me and pleading the same way. After Constanza there was Pastora, the girl from Crete, then Brothers Todor, Petar, and Ivan from the Sila Monastery in Bulgaria, followed by Andreu, Ana's old roommate, followed by Ana. I woke up after my reply to her and I suspected from the annoyed expressions of the other passengers on the plane, I had been singing my dream song out loud.

I had some trouble getting through customs back in the States because of my lack of a visa for Europe. But the guard had probably seen the same thing so many times before, so he shook his head disapprovingly, I sheepishly shrugged, and he let me pass.

I took a shuttle van to my flat on Capp Street in the Mission District of San Francisco not knowing whether I still had a home there or not. I had sublet the flat to a teacher from my school. She was a single woman who was planning to travel to India in the beginning of July when our sublet agreement was scheduled to terminate. I wondered what my landlord, Mark, had done when he didn't receive the rental checks beginning in July. He was my former roommate and we were on good terms, but I really doubted that he would keep the place available for me. After all, a half of a year had passed without any money nor even a word from me. When I got to the house, my speculation was confirmed; a double baby stroller stood before the front door and as I peered through the glass of the door, I saw that a child's safety gate stood at the top of the stairs of what used to be my second story flat. Obviously, there was a family living there now. I pressed the buzzer for the flat below and Daphne, my neighbor of many years opened her door. "David," she gasped as her cigarette fell out of her mouth and bounced off of her black sweater and onto the floor, "I thought you were dead."

"I was dead, but now I have risen," I joked. We sat on the front steps and smoked cigarettes as I told her a sanitized version of my adventures and she informed me that Mark, the landlord, went into a tirade when I missed the rental payment and found out that I had been out of the country for the past eight months.

"But then he got worried about you; we all did. He sublet your flat until the end of the year. But last week they hauled your stuff out and the family upstairs just signed a lease for one year. God, I wish that you had gotten here earlier. The sound of those crying kids and screaming parents is driving me nuts!" Her eyebrows arched and she blew smoke at the stroller standing above us.

"Do you know what happened to my things?" I asked.

"Some of it got dumped; there was a lot of junk. Your buddy, Richmond, took some of it. He`s come by pretty regularly to pick up mail that's been addressed to you. I've been collecting it."

"Thanks Daphne, you`ve always been a good neighbor and friend. Do you have some of my mail now?"

"There's a bit, it looks like junk. Richmond was here just last week. I suppose that he has loads of it." She went inside her flat and brought back my mail and I looked through it. She was right: it was only junk mail.

"Can I use your phone, Daphne? I'd like to call Richmond."

"Of course, David, he'll be so glad to hear from you. He was so worried. We all thought that you were dead."

"I can`t remember his number."

"I have it," she replied. "We`ve been keeping in regular contact trying to solve the mystery of you."

I called Richmond and he was amazed to hear my voice and thrilled to hear that I was back in San Francisco. We agreed to meet immediately at the Uptown Bar, a couple of blocks down Capp Street from my former flat. When I entered the bar, the same regulars were there seated on their same bar stools as the last time that I had been there over a year ago. Upon my entry they casually looked at me, and the bartender, Chett remarked, "Dave, I haven`t seen you here for a while."

"No, I've been out of town," I answered and ordered a pint of Sierra Nevada. The ale tasted exquisite. "Nowhere on God's great earth," I declared, "is there a finer tasting beer than this here."

"It's from Chico," Doc, the regular sitting a few seats to the right of me, mumbled, "Armpit of the Universe, racist white trash shit-hole."

Richmond entered the bar explosively slamming the two doors against the walls and proclaimed, "Bring the fattened calf, kill it and let me eat and be merry; for this son of mine was dead, and has come to life again; he was lost and has been found!" He bought a round of drinks for everyone and stared at me in disbelief like a bug-eyed pink rabbit as I recounted my tales of misadventure over the past year. "God, somehow I knew that you were alive. I suspected that you were in Amsterdam living the high life. I knew that this marriage to Ana business was a joke. No dame is going to bring down the G man. Here's a letter for you, G." he said smirking and bringing out a letter from the pocket of his coat. "Very, very funny, G."

"Why is it opened?"

"I`m sorry, G. I know that it`s a federal offense, but I needed to figure out where you were. I thought you were dead."

I glanced at the letter and was dumbfounded. "It's from Ana," I stated.

"Yeah, that`s right, G, it`s from Ana. Ha, ha. Very funny, G, very funny."

"What are you talking about?" I asked.

"That`s your handwriting, G. I recognize it. You had me going with the emails but when I saw this letter, I knew that the jig was up."

"That is not me, Richmond. This is Ana. Our handwriting is very similar. We are like two peas in a pod.

"Sure, G, whatever you say G-Man. Let's have some more tequila. It's great to have you back."

I carefully read and studied the letter. It was dated May 24, 2002. It read:

David,

I can't believe that you have done this to me after all that we have been through. You go back to your partying. You go back to your loser life in America without me and without your child. I thought that you were real. I thought that you were pure of heart. Remember that bullshit about that wheel of life you told me on the night that we met? Truth, Honor, Justice, Duty, Service, Courage, Humility, Joy - that creed that you supposedly followed. Which of those do you have, you lying, thieving, cowardly sack of shit? You certainly don't have love which is what I said that you were lacking and is what I tried to give to you. I hate you. You're psychotic, but that is not what I hate about you. I hate that you are so weak. May you rot in Hell and may my child never know from what spew she was conceived.

Sincerely,

Ana

I re-read the letter over and over again trying to convince myself that Richmond was right and that I had written the letter. The postmark date was May 24th from Berlin. That`s when in my original delusion Ana and I had flown back to Palma and checked into the Hostel Havana. But that I knew did not happen. I went alone from Germany to the Netherlands. It seemed so clear to me after I retained my memory over the Singel Canal that I had created Ana. Richmond was right - the handwriting looked like mine, even the language of the letter seemed to be mine but somewhere in the back of my mind, there lingered a doubt that the letter was not written by me but by a real live livin' gal named Ana with a bun in the oven.

We drank throughout the night, first at the Mission bars, then at the bonfires at Ocean Beach. Then we drove back to Richmond's flat where I passed out on a mattress in his study. The next morning the sun and a colossal hangover woke me up. I noticed that his computer was on, so I tried my email again. This time it worked; this time I did exist.

Most of the letters came from Ana. The first one was very similar to the letter that I had read at the bar. But as I continued to read them, I noticed that the tone changed from being accusatory to more apologetic. In one letter she wrote, "I know now that you did not run away and abandon us, but I pushed you away. I couldn't confront my fears about our future, so I confronted you and then fled. I wanted you to chase after me and keep me from leaving, but you didn't; you let me go. I've always acted fast and you've always acted slow."

The final letter which was written that morning stated, "Our child was born. It's a girl. I have named her Rose Mary after our grandmothers. She's beautiful: she has blue eyes and blonde hair. She looks like her papa. She's so tiny and so helpless but she's strong. I wish that you could see her. Love, Ana."

I shouted, "It's a girl!" and Richmond and his wife, Eva, woke up, read the email and looked at me disbelievingly. They read all of Ana's emails and laughed.

"Davey," said Eva, "I think that you wrote these letters."

"Look, G," Richmond added, "you must have written this last letter from this computer yourself. You were just too drunk to remember."

"I didn't write it," I asserted, "Ana did."

Over the next few days Ana and I continued to communicate with each other as Richmond and Eva incredulously scoffed at their authenticity. I decided not to share the letters with them anymore because their skepticism began to infuriate me. Ana and I decided that I would not fly out to see the baby, but that they would fly to San Francisco on February 14th, Valentine's Day, to live with me. Meanwhile I needed to find a home for our family and try to get my job back with the school district. We needed to have a home and an income and we needed to get married.

The school district put up a fuss about giving me a teaching position because I had broken the terms of our agreement, but I provided them with a letter from Dr. Van Loon, which attested to my amnesia. Since the holiday break had just ended, it was the beginning of a new school term and there were a few vacancies available. "You can't have your old job back at the alternative school. That's been filled," the woman at Human Resources informed me.

"That's alright," I replied. "It would be like that movie, 'Groundhog Day', doing the same thing over and over again." She studied me with a quizzical expression and then said, "There's a position available at Bounty Island Academy teaching middle school language arts and social studies."

"I'll take it," I agreed instantaneously, "I've been living on an island throughout most of my sabbatical. It'll be good for me to do that again."

She surprised me by answering, "No man is an island."

I added, "If a Clod bee washed away by the sea, Europe is the lessee...any man's death diminishes me, because I am involved in Mankind: and therefore never send to know for whom the bells tolls; it tolls for me. That's John Donne."

"I know, David," she said, "I used to teach language arts myself. Are you going to be alright?"

"I'm great, I'm getting married."

"That's great, David, who's the lucky girl?"

"Her name's Ana," I answered. "She's Spanish... er I mean Catalan..."

"That's nice, David," she said while shooing me out of her office. "Good luck at Bounty Island."

"It will be a pleasure that I will treasure," I quipped as the door closed behind me.

Ana and I decided that I should find a place outside of the city with a fenced-in yard suitable for a family. Richmond had been taking care of my Geo Metro while I was away, so I drove it around the Bay Area to check out houses. At first I thought that I would want a place in Colma nearby all of the cemeteries; it would be quiet there, but instead I found a place on Bounty Island nearby the school.

I drove back to Richmond's flat to pick up my things while he and Eva were away at work. I left him his key and a note that said how disappointed I was in his mocking behavior about Ana and me. I told him that I was moving to Bollywood, where Ana and the baby would join me. I ended the note by writing: Tell my friends that you have seen me, and that soon I will be with my father in Heaven.

My new home on Bounty Island was a plain-looking, small, grey ranch-house with a garage and a fenced-in backyard. It was apart from other residential housing, so Baby Rose's crying would not bother the neighbors and they would not bother us. 'This is much better than my old flat on Capp Street,' I thought to myself as I surveyed the backyard. At Capp Street we would have had to deal with the noisy neighbors upstairs with their dogs yelping, and drunken Mexicans in the garage shack behind the flat, and the junkies in front, and the fire trucks that constantly streamed by with their sirens screaming at all hours of the day and night.

The only building within our vicinity was a deserted warehouse which stood directly behind us. It was a bit of an eyesore, but the rent was cheap, the nights would be quiet, and Ana and Rose would be safe.

The school also seemed like a good change for me. The approach was more traditional than what it had been at the alternative school and I welcomed the chance to make an assessment as to which approach was more effective. Seventh grade Social Studies began with the history of Islam and in the eighth grade we would study American history. Language Arts involved reading and analyzing stories - fiction and non-fiction —from the district-approved textbooks. No more re-inventing the wheel.

The classroom was in a musty-smelling bungalow. The teacher who had been there before me had left it in a state of disarray. Garbage was everywhere. Books were not shelved but were dumped into piles. Dust and grime were in every nook and cranny. I made an attempt to try to clean the room but became overwhelmed with the task and gave up.

The students were a rebellious bunch totally lacking in any sense of discipline. Many of them came from immigrant homeless families, which I found out was a majority of the population living on the island. Bounty Island had been a naval base but after the military moved out, the San Francisco Housing Authority used a lot of the facilities to provide housing for the homeless.

I was given a para-professional who "assisted" me during Social Studies. Ali, a young man with iniquitous raven eyes, would gather some of the boys at a table in the back and tell them stories, while I tried to conduct class. At first, it irritated me greatly because the rest of the class would get distracted and would beg me to let them sit with Ali as he folded twenty dollar bills certain ways so that they depicted the September 11th attacks on the World Trade Center and the Pentagon. The boys in the back would laugh at his origami and then listen intently as he explained to them that the attacks were actually devised by American Jews, who did it so that the American government would go to war against the Islamic nations. It seemed to have worked; we retaliated against the Taliban in Afghanistan and now President George W. Bush had his troops crusading in Iraq against another in the axis of evil, Saddam Hussein.

At first I tried to change what was happening in class by telling the boys that they needed to stay in their regular seats and by talking to Ali privately.

He would always respond with, "You're the teacher; I'm here to assist you." But each time that a new class began, it would be the same thing with the boys joining him at the back table. Finally, I gave up and let him conduct the classes while I sat at my desk reading the newspaper.

In preparation for Ana's and Baby Rose's arrival, I went shopping and bought a new queen-sized bed for us and a bassinet for the baby; also a corner couch with bookend reclining lazy boys, a stroller with a detachable car seat, a changing table, and lots and lots of toys. I hung my tapestries and masks which I had collected from my travels and which Richmond had salvaged from Capp Street and even hired professional cleaners to make our home sparklingly immaculate.

For their arrival, I got to the airport an hour early and stood at the greeting spot with roses for Ana and a stuffed baby tiger for Rose. I watched as other passengers arrived and their hosts greeted them with kisses and hugs and I thought, 'Ours will be better than that.' I played in my head our passion-filled reunion as we ran towards each other in slow motion and kissed over and over again and held each other's faces in our hands.

Their plane which came from New York finally arrived and they entered the greeting area with Rose crying and screaming and Ana looking tired and miserable. I leaned in to kiss Ana's lips, but she turned her face so that all I got was cheek. Neither the roses nor the tiger helped in pacifying either one of them, so we walked to the parking lot as others looked at us with condescending condemnation.

"Here we be," I said pointing to the Metro.

Ana groused, "This won't do. Tomorrow, we'll start looking for a real car; something for a family. This one won't do."

I chauffeured them to our home on Bounty Island as Ana sat in the back with Rose. I tried playing Elton John's 'Your Song', our wedding song, on the CD player, but Ana told me to shut it off.

On the homefront, things did not improve. One look at Ana when she first observed the tapestries and masks hanging about our house told me that their lifespan as interior decorations was very limited.

'This won't do,' I thought for her.

"We need to sleep," Ana said and she dressed herself and Rose in their pajamas. They lay in the bed and I set myself down beside them and looked at their silhouettes in the night. "Turn the other way," Ana said to me. "Your nose is whistling." I rolled over so that I faced away from them as my arm and torso dangled over the edge.

The next morning, I awoke to an empty bed and wondered whether their arrival had only been a dream. I walked into the kitchen and saw their smiling faces turn to me from the table. Ana stood up and ran to me with

Rose in her arms and said, "This is your Papa, Rose. We're home now." She kissed me passionately on the lips as I opened my eyes to see her shining face and noticed that all of my tapestries and masks had already been removed.

"Let's buy a new car," she suggested suggestively, "a family van for the family!" She smiled brightly and clapped her hands together and Rose did as well. So without any breakfast, or a shower, or a poo, I was off to the car dealerships in Daly City looking for a family van.

'Who would have thunk it?' I thought as we were driving back home in our new blue Plymouth Voyager. "The G man driving his very own family van, complete with his very own family. Who would have thunk it?"

We got married at city hall in San Francisco, but Ana insisted that we also do it on the tiny island in Menasha's Jefferson Park on August 11th as we had originally planned, but one year later. Ana still had her dress from our aborted 2002 ceremony; she even brought along the mossy twig that she had found in the Sila Mountains in Bulgaria that she intended to wrap with flowers for her bouquet.

She said that she wanted to come up with unique floral arrangements for the tables at the wedding reception. I said. "American slang for getting married is tying the knot. How about we have a length of rope with a knot at each table?"

"I love it," she replied excitedly. "We can put a rose in each knot. It's elegant in its simplicity."

Invitations were again sent out to family and friends. We used the same painting by Ana of Josiah and Jediah in the mother's womb and the same quotes from the Kabbalah and the Bible but we added, "This time it's going to happen come rain or shine, Hell or high water. Be there or be square."

It wasn't always absolute bliss with the G family, though. Ana complained a lot because I was often very exhausted when returning from the school and I wanted to just vegetate in front of the television with my reality shows – Survivor, Big Brother, The Mole, and Temptation Island.

"You used to write, you used to be creative. Now all you do is watch your stupid American television and eat your junk food munchies and get fat. You are not the man that I fell in love with. You disgust me!" and she would throw a glass toward me which would crash against the wall and shatter into pieces sometimes flying nearby the baby.

Then I would scream, "I can't stand this. I'm leaving!"

Then she would scream, "If you leave, I will kill the baby and myself!"

Then I would turn around and hold Ana's fragile, hyper-ventilating body in my arms until her breathing would become regular again and the storm had passed. We vowed to each other that we would both try to improve; I would be less lethargic and she would control her anger.

But the same episodes would occur again and again. She began to attend classes in anger management two nights per week. She would take the bus into the city and return home refreshed and more optimistic after each session. When she was at home, I would sit at my desk and write my story to please her. There were many tasks to be done around the house as well: pictures to hang, shelves to build, and little Rose to attend to. She was colicky and needed constant attention. We would usually have her harnessed to us as we went about our duties.

Ana was convinced that there were rats on our property, although I never detected any. I bought conventional rat traps, but Ana scoffed at their effectiveness and experimented frequently with something that she called a mubtakker, which she said was Catalan for invention although the word did not sound Catalan. The contraption had two containers, one which held the rat poison. Ana would light the fuse, which she said would then mix the contents of the two containers. I asked her what was in the second container and she replied, "It's an agent to help transport the poison."

"Transport it where?" I asked.

"Wherever the rats are," she answered. But the mubtakker did not seem to be working properly because Ana would curse and throw the materials into the garbage can and then yell at me, "Stop being a lazy bum and do some work!" Then I would head for the backyard because there was always lots to do.

I spent a lot of time working in the backyard because Ana said that it was "not fit for beauty or beast." She often referred to us as that Disney couple or in fits of anger would bemoan the fact that she had married Shrek. I tended to the lawn in the backyard and mended the fence. Whenever I thought that it was safe, I would lie down on the hammock and try to catch forty winks because the nights were always interrupted with Rose's crying.

One day I was lying in the hammock and I opened my eyes and thought that I had seen someone staring at me through the window of the abandoned warehouse. The man's smirking expression did not change as I stared back at him and I realized that there was no man, but it was merely a reflection caused by the sun and the imperfections in the glass. The man seemed to be looking down upon me as if I were a disgrace to mankind for letting Ana mold me into such a pathetic wimp. I tried to convince him that I was not pussy-whipped, that I was autonomous and free, but his smug air indicated that he saw through my pretensions. In anger, I threw the hedge clippers at him and shattered the window and he disappeared. "Great," I said to myself, "now I need to fix that window and get the hedge clippers back before Ana finds out. If I don't trim these hedges, there's going to be hell to pay."

The house cleaning carried over to the classroom and I started to spruce it up as well. I brought in cleaning supplies from home and set about removing the filth accumulated from years of neglect. I was able to get the room shipshape because Ali was handling the Social Studies, so I had nothing else to do during those periods.

One day I found a ball of paper lodged in between a filing cabinet and the back wall. I reached in to retrieve it and was surprised to see that it had been folded to look like the face of a man. Another origami by Ali, I thought, as I studied it more closely.

The face looked familiar although I did not realize who it was until he said, "Don't be a pussy, be a man." It was the same guy that I had seen in the window of the warehouse. I tore him apart and violently tossed the scraps into a wastebasket. One small snippet fell outside of the basket and I picked it up and was about to toss it away when I noticed that there was writing on it; the same strange lettering that I had seen somewhere before and a web address. I would need to investigate this further.

We flew to Wisconsin a few days before the wedding ceremony; final preparations needed to be made. I was surprised at how little interest my family seemed to have for Ana and Rose. I think that my mom was disturbed that the child was born out of wedlock although I assured her that Ana and I had performed our intimate marriage ceremony in Mallorca just days after we had met. She scoffed, "You have such delusions."

"We are not like the others," I argued.

"I agree," she replied. "You're like two peas in a pod."

My family always seemed to be asking, "How are you, David?" and laughing when I expressed my concerns about the preparations for the ceremony.

"What if it rains?" I anxiously asked.

"Then we'll have the ceremony in the pavilion. A lot of the relatives are going to be there. If it's in the pavilion, they'll be able to sit. It'll be alright, David," my sister Sandy assured me, "it will be alright."

The day before the wedding, Ana and I walked to the park and found that algae had come from somewhere and surrounded the island. It stank to high heaven, worse than that tunnel where I had injured my head in Jaisalmer, India.

"If it's like that tomorrow," Sandy reassured me. "We'll have it in the pavilion. The family won't mind."

When I arrived at the park on the morning of the wedding, the algae had gone away as well as the smell from hell. I placed the knotted roses on the tables of the pavilion and wound one long knotted rope with roses around a tree at the ceremonial spot on the island.

I had not seen Ana since the previous day. She had spent the night at a hotel with her family who had flown in from Spain for the wedding before departing to Mexico City for a family vacation. I had planned to see Ana and her family at a party that my college chums were holding in my honor at a hotel, but they never showed up. My friends asked about their whereabouts and joked uncomfortably but incessantly about Ana leaving me alone at the altar tomorrow. My mother, who was beginning to feel the effects of her second Manhattan reassured me, "Don't worry, David, she'll be there tomorrow. You're like two peas in a pod."

The wedding came off pretty much as planned. My brother-in-law, Sal, who had received a license as a justice of the peace from the internet, performed the ceremony. It began with me singing the first verse of 'Your Song' as planned. During the second verse when Ana sang, none of the guests seemed to notice her as she was walking down the aisle: perhaps her voice was too soft. Everyone stood staring at me with dumb grins on their faces that said either, "Jeez this is so great, David's finally getting married," or "This is very, very odd." It wasn't your typical Fox River Valley wedding ceremony.

Ana looked radiant in her homemade white-silken dress and a cape with an attached hood that had small red flowers sewn at the edges. When Sal asked her, "Do you, Ana, take David as your husband in sickness and in health, for better or for worse, from this day forward until the day that you die?"

She answered softly with her luminous eyes burning into mine, "I do."

When he asked me the same question, I answered confidently, "I do beyond the day that I die."

In closing the very brief ceremony, Sal announced, "Ladies and gentleman, I present to you Mr. and Mrs. Geiger." and the congregation hooted and hollered in our honor. Most of the guests were reserved in congratulating us except for my crazy Uncle Ray who kept repeating, "This is great. I'm so happy for the two of you!" and hugged the air out of us over and over again.

The reception was a barbecue and potluck in the pavilion as we had planned with a polka band following the food. Ana's family sat isolated at a single table without much interaction from my family and friends. Ana and I had the traditional first dance and I found it odd that no one later asked the bride to dance. It seemed like your typical family reunion except for the wedding cake, and the slotted box for congratulation cards, and the roses knotted in rope.

We stayed in the basement of my mom's house; my mom stayed at her sister Susie's house with Rose so that we could have privacy. We had both planned to consummate the wedding in bed the traditional way, but we were both so exhausted from the day's proceedings that we instantly fell asleep.

That night I dreamt that Ana and I were living on a farm somewhere. It could have been Wisconsin because we were both dressed in plain Amish garb: Ana wore a bonnet and I wore a straw hat, and suspenders, and a long Amish beard. But we couldn't have been Amish because upon closer reflection I remembered that Ana had a simple, white floral design on her brown dress and my suspenders had thin red and brown stripes. We did not seem to be part of an Amish community. We seemed to be Mennonite.

Ana painted in a large sunlit room and large slanted wooden beams held her artwork. I worked in the neighboring room building frames for her paintings using simple non-electrical tools.

I went to the stable and hitched up the horses to our carriage and our two daughters in their simple dresses and bonnets jumped upon the carriage and we went riding into the forest to find more material for my frames. The forest was enchanted and the girls chased after butterfly fairies while I searched for the perfect wood: not perfect by meaning without imperfections. I searched for wood with imperfections because that wood to me was all the more beautiful.

In the morning when I told Ana about my dream, she said. "One day I hope to be living in the country like that. That is the way it should be. And with two daughters you say?"

"That's how it was in the dream."

"What were their names?"

"I don't remember, but I think that the older one was Rose."

"I thought that the second one would be a boy. I was thinking that we would name him Jacob."

"We have lots of time before thinking about a second child."

"I'm not so sure. I think that I'm pregnant again!" she said very excitedly clapping her hands together.

"How can that be?" said I in shock.

"I think that you know how."

"But you're still breast-feeding Rose. That's a natural contraceptive."

"It's not 100% effective. I want a strong name for this child. If it's a girl, I'd like Magdalena. That's a strong name."

"Wow, I'm speechless. How long have you known?"

"Magdalena, I like it. Let's get some breakfast, I'm starved."

We ate breakfast and then hurried off to pick up Rose. All the while I was still in a state of shock. I had noticed that Ana's belly was getting bigger, but I thought that it was a result of the American diet. We had not been having relations hardly at all since her arrival in February. "Something's afoot," I thought. "Who did it?"

Back in San Francisco conflicts between Ana and I continued to erupt only now they were more intensified. Rather than throwing glasses at me in her fits of rage, Ana's modus operandi changed to destroying my eyeglasses by stomping on them like a cocaine-crazed fitness freak on a Stairmaster. This change in the exhibition of her outrageous fury was safer for the baby and myself but was certainly more expensive.

I continued to retreat more and more often to the sanctuary of my garage and backyard. There was always more work to be done on the van or in the mending of the fence.

On the one month anniversary of our Wisconsin wedding, Ana insisted that we attend the Mill Valley Art Fair in Marin County. I suggested that we go eastward into Oakland, and then take 580 to the city of Richmond, crossing the bay into Marin County. Ana, however, said that we first needed to get some nipple cream at the Rainbow Co-op in San Francisco. "Then we'll have to deal with the heavy traffic on the Golden Gate Bridge," I reasoned. "We can find some nipple cream in Berkeley."

"I want my nipple cream! I don't want to go around Berkeley looking for some other nipple cream. I'm very sensitive now because of my hormones with the baby and Rose's teeth are biting into my breasts. I want my nipple cream!"

So we drove into San Francisco to get Ana's nipple cream at Rainbow. She seemed much more content after we had purchased it. I saw she and

Rose smiling as I looked at them through the rearview mirror. They were sitting in the far backseat of the van as they always did. 'Perhaps I`ll even be able to play some music on the radio,' I thought. 'They look so happy now.'

We drove through the Richmond district on the way to the Golden Gate Bridge and I noticed that I was on Cabrillo Street where Richmond and Eva lived. As we passed their flat, I saw Richmond washing his truck in the front. He looked at us as we passed, but I don`t think that he recognized me because he continued on washing.

I told Ana as we were approaching the bridge, "You know, Richmond was always a good friend to me with a big heart. I should give him a call and see how he`s doing."

"I refuse to let you see him," Ana answered.

"You can`t do that. I can see whomever I choose."

"No, I refuse to let you see him. I refuse to let you see any of your friends. You need to make a choice, them or me."

"That's outrageous, Ana. You can`t tell me who I can or cannot see. And it's unfair of you to make me choose one or the other. You know who else I should call. I should call Lidia."

"Stop the car!" Ana screamed, and I did so. I thought that perhaps there was something wrong with Rose. But I knew that it was more likely that I had struck a very tender nerve by saying the L-name. Ana had always disliked Lidia even though they had never met. She felt some type of irrational competition with her. I moved to the back of the van and we screamed at each other as Rose winced and tried to muffle the sound by holding her hands over her ears. The argument was ridiculous, I knew it. It was a no-brainer to choose between Lidia and Ana. I chose Ana. I loved her. Lidia was a crazy old friend of mine from my Haight Street days that I was still pissed off at for accidentally destroying my journals from India. There was no choice, but I didn`t like Ana giving me an ultimatum.

I screamed, "Who`s the father of the new baby because it sure ain't me!"

Ana feigned calmness and smiled condescendingly. "Of course it's not yours and neither is the first." I sat in shock. I had some earlier suspicions about Rose not being my daughter, but when I saw how much she resembled me, my doubts were removed.

I stepped out of the van and walked away. I walked away like I always did when things got too hot. Ana screamed, "If you leave me now, I`m going to kill the baby and myself!" as she had done many times before. But this time I did not turn around and console her. I kept on walking until I came to the next beam on the bridge and then sat on the sidewalk platform and cried with my hands over my face.

I slowly came to the realization that Ana had been lying to me. Rose was my daughter and so probably was Magdalena. She had only said that to hurt me because I had hurt her. I walked back to the van to set things straight with Ana. As I got closer, I noticed that a police car was parked behind the van. The officers were peering through the windows trying to see if anyone was in the van although it was difficult because of the tinted windows.

"Is this your van?" the officer asked.

"Yeah, I'm sorry. My wife and I had some difficulties."

"Where's your wife?"

"She's in the back with our daughter."

"Open the door." And as I did, the officer's eyes widened and he shouted, "Down to the ground," as he pushed me there on my stomach. The other officer ran to the police car and within minutes there were sirens everywhere. The police shut off traffic to the bridge and fire trucks stood at the end. A large white police truck parked nearby my van and men jumped out of it. Within minutes they said that the situation was clear. There was no harm, the bomb was dismantled.

I asked, "Where's Ana? Where's Rose?"

The officer yelled, "There may be two female co-conspirators. Look for them."

Later I was told by the police that the entire back of my van was loaded with highly-explosive material. They said that the detonator was poorly constructed and thus the bomb never went off. However, according to them, there were enough explosives packed in the back of my van to cause major damage to the bridge. They said that I had stolen the explosives from the warehouse behind my home on Bounty Island.

Supposedly, my computers at home and at school showed high activity in sites associated with homemade bombs. They've been trying to find evidence of my association with Al-Qaeda, since the incident occurred on the two year anniversary of the World Trade Center tragedy. Also found at my home was a manifesto of 1,414 pages that called for the end to capitalist imperialisms. They told me that nearly all of the manifesto were illegible and incomprehensible ravings of a mad man.

The psychiatrist says that I am delusional and have created from my imagination a pregnant wife and daughter. My family and friends agree with him and say that they are sorry for not confronting me earlier about my erratic behavior. I used to protest loudly against them and shout, "They are alive. They're in Africa. She always wanted to get back to Africa!"

Now, however, I don't argue anymore. I spend most of my time quietly reading from the Bible. It provides for me peace and assurance that the truth will prevail.

Given my current circumstance, I am most drawn to St. Paul's letters which he wrote while being imprisoned by the Romans. I was reading his letters to the Colossians and chapter three spoke directly to me.

In verses five to eleven I was told to put off my old nature and put to death all that is earthly in me. Evil desires of passion, fornication, and covetousness should be terminated along with anger, wrath, and malice.

Verses twelve and thirteen told me to put on the new nature, which is in the image of our Creator. I should put on and practice the virtues of compassion, kindness, lowliness, patience and forgiveness.

Verse fourteen (my lucky number) stated, "And over all these virtues, put on love which binds them all together with perfect unity." As I read this, I was reminded of the night that I had first met Ana. We had gotten together at a bar after the concert and I told her about my wheel of life and she told me that my wheel was missing one vital spoke.

I'm in this place that they call a prison for the criminally insane. It's insanity to think that I am insane. I know that these people and these events of the past two years were real. As for being a criminal, well, if love is a crime, then shackle me up and throw away the key. I was loved. The evidence doesn't show it, but I know it. I take the blame for having loved.

Last night my long-departed father appeared before me. Perhaps it was a dream, but it was so vivid that I find it impossible to accept that it did not really occur. He still looked as he did in the old family photographs, but his hair and skin and especially his eyes radiated an essence of otherworldliness.

He said, "Your Father has been following your path since the beginning and has been looking forward to this moment. You have struggled, my son, and now are held captive. Do not despair.

"Soon you will be allowed to go outside of this cell for intervals of time and enjoy fresh air. You have been provided with a guard who will keep you safe during those times. Your captors have been guided to let you outside during the hours of most light. You will need that light to not get lost again.

"Your Father loves you, my son, and anticipates with much affection the coming of the last day when you will be rescued from your imprisonment. Your family will be reunited with you in the end."

I knelt down on the cold cement floor and prayed to my Father. I confessed my faults and gave thanks for all that He has given me. I asked for strength in overcoming my earthly temptations and growing closer to His image. For the first time in my life, it became truly obvious to me that He was with me, He was always with me, He had protected me through my misdeeds, misjudgments, and misadventures and He would protect me now. Tears poured out from my eyes and formed two pools of water on the floor before my knees. The two flowed together into one.

"No man is an island."